SALT RIVER

RANDY WAYNE WHITE

G. P. PUTNAM'S SONS | NEW YORK

PUTNAM
— EST. 1838 —

G. P. PUTNAM'S SONS
Publishers Since 1838
An imprint of Penguin Random House LLC
penguinrandomhouse.com

Library of Congress Cataloging-in-Publication Data

Names: White, Randy Wayne, author.
Title: Salt River / Randy Wayne White.
Description: New York: G. P. Putnam's Sons, [2020] | Series: A Doc Ford novel
Identifiers: LCCN 2019050880 (print) | LCCN 2019050881 (ebook) |
ISBN 9780735212725 (hardcover) | ISBN 9780735212749 (ebook)
Subjects: LCSH: Ford, Doc (Fictitious character)—Fiction. |
GSAFD: Suspense fiction. | Mystery fiction.
Classification: LCC PS3573.H47473 S25 2020 (print) |
LCC PS3573.H47473 (ebook) | DDC 813/.54—dc23
LC record available at https://lccn.loc.gov/2019050880
LC ebook record available at https://lccn.loc.gov/2019050881

First G. P. Putnam's Sons hardcover edition / February 2020
First G. P. Putnam's Sons premium edition / January 2021
G. P. Putnam's Sons premium edition ISBN: 9780735212732

Printed in the United States of America
10 9 8 7 6 5 4 3 2

Praise for the novels of
RANDY WAYNE WHITE

"Hats off to White for combining suspense and madcap adventure with such dexterity . . . Being an under-the-radar kind of guy, Doc Ford is likely not too happy at the way his adventures keep turning up on best-seller lists, but he'd better deal with it; the trend isn't about to change."   —*Booklist*

"'Suspenseful' is a word that has been bandied about to such an extent that it has virtually lost its meaning. . . . But it should be acknowledged that some authors are more skilled at creating suspense than others—and none more so among current practitioners than Randy Wayne White."
                    —*The San Diego Union-Tribune*

"As with every Doc Ford story, the writing is tight and the story fast-paced. . . . [Fans of] thriller heroes from James Bond to Jason Bourne will find a lot to like."   —*Associated Press*

"It's surreal and whacky, but darn scary and suspenseful, too . . . . Mr. White delivers once again the thinking person's thriller his readers have come to expect, along with excellent management of pacing, settings, and characterization. It's a winner."   —*Florida Weekly*

"With Randy Wayne White, one gets not only a dead-on thriller, with all the twists, surprises, and action one expects, but a sense that each of the Ford books is a chapter in the development of one of the most compelling characters in the genre."   —*Miami Herald*

"A trip to the Gulf Coast with Doc Ford is never dull . . . and White doesn't skimp on the action. . . . This marine biologist increasingly lets his clandestine life as a government operative take him away from his quiet Sanibel Island home [and White] continues to find fresh ways to bring Ford into the chaos of world politics."   —*South Florida Sun Sentinel*

"Anyone who insists that mysteries cannot be 'real' literature should be duct-taped to a chair and handed Randy Wayne White."   —*The Washington Times*

TITLES BY RANDY WAYNE WHITE

DOC FORD SERIES

Sanibel Flats

The Heat Islands

The Man Who Invented
Florida

Captiva

North of Havana

The Mangrove Coast

Ten Thousand Islands

Shark River

Twelve Mile Limit

Everglades

Tampa Burn

Dead of Night

Dark Light

Hunter's Moon

Black Widow

Dead Silence

Deep Shadow

Night Vision

Chasing Midnight

Night Moves

Bone Deep

Cuba Straits

Deep Blue

Mangrove Lightning

Caribbean Rim

Salt River

HANNAH SMITH SERIES

Gone

Deceived

Haunted

Seduced

THE SHARKS, INCORPORATED SERIES
FOR MIDDLE GRADE AND YOUNG ADULTS

Fins!

NONFICTION

Introduction to *Tarpon Fishing in Mexico and Florida*

Batfishing in the Rainforest

The Sharks of Lake Nicaragua

Last Flight Out

An American Traveler

Randy Wayne White's Gulf Coast Cookbook: With Memories and Photos of Sanibel Island

Randy Wayne White's Ultimate Tarpon Book

AVAILABLE EXCLUSIVELY AS AN E-BOOK

Doc Ford Country: True Stories of Travel, Tomlinson, and Batfishing in the Rainforest

FICTION AS RANDY STRIKER

Key West Connection

The Deep Six

Cuban Death-Lift

The Deadlier Sex

Assassin's Shadow

Everglades Assault

Grand Cayman Slam

FICTION AS CARL RAMM

Florida Firefight

L.A. Wars

Chicago Assault

Deadly in New York

Houston Attack

Vegas Vengeance

Detroit Combat

Terror in D.C.

Atlanta Extreme

Denver Strike

Operation Norfolk

For Georgia Jeff,
a fellow wanderer and wonderer

The coast [of Southwest Florida] is all in ruin because in these four or five leagues of sea there is barely 1.5 fathoms of water where many fish are dying.

—Juan López de Velasco,
Spanish cartographer,
journal entry, 1575

We are born alone, and we will die alone. This, the most basic of truths, was revealed to me when, a week after I left for college, my parents moved to East Hampton and failed to provide a forwarding address.

—S. M. Tomlinson,
One Fathom Above Sea Level

DISCLAIMER

Sanibel and Captiva Islands are real places, faithfully described, but used fictitiously in this novel. The same is true of certain businesses, marinas, bars, and other places frequented by Doc Ford, Tomlinson, and pals.

In all other respects, however, this novel is a work of fiction. Names (unless used by permission), characters, places, and incidents are either the product of the author's imagination or are used fictitiously. Any resemblance to actual persons, living or dead, or to actual events or locales is unintentional and coincidental.

Contact Mr. White at www.docford.com.

AUTHOR'S NOTE

Before thanking those who contributed their expertise, time and good humor during the writing of *Salt River*, I want to make clear that all errors, exaggerations, or misstatements of fact are entirely my fault. This applies particularly to those who helped guide me through the morass of data (and often politically charged misinformation) on harmful algae blooms known as "red tides" in saltwater regions, or "blue green algae" when referencing cyanobacteria outbreaks that occur in, but are not restricted to, freshwater areas.

Organisms that contribute to destructive algae blooms are found in most water environs, salt and fresh, throughout the world, year around. "Pollutants" they are not. Indeed, the global food chain would collapse without these microorganisms and macro algae. Keep this in mind the next time you read about small quantities of "red tide organisms" found at your local beach. This is not news. The micro flora are always present—and, sadly, so is the hysteria associated with the word "algae."

There isn't much that biologists agree upon regarding harmful algae blooms (HABs) save for a worldwide consensus that the phenomenon, while naturally occurring and massively destructive, can be enhanced by human activities. The degree to which humans cause, or contribute, to these events is at the historic epicenter of disagreements so passionate that opinions too often have more in common with theology than science.

In this book, the fictional Doc Ford attempts to provide readers with an overview of the subject that is dispassionate and, above all, factual. This was a challenge. As I explained in an editorial I wrote for the Sunday *New York Times* (September 29, 2018): "During my 50 years on this coast, I've experienced four killer algae blooms as a fishing guide (1974, '82, '96 and 2004). As a novelist, I've researched the subject, yet my understanding lacks the certainty or rage of those newly acquainted with these blooms." [https://www.nytimes.com/2018/09/29/opinion/sunday/red-tide-florida-tourism.html]

In other words, the more I learn, the less likely I am to be persuaded by those whose convictions are unshakable, for they invariably have a financial stake in whatever "solution" they advocate. This includes organized camps representing the phosphate, sugarcane, and agriculture industries as well as low-profile developers who view agriculture as a waste of acreage that would become a goldmine if bulldozed and transformed into golf courses and gated communities.

This is another element to keep in mind when ferreting through arguments regarding the solutions to red tides.

The newer, booming "environmental industry" also has a stake in the controversy. According to Environmental Business International Inc., a publishing and research firm, the industry grew by 4.8 percent in 2017 and produced $370 billion in annual revenue. This amount dwarfs the $10.1 million collected in 2016 by the Everglades Foundation, one of fourteen Florida-based nonprofit organizations that have a vested interest in the causes and effects of harmful algae blooms. I do not doubt the altruistic motives of these groups, nor do I think it unfair to acknowledge a simple fiduciary fact: to survive, to continue their good work, each must motivate the public sector to provide funding.

In this novel, you will meet Mack, the owner of Dinkin's Bay Marina. Mack has strong opinions on this subject. Even the unflappable Marion Ford cannot convince Mack that hysteria mongering has become a dangerously misleading fundraising tool.

For decades, I've collected newspaper accounts and research on algae blooms that date back to the 1800s. My file contains hundreds of clippings, many acquired at Florida libraries, after scanning through reels of microfiche. The historic overview they provide suggests a predictable cycle, and that cycle has not changed much. When acres of dead fish begin to wash ashore, there is a sustained, communal panic. Civic leaders demand action—and an explanation.

A few examples: According to a study issued by the University of Miami in 1955, a series of lethal red tides between 1844 and 1878 were, according to local fishermen, caused by a "poisonous" flow of freshwater from the Everglades into Florida Bay. A December 1918 headline in the *Punta Gorda Herald* asserted "Seismic Explosion Under Gulf Kills Many Fish Between Boca Grande and Marco." In July 1937, the *St. Petersburg Times* suggested that "the discharge of chemicals from freighters at Port Tampa" was to blame for the sudden death of "fish and eels rarely caught." An article in a November 1940 edition of the *Fort Myers News-Press* claimed that a massive fish kill was the result of a mysterious "subterranean disturbance." A *Miami Herald* article, dated February 1954, referenced the devastating red tides of 1947–50, and reported that scientists had traced the cause to excessive amounts of phosphorus found in the Peace River. A year later, in February 1955, the *News-Press,* under the optimistic headline "Red Tide

Seen Under Control in Three Years," cited a study that concluded that phosphate had nothing to do with red tide, then reassured readers that "government scientists" had discovered that dusting algae blooms with copper sulphate (sic) was an inexpensive and effective solution.

Problem solved? Of course not, and it is ironic to note that, as recently as 1989, the idea of dusting algae outbreaks was revisited—but with phosphatic clay, a residue produced by Florida's controversial phosphate industry.

The list of researchers from whom I've culled information is lengthy, but I would like to give special thanks to Dr. Brian Lapointe of Harbor Branch Oceanographic. Dr. Lapointe possesses the rare ability to process the opinions of those with whom he disagrees, to accept them as integral to a valid historical overview, and then distill even the most complex subjects in a way that is fair-minded, objective, and understandable even to a layperson such as I myself. Dr. Karen Steidinger also deserves special thanks for her concise responses to what, to me, seemed complex questions. Dr. Steidinger is acknowledged worldwide as an authority on dinoflagellates and harmful algae blooms. Indeed, her scholarly impact on the subject is so profound that the scientific name for Florida's red tide organism, *Karenia brevis*, was named in her honor. As mentioned previously, all, if any, misstatements of fact in this novel are entirely my fault, not theirs.

AUTHOR'S NOTE

Insights, ideas, and medical advice were provided by doctors Brian Hummel, my brother Dan White, Marybeth B. Saunders, Peggy C. Kalkounos, and my amazing nephew, Justin White, Ph.D. Local consultants on far-ranging topics include tennis guru Nate Dardick and "Captiva" Jeff Brown.

Pals, advisors, and/or teammates are always a help because they know firsthand that writing and writers are a pain in the ass. They are Gary Terwilliger, Ron Iossi, Jerry Rehfuss, Stu Johnson, Victor Candalaria, Gene Lamont, Nick Swartz, Kerry Griner, Mike Shevlin, Jon Warden, Davey Johnson, Barry Rubel, Mike Westhoff, and behavioral guru Don Carman.

Bill Lee, and his orbiting star, Diana, as always, have guided the author safely into the strange but fun and enlightened world of our mutual friend, the Rev. Sighurdhr M. Tomlinson. Equal thanks go to Albert Randall, Donna Terwilliger, Wendy Webb, Rachael Ketterman, Stephen Grendon, my devoted SOB, the angelic Mrs. Iris Tanner, and my partners and pals, Mark Marinello, Marty, Joey, and Brenda Harrity.

Much of this novel was written at corner tables before and after hours at Doc Ford's Rum Bar & Grille where staff were tolerant beyond the call of duty. Thanks go to Andrew Willis, Jim Rainville, Ashley Rodeheffer, Carle Mitchell, Chester Steven Chance, Jim Green, Justin Schirmer, Lisa Kendrick, Michelle Gallagher, Justin Harris, Sarah Carnithan, Scott Hayes, Katy Forret, Blake

Colbert, Tyler Wussler, James Sharp, Kirsten Blazo, Yvonne De Montes, Big Boston Brian Cunningham, and Sergio Ramirez.

At Doc Ford's on Captiva Island, many thanks to Joyous Joy Schawalder, Misael Guzman, Adam Traum, Ryan Cook, Braulio Mendez, Robert DelGandio, Dear Erica DeBacker, Carey Galantino, Donald Yacono, John King, Ray Rosario, Krystal Bovan, Adam Johnson, Jahlil Poindexter, Sam Uscanga, Ivan Riverol, Shelbi Muske, Scott Hamilton, Tony Foreman, and Cheryl "Key West" Erickson.

Finally, thanks to my amazing sons, Lee and Rogan, for helping me to finish another book.

Randy Wayne White
Casa de Wendy
Sanibel, Florida

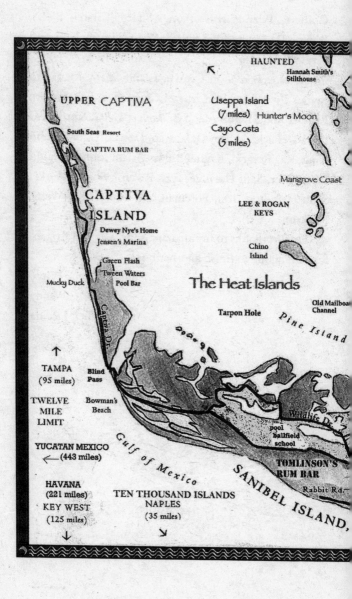

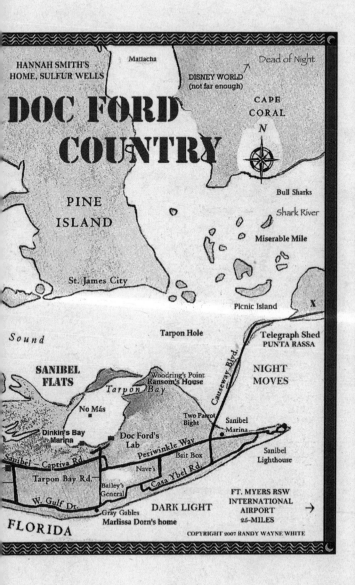

ONE

It started in the galley of my wobbly old house during a lightning storm that fried a nearby transformer. A sizzling boom rattled the windows. Combusted ozone drifted bayward and sweetened the air while rain hammered the tin roof.

The lights went out.

"Perfect," my boat bum pal, Tomlinson, said. "Natural disaster is humanity's last hope. The internet has butt-ravaged us all and looted our privacy. I say bring on the pale rider. Might as well have another beer, huh?"

It was late but didn't feel late. In July on Florida's west coast, the sun doesn't set until almost 9. I waited in darkness for several seconds expecting my generator to kick on. It did not.

"If I don't get the darn thing started, my fish will be belly-up in an hour," I said. "And keeping fish alive has been tough enough lately. There's a kerosene lamp in the cupboard. Help yourself."

I'm a flashlight snob. Spend enough time in Third World countries, the dark becomes a foe. I have a phobia about being without a solid little LED handy, so they're in every room—including one on the bookcase, which I found before going to the door.

"Try not to burn the place down," I said.

"You're coming back, aren't you? I was just getting to the weirdest part of the story." Tomlinson had a little plastic lighter out. The way he stumbled around in the gloom, arms outstretched, reminded me of a scarecrow Frankenstein.

"It gets weirder? Good god," I said. "Shouldn't you be talking to a priest or something?"

"I *am* a priest," my Zen Buddhist buddy reminded me. "We're not into the whole confession thing—too risky, the way some monks are wired. Besides, donating to a sperm bank can't be considered a sin. Not two decades ago anyway . . . can it?"

I replied, "Forty-some donations in less than a month? If it's not a sin, it should be a felony." Going out the door, I added, "There's a six-pack in the fridge—but leave at least one for me."

I switched on the flashlight and crossed the breeze-way to an adjoining structure, all built under the same tin roof. I call it my lab because I'm a marine biologist, and that's how the room is used. Inside was a row of tanks containing fish and other creatures that I collect and sell to schools and research facilities. I was careful with the flashlight. Deer are not the only animals that can be stunned by a bright beam. I'd read a recent study on retinal bleaching in benthic fish. Dazzling submersibles with video cameras are new to their ocular DNA.

I panned the light to a workstation where there were test tubes in racks, a microscope, other lab tools, and a desktop computer. A sign on the far wall read *Sanibel Biological Supply*—the name of my business.

For no rational reason, I confirmed that aquarium pumps and aerators do not work without electricity. The word *methodical* is preferable to the newer label, which is *OCD*. I unplugged the computer, went outside to the breezeway, and stood at the top of the stairs. The clouds throbbed with light. A storm cell freshened and battered the tin eave above my head. It was like standing behind a waterfall.

Through the screen door, I watched Tomlinson light a kerosene lamp. His long, stringy hair became a hood— a medieval monk, gaunt-faced, who carried the lamp to the fridge and rummaged for a modern version of beer.

"Want me to put a pot of coffee on?" he called.

"I'm not going to bother with rain gear," I replied. "I'll get soaked no matter what. Looks like the marina got knocked out, too."

Down the mangrove shoreline, Dinkin's Bay Marina was a community of shadows. A yellow mercury light flickered in its death throes. It showed a wedge of rooftop that was the marina office. Along A dock, a couple of the larger yachts had switched to battery power. Their windows cast blue oil-painting swirls on the bay and just enough light for me to notice an oddity. Someone was wading the mangrove rim headed my way—a beanpole person sheathed in glittering plastic as translucent as dragonfly wings. That was the impression anyway.

Internal alarm bells sounded. I checked my watch. Who in their right mind would be out in a storm two hours before midnight?

There was no benign explanation. Mack, the marina owner, always locks the gate by 10 on weekdays. Today was a Monday in July, the steamy off-season for tourism on Sanibel Island. And the dozen or so marina residents were savvy enough to stay safe and snug, buttoned up aboard their floating homes.

I am wary of strangers. More so on this rainy night because, three days ago, I had returned from a jungle rendezvous in Guyana, South America. It was unlikely, but a cadre of traffickers might be seeking revenge for the business I had completed there.

I went back into the house, telling Tomlinson, "Changed my mind. I'm going to grab my foul-weather jacket."

"A night as warm as this," he said, "you're better off

going *au naturel*. Good for the hair, and it cuts down on laundry bills. Take it from an old sailor."

I went past him, threw a curtain aside, and entered the cubbyhole that is my bedroom. "Are you expecting visitors?"

"Tonight? What time is it?"

I told him.

"Nope, but I haven't given up hope. It's still early. How about we pop over to the rum bar and grab a pint? I can finish my story."

"I'm not sure I want to hear it," I said. "Hold on a sec."

My pal kept talking. "Geezus, Doc, twenty-some years ago if sperm banks had posted warnings about DNA testing down the road, I would've dated the damn nurse and gone back to drugs instead of whacking off in a jar. She—this nurse—was very strict about no drug use. Not even weed. I needed the money. Plus, my god, the woman had the face of a saint and the hands of a dairy-maid. These days—or so I've read—they actually have a machine that—"

I interrupted. "I've got to use the head. Do you mind?" and pulled the curtain closed.

That shut him up.

I zipped on a foul-weather jacket, commercial-grade, made by Grundéns. After confirming that Tomlinson had returned to the table, I knelt and unlocked my private hidey-hole. It is the equivalent of a fireproof safe built into the floor. There, among false passports, a few treasured artifacts, and a newly rendered stack of one-ounce gold bars, were several weapons. Three were conventional firearms, two were not. As backup, I chose a Sig Sauer P365—a pistol small enough to carry unnoticed three hundred and sixty-five days a year yet that packs enough firepower to keep the owner alive for years to come.

Its clip-on holster slipped easily over my belt.

A less conventional choice was a military-grade laser. The gadget resembled a flashlight. It was silent, defensive in design, and not lethal. But it was also illegal. Either way, I had to be selective regarding usage. Hopefully, the person I'd seen was a drunken friend. Or a friendly drunk who'd lost his way.

I flushed the toilet and stepped through the curtain.

"Hey," Tomlinson asked, "where's Pete? It just crossed my mind he might be out there swimming around in this storm."

My dog, Pete, a retriever of murky lineage, had been staying with Luke O. Jones, a kid who works for me when I am away. I explained this with an edge that did not invite more questions.

"Another one of your mysterious trips," my friend responded. "Let me guess: Hannah got mad and dumped you again? Don't worry, bro. If she did, she'll come around."

Hannah Smith was Luke's aunt, a first-rate fishing

guide and my sometimes lover—when she wasn't miffed at me about something. And usually for good reason. Twice I had asked the woman to marry me. Twice, she had declined, which, on one level, was a relief. I'd made the offer. Me, the noble bachelor, had tried to do the right thing. But, on a deeper, more private level, I still nursed the hope she would come around.

I ignored Tomlinson, so he followed me across the room. "Hey, face it, she's a new mother. And you were doing a pretty good job as father, too—until you disappeared for two weeks. Women have a thing about foolish consistency. Want me to give her a call and try to smooth things over?"

Relationship advice from a guy who'd sought romance at a sperm bank? No thanks.

I said, "Save it for the mothers of kids you've never met," which was cruel, and I knew it. I stopped at the door. "Sorry, pal. That was unfair."

Tomlinson sighed in a way that communicated remorse. "No, you're right. The sperm bank business, truly a dumbass thing to do. But I didn't know, man, how could I? Screw the obvious fiscal responsibilities—I've got plenty set aside—but the emotional scars for those kids . . . Wow! You're the least emotional guy I know, so I could use a fresh eye." My friend paused. He noted the time I'd spent alone in my room, then consulted the nearest darkness of a window. "Hey, dude—who's out there?"

In response to my silence, he added, "Just because I can't see a gun doesn't mean I don't know you're packing heat."

"Packing heat?" I chuckled. It broke the tension. On a shelf near the door was a handheld VHF radio in its charger. There was mosquito repellent and other boating necessities including a small night vision monocular in a canvas military case. I unzipped the case, saying, "If Al Capone arrives, tell him to stay away from the windows until I get back. You, too, okay?"

I have a friend, a specialist in tactical optics, whose company recently moved from Phoenix to El Paso. When their engineers come up with a new gadget, he sends me a prototype to field test. NVD is the acronym for all varieties of night vision devices. The palm-sized scope in my hand was a hybrid mix of thermal imaging and forward-looking infrared—FLIR.

I returned to the breezeway steps. Rain had slowed and shaded the black mangrove shoreline. The person I had seen was no longer there. I tilted my glasses and put the scope to my eye. Shadows were illuminated as if by a bright jade lens. I scanned the area between the marina and the rickety boardwalk that is the only access to my house. If someone had mounted the boardwalk, trip wire beams would have sounded an alarm. But it was possible the person had waded into deeper water and was now hidden beneath the platform on which my house sits.

Or was it?

With the click of a button, I switched to thermal imaging. Green daylight became a Kodalith of contrasting blacks and grays. Spaced along the shore were glowing splotches of red. Mud had retained the heat from my visitor's feet. The footprints veered away from the water into the mangroves. Limbs there were adorned with occasional thermal handprints, smudges of color like luminous paint.

The person was heading for the road where I park my truck.

I went down the steps in the rain to a lower platform that also serves as a dock. My boat, moored beside the lab, strained at its lines in darkness. I studied trees that bracketed the boardwalk. A web of lightning confirmed no one was waiting in ambush. Thunder accompanied me across the boardwalk to a path through the mangroves. When my truck came into view, I stopped and used the trees for cover.

No sign of my visitor, but the hood of my truck was open.

What the hell?

There is a protocol, a color code of awareness. I transitioned from stage yellow to orange—a potential threat

RANDY WAYNE WHITE

had been identified. But what was the threat? A fisherman who wanted to steal a battery for his broken-down boat? Or some goon sent by Guyanese traffickers?

Odds were against the latter. The aliases I had used in South America had been randomly generated by professionals in the field. I had been provided documents to match—none of which, theoretically, could be traced to me.

Theoretically.

Tomlinson's lament about cyber-assaults on our privacy was a reminder that, in these noisy, intrusive times, the Theory of Anonymity—a statistical model created by clandestine experts—would soon be an anachronism, if it wasn't already.

Rain fauceted off the mangroves. Fat drops pelted the hood of my slicker. I pushed the hood back and took out the tactical laser. It's a complex bit of machinery but simple to use. The arming switch is shielded by a cover. When a blinking red LED confirmed the unit was ready, I toggled down to five-meter range—the lowest power— and approached my truck.

A quick search suggested that my visitor was up to no good but had been interrupted. Thermal imaging revealed a few footprints that were fading fast because of the rain. I followed them around the gate, through mangroves, into the marina parking lot, where they disappeared.

Odd. Why would a thief, or possibly a killer, choose

to be boxed in? I could think of only one reason—my visitor had come by boat.

I would have to hurry to get a glimpse.

Dinkin's Bay Marina is among the last of what were once called fish camps, which is to say it is a small area and the buildings are not giant galvanized barns. Mack is the owner. His house lay in sleepy silence beyond a ficus tree that separated it from the Red Pelican Gift Shop. No one was out in this heavy summer drizzle. But windows in the apartment above the marina's office glowed with the stark glare of a Coleman lantern.

Good. Jeth Nicholes, one of the fishing guides, was awake if help was needed.

Jogging, I used the building for cover, then peeked around for a view of the docks. The bay was leaden. Clouds flickered with thunderous regularity. I crossed to the shelter of a roofed area where bait tanks were bracketed by a pair of picnic tables.

I should have checked behind me. I didn't. From the shadows, an unexpected voice said, "We're both trespassing, but I'll call nine-one-one if I have to. Find someplace else to steal a car or, I swear to god, I will."

A woman's voice—tough, aggressive, not scared. I was so startled I jumped and spun around. It was the beanpole person I'd seen earlier sheathed in a translucent rain jacket. She was sitting, a vague gray shape, legs crossed.

"Geezus, you scared the crap out of me," I said. "Who are you?"

"Who are you?" she shot back.

"I live here, so take it easy. Did your boat break down? I can help find a battery if that's what you're after."

The woman's attitude was instantly transformed. She stood and stammered, "You're not . . . You're not him, are you? I'm sorry. I should've called, but . . . Well, how could I?"

Not only was it dark, my glasses were fogged. "Watch your eyes," I said. I used the flashlight, pointing it down so as not to blind either one of us. "Who're you looking for?"

The woman, mid-twenties, a rope of sodden hair over her right shoulder, was as tall as me. And her eyesight was better. "My bad," she said. "You . . . You must be his friend, the marine biologist, Dr. Ford . . . Dr. Marion Ford? He mentioned you in the foreword when they reissued his book."

"Book? Whose book?"

"You know . . . *him*. I've read it at least five times. Please don't tell him I'm here."

I relaxed a little. "The famous mystic and author," I said, smiling. "You snuck in hoping to meet Tomlinson. That explains part of it, I guess. What's your name?"

Delia something. Her last name was complicated. Kurrentanos, possibly—Greek, Mediterranean. She was one of Tomlinson's fans, nothing more. This was not unusual. Years ago, while institutionalized, my pal had written a valuable little book, *One Fathom Above Sea Level*—"a philosophical guide to kindness," as he describes it. Over the years, the book has accumulated a small, sometimes fanatical cult following. Many a starry-eyed female devotee had shown up at the marina unexpectedly hoping to meet their hero.

"Why so late—and during a storm?"

"I didn't mean for it to happen this way," she said, and pointed. "My boat's out there. It's a twenty-two-foot Catalina. I thought I'd be here by sunset, but that squall caught me. I had to tack and jibe the last five miles. No motor—a purist," she added with a hint of self-importance. "I thought Mr. Tomlinson might like that."

Purity is not a quality I associate with my friend. I let it pass. "Is there enough room on a boat that size to sleep tonight?" I asked. "You've got to stay somewhere. What about dry clothes?"

"I'm cool. Don't worry about me. I'd just gotten anchored when the power went off. There was no one around, so I waded ashore when I saw someone light a lamp at what must be your house. A taller man, long hair—I thought it might be him. But he lives out there, right?" Again she pointed. "I didn't want to intrude, so I set up closer to shore."

A strobe of lightning illuminated the brackish lake that is Dinkin's Bay. Tomlinson's old 42 Morgan floated aloof and alone on its distant mooring. A smaller sailboat was anchored not far from the mangroves.

"Delia is it? If you don't have a swing keel board," I said, "you'll be aground when the tide goes out."

Her confidence returned with a hint of aggression. "I'm not exactly a beginner, Dr. Ford. And I don't need advice from a stinkpotter on how or where to anchor. I saw that monster powerboat next to your house. Just promise you won't tell him, and I'll be out of here."

Stinkpotter. The last time I'd heard that condescending term was at a preppy yacht club in Palm Beach.

"I have a thing about lying—especially to friends," I said. "Don't worry. Tomlinson likes meeting his fans. So why not dry off, get some sleep, and stop by in the morning? You can explain why you were messing with my truck over breakfast."

"Your truck?" she responded. "That wasn't me. That's who I thought *you* were—a car thief. There was a guy. I saw him. He ran off when he saw me."

This was disturbing news. "A man? What did he look like?"

As I spoke, I tilted the flashlight and got my first veiled look at the girl's face—a face with sculpted features that reminded me of an old painting, not a friend or an acquaintance. But her blazing eyes, the shape of her ears, and the way she tugged her hair were all too familiar.

"Good Lord . . . you're not just a fan," I said gently.

"What do you mean?" she responded, but knew exactly what I meant. "I am a fan. Sort of, I guess. We all are—seven so far, according to the DNA thing we subscribe to."

DNA. That explained it.

"*Seven?*"

"Probably more, but like, who the hell really knows? It's been the strangest month of my life, Dr. Ford. I'm not asking you to lie. Just hold off telling him until we can meet in our own way. Tomorrow, like you said."

How could I refuse such a simple request from one of Tomlinson's daughters?

TWO

Tomlinson had carried the lantern into the lab and was gawking out the bayside window when I returned.

"A 22 Catalina," he remarked, referencing the sailboat that had recently arrived, and the girl who was aboard. "Who's that tall drink of water? You should've invited her up."

It's possible that I imagined his locker-room leer, yet I let it go until he added, "Even from this distance, I like her swagger. Cripes, Doc, now she's . . . Well, that woman's got hands made for the tiller, I'll say that much."

"Get away from that window," I snapped.

"Huh? All I meant was—"

"I know what you meant. Since when did voyeurism

get added to your list of weird-ass kinks? And blow out that damn lamp. You can't hear the generator running?"

I switched on a light and found Tomlinson staring at me as if I'd gone mad. "Who blew a grumpy pill up your butt?"

"Hands made for a tiller," I parroted. "Like you're some dumb high school jock. Women at this marina have a right to privacy—even around you."

"Well, thank you, Gloria Steinem. Hey, man, shallow up. Before you boil the tar and get the feathers, come look for yourself." He slid the curtain aside and motioned me to the window.

I approached reluctantly. Below, beyond the mangroves, Delia was sculling her little sailboat toward deeper water, both hands on the rudder post. A flicker of lightning showed that she still wore the baggy rain slicker.

"Oh," I said. "*That* kind of tiller."

"Apology accepted." My friend smiled. He scooted closer to the window. "A minute ago, I watched her pull anchor with one hand and use the other to row herself upwind. Amigo, that's some old-school sailing right there. Why're you in such a pissy mood?" A moment later, he added, "Good, she's anchoring again. I want to meet that girl. What's her story?"

Rather than lie, it's wiser to stick to the truth, then quickly switch the subject. "She's one of your fans. The rest, she can tell you herself. Take a look at what I found planted on my truck." At the lab's workstation, I switched on another light and placed a small rectangular device on the desk. It was a GPS transponder on a magnetic base.

Tomlinson's mind remained on our new arrival. "A fan of my book? Hmm . . . and a kick-ass sailor, too. What's she look like?"

I said, "Nothing like you, thank god. Knock it off and pay attention. Someone stuck this under the back bumper. They want to track me. They had the hood open, too, then got spooked and ran."

He gestured to the window. "It couldn't have been her—not if she's simpatico with my books. They tend to be gentle, spiritual beings. Highly intelligent. What's she like? From a distance, a pretty nice body, I'd say."

"How the hell would I know? And enough with the crude remarks, okay? We only talked for a few minutes. Stick to the GPS. There's a long list of people who might have a reason to want to know where I am."

Tomlinson hoped I was about to open up regarding my recent visit to South America. It was in the eagerness of his laid-back reaction. "Hey, cool. If you need to rap or get something off your chest, I'm all ears. Or not . . . Whatever . . . How dangerous are these dudes?"

I replied, "When the internet reboots, I'll look up the make of the transponder. That might tell me something. I don't know . . . Could be the Bahamian government, maybe."

This was a red herring, but a possibility. I was referring to the recently rendered gold ingots in my floor safe—and an additional hundred pounds of gold, twenty-two karat, that lay hidden beneath my dock in the form of a mooring anchor.

The windfall was a recent acquisition. Tomlinson was the only person I'd shared the story with—not solely out of trust, although I do trust him. As a small-time ganja merchant, he's also had a lifetime of experience at money laundering. Dodging taxes wasn't my intent. But how does a low-profile biologist liquidate two million dollars in gold, then declare it as income?

Slowly, carefully, a few thousand dollars at a time, was the answer. As a result, my lab was now equipped with an acetylene torch, a jeweler's oven, and graphite molds in various troy-ounce sizes.

"Bahamian spooks, that makes sense," Tomlinson reasoned. "You're a rich man now—and you can always go back to fatten the kitty if you want more." He said this in an odd, testing way. "You know what that means, don't you?"

I got up. "There's got to be at least two beers left. Want one?" Then, at the door, I listened to him explain, "Dude, I grew up wealthy. Take it from me, even the best of us are potentially dangerous. Greed isn't a financial issue. It's the most common of human flaws."

I stopped. "I don't feel guilty about stealing from a thief, if that's what you're hinting at."

"I'm talking about me. All of us. That's why I'm sort of excited about this DNA test thing. When the internet's running, I'll show you emails from my test tube heirs . . ." He turned to the window, more interested in our recent arrival than his claims of munificence. "Doc, this might be my best last chance to give it all away."

In the morning, puttering out the harbor in my fast, open boat, I got my first daylight look at Delia with the complicated last name. She was atop the cabin of the little Catalina, hanging out laundry to dry. Her bikini top consisted of two swaths of cinnamon handkerchief that tinted the olive glow of her skin. A tall woman, almost six feet, with a spill of glossy, cherry-black hair. She had a body that, at first glance, I knew would cause Tomlinson to make an absolute ass of himself if I didn't intercede.

She waved in a *Hello, new neighbor* way. I waved in response.

On the docks, the fishing guides—Jeth Nicholes, Neville Robeson, and Big Alex Paine—speared me with looks of pure envy. This confirmed my assessment of Delia's physical attributes. Immediately, I turned away from the channel and idled another hundred yards to my friend's sun-bleached Morgan, the name *No Más* in script on the stern.

"Are you awake?" I called.

My pal came yawning up the cabin steps. "Yeah, man. I was just braiding my hair. What do you think?"

"Geezus." I grimaced and gestured to our audience on the dock. "Get some clothes on, for god sakes—at least a towel."

Delia was watching, too.

He abandoned the Rastafarian clump of hair he'd been frizzing. "Whoops! My bad." He reappeared wearing baggy surfer's shorts. "What's shakin', Elvis?"

"I don't make promises unless I intend to keep them," I said. "You know that."

"For sure, amigo. Good ol' Marion Ford—the last honest hall monitor at the school for wayward boys." He sniffed and gave a long sigh as he refocused on Delia, who, even from a distance, was stunning. His eyelids drooped. A second deep breath communicated pain, and he wet his lips. "Dear heaven above . . . what a beautiful vision to behold. The girl loves my book, does she? Hot damn, Sam. My cup runneth over, methinks."

"Your cup needeth a shock collar," I responded. "That's why I stopped by. There's something you need to know."

Tomlinson seemed not to hear. "In a way," he mused, "I hope she chooses not to become one of my Zen students. I have very strict rules about fraternizing with students. Although, let's be honest—I've broken them a time or three." After another painful sigh, he added, "If this is another one of God's shitty morality checks, all I have to say is, Thank you, Jesus . . . There oughta be a law, huh?"

"There is," I said. "Don't look at her, dumbass, look at me." He did. "Remember what we were discussing last night?"

"Uhh . . . no."

"DNA? The fertility clinic? She's your daughter, you bonehead. One of them anyway."

Shock registered as a question. *"What?"*

I said it again.

My pal recoiled with an expression of self-disgust. "Oh man. That's just freakin' cruel, if you're joking. Please tell me you're joking. Wait, you're not . . . Are you sure?"

"She asked me not to tell you. I'm only doing this because I know what an idiot you can be."

"My *daughter?*" It was too much for him to process. "Geezus, God has smitten my wicked ass once again." He wheeled around, suddenly dizzy. "Oh, this is just . . . Know what I am? Lowlife scum is exactly what I am. I've been eyeballing that innocent young creature all morning. I should be lassoed and put in a cage for some of the god-awful scenarios that went through my head. And just now, in the cabin, I . . . I almost—"

Tomlinson put his hands on his stomach as if about to retch. He flapped his arms and sat heavily on the starboard bench. "That does it, man. I'm done with sex. I mean it. Total celibacy until we get this whole DNA mess sorted out. Doc—promise you'll help. We both know how weak I am."

"When you meet the girl," I said, "don't bother acting like you're surprised when she tells you who she is. You're a terrible liar, and I'd prefer not to add another lie to the mix." I throttled my boat into reverse and pulled away.

"Dude . . . you're not leaving? Wouldn't it be better if you introduced us?"

"Put some clothes on and invite her to breakfast," I called over my shoulder. "Relax, be yourself. The girl's smart enough to know she could've done a lot worse in the gene pool lottery."

I exited Dinkin's Bay at cruising speed and turned east toward the Sanibel Causeway. The bridge is a series of arches linked by strands of beach and passageways of blue that funnel into the Gulf of Mexico. There were only a few boats out on this heat-dense morning. Highway traffic was sparse—a seasonal rarity I'd been counting on.

I was about to set a trap.

On the console, open to satellites above, was the GPS I'd found on my truck. If the person or parties tracking me were applying tight cover, my boat would soon blend with the snail's flow of cars on the causeway. If someone was sent, they would arrive expecting to find my old blue Chevy pickup, unaware I was watching them from the water.

Whoever had done it had botched the job by leaving my hood up. I was not dealing with professionals.

They were.

At Woodring Point, I hugged the shoreline, ran beneath power lines along Bay Drive, then turned northeast parallel to the bridge. Car traffic would provide cover when viewed from a satellite. Years ago, dredges used to build the causeway had created two mini islands and cut winding, unmarked channels through the shoals. I crossed the flat to where casuarina pines shaded a parking area and a public restroom. In three feet of water, I shut down and drifted along a strand of white beach.

No one around, just me. Had this been a Sunday in March, the place would've been packed with a cheerful circus of RVs and charcoal grills. This was a Tuesday in July—but the heat was not the only reason for the absence of visitors. Southwest Florida was just beginning to recover from months of a toxic algae bloom that, generically, is referred to as red tide. It is a cancerous natural phenomenon, exacerbated by human-borne contaminants. Influences are still a matter of rancorous debate, but it is generally agreed that during these blooms, algae dies, sinks to the bottom, and the process of its bacterial decomposition depletes the water of oxygen.

Fish and filtering species literally die of suffocation.

Every ten to fifteen years it happens, according to re-cords I have long collected. And every cycle it seems the harbinger of an environmental apocalypse. That is as true today as it was in 1857, when locals referred to it as a poisonous plague, and in 1947, when Navy warships were summoned to blow hundreds of acres of dead fish out of Tampa Bay.

This year, however, was the most destructive red tide I'd experienced. And, unlike dead fish, internet images of the mess had lingered months after the worst was past. Bloated corpses of bottlenose dolphins, dead sea turtles— photos of these amid mounds of decomposing sea wrack had displaced reality via social media. Tourism on the coast had taken a massive hit. Thus the scarcity of boat and car traffic.

I nosed onto the beach, put the GPS transponder into my pocket, and slipped over the side into the water. Near the public restroom, I knelt to tie my shoes. Once the transponder was hidden under a scoop of sand, I re-turned to the boat and began fishing not far from shore. The meadow of turtle grass there is in five feet of water— ideal for an 8-weight fly rod with a floating line.

I drifted in the heat until I lucked into a mixed school of ladyfish and spotted sea trout. Ladyfish are superb fighters. Sea trout, a member of the drum family, are more of a visual pleasure than a sporting challenge, but they're pretty good to eat if not overcooked. Better yet, they are among the last species to rally after a prolonged red tide.

This was an encouraging sign.

Fishing kept me busy through a few false alarms. A van with a mother and children arrived, then an SUV with a nervous couple possibly looking for a secluded place to continue their affair.

Half an hour and several nice sea trout later, my trackers arrived from the mainland in the form of a hefty Harley-Davidson carrying two helmeted riders. A big-shouldered male sat at the handlebars. He wore a checkered racing helmet, silver on black, full-faced. A female, riding aft, watched the screen of her cell phone and voiced directions into a wireless system built into the helmets.

I couldn't hear them, nor did I show any interest. They did a slow pass. They made another pass, then circled back and stopped near where I'd hidden the transponder.

Body language told a story. The woman was insistent: *Damn it, the blue truck had to be around here somewhere.* The man was impatient. As a pair, they took a look inside the public restrooms. Unfortunately for me, they still wore helmets when they remounted the Harley and sped off toward Sanibel.

After that it was a race, me against them. I retrieved the GPS, slung myself into the boat, and motored full throttle back to Dinkin's Bay. By the time the Harley rumbled into the marina parking lot, the magnetic transponder was under the bed of my truck. I watched from a mosquito haze in the shadows of mangroves.

Again, they did a pass by, circled back, and stopped. Body language communicated confusion, then irritation. The woman pantomimed throwing the GPS tracker away. *This damn thing can't be trusted!* The man seemed accusatory. *How'd you screw up such an easy job?*

The bike was too far away for me to get the license plate, so I took a chance. I exited the boardwalk and stepped out into the sunlight. I offered a friendly wave and approached. The man, helmet visor down, took one look, nudged the woman, and they sped off.

I felt a little better after that. They were bungling amateurs. In my mind, this eliminated cartel traffickers from Guyana as my adversaries, but nonetheless left a long list of thugs I'd offended over the years.

I have lived an unusual life.

More likely, I decided, they were treasure hunter types on the scent of a shrewd operator named Jimmy Jones. Jimmy had been the hottest high-tech treasure hunter in the business for a while. National magazines ran cover stories. There had been documentaries on the so-called engineering wizard who'd solved the impossibility of salvaging wrecks in water that was two miles deep.

But Jimmy was a thief at heart. He had used his notoriety to attract big-time investors and bilked them out of millions. And then one day he had just disappeared.

With him vanished many tons of Spanish and Dutch gold that archaeologists considered to be a treasure trove of history.

It took the feds years to finally nab the guy, and they offered him a deal: Reveal where he'd hidden the stuff, then maybe a better deal and bail could be discussed.

One of Jimmy's investors was more succinct: Draw a map or die in jail.

The infamous treasure hunter had refused. Bad choice. He had been found in the showers with his head beaten in. To the feds, the location of the stolen gold remains a mystery, although a few savvy insiders still suspect that Jimmy's ex-girlfriend might know where to look.

They are right.

Several months back in the Bahamas, I got lucky. I learned an interesting detail that insurance agencies and several governments had dismissed as unimportant. Jimmy, while a student at MIT, had worked part-time at a place that manufactured commercial mooring buoys.

Mooring buoys.

The rig is used worldwide—a big floating ball connected to a chain with a heavy lead weight below. A mooring buoy is the quickest way to secure a boat where there is insufficient dockage—standard tackle in the islands.

This detail had provided a working theory that proved correct. Jimmy had melted a cache of stolen artifacts into mooring anchors—spoon-shaped plates that weighed fifty kilos each. I'd found dozens of them buried in the sandy shallows, hidden in plain sight.

By then, I'd also met Jimmy's ex, a smart, mousy woman whom I had helped to disappear.

I've had few lucky windfalls in my life, but nothing compared to this discovery. Do the math. One hundred and twenty pounds of gold equals seventeen hundred–plus troy ounces. Multiply that by the daily bullion price, minus the standard ten percent dealer's fee.

The anchor plate I'd stolen from Jimmy, the thief, was worth in excess of two mil. I'd returned with only one plate, flying solo in my little Maule four-cylinder seaplane. And dozens more were still out there just a two-hour flight away.

But why risk it? I was rich by my standards, and living under the radar has been a lifelong necessity. Not that it has been easy in recent days. At a boat show in St. Pete, I'd been tempted to buy a stunning Marlow Havana, 37 feet long and powered by a triad of Evinrude outboards— 750 horsepower. I couldn't take my eyes off the damn thing, but the same would be true of anyone who knows boats. That's precisely why I didn't buy it.

At the Ford dealership in Fort Myers, I caved a little when I test drove an F-150 Raptor. In comparison to my old blue Chevy, it was an off-road rocket ship designed to survive the wilds of Baja. So I'd made a down payment on one in volcanic gray, but minus all the *Look at me* Raptor badges. Delivery date was a few months away. I still had time to change my mind.

The toughest test, though, was the urge to buy a new seaplane. My small, usually reliable Maule M-5, a four-seater, the fuselage blue on white, had been in the shop for nearly a month. Both pontoons had sprung leaks, and there was a carburetor linkage problem that even my ace mechanic, Ricky Hilton, had yet to solve.

I'd been grounded—an inconvenience I had to live with as if there was no alternative.

Keep it simple, stupid is an old reliable credo. Now that I had money, greed was an intuited enemy. The urge to expand, add more and more to my pile for money's own sake, was a bad idea. It had a cancerous parallel to all sorts of lethal phenomena—the recent red tide included.

Tomlinson, the son of a billionaire, was right. When big money is involved, even the best people can become dangerous.

It gave me something to think about on my way back to the lab. When the timing was right, I decided, I would remind my pal that this maxim might also apply to his new list of DNA heirs.

THREE

Delia's last name was Carapoulos, spelled with a *C*. Until a month ago, she had believed her parents were of Greek and Swiss descent, but was now in emotional limbo. The same was true of the six half siblings whom Delia had yet to meet but knew through a DNA website that offered subscribers the seemingly harmless opportunity to discover their genetic roots.

Most of the siblings, Delia had told Tomlinson, went by first names only. As a group, they were still in shock over the news yet intrigued when one of them discovered the identity of their true birth father. An email address had been provided by the cult author's publisher—with the author's blanket permission, of course.

Tomlinson shared all of this in a rush as he tugged his

hair and paced around the lab. It was a Wednesday morning. The squall had washed the air clean and flattened the bay into a blue-green gel.

I said, "I warned you about spitting into a test tube and sending it to an international data bank—especially a guy with your history." Months ago, when the DNA craze had swept the island, I'd warned several marina locals—all friends. Our tropical boat bum culture is a freewheeling, randy lot, so why invite attention from the past? Returns were still coming in, and reviews regarding the results were mixed.

"That's exactly why I didn't send the damn tube in," he responded, "so back off, boogaloo. Besides, wouldn't have mattered anyway from what Delia told me. Doc, meeting her was the strangest hour I've ever spent in my life—and that's saying something."

"You've set the bar pretty high," I said agreeably. I was at the desk reading a research proposal, *Trophic Ecology of Large Coastal Predators Along Florida's Gulf Coast*. It had to do with sharks eating bottlenose dolphins, possibly caused by reduced food sources as a result of the red tide.

"The poor girl didn't know whether to hug me or tell me to burn in hell for being such a thoughtless, no-good dilettante. So she did both."

"Dilettante?" I said. "That's an unusual choice of words, but okay. Shows she's smart. Most people tumble for your spiritual Zendo persona right off the bat."

"This is serious, bro."

I wasn't joking, but eased off a tad. "Sorry. This has got to be tough on all of you. What else did she say?"

Tomlinson straddled a chair and plopped down opposite me. "The mood swings, man. She quoted a few favorite lines from my book—a real spiritual connection. We both felt it, no doubt. *Zap!* Electrical, you know? But she doesn't look much like me, I don't think."

"No, thank god," I replied.

"Dude, don't be mean. Her ears, some of her mannerisms, even her voice, reminds me of a classier female edition of yours truly. But, holy cripes, moody. She'd fester back on what she called the lie she has been living and get stormy cold. How could her parents do this to her? And who the hell was I to impose my genetics on her and umpteen other kids I didn't give a damn about and, hopefully, would never meet."

He continued. "Those were her words, not mine. I felt so guilty, I booked her a nice room on the beach for a couple of nights. The poor thing sailed all this way to meet me, no AC on her boat, and the damn 'skeeters about ate her alive last night."

My friend was suddenly teary-eyed.

"Take it easy, ol' buddy," I said.

"Damn it, though, Delia's right. I don't know if I can handle it, Doc, meeting them one at a time like this. And what if those kids want to include their mothers? Worse, their fathers—the real ones, men who worked their asses off to raise them? Geezus frogs, who'd've thought that whacking off in a jar was more dangerous than sleeping with married women?"

I pushed aside the paper I'd been reading. "Geographically, the other six siblings, where are they from? Wait—start at the beginning. If you didn't do the DNA test, how the hell did they find out their biological father was a sperm donor?"

Tomlinson settled back and explained how things had been when he was a younger man. After getting a Ph.D., he'd bummed around California, refusing to accept money from his estranged East Hampton family. Drugs—cocaine, heroin, LSD—he'd tried them all and ended up in a Berkeley psych facility. Nearby was Mensal Cryonics, a Boston-based firm with sperm bank clinics in California, Miami, and Atlanta. They targeted an upscale clientele. Donors were carefully screened with an emphasis on high IQs and success in both scholastics and athletics. Thoroughbred genetics, is what the company was selling.

"At the clinic, I had to document everything," he went on, "from my varsity letters in high school to my college curriculum vitae. Did I mention the nurse took a shine to me? So she definitely cut me some slack regarding my past, but that was a wise business decision, she claimed. Us tall Scandinavian types with Ivy League degrees were their bestselling models. Like picking out a car, you know? Couples who couldn't get pregnant got a list of options—eye color, hair type, ethnic background. Did they prefer a chess champion or a baseball star? It was a small clinic, and you know what a drag it can be to be cooped up in an office all day. The nurse—maybe just a clinician, I don't know—she was forty-five going on eighteen, so we played around and enjoyed ourselves, but still got the job done."

I asked, "How many times did you, uhh . . . More than forty, you told me."

Tomlinson was unsure. "Hydration became an issue, I remember that much. The nurse said I was the equivalent of a Cadillac Coupe de Ville, fully loaded. And that's how I was listed in the clinic's catalog—as Deville—along with a sort of bio. Donors were assigned a single fake name—sort of like pro wrestlers. So I assumed it would stay that way because of how the procedure worked."

"Because it was just you and the nurse, alone in a room," I suggested.

"No. It's the way female clients were inseminated. The procedure was called"—he had to search his memory— "complex insemination? No, it was called confused insemination. That was the term. *Confused* because the clinics intentionally murked the outcome. Here's how."

He explained that Mensal Cryonics had a strict protocol. Clients were instructed to have intercourse the day before the insemination procedure and the day after. To increase the odds of the male partner actually impregnating the female, he, too, contributed a sperm sample. It was then mixed with the anonymous donor's sperm.

A similar protocol was used if the eggs were fertilized

outside the female's body prior to being injected into the uterus.

"Geezus," I said. "I had no idea. In a way, it's kind of creepy, but statistically, I guess, it makes sense."

"Creepy, even when you think it through," Tomlinson said. "There was a real chance that the father actually *was* the father. A psychological boost, you know? And if the guy was shooting blanks, the happy couple got the deluxe model instead. Not that I gave it much thought at the time. It paid more than selling blood and was a heck of a lot more fun."

I asked the obvious: How did Delia and the others track him down?

Tomlinson's reaction suggested self-contempt. "'Cause I was a thoughtless idiot who didn't bother to read the fine print. Mensal Cryonics was one of the first to require that donors allow their personal information to be released—upon request, of course—when the children they'd sired turned twenty-one. But hell, back then what were the chances? I didn't have a clue until a month ago when I got what I thought was a crank email from a guy—my son, turns out. Online, he'd already made contact with three of his DNA siblings. They have this sort of chat page thing. But he was the first to contact the clinic and demand my personal information. There are a ton of Tomlinsons in the world, but only one adult male, apparently, named Sighurdhr Mantle Tomlinson. After that, finding me wasn't too hard."

"The guy—what do you know about him?" I asked.

"My son, you mean? A nice kid, seems like. Well . . . he's in his mid-twenties and has a divinity degree from Carolina Christian. The Right Reverend Chester Pickett— a freakin' Baptist via the U.S. Marine Corps. Isn't that a kick in the pants? Chester's acted sort of as spokesman for the group. Before he found out my name, he and the others referred to me as Johnny. Get it? As in Johnny Appleseed? Or Capt. Monkey Spanker. That still hurts my feelings for some reason."

"This was a month ago? You didn't mention it to me. Have you heard from all six? Or is it seven?"

Tomlinson replied, "I guess I thought it would blow over—which proves I was in denial. At first anyway. Then I got more emails while you were gone. Man, what a stunner. So I started to rethink the situation." He made a fluttering noise, overwhelmed. "So far, seven. But maybe seventeen or more, for all I know. Geographically, most of the kids still live in states where there are Mensal clinics—one in California, one near Boston, and two from Florida. Delia was born in San Diego, but her folks moved to Tampa when she was a girl."

"Had she emailed you?"

"Nope. I didn't know about her until today, but I've heard from a son in Gainesville, and another outside Boston. The only one who seems happy about the big surprise is a daughter who lives in Arizona . . ." My friend managed a smile. "She's a real pisser, that one. Imogen, age twenty-four. Just graduated from Sedona College of Holistic Medicine. Cool, huh? I got my third email from her yesterday. Lots of emoji kisses. And an idea I tried to bounce off you last night, but you split."

"Bounce away," I said.

"You ready for this? Imogen, the Arizona girl? She wants to have a reunion. All seven of us—or anyone who wants to come."

"You've never met these people. How can you have a reunion?"

"We've got to call it something. Conclave? That doesn't sound right. And meet and greet is definitely out. That's a homograph just begging for an ugly twist."

It took me second. "Oh yeah . . . *meat* and greet."

Tomlinson winced. "Yep. Imogen suggested Florida since three of the kids live here already. I'd have to pay her way, of course. They—the six or seven of them—they've been discussing it back and forth over the chat page they use. A couple of the kids, though, want no part of it. Imogen's the only one who's really stoked. She's never been to Florida."

He got up, began to pace again, and referenced a daughter he hadn't seen since his acrimonious divorce fifteen years ago. "Let's face it, pal, I haven't been much of a father to Nichola and I knew she was my kid from the get-go. The girl still won't talk to me, and I don't think that'll change. So, I'm trying to view this as a chance to redeem myself. God knows, if anyone needs redemption, it's me." For an instant, he made eye contact. The inclusion *You, too* seemed implied.

"Doc," he added, "I'd like you to talk to her as a favor to me. It was her idea."

"Who, Nichola?"

"No, coconut head. Spend some time with Delia. This morning, I tried to win her over to the idea of a reunion. She balked. So, as a sort of character reference, I used you. Even gave her a couple of your research papers to read. She called from the hotel. Maybe you could take her fishing or something."

"No thanks," I said. "It's ninety in the shade out there. Besides, I don't want to get in the middle of this mess."

"Come on, Marion. Delia was impressed by your research work. Says you're a dispassionate clinical thinker. I told her, 'No shit, Sherlock,' which at least got a laugh. You know me better than anyone, man. She just wants to . . . Well, I'm not sure why Delia wants to talk, but she does."

I said, "In other words, she doesn't trust you."

"Bingo," Tomlinson replied. "Would you mind?"

I gave it some thought during my noon workout session. Noon in July because I'd found my endurance lacking in the jungles of Guyana, and that's the way it starts. We lose a step over months of modern living. We indulge in carbs, desserts, too many beers, and our caveman brain records the data as a season of plenty. Time to hibernate, pile on the pounds. In fact, that lost step is the first concession to decay.

It's inevitable, of course, the aging process. But the caveman brain, if ignored, also interprets sloth as symptomatic of surrender. The body is mindless machinery. It always prefers the laziest path of resistance before the final stop, which is the grave.

Not today, I told myself.

It is a one-point-four-mile straightaway from the Dinkin's Bay gate to the end of Tarpon Bay Road. I did it in a respectable twelve minutes. There, the beach curves east and west. I chose the deepest sand, of course. Alternately, I jogged and sprinted west another mile until I damn near collapsed in the heat. This was near the West Wind Inn. A turquoise pool and umbrellas at the tiki bar beaconed. I stumbled up the bank, over putting-green-groomed grass toward restrooms located beneath the pool bar deck. I almost made it. Almost. Midway, I stopped, turned, and upchucked in the bushes.

Fortunately, the few people lounging around the pool didn't notice. But above me, from the bar, a woman's voice beckoned, saying, "Are you okay, mister? Want me to call nine-one-one?"

My glasses were fogged. I removed them and looked up at the blurry figure. "Huh? No. Just need a couple bottles of water. I've got money. Is the bartender up there?"

In my confused state, the voice, weirdly familiar, funneled down as if through a tunnel. "Oh my god . . . You're Dr. Ford. I thought you had more sense."

It was Tomlinson's daughter, I realized. "Nope, not me. No sense at all," I replied, and attempted a smile. My hands were on my knees in what military types call the leaning rest.

There was the clatter of a chair. "You're so pale . . . white as a sheet," Delia called. "Hang on. I'll bring you some ice before you pass out."

"Don't be silly," I insisted. That's when the ground rushed up to meet me and I damn near did.

O n my way back to the lab, Tomlinson exited the parking lot on his fat-tire bike. Decorations included peace signs on the fenders and a basket on the handlebars stamped *Fausto's, Key West*.

"Geezus, you look like hell, bro," he said. "Don't tell me you went for a run at this time of day. You out of your freakin' mind?"

I had already been lectured on the dangers of heat exhaustion by Delia. The girl turned out to be a twenty-five-year-old Eckerd College grad who'd majored in chemistry with a minor in marine science. She had also pampered me with ice and Gatorade while scolding, "The trouble with biologists your age is, you guys spend all your time indoors at a computer or a microscope. No I-R-L experience—in, like, real life, you know? Pilates or yoga, that's what I'd recommend. Start slow, and work your way up to jogging."

To Tomlinson, I said, "I'm taking your daughter out in the net boat around sunset. How do you want me to handle it?"

"You talked to her?"

"At the West Wind. I went to the pool to cool off and there she was. It's up to you. How honest do you want me to be? I'm not going to lie to her, but I can try to avoid the rough patches."

"Hell, tell her the truth and let the facts fall where they may," Tomlinson said, then decided, "No . . . wait." He walked his bike into the shade while he reconsidered. "What rough patches?"

I said, "Do you really need a list?"

He scratched at his temple where there was a scar that resembled a figure eight. "Well . . . I see no need to mention that I've been busted for drugs, and sold my share of weed. That would set a bad example. I don't want a child of mine thinking it's okay to smoke. Bad for the lungs, man. Even I know that."

"Got it," I said. "Anything else?"

"Well, these days the whole drug scene is risky. LSD tabs—you can't trust that crap. It's cooked by methheads and skanks—amateurs, not true cortex explorers. Drugs, totally out. That's a definite no-fly zone for kids Delia's age. Don't you think?"

I said, "Gotcha," and started away.

"Oh—" Tomlinson snapped his fingers. "One more thing. I wouldn't mention that murder charge. We both know it was totally bogus."

I turned. "Yeah, that's what I figured."

"Good. Then you'd have to get into the whole jealous husband thing. Infidelity, screwing around, and jumping out of windows at midnight. That kinda crazy shit. I'd just tell the girl, sure, your birth father hasn't lived a perfect life, but he's the sort of man who strives for the wisdom to learn from his mistakes."

He took another second to ponder. "In fact, I'm on my way to the West Wind now. Maybe I'll just tell her myself."

"Good idea," I said.

"Doc?" Again, I pulled up. "Did you two hit it off? Not romantically, of course—at least, I hope not." Tomlinson scowled at me for a moment. "Dude, that would be breaking the rules. Same with the other yahoos who were ogling Delia at the marina today. Hands off, understand?"

I said, "Dude—if the world played by your rules, there would be fighting in the streets. We met by accident. I pushed myself a little too hard, and she thought I was suffering heatstroke. Which I wasn't, of course.

She's a nice girl but, frankly, sort of condescending and with an attitude. She brought me a bag of ice and made me cool off in the pool. That was it."

The scowl vanished. "What do you expect of a girl who has genetics from the à la carte menu? Does she seem to trust you?"

"She thinks I'm a bumbling nerd," I said, "with no real-life experience. She used some dumb acronym—*I-R*-something. Doubt she thinks I'm smart enough to be tricky. But at least she doesn't say 'like' every three or four words."

"Perfect." My friend, nodding, smiled as if satisfied. "When you come right down to it, Doc, I think the less our kids know about us, the better."

In the afternoon, I walked to the marina. It was near closing time. Mack, the owner, was behind the counter chewing on a cigar. He is a large, squat man, balding, who claims he migrated from New Zealand to the goldfields of Australia, then invested his profits in Sanibel. Along with owning the marina, he'd recently purchased a cluster of fifties-era beach cottages, formerly a nudist colony.

"Damn idiots," Mack muttered, his accent muted by many years in the States. He was focused on a laptop near the register.

I got a quart of beer from the cooler and placed it on the counter. "Still problems getting building permits?" I asked. He'd been trying to remodel the cottages and wanted to change the signage out front from *Grin-N-Bare-It Resort* to something more tropical.

"Always problems when you deal with the city," Mack growled. "But what really pisses me off is, there are idiots among us who won't let that damn red tide go away. Business was down twenty percent all summer. And now, when it should be getting better, our local so-called experts posted this."

He swung the computer around for me to see. It was video of beach carnage shot months ago during the worst of the algae bloom. A dead false killer whale lay amid piles of bloated fish. The YouTube caption urged viewers to donate to a local conservation group to "Fight Big Sugar" and pollution from Lake Okeechobee.

"Sanibel hauled three hundred tons of dead fish off the beach," I reminded Mack. "Water quality still isn't great. And it's not like it didn't happen—you know how fast people forget."

The man's face reddened. "Right, mate. But it's not happening now, and this goddamn lie was posted today. That's my point. Silly fools don't realize that if businesses like mine go broke, who's gonna fund them and their damn staff? They're pissing on the bankbook in their own bloody nest."

On the laptop screen's search window, I noticed an

oddity. Mack had been researching gambling laws in New Zealand, as well as the culture of the indigenous people there—the Māori Tribe.

"Are you thinking about selling out?" I asked.

He seemed not to hear. "Cheeky do-gooder bastards," he fumed. "We've never asked the media to lie—tourists aren't stupid. Pull a trick like that, they'd never come back. Every business owner on the islands understands that. But why do these idiots beg for money by publishing this crap when the beaches are clean and the fishing's good again?" He turned the computer his way and looked up. "Fishing is good again, isn't it? Have you done a flyby lately?"

"Can't," I said, "my plane's down for repairs. But I'm taking my net boat out around sunset, and I'll do a drag for forage fish."

Mack's reaction asked *Huh*?

"Forage fish—small stuff that bigger fish eat," I said. "Menhaden, ballyhoo, pinfish, mullet. Without them, the whole fishing pyramid collapses. It's a lot better than it was, I can tell you that much."

He seemed satisfied, then motioned with the cigar. "Got a minute? I want to show you something else. Between us, okay?"

I followed him through the fish market outside, then into his private office. After a peek out the door, he locked it and took a seat at his desk. "What do you know about gaming casinos?"

Casinos? Maybe he really was thinking about selling the marina. "They're smoky," I said. "And it's *gambling*, not *gaming*. Using a sham name doesn't make it less of a dirty business. You're thinking about opening a casino? Mack, that's just nuts."

"I thought you'd be more open-minded," he replied patiently. "Doc"—he chewed at his cigar for a moment—"there's a lot you don't know about me. Well, let's face it, everyone at this marina has their little secrets."

His smile suggested he knew things about me that were best not shared.

I didn't doubt it. And I knew a lot more about Mack than the man realized. He hadn't made his money in the goldfields of Australia. He'd left Tasmania, where he was wanted for assault, racketeering, and running an illegal carnival show. Mack hadn't migrated to Florida, he'd fled.

"We're all human," I responded amiably.

"You're bloody right about that, mate," he chuckled. "I'm going to tell you something that only two of my girlfriends know. Have a look at this." He reached behind him and placed a carved wooden spear on the desk. The thing was beautiful. It was glossy amber with intricate designs etched into the knob and along the shaft. "This is considered to be a power totem in New Zealand," he said, lowering his voice. "Handed down by kings."

I waited for him to nod permission before taking the spear into my hands. "From the Māori Tribe?"

"My ancient ancestors," Mack said.

"Your what?"

The man seemed to puff up, shoulders back, in his chair. "That's right—I'm part indigenous Pacific Islander. You're a scientist, maybe you can tell me. Does that mean, legally speaking, I might also be considered a Native American? I'm a legal citizen of this country, after all, and people did migrate here from the Pacific. There was a show about it on the Travel Channel."

I started to laugh. Couldn't help myself. "Geezus, Mack, I get it now. A gambling casino like the Seminole and Miccosukee tribes run in the Glades. How long has it been since you got your DNA test back? A few days? I told you those damn things would be nothing but trouble."

My friend, offended, took the spear from my hands. "That's a shitty thing to say. I've always suspected I'm part Māori. In my heart." He banged his chest with his fist. "Where it counts. It's something a Caucasian wouldn't understand. The DNA thing only confirms what I've always known—legally speaking."

"Take it easy," I said. "What percentage Māori? Look in the mirror, it can't be much."

Mack turned as if to spit into the trash can. "Whiskey is still whiskey no matter the proof. I thought you'd be better informed. There are studies that prove that Pacific Islanders share some of the same DNA as tribes in the Americas.

Marion"—his tone becoming confidential—"this could be a bloody gold mine. I've done some checking. The New Zealand government doesn't give our people a break when it comes to opening a casino. But in the U.S., a few of our native tribes are getting rich."

Our people, our tribes? It took some effort to compose myself.

"What are we talking about, less than four percent Māori? I don't know how it works, but Tomlinson might. We've got some Miccosukee friends who I can ask. The gambling business, though, you don't really want any part of that."

"I'm two point five percent," Mack conceded, and some of the air went out of him. "I know . . . it was just an idea. This red tide mess has really got me down. And so has battling to get permits to fix up cottages I own, not some bastard with a clipboard. Even the way they are, the rooms are nice enough we could open tomorrow if they'd let me change the sign and wire the place for internet. Maddening crap, and it never seems to end. Makes me want to pull up stakes and run sometimes. You ever feel like that?"

No, not lately, but I played along. "Sure. Who doesn't?"

"Guess you're right," Mack mused. He eyed the wooden power totem, lofted it briefly like a spear. "Nice, huh? Since I was a kid, I've wanted one of these. We lived near a tribal area, North Auckland. They performed for the tourists. At night sometimes, particularly when there's a storm, I can still hear their drums pounding in my ribs. Makes me want to strip down to my shorts and hunt by the light of the moon. I've always been that way—a Māori in my heart. A hunter. So how the hell did I end up a fat old man behind a cash register?"

I waited while he drifted off for a few seconds, stroking the wooden totem.

"Doc?"

"Yeah, Mack."

"Between us, I bought this damn thing on eBay," he said. Wincing, he placed the totem on the desk. "It's kinda embarrassing, you know? But I trust you not to peach on me, mate. I'm gonna mount it over the counter. How do you think it'll look?"

"Like it was made for a Māori king," I said, which was the truth.

On my way out, he stopped me in the doorway. "I should've asked," he said. "I haven't seen Hannah around in a while. How's she and your son doing?"

It wasn't common knowledge that the child was my son. It was Hannah's preference—for now. I chose not to view his inquiry as a subtle reminder that entrusting a secret is a dual agreement.

"I've got babysitting duty after I get off the net boat," I told him. "I'll say hello to them both for you."

FOUR

Delia seemed at home on my creaky, flat-bottomed bay shrimper. It is 30 feet long, built of heavy cedar planking and brass screws, an old workhorse I'd bought in Chokoloskee years ago. With its twin booms and the nets raised, the vessel resembles a floating pterodactyl. It's as solid as a slab of cement. And just about as nimble.

"Cool boat—kinda old-timey-looking," the girl said despite the thumping diesel.

Experience can be gauged by the little things. Delia didn't step aboard without asking permission. She avoided the common rookie irritants such as trying to help when help wasn't needed or suddenly standing up once we were under way.

Another encouraging sign was that she was dressed

for work, not a beach outing. But her khaki cargo shorts and maroon fishing shirt seemed to emphasize, not disguise, an ample sexual dimorphism that, under other circumstances, might have caused whiplash to a passing male.

At first glance, Delia was a beautiful young woman with a healthy pelt and muscularity. But a drawn, serious expression dulled her face and begged for horn-rimmed glasses that she did not wear. It was her eyes, gray-blue, that suggested a life of responsibilities and constant worry.

"How long have you been sailing?" I asked over the machine-gun putter of the engine. It was an hour before sunset with thermal heads dissipating over the mainland. She stood to my right, her hand on a towing boom. We had exited Dinkin's Bay, headed for an expanse of shallow seagrass off the Intracoastal, west of Marker 13A.

"Since I was a kid, I've loved it," Delia said. "The Catalina was my graduation present from the fam. I keep her stocked with clothes and personal stuff in case the wind's right and I want to take off on a whim."

We talked about sailing for a while—her childhood in San Diego, then Tampa—but with the careful superficiality of strangers at a dinner party. When she got to the part about why she'd chosen Eckerd College in St. Pete, across the bridge from Tampa, she parted the curtain a bit.

"Five years ago, my father was diagnosed with—well,

he's been sick off and on. So I wanted to stay close to home, plus Eckerd has one of the best teams in the Intercollegiate Sailing Association. Now I've got a decision to make. Should I stay in the area or . . ." She shrugged. "This whole month has been a blur. I have a phobia about hurting people's feelings, you know? I still haven't told them."

"Your parents, about Tomlinson?" I asked. "Well, they certainly knew you might find out the truth someday."

Her response was a classroom primer on fertility clinics. It included what I already knew about "confused insemination."

"As far as my mom and dad are concerned," she continued, "I'm their daughter in every possible way. Period. A week ago, I chose a drop-dead date and promised myself I'd do it. Just march in, sit them down, and talk as adults. Instead, I got in my boat in a sort of panic. All this crazy stuff in my life has been building up. Waiting to hear about jobs, problems with this guy—a boyfriend, sort of—then this. I was twenty miles south, off Sarasota, before I finally admitted to myself that I was on my way to Sanibel. Like, you know, what dafug? I knew my birth father lived here. It's in his publisher's bio."

The girl sniffed, tugged at a strand of hair in a way that was spooky, then considered the bundle of braided shrimp net above her head.

"How's that for too much information?" she joked. "Nice of you, though, spending time with me, Dr. Ford.

This should be interesting. At Eckerd, I helped with a project on sedimentary development—core digs, all along the coast. But never a fish survey. It might help me land one of the internships I applied for."

I was watching the depth finder. North of us, in the late sunlight, channel markers caught the sun, bright red and green reflectors. On the Intracoastal, a flats boat angled our way while a go-fast Scarab beelined toward the causeway. This reminded me to asked Mack about recent visitors on a Harley.

"You can drop the doctor stuff. Call me Marion," I said. "Or Doc. Wait until I get the nets out, then feel free."

"Free to what?"

"Ask me anything you want about Tomlinson. It'll be quieter out here. I agree with your reasons—in a clinical sort of way. We can talk in private."

"I don't see what you mean about 'clinical.'"

I said, "You're trying to understand who your birth father is. Emotion—well, in my opinion anyway—only confuses the issue. And I think you're right. Sometimes the best way to assess a person's character is by talking to their friends."

"Assess?" Delia was mildly offended. "You mean, like, judge him? No, I just explained that I have a phobia about hurting people. I don't know why. Or, like you said, emotion just screws up our thinking. Anyway, this morning at breakfast, I wanted to open up to the guy but

I couldn't. I . . . I heard a rumor, Dr. Ford. If it's true, he needs to be warned. Or at least a chance to explain."

I was confused. "If what's true? Are you talking about Tomlinson?"

The girl confirmed it, saying, "He seems like such a sweetie. How could he not be to write as beautifully as he does? But you have to admit, the dude comes off as a little bizarre. The way he is, almost childlike, it sort of scares me. And he dodged a lot of my questions. If he didn't have something to hide, why wouldn't he just open up and share?"

I reduced speed and held up a finger, meaning *Give me a second.* At idle, I cranked the booms down. Tickle chains clanked, the winch creaked. Delia helped deploy the otter boards. Twin trawl nets sank to the bottom and blossomed into funnels. Our conversation was put on hold until the boat settled into a slow turn that, to jetliners above, would appear as a dusty furrow on a sunset sea of bronze.

I opened the ice chest, aware but unconcerned about the fast, blue-hulled flats boat that would soon pass nearby. "Water, beer, or Diet Coke?" I asked.

Delia, backdropped by the sun, got up and selected a bottle of Corona. She hefted it as if toasting me, her host, but was visibly uneasy. "Okay," she said after a long drink. "Here's the thing about Tommy—that's what he wants me to call him, Tommy—I don't know if I can handle that. Anyhoo . . . this morning, I asked him if he had any past, uhh, like health issues. As the child of a third-party donor, we have the right to know, don't you think?"

"Of course," I said. "Medical history on the paternal side has to be a concern for anyone in your position."

"And there are hundreds of thousands of us," Delia agreed. I realized she was referring to the number of children fathered by sperm donors as she took another drink and waited for the alcohol to move through her. "There's lying by commission and then there's lying by omission. That's what I was taught. Anyway, I might have had the balls to warn him if Tomlinson hadn't pissed me off by evading that one simple question."

I said, "Warn him about what? As far as I know, the guy's healthy as a buffalo."

"You sure?"

"Well, I'm not his physician. About his health . . . What's the rumor you heard?"

"Not a rumor." The girl stepped closer to study my reaction. "It's something we found out—Tomlinson spent six months in a California psych ward. Electric shock therapy, probably drugs, too, around the same time he was donating his . . . selling his sperm to the fertility clinic. One of us—I don't know the name yet—got his medical records somehow. You're his closest friend, but you didn't know?"

I bought some time by looking from the go-fast Scarab to the blue flats boat angling our way. "I'm aware he went through some tough times when he was younger. A lot people do. Did he deny it?"

"I didn't ask specifically, just if he'd ever had to see a shrink. He gave me some dumb line about learning from his mistakes. That was a bullshit answer. Marion . . . *Doc* . . . this is important to me—to all seven of us—and however many others that man has fathered. There are five types of mental illness that can be traced to the same inherited genetic variations. But . . . why the hell am I telling you?"

"I'm interested," I said. "Keep going."

"Then I will. There are at least five mental disorders that include depression, bipolar disorder. My god"—she was getting angry—"schizophrenia, for Christ sakes. You don't think I've doubted my own mental health since I got the DNA thing back? My whole life, I've had to fight a sort of . . . not depression, exactly. More of a shitty sort of cloud that scares me sometimes. And what about *my* children?"

The girl had a right to be angry. When I told her, "Fair enough. I promise that Tomlinson will talk to you, and he'll tell the truth," she put a fist to her lips, hesitated, then gave me a quick, impulsive hug.

"Thanks . . . even if you're wrong," she said. "This isn't easy . . . And there's something else, something I didn't tell him but need to. That rumor I mentioned?"

A week ago, she explained, the seven half siblings had received an email from an attorney asking them to join in a class action suit against the fertility clinic. Named in the suit was a long list of Mensal Cryonics donors, among them, Sighurdhr M. Tomlinson. The rumor was, she said, the lawsuit was real but they hadn't confirmed the authenticity.

"A lawsuit demanding what?" I asked.

"Money, probably," Delia replied. "Is there any other kind? One of the bio sibs, my half brother—he's the minister of a small church in North Carolina—he suggested we vote on what to do in case the suit isn't bogus. So far, the vote is four against joining the suit until we have a chance to get to know him, you know, our birth father. The other two sibs, I think one's too embarrassed to get involved. And the other, a guy I think from his chat posts, he already sounds a little nuts. Psychotic, even. Understand now why I panicked and came here?"

"Psychotic, as in dangerous?" I asked.

The girl shrugged the question away until I pressed her for an answer.

"I don't know. Psychotic, as in crazy, I guess. These long, rambling posts about us being spied on, wiretaps. That we're being set up by some evil government agency. According to him, donor siblings around the country are starting to unite, they're so pissed off at the system."

"Do you have a name?"

"Well . . . no. At first, we all went by the numbers assigned by the DNA chat room. The minister—his name's Chester—he was open from the start. And I have a bio sister in Arizona, Imogen. She's sounds a little ditzy, too, but not in a bad way. She can't wait to meet us all—like this is a party, nothing to worry about. Which is . . ." The girl paused. "What's that stupid saying about the apple falling from the tree?

"Dr. Ford?" Her tone demanded honesty. "I'm going to tell you something, like, no kidding around. I'm scared."

"Of what, Tomlinson?"

"No—yes—well, maybe. Scared of me, of what's inside. I hate the feeling there's something in my brain that, down the road, I can't control. I want to live a long, healthy life, and I hate drama. Everyone's a little screwy. No shit, right? But tell me this now. Is Tomlinson a good person? You know what I'm asking. Deep down, the whole package?"

"One of the best," I replied.

The girl stared as if expecting me to blink. Instead, I confirmed the truth by giving her arm a squeeze, then stepped away and looked toward the sound of an outboard motor.

"Uh-oh," I said.

The blue flats boat was close enough now, I recognized the boat and the driver. It was a pristine 21-foot Maverick—a fast, shallow-draft skiff—that I will always regret selling. At the helm was a lanky, dark-haired woman, shapely in a T-shirt, wearing Polaroids and a visor. I stood straighter and waved. In response, the woman glared at me and my passenger, then ignored us.

It was Hannah Smith, the celebrated fishing guide and mother of my child.

"Oh . . . perfect," I murmured.

Delia sniffed and returned Hannah's glare. "Damn stinkpotters," she said. "Well . . . at least give the lady credit for running her own boat."

At sunrise, I left Hannah's dock across the bay from Sanibel. The route took me east toward an unmarked swath known as the Mailboat Channel. Before Florida was lacerated with asphalt, back bay access was how mail was delivered along the coast. Off York Island, I slipped the channel and turned toward Dinkin's Bay, where mangroves were honey-glazed by fresh morning light.

I had left the bay shrimper at home in favor of a recent acquisition, a 26-foot Pathfinder. It is a favorite among Florida's light tackle guides, so less conspicuous than a Marlow or my previous high-tech ride. Skip Lyshon at Pathfinder had built it to my specs. The skiff is painted Whisper Gray and loaded with the latest fishing gizmos. As a favor to me, it was also outfitted with an extra long-haul fuel tank and special electronics unique to my needs.

I didn't plan to fish that morning but, spend three hundred days a year on the water, the rare can't-miss intersection is bound to plow across your path.

It happened. The bay was calm, a neon gel. I saw

sparks in the distance. I dropped off plane and killed the engine. Momentum drifted me toward a glittering carousel of scales and tails that was a school of tarpon.

I readied a fly rod, then deployed a potent little trolling motor and steered toward them.

Years ago, after I'd lost and landed a few, I stopped thinking of tarpon as fish. They now move into my mind collectively as a singular being—*Megalops*, a creature with giant, primal eyes—that has survived, unchanged, since the Jurassic period when only tarpon and other dinosaurs populated the Earth. As a genus, *Megalops* is pure and tidal, indifferent to time or the brevity of one's own life.

Grinning, I got ready to cast.

Ahead, water bulged with a slow passage of shadows. The shadows schooled closer, then vanished, only to reassemble on the surface as a conga line of chromium scales. They were out of range, but what the hell? I double hauled and offered the stragglers a Mylar-laden streamer to eat. On the retrieve, the lure resembled an absurd water spider—until it was inhaled by what felt like deadweight.

I lifted. Beneath the surface, *Megalops* spun an incandescent circle. Then the animal vaulted free of its world, high into mine, mouth wide, gills clattering with the resonance of bone. For a frozen instant it paused in midair, a silver folklore framed in blue, then threw the hook and fell. The sound resembled the percussion of a refrigerator falling from the sky.

By the time I recovered, *Megalops*, as a tribe, was gone.

On my way back to the lab, I nudged up to Tomlinson's sailboat. He was using some kind of purple goop to remove wine stains from the teak railing. "How was your night?" he asked, aware that I had stayed at Hannah's place taking care of our son.

"My night went from cold to frosty, not counting windchill," I said cheerfully. "But I haven't given up. And the boy likes me. He's way ahead of the curve, I think, when it comes to motor skills."

"Aren't they all?" my friend said, smiling.

The smile faded when I said, "Ol' buddy, you've got to tell Delia the truth about your past—including your summer vacation in a psych ward. The others deserve to know, too."

"Christ . . . all of it?" He glanced toward the little Catalina sailboat that was still anchored near my house. "Dude, get real. No kid wants to know the truth about her dad."

"You'll never see her again if you don't. Leave out the felonies and the womanizing—for now," I suggested. "Your medical history, though, you've got to lay it all out for them."

"Not one kid at a time," he groaned. "My balls haven't left the cave since I took Delia to breakfast this morning. She's as intimidating as my first Mother Superior." He slammed down a sponge and stood on boney legs. "Man, that does it. Give me a ride to the marina. I need to talk to Mack about his cottages."

"You're thinking about renting them for . . . Are you still calling it a reunion?"

"An intervention, more like it, if I drink all the rum it'll take for me to deal with this one kid at a time. Geezus, yes, rent the cottages. You're a little slow at the helm today, poncho."

"Not until you get some clothes on," I reminded him.

Tomlinson did a quick downward inspection. "Oh, yeah. Forgot. Mack's cottages, it's not a nudist colony anymore, is it?"

I was in the lab at the computer scrolling through a list of messages posted by Tomlinson's DNA progeny. Delia had provided a link and her personal password—but reluctantly.

I said to her, "The guy you described as psychotic, I don't see that he's posted anything strange on this chat page. In fact, from what you told me, I expected a lot more interaction between you and the other six siblings."

The girl sat across from me, going through my folder of newspaper articles and studies, all dealing with red tide. "That's because most of the posts were deleted," she said a little sharply.

I wondered if her tone was intentional or if she was

simply focused on reading. "You deleted the posts because they were weird?"

"Of course not."

"Then why?"

Delia, not looking up, said with exaggerated patience,
"I'll walk you through it. Find the upper right-hand corner of the webpage. You'll see a preferences icon there.
Kind of a gear-looking thing. Drag down, you'll
understand—I hope so anyway."

I did. A list of options appeared. One was labeled *Disappearing Messages*. That link opened another list of options. Members could allow their posts to remain public
or have them automatically disappear once the posts had
been viewed. Or the author could limit the amount of
time the posts were readable, from five seconds to five
minutes, even as long as a week.

"You didn't happen to take screenshots before his
messages disappeared, did you?" I asked.

"No," she snapped. "Why would I? I didn't say he was
dangerous, just paranoid. The guy—whoever it is—he
posts something, I get one look at what he wrote and it's
gone. It's the same with most of us now."

I replied, "All the more reason to keep a record. People seldom seem dangerous—until they are."

Delia lowered the folder in a huff. "I didn't realize
you're an expert. I'm surprised. How many dangerous
people does a biologist meet in one lifetime?" She chuck-

led as if it was funny, not sarcasm. "Sanibel Island is overrun with, what, bike thieves?"

"Oh yeah, I live a pretty quiet life," I agreed but wasn't done. "Is there a way you can find out the person's name? Maybe he's made contact with some of your other siblings. Can't hurt to try, can it? And I wouldn't mind seeing a copy of that class action lawsuit email, while you're at it."

She spun the folder onto the desk that separated us. "I don't understand why you're so interested. I appreciate you trying to help and all. And you have. Tomlinson—I can't call him that ridiculous name Tommy—he and I are finally going to talk, so thanks. But that's enough help for now."

"Can't hurt to have an outsider's opinion, can it?" I countered.

"When it's not needed, yes. Look, Doc . . . Marion . . . it's not like you're a psychologist or an internet expert or, I don't know, a security dude. In fact, it's really none of your business."

Mood swings. Tomlinson had warned me. "That's what biologists do," I disagreed gently, "study living organisms. Internet security and stuff, sure, that's way out of my field, you're right. So think of me as a curious old snoop."

"A snoop, huh?" The girl was dubious.

"More like an obsession if I don't catch myself," I

said. "I've never done a crossword puzzle in my life because I know I'd be hooked. Find an unfinished *Times* in an airport, I'd miss my flight. Sort of sad, really. I straighten paintings in public buildings. I pocket litter when I go for runs. If I hear about a person behaving oddly—your half sibling, for instance—my mind won't let go until the behavior makes sense." I winked and added, "Maybe I'm the one who needs a shrink."

Her manner softened. "Sorry, Doc. The real reason I'm pissy is, well . . . you broke a rule and I let you get away with it."

"Oh?"

"Damn right, you did—a rule my parents' generation doesn't know about, apparently. You asked for my password. I should've said no, or at least explained. That's like asking for the key to someone's diary, but I didn't want you to think I had something to hide." She poofed—a blowing noise—exasperated. "Maybe we both need shrinks. Honestly? I'm the same, obsessive. At night, I lie awake fixated on the stupidest things and worry maybe I'm losing my mind. Particularly since I found out that my father is a hippie mystic with a history of drug abuse."

We discussed obsession for a while, a friendly back-and-forth about the silly oddities of orderly, driven people. Then returned to the subject of Tomlinson. Delia consulted her electronic sports watch. "He's supposed to be back around four, and we're going for a long sail. I haven't been aboard his boat yet. The wind's supposed to swing northeast and blow fifteen to twenty. Think it'll be okay?"

"He's the best sailor I know," I said. "Well . . . maybe the second best, now that I've met you."

This seemed to broker a friendly covenant. "I think you're a nice man . . . Doc . . . for a harmless old snoop." She waited for me to laugh, then referenced the folder she'd been leafing through. "Mind if I take this to read tonight? It's really interesting, especially the old newspaper articles. The ones from the late 1800s and the turn of the century—red tide even back then."

The folder was in the girl's backpack when she stood and shared a fist bump on the way to a window where there was a view of the marina.

Her smile broadened. "Who are they? They're gorgeous."

In the parking lot were two girls in matching sundresses. They were Maribel and Sabina Esteban, ages thirteen and ten. The girls were on their way to Bailey's General Store, judging from the baskets they carried.

"Sisters," I said. "Cuban American. They live at the marina on a houseboat with their mother. A nice family. They help me around the lab sometimes."

"I'm envious," Delia said.

"I'd offer to hire you, too," I said, "but selling fish to Science Departments isn't as profitable as, say, selling sweepers door-to-door."

We were having fun, back on good terms. There was still a lot I wanted to know—particularly details about the lawsuit—but it would have to wait.

Delia looked back as if inspecting the lab. Her eyes took in a bubbling row of aquaria bright with sea corals, tunicates, and captive creatures that moved in unison or foraged alone. She also noted the baby chair and changing table in the corner.

"You seem to be doing just fine," she said. "I was talking about those little girls. I'd like to have children myself one day, and, well, you know what my concerns are. It's so sweet the way those two walk in step, holding hands."

"Down there, holding hands is customary for women, not just sisters."

"You've been to Cuba?" She asked the way most people do, a mix of surprise and envy in her tone.

"I've flown over it a few times," I said.

"In your own plane? I heard you had one."

"Just a small amphib. It's down for repairs, but, no, I meant flying commercial." This was a misleading truth that I might have amended if the wall phone hadn't rung.

It was Tomlinson. He sounded as if he'd been hyperventilating.

"Lock Delia in the house and get your ass over here," he said in a panic that carried across the room.

"Where?" I asked.

"Mack's cottages, where you think? One of her DNA

brothers showed up and he threatened to kill us all. I can't call the cops on a guy who might be my son, so hurry up. And bring a gun."

Delia was eavesdropping. "My god, this can't be happening. He's not serious about the gun?"

She spoke to my back while I headed across the breezeway, into my cabin. I returned wearing a baggy shirt, unbuttoned, over a tank top and khaki slacks.

"Tomlinson gets excited, he gets dramatic," I said, tightening my belt. "Stay here, I won't be gone long, I hope."

No way. Delia insisted on going. In the truck, she tried to reassure herself as I drove to West Gulf and turned left. "He probably blew it all way out of proportion. Besides, that's just crazy. Why would a biologist own a gun?"

FIVE

Mack's old Lincoln Continental sat in the sandy shade of coconut palms. No other vehicles around, just Tomlinson's bicycle and a rusty swaybacked golf cart used by marina employees. We stepped out into the heat and dozy bird sounds of the July afternoon.

Delia was nervous. "Maybe everyone has calmed down," she suggested. "God, I hope so. I've never met any of my bio sibs. And why would he threaten to kill . . ." She dismissed the possibility. "It can't be true."

Kill Tomlinson, her birth father, she meant.

The safest way to handle the situation was to ask her to stay in the truck. When I did, she refused with a curt profanity meant to put me in my place. I scouted ahead, then returned, saying, "Stay behind me."

The wind freshened. A flotilla of charcoal clouds scudded inland and muted the sunlight. The collegiate sailor had been right about the weather changing.

We crossed into a postcard setting of Florida from the 1960s. There were six tiny cabins, whitewashed and trimmed in fresh pink, built around a commons. There was a gas grill, a shuffleboard court, a weedy patch of white sand for volleyball, and a large one-story club-house. It was CBS brick and stucco, also painted white and conch shell pink, and large enough for potlucks or bingo, with room to seat fifty or more.

Mack, red-faced, exited as we approached. He wore a carpenter's apron. The sound of a power saw inside echoed off the linoleum.

"Well, the mystery of Sasquatch, the Abominable Snowman, has been solved," he said with mock humor. "Tomlinson, in his travels, has apparently sired a race of giant lunatics. You just missed one of his prodigal sons."

"What kind of car was he in?" I asked.

Mack kept talking. "I called the cops anyway, and I hope they catch the crazy picaroon. He threatened to burn the place to the ground—as if I'd rent to him or any of his spawn. The whole family's batshit crackers."

Through the entire speech, he ignored my attempt to hush him.

He noticed Delia. Mack's expression asked *Who's she?* before he apologized, "Sorry about the language, miss.

We're discussing one of our local nutcases. Nothing to fret about."

Delia, furious—or stricken—demanded, "Where is he?"

"Which one?" Mack asked. "My dear, you don't want to involve yourself with—"

"I'm no damn *dear*," she interrupted. "I'm an adult who asked you a simple question. The person you described as a gigantic lunatic, where is he?"

"Not gigantic, a giant," Mack said. He was unnerved by the girl's anger. "The crazy bast— This person, the guy, had to be close to seven feet tall. Had hair down to his hips like a Viking, calm enough at first, then started . . . Well, don't worry. He won't—"

A nearby cabin door banged open and Tomlinson appeared. He was surprised to see Delia, but handled it. "Perfect timing," he called in a cheery way, yet looked exhausted. "Mack, meet Delia—Delia Carapoulos. Isn't she a beauty? Delia's one of my daughters, just graduated from Eckerd with top honors. That ought to put your mind at ease about the whole fam-damn-ily being nuts."

It did not. Mack, however, as a businessman, knew the wisdom of concealing anger in the hope of future gains. Instead of another nasty reference to genetics, he said, "Congratulations, Delia. Young lady, you're welcome here anytime. Sorry for the upset." Then fixed Tomlinson with a mean look. "As for your other *sprog*, please tell Mr. Deville—or whatever his name is—I don't care to see his ass on my property ever again."

*D*eville?" I asked Tomlinson.

We were in a cottage, just the three of us. Delia had not reacted to the name assigned years ago at Mensal Cryogenics, so I mouthed the question while she was in the bathroom.

The mystic boat bum gestured, palms out, as people do when mystified. "That kid was spooky as hell," he whispered. "No way am I going to tell her all of what just happened. My medical history, sure, but some of the vicious things the guy said would knock her off her pins. 'Diseased genetics . . . A bloodline so vile, we should all be napalmed.' Crazy kimchi like that. Doc, he not only knows my donor name, he found out how Granddad made his fortune."

My pal leaned his head into his hand. "Blood money, and the kid was right. *Kid* indeed," he added softly. "The guy looked more like the offspring of a Russian Cossack who'd screwed a grizzly. But it's possible that he is my son. I suspected it the moment he—"

A toilet flushed.

I asked, "What kind of car is he driving?"

Tomlinson shook his head, unsure. "And he knows I

inherited a bundle of money. Said I was plutocratic vermin for not giving it all away. A *plutocrat* . . . Geezus, lecturing me, of all people. Mack was right there, he heard it all."

"You inherited a bundle when?" I asked. This was news to me.

The bathroom door opened. Delia stepped into the room, wiping her hands with a pink-flowered towel. "Deville—that's French, isn't it?" she said, not with distaste but concerned. "Please tell me I don't have siblings spread all over the whole damn world."

"Good heavens, no," Tomlinson said. "Well . . . at least it's unlikely. I don't think FedEx offered overnight to Europe in those days. Why don't you have a seat, dear? We have a lot to talk about."

"Tommy . . . Tomlinson . . ."—she was folding the towel—"I'm not sure I want to. I can't take much more of this. If you think—his name can't really be Deville. But if you think he's dangerous, maybe it's best if I go back to my boat and we never see each other again." She took a moment to get control of her breathing, then changed her mind. "No. I didn't come this far to run away. I deserve to know the truth about what just happened. About you, me . . . Everything."

Her eyes sparked when she turned to me. "Marion, I'd like you to stay. Someone needs to keep it real around here."

I waited for my friend to nod his consent. He didn't.

"Start without me," I said, getting up. "I'm going to take a quick walk around the area first—just as a precaution." Facing Delia, I tugged the back of my shirttail into place, then went out the door.

Outside, through the thin clapboard of the cottage, I heard the girl ask, "Who is Dr. Ford? I mean, *really*?"

I did a loop around the property, impressed by the improvements. A hot tub had been added next to the tiny swimming pool. Walkways were lined with whelk shells. One by one, I peered into the five empty cottages. Dusty bamboo furniture had been replaced with glass-topped rattan and overstuffed couches in garish hibiscus patterns of yellow and lime green.

No sign of the man who claimed to be Tomlinson's son.

Near the pool and hot tub was a grove of mango and avocado trees the size of oaks, limbs sagging with fruit. I pocketed a mango, checked the bike path on West Gulf Drive, then returned to the clubhouse, where Mack had just finished hanging a wide-screen TV. The building, built in the days of nuclear panic, was as solid as a bunker and ten degrees cooler when you stepped inside.

"What happened to the police?" I asked.

"Canceled them," he replied. "Decided it's not worth the trouble. Cops and the Zoning Department are next door to each other, and you know how people talk." He looked around and spread his arms to indicate all the progress he'd made. "What do you think? Cable for internet should have been laid a month ago, but the bastards still haven't said yes."

Transport a small gymnasium from Ohio to Florida and you'd have something similar. It was decorated with taxidermied fish, brass nautical lights, and lots of typical bar signage—*Cuba: 200 Miles . . . Let's Get Ship-faced*. Behind the bar was a kitchenette similar to those found at a VFW or Moose Lodge.

I said, "Looks like you're about ready for the Grand Opening." He had waved me to a lacquered bar, where there were stools. I took a seat and accepted a bottle of water from the cooler. "You mind telling me what happened?"

Mack popped a bottle of Steinlager, sat across from me, and summarized. He had been here, discussing the possibility of Tomlinson renting the cottages, when an NBA-sized man had appeared in the doorway and introduced himself as Mr. Deville.

"That struck me as odd from the start," Mack said. "No one introduces themselves as Mr. these days. And the way he was dressed—a black robe, like a priest, but with bleach-blond hair to his waist. A full beard, too, ragged-looking."

A rock 'n' roll star, that was Mack's impression. Or some kind of hippie preacher. With all the hair and his size, the man could have played Sasquatch on reality TV.

"Turned out, he'd been outside the door for a while,

listening," Mack said. "He was polite, at first. Very formal, but aggressive in that quiet way some men have—damn near crushed my hand when we shook. I thought Tomlinson was going to faint when they stood almost eye to eye. The guy—Deville—put his hands on Tomlinson's shoulders, said, 'Hello, Daddy-O,' and gave him a kiss full on the lips."

"How did Tomlinson react?" I asked.

Mack shifted uncomfortably on his seat. "Stunned, I suppose. It was a smothering kind of kiss, like that picture of the sailor and nurse in Times Square when World War Two ended. In Sarasota, there's a giant statue of them kissing, and Deville is damn near as big. He shook Tomlinson like a rag doll, a huge, mad grin on his face, then let him go."

After that, the scene escalated, according to Mack. Rapid-fire, Deville had accused Tomlinson of all kinds of crimes, murder included.

"Ridiculous, batty things," Mack went on. "Claimed Tomlinson's grandfather was responsible for the deaths of millions of people. Something about inventing a gear or motor—I don't know—that allowed a machine gun to fire through an airplane propeller. 'Built your fucking fortune off the corpses of young men,' the crazy S-O-B said. By then, he was screaming, pacing back and forth like a lunatic."

I cleared my throat without comment. Some of the accusations were true.

———

Finally, Mack had had enough.

"I picked up a hammer and told the sonuvabitch to get off my property. When I did, the guy turned on me. A wolf—you know how their eyes blaze?—he was like that, only his eyes were blue. When I dialed nine-one-one, he threatened to burn this place to the ground if I let Tomlinson—Daddy-O, he called him—hold a reunion here. Then stormed out."

I asked a few questions. Deville was in his mid-twenties, according to Mack, six-six, or taller, and close to three hundred pounds. He hadn't heard or seen a car, so maybe the guy had walked or come on a bicycle.

"Or had a driver," Mack suggested. "He was wearing a gold Rolex, the big one with diamonds, so he's got some money. Or he's a thief."

"What about shoes?" I asked. A man in a robe could wear six-inch lifts. He could also dump the robe, his wig, and walk away normally dressed, bald and half a foot shorter.

Mack was getting impatient. "What the hell's it matter? But you know"—he gazed around the room—"the guy might have come up with a good idea before he started to rant. He told me this place was a gold mine, if I marketed it right. Seemed to know his p's and q's when it came to business. Said I should advertise the cottages as an internet-free zone—nothing else like it in Florida. Sounded idiotic, at first, but now? Well, I'm not so sure."

"You told him about your cable problems?"

"Already said the guy had been at the door listening. 'Make people pay for what you *don't* have,' he told me, but then had to go and get nasty, added, 'including a brain.' That's when I started to get bloody well pissed."

Mack took a cigar from the pocket of his floral Hawaiian shirt and bit off the tip. "Guy's an asshole, and the spitting image of Tomlinson if he lost a hundred pounds. Like they say, madness runs in the blood. If he ever comes back, I'll lay a little Māori on him instead of bothering with a damn hammer."

The owner of Dinkin's Bay Marina got up, found his lighter, and started for the door, asking, "What do you think?"

"Call the police, let them take care of it," I said. Outside, the wind had turned. Palm fronds were frosted with a sudden northeast breeze.

"No, about the internet-free zone. Maybe the weirdo has a point. A niche market, like he said. Some folks are fed up with all the constant electronic garbage. People with enough money to pay for what they can't get anywhere else."

Mack lit his cigar while the pros and cons played out in his mind. He puffed a few times, then smiled through the smoke. "Sure . . . make the place exclusive. Charge more for what we *don't* have. Bloody brilliant, you ask me. And tell the Zoning Department to kiss my ass."

A marina employee, shirtless and heavily muscled, came down the drive pushing a wheelbarrow. "Where was Figgy during all this?" I asked, meaning Figueroa Casanova. The man, just over five feet tall, had suffered monoxide poisoning as a child in Cuba. He also smoked a lot of weed. One or the other had blunted his intellect, and possibly his growth, but Figgy was hardworking, a gifted amateur shortstop, and among my favorite people on the island.

Mack, lost in the idea of an internet-free resort, waved the question away, saying, "Ask Figgy yourself."

I intended to. As I started toward the road, Delia and Tomlinson exited the cottage. They faced each other, hugged in a brief yet personal way, Delia red-cheeked from tears but happier than she'd been.

Tomlinson called, "We're going for a sail this afternoon and it's getting late." This was followed by a searching look that inquired *Any sign of Deville?*

My wordless response was *Nope.* "Take my truck," I suggested. "I'll use the bike and see you back at the marina."

Figgy watched Delia get in on the truck's driver's side and pull away. "Wow! That lady sure has some nice *chichis*," he said in Spanish. "I like the way they bounce, you know? Makes me hungry for mangoes."

He had already told me he hadn't seen a stranger on the property, with or without a black robe. The little Cuban had slipped off to the beach to smoke a joint, then spent an hour helping kids build a sandcastle.

"She's Tomlinson daughter," I warned.

Figgy misread this as ignorance on my part. "Doc, my friend, every girl is someone's daughter. Don't you know that simple fact? . . . Think she likes baseball? I might invite her to play catch and smoke a *pitillo*, if she comes back to the marina."

The rumble of a motorcycle drew my attention—a Harley, possibly, carrying just one, not two, helmeted riders. My truck had just turned right on West Gulf, and I'd forgotten to remove the GPS transponder from beneath the bed.

"I'm an idiot," I murmured.

"No, I make the same mistake before I learn about life," Figgy reassured me. "Same with everyone, girls and boys. We all got parents. My papa, I never met him, but I'm pretty sure he was someone. You know, an hombre, 'cause that's the way it works. In Gringolandia, they don't teach this in schools?"

The mango I'd picked was in my pocket. I gave it to Figgy, and said, "Gotta go."

A man, mid-thirties, wearing slacks and a starched collared shirt, was peering into my truck until I surprised him from behind on Tomlinson's beach bum bike.

"Where's your motorcycle?" I asked, coasting to a stop. We were on the mangrove side of the boardwalk to my lab.

He was startled yet his puzzled reaction seemed genuine. "What? No . . . my car's parked at the marina and I walked. Are you Dr. Marion Ford?" The accent was Midwestern, a generation removed from some New York barrio.

"Depends on who's asking." This was said in a friendly way.

From a computer bag the man produced a business card. "I'm with the Internal Revenue Service," he said. "Special Investigator Leo Alomar. Nice to meet you, Dr. Ford."

I took the card as if unaware he intended to shake hands. If it was a fake, the card was well done. His name was in raised letters below the embossed stamp of the U.S. Department of the Treasury.

I handed it back to him. "Must be interesting work, Mr. Alomar. But don't you folks usually phone for an appointment or send something in the mail?"

"Call me Leo," he said. "This isn't official, I just happened to be in the area. Can you spare fifteen minutes?"

Amused skepticism was my response.

He waited out my silence. Finally, he gave in. "Okay, there you go. Smart. I admire that. All right, cards on the table. I came to see you. We can make it official if you want, Doctor, but it's better this way. A private talk just between us. Off the record. How's that sound?"

"Darn nice of you, Leo," I said, "but if I screwed up a tax form or something, why keep it a secret?"

He didn't expect that. "Not secret. I didn't mean . . . Well, let me put it another way. What it doesn't say here"—the card again—"is that I'm a Special Investigator with the IRS Whistleblower Program. Ever hear of it?"

"Nope," I said. "And, frankly, I doubt it exists. What are you really after?"

The man maintained his composure. He turned toward my stilthouse. "Do you have a computer? How about I wait out here while you go inside and look it up?"

I had gauged the man's age, his size, and was heartened by the absence of scar tissue around his ears. The fact that he looked nothing like Tomlinson was a bonus, as was an intriguing oversight. He had failed to offer his ID and Treasury Department shield even though I had just called him a liar.

"In this heat?" I said. "Come inside with me."

"There you go," the man said again, and was delighted when the IRS webpage proved me wrong about the Whistleblower Program.

SIX

Special Investigator Leo Alomar—or whoever he was—explained that anyone can call an IRS hotline, accuse a person or company of tax fraud, and remain anonymous throughout the process. If an individual or company is found guilty and has assets of more than two million dollars, the whistleblower, depending on the court's findings, can be rewarded with fifteen to thirty percent of whatever the IRS recovers in fines or auctioned assets.

We were in the lab. Alomar had taken a chair at the workstation, where there is a sink, an emergency eyewash, a Bunsen burner, and a rack of Pyrex in utilitarian sizes. I sat across from him at the computer, confirming that everything he'd said thus far was true.

I'd also skimmed ahead regarding the Whistleblower/ Informant Awards Program. What I learned was interesting . . . and troubling.

The IRS wasn't as fussy when it came to accusing individuals. As long as informants turned in people with annual gross incomes of more than two hundred thousand dollars, the process, the rewards, and the promise of anonymity were much the same.

I said, "Leo, take a look around. Do you see two million in assets here? Good luck, if my business is what you're after. And if you're recruiting informants, you picked the wrong guy. I suggest you target people who're already ass-deep in debt to the IRS." I rolled my chair back, done with the conversation.

He stopped me with a sharp look. "That's exactly why I'm here, Dr. Ford. You're not ass-deep yet, but you soon will be." Slowly, his thin smile faded. I had failed to react. "Think I'm bluffing? How about we go over a spreadsheet of your income versus expenditures over the last three months? I've got it right here in my briefcase."

"Fine," I said. "While you're at it, pull out some ID. I don't think I've ever seen a Treasury Department badge before. Did they run you through the pistol course at Glynco? I hear it's pretty tough."

I watched his face change. I waited while he fumbled around in his head, unsure if the question was a trap. Starched confidence was displaced by impatience and an involuntary thrumming of the left foot.

"Let's stick to income versus expenditures," he said. "You're in enough trouble as is, unless we can come to some sort of agreement."

"Agreement?"

"There you go. It's something I'm authorized to offer if you cooperate."

I got up and walked to the phone. It is an outdated wall model, hot-wired, which is a necessity in a building with double thick walls and a tin roof.

"What are you doing?" he asked.

"Calling the police," I said.

Leo Alomar—or whatever his name was—got to his feet so fast, his briefcase fell to the floor. "Goddamn it, Ford, I'm trying to do you a favor. This needs to stay between us."

I paused with the phone to my ear. "Give me one good reason why an agent from the Treasury Department doesn't want the police involved?"

He gave me two. A name—Jimmy Jones, the infamous high-tech treasure hunter, a felon, who had been beaten to death in jail.

"I was on the team that helped bust that Ivy League prick," Alomar said. "We net-worthed him—Al Caponed him, we call it. A ton of gold is still out there waiting to be found, as you damn well know." He waited for that to sink in. "Don't deny it. My contacts in the Bahamas confirmed that you and your seaplane spent a month there around the time that Jimmy's ex-girlfriend disappeared."

"What's your name?" I asked. "Your real name?"

The man said, "Give me twenty minutes to explain. It'll be the smartest investment you ever made in your life."

I hung up the phone.

Tomlinson's sailboat, *No Más*, isn't large by blue-water standards but sizable for a brackish area like Dinkin's Bay. It has a twelve-foot beam, weighs nine tons, and requires a substantial depth to keep its keel off the bottom.

Watching *No Más* beat its way upwind, mainsail and jib hunting from port to starboard, was entertaining. It was a zigzag battle that Delia, at the helm, finally won after a long reach that skated the boat clear of shoals at the mouth of Dinkin's Bay. Tomlinson was a shirtless stick figure in the distance, his hair wild in the late sunlight. The yellow dinghy tethered off the stern resembled a miniature comet's tail.

Leo Alomar—he insisted that was his name—asked, "Doesn't the fool have a motor?"

We had moved outside to deck chairs, leaving recording devices—phones, pads, and computers—behind by mutual agreement. The transition had provided me time to throw a towel over the acetylene torch and other gold-rendering tools in the lab.

"He has one, but she doesn't need it," I said.

The man either didn't hear or missed the significance of the pronouns, for he wondered aloud about Delia, "How could a woman so young afford such a boat? Must be loaded, huh?"

I said, "All you need now is an informant to provide her name. Is that how this works? I make a call, you tear that girl's private life apart, and, with luck, we split the profits? I don't see much difference between people like you and treasure hunters."

Alomar, despite the relentless tapping of his foot, wasn't offended. "How so?"

"You both keep throwing darts at a map until you strike gold—usually at the expense of people who don't know a damn thing about what you do. Or how you do it."

From my chair, I could see the marina docks. Figgy was near the boat ramp, lobbing a baseball with a college-aged kid, probably here on vacation. Jeth was outfitting a family of four with kayaks and life jackets. The go-fast Scarab I'd seen yesterday had just refueled and was idling out in the channel, engine burbling like a dragster.

I got to my feet, stood there for a moment, then walked to the railing. At the wheel of the Scarab was a huge man, a sun hoodie over his head. No one else aboard, just him, unless a passenger or two were inside the cabin. Other details vanished when the boat rocketed toward the mouth of the bay where *No Más*, now tacking to port, was still visible.

"Are you ignoring me, Dr. Ford, or are you going to keep playing dumb?"

Alomar, I realized, had asked me something. I continued to watch until the Scarab exited the bay and turned right, the opposite direction of *No Más*.

"You've got fifteen of your twenty minutes left," I said, returning to my chair. "Jimmy Jones . . . I recognize the name, but who doesn't? The guy made headlines a few years back."

Fingers drummed the arm of the teak chair in sync with Alomar's tapping foot. "Look, Ford, I know you were one of the last people to see Jimmy's ex before she disappeared. Lydia Johnson—skinny little mouse of a woman. I've got security cam video of you together at the mailboat dock in the Bahamas. That's the last time she was seen, somewhere between Cat Island and Nassau. Why not just drop the act?"

It was hot, an hour before sunset, but there was a breeze. Alomar was a heavy sweater. His chambray shirt was soaked. I added this detail to his nervous tapping and wondered what kind of drug he was hooked on— oxycodone, a prime contender.

I said, "Now you're accusing me of murder?"

"I don't investigate homicides." He said this as if he were giving me a pass or didn't care one way or another. "Two Christmases ago, an associate interviewed Jimmy— before that con used his head as a piñata, of course. From the beginning, Lydia was the key to this whole thing.

She knew where Jimmy stashed what he stole from his investors—three tons of gold ingots and coins off the SS *Panama*." He fixed me with a hard look. "Minus, of course, whatever you took. I'm guessing you chose coins over ingots—the historical value makes them worth more. Like I said, you're smart."

Leo Alomar was confident that he had my attention. "It's all in my briefcase, if you want to see it. We've got all kinds of ways of flagging illegal income. That boat show you went to in St. Pete? The big yacht dealers? We set up autonomous card readers at the gate. Nobody has a clue. A guy like you walks in and starts shopping for a million-dollar boat, the system immediately harvests your chip cards and electronics. If income and credit don't mesh with the price of the boat, your data is linked to a tracking system. That's how you were flagged. There's something else odd about you, Ford."

"Hopefully, more than just a few things," I replied.

"A comedian," he said. "What I realized is, there are no pictures of you on the internet. As in zero. That's not the sort of thing that happens accidentally—another red flag." He gave it a dramatic beat. "So far, I'm the only one who's made the connection between you, Lydia, and the Bahamas. See what I mean about already being in ass-deep? No one else has figured it out—yet. That's why I wanted to keep this a private discussion."

I had noted his nervous involuntary tweaks and twitches, but had already made up my mind about Alomar on a visceral level. We all do it in the blink of an eye—assess strangers as potential friends or foes or as meaningless passersby. Intellectually, of course, we then select data to support our first instincts. To do otherwise would be to admit that, at base level, we are nothing but primates with an inflated sense of ethics.

I consulted my watch. "You never did answer my question about Glynco. Is the firearms course there as tough as they say?"

The man's face colored. Hands tightened on the arms of his chair. "What the hell does that . . ." He sat forward. "Are you too stupid to see what I'm getting at?"

"Apparently," I said. "Alomar, you've got five minutes left to help me understand."

"I'm the only one who *knows*," he repeated, "about what you and Jimmy's ex found in the Bahamas. And here's the good news—I don't give a damn about how much you took. Keep it, maybe even take a percentage if we partner up. Is that plain enough for you?"

"Partners in crime, huh?" I said.

He misinterpreted my musing tone. "There you go— and call me Leo from now on, okay? See, there's no such thing as crime in the tax racket. Just criminals dumb enough to get caught. And we won't. But here's the deal . . ." He leaned closer. "First, you have to tell me where it is. I want GPS numbers and two weeks to check it out on my own. Be straight with me, this whole IRS mess will go away. What do you think?"

He extended his hand to close the deal. I stared until he lowered his arm. "I don't doubt you worked for Jimmy Jones or maybe even the Treasury Department at some time in the past. What happened? Get caught pulling a stunt like this? I'm careful about who I do business with . . . Leo."

"What's it matter as long as I have the right contacts and know what I know?"

Again, he extended his hand. I ignored it.

"One more question," I said. "Did you plant a GPS transponder on my truck?"

It threw him. "Huh?"

I repeated the question.

"Good god, no. You kidding?"

Leo, for once, was telling the truth. "How much gold did you say that guy Jones stole?" I asked.

"Wait," he said. "What the hell are you talking about? A GPS on your . . . This happened recently?"

"Three million dollars' worth?" I asked, getting to my feet. "Or was it three tons in gold ingots? Either way, that's the kind of money that could get a man killed."

Leo had a mean streak. He got up. We stood eye to eye. "Hey, hold on here a second, Ford. Are you threatening me?"

I backed away a step. To him, a minor concession. For me, a way to create enough space to move. "Think about it," I said. "Someone planted that transponder on my truck. If it wasn't you, that means you're not the only one who's wrong about my involvement in all this." He still didn't get it. "Leo, whoever it is, if they suspect me, they already know about you. How else could they have found me?" I waited for a light to blink on in his head before asking, "Who are your confidential informants?"

He murmured, "Sonuvabitch. One of them planted the GPS, you think?"

"There you go," I replied. "You need to watch your ass, Leo."

SEVEN

Nautical twilight is the term astronomers use to describe the pearly purple time between dusk and nightfall. The sky turns to indigo and stars pierce the last lemon glow of sunset.

That's when I began to worry about Tomlinson and Delia. It was nearly 9. *No Más* had yet to return.

On the wall near the phone hangs a VHF marine radio. White coaxial leads to an antenna mounted high atop the cistern of my old fish house. When conditions are right, the signal carries line of sight for twenty miles, occasionally more. Typically, Tomlinson turns off his cell phone but continues to monitor VHF channels 68 or 72.

I hailed him at 9. No response. I tried again half an hour later. Same thing. By then, it was dark. A copper moon, three days before full, drifted low over the black mangrove fringe of Dinkin's Bay.

From the kitchen, Hannah Smith reminded me, "Marion, he's a grown man, for heaven sakes. Leave them alone." I knew what was coming next and it didn't take long. "Or are you more worried about his daughter? Delia, you said? She's very fond of you, from the way you two hugged, but, either way, I'm fine with it. Our agreement, I mean. But . . . Well, I'm not going to say what's obvious."

Isn't she awfully young? is what my sometimes lover had been too tactful to ask. Good. I took perverse pleasure in this subtle display of jealousy. Our "agreement" not to continue what had been an exclusive relationship was all Hannah's idea. Caused, although she would not admit it, by her suspicions that my occasional need to drop everything and disappear for weeks at a time signaled illegal commerce of some type. Or, perhaps, there was another woman—or women—sequestered away somewhere, which, in her mind, might explain the lies I had to invent to explain those disappearances. Hannah was one of the rare ones—a man's woman in every way. The drawback was that she understood—or thought she did—the innate duplicity of men.

I had cooked dinner, so she was tidying up. Camp rules. I'd made Caribbean fish stew. It is an exotic name for a simple recipe. Marinade a prime grouper or snapper fillet in chicken bouillon, grated ginger, sea salt, and thyme. Sear the fillets in oil that is smoky hot, then simmer in the boullion roux. Add fresh onion, tomatoes, a sliced green pepper, a jalapeño or three, and, on this occasion, lots and lots of garlic. Fried plantains and rice had been our side dish. Chilled mangoes from nearby Pine Island had provided dessert.

Hannah is a tall, busty woman, narrow-hipped, with shoulders that allow her to wear men's shirts, no problem. Tonight, though, she had changed into light cotton slacks and a frilly green blouse that showed a hint of cleavage—a tasteful amount, of course, suitable for her second date with a man I had yet to meet and didn't, by god, want to.

I tried to turn the tables by asking, "Why are you going out so late? Not that it's any of my business."

"You have every right to know what time I'll be back to collect Izaak," she responded. "There's a special Mass at St. Isabel's, then we'll probably stop for ice cream. Is midnight okay?"

Collect? This was an unusual choice of verbs for a woman who was Old Florida, a devout Christian who spoke with a drawl. People from the South *carry* or *pick up*. They do not *collect*. Who the hell was she dating, a vacationing Brit whose itinerary included a fling with one of the locals?

Male territorialism is another primate-based taboo. It must be smuggled beneath a camouflage of reason. "I'm not an expert," I said, "but I thought Christmas was the only time they held Midnight Mass. Sort of strange, when you think about it—and on a Wednesday. How well do you know this guy?"

"Marion?" She came toward me, a dish towel in her hands, her expression maddeningly soft with empathy. Affection, too, I had no doubt. "I'm not going to fight. We're going to be fine, you and me. And Izaak is going to grow up proud of us both—especially his brilliant daddy. You've got to trust my judgment. Both of us, for now, we need our personal space. A peaceful time. Okay?"

Space. Geezus, what a dumb, nebulous term for what constitutes strict emotional boundaries.

"Just like we agreed," I said agreeably. "Even so, it can't hurt to check the schedule of events at St. Isabel's. Or maybe you already did. You know"—I let her see I was giving the subject careful thought—"I'd almost bet that I'm right about that Midnight Mass only at Christmas thing. The guy you're seeing, it could be he's, well . . . more interested in ice cream than going to church."

Hannah's look of concern provided a depth of caring that was undeserved, considering what I'd just insinuated.

"It's a special Mass," she said, "for the victims of what's been going on. Catholics, I'm not sure how many churches—dioceses, I think they're called—they've been asked to hold prayer vigils tonight."

Hannah was Baptist, not Catholic, but I was done behaving like a jerk. "Then I'm sure it's okay," I said. A moment later, though, I had to ask, "What victims? I haven't been following the news because . . . well, I've been away on business."

Fifteen days I had been gone in Guyana. She had been furious at me in her quiet way for disappearing without notice but had let it go.

"Day before yesterday," she said, "two people were killed when a bomb went off at a clinic in Miami—one of the suburbs, I think. There's been several attacks, I don't know how many dead."

I zeroed in. "You're taking about abortion clinics, right?"

Hannah had been following the story. "No, a different kind—fertility clinics, some call them. You know, for couples who can't get pregnant? They're holding a special Mass because, in Atlanta, a man broke in after hours and attacked three employees with an axe. One survived long enough to say the guy was dressed sort of like a priest—but with a hood."

She grimaced, internalizing the horror. "Just awful to think about. There's no proof he's a priest, but you know how the news is these days. The Catholic Church is being blamed for the actions of one crazy person. So that's why I—my friend and I—we want to attend services at St. Isabel's tonight."

She stepped closer, her manner serious. "Doc, please

try to understand. I know that people make fun of people like us—Christians, I mean. I'm used to it. And don't care, because I really believe there's power in attending services. In Christ—or whatever religion you are—especially when people pray as a group." She hesitated. "One day I hope you come to know the peace it can give you, Marion. To at least open your mind . . . It would mean a lot to me."

People like us—Hannah had included the man she was meeting, but had yet to use his name. Fine. And I was too damn stubborn to ask.

So what can you do when your stomach knots with a primal response that borders on pain? You refocus and escape to the starboard side of the brain. It is a large and linear space, a hemisphere not shackled to emotion.

I asked, "Did the survivor provide any more details? You said one crazy person. Are the cops sure it's not a group of some type?"

I was thinking about the man who had introduced himself as Deville.

This was not what Hannah had hoped to hear. Disappointment registered, then resignation. Her expression told me *You'll never change.*

"I'm more concerned with the poor folks who've suffered," she said. "But tonight, if you want, I'll find out what I can." Then, with a sly look, she offered to make peace in a way that was irresistible. She cupped a hand to her mouth, sniffed, then grinned. "Garlic—you troublemaker you. And don't pretend it was an accident you added three times more than what that fish stew needed. Lord knows, He broke the mold when He made you."

The knot was gone, displaced by the clarity of a new objective. I laughed, and reached for the mother of my son, saying, "Look, just be careful, okay?" and gave her a tender kiss on the forehead.

When she was gone, I went to the computer. By 10 p.m. I knew what little there was to know about three fertility clinic attacks—Charlotte, Atlanta, and Miami. Two were Mensal Cryonics franchises. The third was owned by an entity called Preferred Cryobank International. All provided a full catalog of options, from artificial insemination via unknown donors to in vitro fertilization.

In vitro, from the Latin *vitrum*, meaning *a shell that could be pierced*—I had to look it up. This was a more complicated process. It required follicle aspiration, an outpatient procedure. Next, multiple eggs were fertilized in a lab. A few days later, the live embryos were transferred into the client's uterus via a catheter tube and a syringe. In both protocols, the female was first given fertility medication to increase the number of eggs she produced during ovulation.

My notions of romance and sex went out the window. But these options had made tens of thousands of infertile couples very happy.

Not all involved agreed, however. A manifesto posted

by one or more of the attackers condemned the clinics as "creationist orphanages" that marketed test tube babies to the highest bidder, indifferent to the child's "true destiny in a future or past life."

The exact wording. Geezus, how could reading this nonsense not bring Tomlinson's situation to mind?

No Más had still not returned. Now I was thinking about Deville and the Scarab go-fast boat I'd seen earlier. Twice I hailed my pal on the radio without results, then tried his cell. Next, I made an apologetic call to aviation mechanic Ricky Hilton. My Maule amphib was still waiting on parts, but, tomorrow, he had to deliver a Cessna to St. Pete.

"The owner will be with me," he said, "and needs the hours. I don't think he'd mind flying a grid while I look for Tomlinson's boat. Any distinctive markings? Even at five hundred feet, you know those damn things all look the same."

I had already consulted a chart and extrapolated the probable course and speed. "I'm not really worried," I said. "He and his daughter probably ran aground or fell into the Heineken trap and anchored for the night. But, yeah, if you don't mind, they'd be somewhere between Captiva and Boca Grande Pass. Unless . . ." For the first time, it crossed my mind that the duo might have decided to sail to St. Pete, where Delia lived. It didn't make a hell of a lot of sense, but the girl had said she liked taking off on a whim. "Even if they sail all night," I amended, "the farthest north they could be is some-where off Sarasota."

"Think you ought to call the Coast Guard?" Ricky asked. Then changed his mind, and said, "No, definitely not." We both knew what the Coasties might find if they boarded *No Más*. A drug stash.

I had already thought it through. A better choice, if law enforcement was needed, was Chris Bannister, a dep-uty sheriff stationed on Captiva Island. Chris was a good man. Almost everyone on the island had his cell number, including me, and he had quick access to a patrol boat.

Ricky had another idea. "Hey, how about I call one of the Sundown Patrol guys and see if they noticed any-thing unusual this afternoon. You said Tomlinson left around seven? He would have been on their route."

The Sundowners Flying Club is a local institution. They are civilian pilots who every day around sunset fly a coastal loop in search of vessels in distress.

"I'd appreciate that," I said, then described *No Más*. It was a nondescript vessel save for the Conch Republic flag Tomlinson sometimes flew off the stern. Oh, and the yellow inflatable dinghy he used as a tender.

"If you have a picture, text it," Ricky suggested. "I'll send it along to a couple of Sundowner guys I know."

I did, and was going over charts when I heard the first purring alert that Baby Izaak was about to awake. Breast milk was in the fridge. It was time for a diaper change. I lifted the warm density of my son and not for the first time marveled at the infinite possibilities encased in a body so tiny, so fragile.

I touched my lips to his cheek. The boy balled his fists, yawned mightily, and was soon asleep. I was stretched out beside him and had nearly dozed off myself when, half an hour later, Ricky called back. His Sundowner pal had seen a vessel similar to *No Más* inside Captiva Pass. It had been anchored in a shoal area where sailboats that size seldom ventured.

"That's the only reason he noticed the boat," Ricky said. "Do you have a chart? You know the area, but I can pinpoint it for you."

"What about people aboard?" I asked. "That yellow dinghy would've been easy to spot."

"I don't know," Ricky said. "The boat didn't appear to be in trouble, so they didn't circle back. I can call him again, if you want, but, like you said, if it was Tomlinson, they probably had a few beers and anchored for the night. He knows the waters around here better than most."

I carried the phone to the desk and marked a spot on the chart. It was twelve miles north of Dinkin's Bay and only a few miles west of Hannah's home in the fishing village of Gumbo Limbo. I knew the area well—Captiva Shoals, it is called, a tricky waterscape of cuts and oyster bars. Six old empty fish houses similar to my own stand in the shallows. They are weekend retreats for locals who hold the leases, but since there's no fresh water or electric, the cabins were usually empty and locked tight.

At first, the scenario made sense. Hole up for the night. Have dinner and a long, private talk. Then it didn't make sense because of what I saw on the chart and a mosquito buzzing around my ear. This was deep summer, the hot, muggy reminder that Florida is a hostile host and damn near uninhabitable without the modern niceties we have imposed upon it.

Why hadn't they sailed a mile or two farther to Cabbage Key or Useppa Island? This time of year, both were like ghost towns. Plenty of privacy, and, on Useppa, awaited the advantages of a graceful old inn for dinner, with a full bar, screened porches, and AC.

Well . . . Tomlinson was a minimalist. Maybe Delia was, too.

This seemed reasonable until I reviewed details about the attacks. The first was two weeks ago in Charlotte, North Carolina. Five days later, a clinic in Peachtree City near Atlanta was the target. Both attacks had occurred shortly after closing time. Two RNs, two clinicians, and a doctor had been hacked to death with an axe. No witnesses, no video cam footage, and the lone survivor had not lived through the night.

Then, two days ago, it was Boca Raton, north of Miami. The perpetrator had become more sophisticated. He had sent or planted a bomb, and added two more scalps to his belt.

This target wasn't a Mensal clinic. It was owned by Preferred Cryobank. Was that significant? I thought about it while also trying to recall the name of Tomlinson's biological son, the minister in North Carolina. Cryobank could not have been chosen randomly. Unlike an axe, a bomb requires expertise, planning, and time.

This suggested that maybe two or more people were involved, united by a mutual obsession. And the time line marked their route from North Carolina to Georgia, then into Florida.

North Carolina.

What the hell was that kid's name? Chester something, Tomlinson had said. The Right Reverend Chester . . . The minister of a small church, Delia had said.

My mind blanked on it. So I went to the computer and tried a backdoor approach by typing in all the little threads. This was diversion enough to free my memory, and the name came to me even before I hit the search button.

Rev. Chester Pickett smiled back from his church Facebook page—Friendship Baptist, a congregation of fewer than a hundred—*All Faiths Welcome.*

The man was angular, gaunt, and distinctive, with his long red beard and hollow eyes. Pickett was a former Marine who'd seen action in Afghanistan. That explained the beard, which hid facial scarring, but also the wheelchair and what might have been a prosthetic hand. The church activities calendar proved that as of two days ago, at least, he had not left his home region near the Pee Dee River.

Rev. Pickett was not Mack's Sasquatch—the man who had called himself Deville.

It was 11:15.

I got busy. I texted Tomlinson's cell with the info Ricky had provided and said I was on my way. The message might interrupt whatever was going on and scare off an attacker—if there was an attacker. By the time an electronic alarm announced Hannah's return, my boat was iced and provisioned with equipment I might need . . . And a few items I hoped I would not.

Our exchange was awkward. She spoke of how nice the service was. Her "friend" wasn't mentioned. I described my evening as uneventful with a breeziness that only magnified the tension we felt.

It got worse when I offered to follow her home by water. It was a reasonable offer, I thought, and also a good excuse. The woman came and went by boat, seldom drove her SUV. I'd be heading that direction anyway the moment she took off.

Hannah is not the chatty type, but articulate in a comfortable, Southern way. Never had I seen her struggle to find the right words. "Well . . . thing is, Doc, I, uhh . . . I won't be . . . See, we are going home, Izaak and me—of course we are—but I'm leaving my boat here tonight . . . Now, don't get the wrong idea . . . I mean, really, you know better than *anyone* how I am when it comes to *that* sorta thing . . ."

This attempt to poke fun at her own cautious sexuality fell flat, and Hannah knew it. "I'm sorry," she said, and began gathering Izaak's things. "I don't blame you for thinking what you're thinking, but you're wrong. I wouldn't do that to you or our boy. What happened is, my friend offered to drive us because there's a chance of rain tonight. It seemed like a good idea, so I said yes."

On this evening of clear sky and moonlight, I hadn't thought to check the weather. To check now, in Hannah's presence, was to risk humiliating us both.

A step to my left provided a view of the mangroves that hedge the parking area. A fragment of headlights pierced the foliage. A car was waiting for her. The decision had already been made.

"That's smart," I said. "Keeping you two safe is all I care about."

She declined my offer to escort her beyond the mangroves, and it was a relief to be in my boat, alone, cruising through darkness, attached to nothing but water and a swath of moonlight.

At the mouth of Dinkin's Bay, an easterly flare of lightning was a comfort, not a concern—Hannah had not been lying about the weather. It also illuminated an unexpected hazard ahead—an empty kayak, so low in the water that I wouldn't have seen it otherwise. I dropped off plane and used the spotlight. Reflective letters told me it was from the marina.

Odd. Mack, Nick, and Figgy were fastidious when it came to storing and logging the comings and goings of rental boats.

I got a line around the thing, secured it in the bushes, and got under way again.

An oversight, I told myself. The other possibility was too troubling to entertain. Someone—Deville, possibly—had stolen the kayak, then abandoned it after flagging down Tomlinson and Delia as they had exited the bay aboard *No Más.*

EIGHT

No Más was where Ricky said it would be, two miles inshore of the Gulf, near a row of stilthouses. Viewed beneath stars after midnight, the structures resembled skeletal birds that had no eyes. Without directions, I might have missed it. The boat was far off the main channel, no lights showing, not even the required white anchor light atop the mast.

Tomlinson isn't fussy about his own well-being, but he never would've put the life of a passing boater at risk.

Something else was amiss—the little yellow outboard dinghy was gone.

I slipped the 9mm Sig into a holster belted to the small of my back. The NVD monocular was in a console drawer. It snapped securely onto a headband that positioned the lens over my left eye. With the moon, I hadn't needed it despite hillocks of squall clouds over the mainland.

Flick a switch, nighttime through a green lens became high noon. Overhead, stars multiplied by the tens of thousands. Satellites sparked thin robotic threads, and the flickering distant storm became volcanic, boiling with electricity.

There was no sign of life aboard *No Más*.

On the T-top of my boat is a wireless LED Golight, military-grade. An infrared cover makes the beam invisible to those not equipped with night vision. It could light up a stage, yet actors would believe they were in total darkness.

I used the Golight to scan. The sailboat's cabin door had been left open. As I idled closer, I probed the length and breadth of her. Still no hint of human activity. I knew I'd have to step aboard eventually and dreaded what I might find.

I tied off. Inside the cabin, there was no blood, no bodies, no obvious signs of chaos aside from what is typical on a boat that is used as a floating home. Delia had left her computer bag, with her purse and laptop inside. Tomlinson had left his biker's wallet and cell phone. Surprisingly, his cell was on. I swiped it open and searched for unchecked messages. There were none, which meant the text I'd sent had been read.

Why hadn't my pal responded?

The forward berth was empty. Sheets had been ripped

off the bed. There was also a roll of duct tape—a disturbing find—which went into my small tactical bag. On the chart table were rolling papers, a bong, and an open Ziploc filled with weed. The scent of patchouli was overwhelmed by recent marijuana musk.

Delia hadn't struck me as the smoker type. And it wasn't likely my pal had revealed this personal weakness to a woman already spooked by the genetics of her biological father.

Where had they gone?

Topside, a mile away, Useppa Island was a dome of black trees sprinkled with a few lights. In winter, a hundred vacationers might be staying there. In July, there are only a couple of full-time residents, and most of the restaurant staff are ferried back to the mainland after it closes at 10.

Closer—much closer—were the old fish houses.

I returned to my boat and deployed the electric trolling motor. With the wireless remote looped around my neck, I started toward them under the cover of rumbling distant thunder. A century ago, before refrigeration, the Punta Gorda Fish Company had built similar houses along the coast. They chose shallow-water spots with a channel. After jetting in pilings, a platform was constructed. On the platform, two small cabins were bolted fast. One cabin was to house fishermen. The other was insulated with double-thick walls to store fish.

The cabins ahead were battered remnants of what

they'd once been, reduced in size, patched with plywood, all windows shuttered. Because they'd been built in a wobbly row, two of the cabins were blocked from view until I rounded an oyster bar that shielded them to the west. One by one, I painted them with infrared. White birds, unaware, roosted in nearby mangroves. No sign of Tomlinson or his dinghy. Before speeding off to check the docks at Useppa, I gave the cabins a last try by switching to thermal vision.

The sudden change was remarkable. Stars, distant lightning, vanished. Thermal imaging is indifferent to light. It sees only heat. Internal circuitry converts degrees of infrared to colors. The spectrum ranges from heartbeat red, to orange and cold, cold blue. Tin roofs of cabins were a warm copper. Pine siding, an icy gray. The roosting birds appeared as vascular red specks.

Nothing unexpected until I found the largest cabin. It was about midway down the row, capped with a wooden cistern. One of its shuttered windows was framed with thermal yellow.

Body heat. Someone was inside.

A splotch of red appeared in a silver frame that opened, then closed. The person had cracked the shutter to peek out. Bad timing for me. It was possible I'd been seen because of the moon.

I motored closer. Tomlinson's dinghy came into view. It was tied in the shadows of mangroves on the north side of the cabin. Its little 15-horse motor glowed with recent heat. There were other warning signs. A padlock and hasp on the cabin's front door had been sheared away as if by the stroke of an axe. On the overhead lintel, a large human handprint was still visible. It was a ghostly, fading petroglyph shaded amber.

That person inside, I realized, might be watching me. I tried to imitate a bumbling fisherman as I fired the outboard and roared away, my running lights bright. Halfway to Useppa, I stopped and called my deputy sheriff friend, Chris Bannister. As we spoke, I could look south and see the white glow of Captiva Island, where the man lived.

"Just say the word," he said after I'd explained my suspicions. "But Doc? Stay out of this if it turns out you're right. Call *me*—I monitor VHF—or by phone."

I said, "If you don't hear from me in thirty minutes, something's wrong."

Using the trolling motor, I returned to the stilthouses— but this time, mangrove trees screened my arrival.

Mosquitoes blossomed from the trees as I approached on foot. Roosting birds—white ibis and a great blue heron—flushed with the roar of lions. Until then, the cabin had resonated with a lone male voice that suddenly went silent. It wasn't Tomlinson's voice. Whoever it was had been lecturing in a feverish rage.

I crouched, hoping the lecture would continue. It didn't.

At the side of the cabin, a shutter opened. A fragment of light speared out and searched the foliage a few yards to my right. When the shutter closed again, I crunched my way across the oysters and ducked under the house. Water was up to my thighs. There was enough headroom to stand.

Above me, inches away, heavy feet thumped their way to another window. A flashlight startled a cormorant, and nearly found my 26-foot Pathfinder. I'd left the trolling motor running because the remote around my neck allowed me to control the boat from a distance. With the wireless toggle, I canceled the electronic anchor command—Spot-Lock, it's called. The touch of a button sent the boat gliding out of sight. Another button stopped the vessel and reengaged the GPS anchor system.

After a long, quiet moment, I was relieved to hear Tomlinson speak. Muted by thick planking, he said what sounded like "Just birds, man. Come on, you're all strung out." Then something about "cut this shit out and let's go back to the boat." Or possibly "cut this shit off," which suggested his hands might be taped or tied.

The man thumping around above me had an oddly high, acidic voice. "I think your boyfriend ran away, Daddy-O. Goddamn it, I shouldn't have waited." More heavy footsteps, then I heard the bang of something metallic on the floor. "Too bad. I wanted him to be here for the weenie roast—get it?" The voice laughed and repeated the punch line. "Well, hell . . . the dude probably called the cops already—that's on your head. Means I'll have to split before the fun starts."

Delia spoke. I couldn't decipher her words, only the phrases "You can't do . . ." and "This doesn't solve . . ." It was the voice of a reasonable woman about to succumb to panic.

The man, still laughing, said, "Sister, I already have."

Drip-drip-drip—liquid began to drizzle down through the floorboards into the water. The drops followed a seam in the planking in step with shoes crossing the room above. Was the guy pissing?

No. The familiar odor was an electric jolt to the back of my neck. It was diesel fuel. Tomlinson kept a spare can aboard for his underpowered little Yanmar engine.

The lunatic was about to torch the house.

I wore gloves. Barnacles, like glass shards, covered the pilings. I slogged and stumbled to the dock and heaved myself up. Wood pilings are sensitive to vibration. I forced myself to move slowly. Hopefully, there was time. In an enclosed space, gasoline, as an accelerant, explodes like a bomb. Diesel is different. Diesel fuel can be hard to light with matches. Maybe the guy didn't know enough to soak a rag or a ball of paper first to reach the necessary flashpoint.

———

I went up the stairs. Inside, the voices of Tomlinson and Delia were muffled, but I heard my pal say clearly, "Goddamn it, leave her out of this."

A string of distracted profanities suggested that their captor was getting frustrated. There was the odor of petroleum smoke but no crackling of flames. Perhaps it was the challenge of starting a fire with diesel. I used the noise he made as cover and attempted to open the door. It was locked on the inside. When I tried to pry it open, I heard the heavy clang of something falling to the floor—possibly an old-fashioned bolt on a string.

The cabin went silent.

So much for the element of surprise.

In my pocket was an LED flashlight. I cracked open the door, drew my pistol, and stepped into the shadows of a room, where, on the floor, several sputtering rolls of toilet paper were struggling to burn. They had been arranged in an odd circular pattern. A six-volt lantern showed Tomlinson's face in half-light. He was in a bamboo chair, wrists taped, legs free. Delia sat with her back to me, not bound, but her eyes were fixated on an interior door that had just closed.

I crept closer, gun out. A haze of black smoke caused my pal to squint when he saw me. His eyes widened—a warning that made no sense until he yelled, "Behind you!"

Too late. A withering impact drove me sideways. The flashlight went flying, but I held on to the pistol. I spun in time to duck beneath the path of what I feared was an axe but turned out to be a hammer. My attacker, a lanky silhouette, swung again. I juke-stepped back. It provided the microsecond needed to decide not to shoot the son of a bitch. Not yet.

Delia hollered something frantic as I holstered my pistol. Hands free, I slipped under the arms of a man who was taller, but not as wide, and dislocated his elbow with a quick *Come along* cradle. The joint made a distinctive pop.

The hammer tumbled to the floor.

The man bellowed and charged. I dropped to my knees. A double-leg takedown, the move is called in wrestling circles, and this guy was no wrestler. Not much of a fighter, in fact. I hefted him briefly off the floor, then bulldozed him out the door and gave him a push. The deck railing there was kidney-high. The crossbeam shattered upon impact. The man clawed the air, falling backward, his scream cut short when he hit the water.

I didn't bother to look down. An accidental drowning could be explained. And the guy was welcome to try to outrun me in Tomlinson's dinghy.

A more pressing issue was the fire. A breeze from the squall and the open door combined had finally set the toilet paper ablaze—but manageably because of my gloves. To Delia, I yelled, "Are you hurt?"

She hollered back, "No, but we've got to get him out

of here," meaning Tomlinson, who was on his feet but still taped to the chair. It was hard to breathe because of the fumes, and harder to see.

Under the sink was a bucket. Dousing the flames would only cause more smoke, so I used the bucket as a basket. I gathered the burning rolls in a rush, carted them outside, and dumped them over the broken railing.

The man had vanished.

"Where'd he go?" Delia demanded. I had cut Tomlinson free and steered them both outside with the help of my flashlight. She coughed and shielded her eyes. "Are you a policeman? Thank god you found us."

She had yet to recognize me, I realized.

"He's in the water somewhere," I told her, then asked Tomlinson, "The guy Deville—does he have a gun? If he does, both of you stay low until I say it's okay."

Tomlinson replied, "It's not him. I don't know who the hell . . . No, Deville's a lot bigger."

Delia argued, "How can you be sure? He was wearing that thing over his head—a stocking or whatever it was." She turned from her biological father and finally recognized me. "Oh my god . . . *Marion*?" She was stunned. "How could . . . I can't believe it's you."

Below us, the man—whoever it was—got the little outboard kicker started on his third try. From the shadows, Tomlinson's dinghy appeared. It puttered slowly at first, then faster, but not at a speed equal to the two-stroke wail of the engine. For a few seconds, I followed the dinghy with the flashlight. I got a vague look at a tall, boney man wearing a black hood or stocking cap.

He was driving east, away from the Intracoastal channel, possibly toward the only smattering of lights visible—the fishing village of Gumbo Limbo, where Hannah and Izaak lived.

I said to Tomlinson, "Move, get your ass in gear. We've got to make sure the fire's out, then I'm going to follow that lunatic."

When he tried to interrupt, I told him he could explain it all to a deputy sheriff after I'd taken them back to *No Más*. "Chris Bannister—you know him. Tell Chris what happened, and I'll be in touch by VHF."

We were aboard the Pathfinder, planing toward the sailboat, when Tomlinson slid over and confided, "I don't want to hang an attempted murder rap on the kid—whoever he is. He needs a psych ward, not prison."

Delia sat on the forward seat, her hair wild in the wind, unable to hear.

"Kid?" I said. "Knock it off. The guy's dangerous. You can't ignore what just happened." I'd just hung up the phone after another conversation with Chris. He was on his way, and had offered to get a department helicopter involved if needed.

Tomlinson was serious. "Marion, listen. It wasn't the same guy, but there has to be a connection. At least talk to him first. Find out, Deville and him, what do they really want?"

"To kill you—that's not obvious?" I said. "What I don't understand is, why did you let him get on your boat to begin with?"

"Let him?" Tomlinson snapped. "Whoa! Back off. The dude stowed away in the forward berth. Before we got aboard, he musta swam out to my mooring or used a canoe—I don't know. We didn't even know he was aboard until we came about off Captiva. That was two hours ago."

"Didn't notice him on a forty-foot boat?" Police would be dubious. And so was I.

"Yeah, man. Just off Captiva Pass. Suddenly, there he was. At first I was, like, be cool, be nice, the more, the merrier. The guy—his size, his hair—nothing like Deville this afternoon. He'd fired up the bong, but—wow!—things went south from there."

I almost laughed. "In other words, your biological son changed wigs, you got stoned together, and you two bonded before he tried to burn you alive. Stop trying to protect him."

"I'm not," Tomlinson insisted. "The kid, his brain's eaten up with demons, the kind cooked up in a meth lab. He went into this whole rap about ancient alien spirits. Animal deities. Rats especially—they talk to him at night. He never sleeps, so he gets cranky. Doc, you get him calmed down, he might open up to me."

Cranky? Only Tomlinson could redefine murderous intent with an adjective from *Leave It to Beaver*.

"Then accuse him of grand theft and arson when you talk to the police," I said, done arguing. If I was right about the fertility clinic murders, it would be enough to put the guy away. I didn't want to hear any more details.

"Save it," I told him when he opened his mouth again. "I'm in sort of a rush."

In the bays of Southwest Florida, ribbons of imploded limestone form channels that are unmarked, known only to locals. The channels start and end without notice except for subtleties of surface tension—a swirling current, a sudden slick, an eddy coming off a ridge of oysters that can rip the bottom out of a boat.

In the backcountry, a straight line is almost always a dangerous navigational choice.

Tomlinson's "troubled kid"—Deville, in my mind— had escaped east toward the nearest lights, unaware of what lay between the fish houses and the village of Gumbo Limbo.

That's the trail I followed, alone, in my fast open boat.

Ahead lay a tangle of mangroves that appeared as a low lone wall of shadows. In truth, it was a slalom course of islands, mostly swamp. If the guy managed those, there were sandbars surfacing with this falling tide. And corridors of rock that funneled boaters into a little marina that wouldn't open until dawn.

In a space of only a few miles, there were plenty of places the man could hide—or ruin an engine. I didn't care as long as Hannah and our son were safe. The odds of him stumbling onto them were slim, but it was possible. I had to get to Gumbo Limbo before Deville did, and he'd had a twenty-minute head start.

I had switched out my running lights, all electronics off save for the radio when I left *No Más* behind. Now I was doing fifty-plus in good water, thirty-five in thin areas where crab traps littered the flats.

Night vision allowed me to see what Deville could not.

Hillocks of mangroves blurred past—Little Wood Key, Josslyn, and Part Island. A squall wind sparked overhead. A lone cloud the size of a sailing ship slowed and strafed me with pellets of rain.

The rain intensified, then was gone. The cloud plowed a black comet's tail that scarred the water's surface at a speed I could not match. Inside Rat Key, I turned north toward the high palms of Gumbo Limbo and didn't shut down until I had a clear view of Hannah's dock.

I felt some tension go out of me. Hannah's refurbished cruiser, where she'd lived before having a child, was moored in darkness. It lifted and rolled when my wake surfed shoreward. There was no yellow dinghy tied nearby.

Across the road, built atop a high shell mound, was the house where Hannah had grown up and now lived. A room had been transformed into a nursery. Her mother—a likable but contentious eccentric—had moved into a tiny guest cottage at the back of the property. The wraparound porch was dimly lit.

I shifted into neutral with the indifference of a man who wasn't spying on his ex-girlfriend.

On the porch were silhouettes. Two people stood alone, perhaps face-to-face, but at a distance it was impossible to be sure. In the shell drive, parked next to Hannah's SUV, was an unfamiliar car—foreign, a mid-sized sedan, white or possibly silver.

Her friend, after delivering mother and child safely home, had been allowed to stay.

It was 1:35 in the morning.

In my abdomen, a residual tension returned. The silhouettes embraced—a kiss, then a longer kiss. The people parted. Porch lights blinked out. The silhouettes, vague as smoke in the moonlight, seemed in a rush to rejoin.

Maybe they did. I turned my back and continued on to the marina. The docks there catered to commercial fishermen, not the yachting set. A sailboat dinghy would have stood out.

No luck.

The channel into the basin is a limestone corridor, rocks on both sides. A few years earlier, I'd witnessed a fatal boat crash here. A dangerous stretch. Easy on the throttle, all running lights bright.

I left Hannah and her new friend behind and didn't

switch off the lights until I had cleared the rocks and turned toward the fish houses. They were two miles away, screened by mangrove shoals. A rhythmic blue halo above the trees told me that Deputy Bannister had found *No Más*.

Good. No matter what Tomlinson claimed, there was evidence of arson. That would attract more police boats and possibly the chopper Chris had mentioned.

I reached to make contact by VHF, then caught myself. Deville—whoever he was—had to be somewhere nearby. I was in no mood to be sent home by my deputy friend, so why not poke around on my own for a while?

It was an obvious rationalization, but the odds were on my side. Deville had probably run aground. He was hurt. I'd heard his elbow pop when I'd locked him in an arm bar. The man was not only lost, he was in pain.

So where was he . . . ?

At night on the water, inexperienced adults regress. The instincts of a child take over. They panic and try to outrun storms. In the darkness, they steer toward the nearest lights without a thought to the hazards that lie between.

I dropped off plane and drifted. You don't have to be a madman to think like one. Behind me, Gumbo Limbo sparkled through a veil of palm fronds. Shallow water had probably barred the man's access, so the next closest haven would be . . . ?

My eyes searched from south to north. On the horizon, incandescent balloons marked the strongholds of habitation. There were several, all too far for a dinghy-sized vessel save for one—Useppa Island. It was a hundred acres of pre-Columbian shell mounds and shuttered vacation homes.

A man who was hurt and haunted by ancient aliens might find Useppa a calming sanctuary.

And if he didn't?

That was okay, too.

NINE

The yellow dinghy was on the east side of Useppa Island. Deville had run it onto the beach rather than bother with the big commercial dock that years ago had been a popular spearfishing spot for local kids.

Maybe it still was. Water was deep there, boat traffic rare. A forest of pilings attracted the biggest of many species, including bull sharks and hammerheads from nearby Boca Grande Pass.

I tied up to the dock and used the infrared LED to search the beach. The dinghy was a mess of mud and mangrove detritus. A bent propeller proved the motor had been abused. I'd been right about the guy running aground.

Deville had had a long, tough night. And he had to

know it was nearly over. Another police boat had found *No Más* to the south. Blue lights bounced off clouds that sailed the squall closer. Low, in the east, a laser beam scanned the water. A police helicopter was speeding our way.

This was another opportunity to make radio contact. I should have done it. Should have called Chris, my deputy friend, and admitted that I had found the fugitive. But VHF is a public conveyance. Every cop listening would hear, and the whole scrambled force would ascend on the island. How would a madman respond to a cavalry of noise and flashing lights?

Deville, with his crippled arm, was beaten, probably exhausted. I decided to go it alone—quietly. "Try to reason with him," Tomlinson had urged.

Okay. I would try. After securing my boat, I took the precaution of pocketing my keys, then walked down the shoreline to the dinghy. As a second precaution, I disconnected the dinghy's fuel hose and opened the cap of the plastic gas tank.

An elegant whitewashed stairway led uphill to the Collier Inn, a fishing lodge built in the early 1900s. Banks of windows, three stories high, reflected a silent bolt of lightning as I ascended. The wind freshened. To my left was a patio shaded by ficus trees. To my right was the entrance to the dining room and bar. In the breeze, the door swung wide. Broken glass suggested that Deville was inside.

No. I found him several minutes later, curled up, naked and weeping, on a lounge chair by the pool. He shielded his eyes from my flashlight. "You're the man who broke my arm," he bawled. "I hate you. Don't hurt me anymore. *Please*. I don't want to fight."

It was the voice of a child.

Beside him on the deck was a pile of towels. He'd stolen a bottle of vodka and gone for a swim in the pool.

"You mind showing me your hands?" I asked. I didn't say it gently, but there was no need to spook him by shouting orders.

"What?"

"Both your hands. I want to make sure you're not hurt."

He mumbled a slurred profanity but did it, fingers spread wide.

I holstered my pistol. "What's your name?"

Again, his response was childlike. "Jayden. What's yours?"

"Get your clothes on," I told him. "You're going for a boat ride. I'll stay here and keep you company until it's time to leave."

"Too tired," he said, and lay back.

Finally, I did the smart thing. I called Chris Bannister on my cell and got voicemail. While I left a message, Jayden began to babble about his clothes. He didn't want to put them on. They were filthy, diseased, he said, infested with bugs that had eaten his flesh. "Those fuckers have to be burned. Seriously, man." He sat up abruptly. "The disease, once the bugs get in your ears, they eat right through to your brain. Chlorine"—nervous fingers waved hello to the swimming pool—"is the best way to kill them. But they don't die. Not really. Fire's the only answer. What I should have brought was a pipe bomb. I've still got two in my car, but they're too damn, you know, hard to hide."

Pipe bombs? If true, this was enough for police to suspect he was involved with the attacks on the fertility clinics.

I got my first clear look at the man. He had a haggard oval face, curly black hair. Mid-twenties, tall, not lean or fat, but soft, an adolescent pudginess. Tattoos snaked up his arms, a geometry of symbols intersected by lines. Aside from his height, I saw no genetic similarities to my friend.

"What makes you think Tomlinson's your biological father?"

"Who?"

I repeated the question, and added, "What's your last name?"

He responded, "That's a big negatory, man. But my test tube daddy was a monster just like him. We call them all that—Daddy-O. All of us, we're experimental units, test tube brats. But we *are* the chosen ones. Oh, trust me, the world will understand one day."

Jayden's eyes communicated a feverish certainty.

"Then why try to kill him?"

"Why not? Tomlinson—that's his name, right? He poisoned the DNA of a friend of mine. Same thing—spawn monsters, all of the Daddy-Os. And we've, like, finally united to become the King Slayers. King of Thrones—that show's reality, you know. We were all placed here by the same galactic creator. You probably didn't know that either."

After a gulp from a bottle of vodka, he coughed and took another long drink. "Oh, puke city," he moaned, then clutched his stomach, turned, and dry-heaved. Several seconds later, he looked at me with watery eyes. "See? It's working. Smoke purifies . . . Dude, what's your name?"

"Ford," I said. "Get your clothes on, please."

"Ford." He thought that was hilarious. "Sure, Mr. Ford and Mr. Cadillac. You could at least thank me for saving your life. Tell the police that. Tell them I saved your ass and tried to burn the world clean, okay? I'm done with this crazy shit. I just wanna go home."

Another absurdity—until I followed his gaze to an old clapboard building next to the pool. A window there bounced with a smoldering orange flame.

Christ, he'd set the place on fire.

"Let them burn," he yelled as I sprinted away. "They're my clothes, don't touch them. The bugs will spread and everyone on the planet will die."

Inside, among fishing rods, swim fins, and patio furniture, he had piled his clothes on a can of Sterno and lit it. Fortunately, he had all but smothered the flame. I stomped the fire out, and was gathering the mess, when I saw the man, still naked, cross the window in moonlight, a towel hanging from his right hand.

I turned toward the open door, saying, "Thanks, Jayden, I can use that," meaning the towel.

Jayden, eyes wild, dropped the towel and his childlike act. In his hand was a pneumatic speargun he'd probably found in the same room. "You're even dumber than him." He grinned, and aimed the gun at my face. Shrewd, the distance he maintained—close enough to shoot me, but not so close I could lunge and strip the weapon away.

My right hand found the Galco holster belted to the small of my back. "Aren't you in enough trouble?" I started to say, and that's when he fired—a metallic ping.

I ducked. If I hadn't, I might have died. Instead, the stainless shaft, double-barbed, pierced the soft area beneath my left trapezoid muscle, close to my jugular. The shock more than the impact knocked me to the floor.

"Told you what would happen," he yelled. Then came at me, speargun raised like an axe in his good hand, while the arm I had dislocated dangled at his side.

A dazed sense of unreality spun the ceiling. I watched from above, every next move in slow motion. He feinted left and right, trying to get a clean shot at my head with the butt of the gun. I kicked at his shins. Twice, he hammered the floor near my ear. It was a sickening exchange because the spearhead had gone through me and I was tethered to the shaft by a nylon line. Each time he swung, the double barbs deployed and buried themselves deeper in the back of my neck.

He knew it. When I tried to stand or reach for my pistol, he pulled the line taut and dragged me into submission. The pain was searing if I resisted. On my knees, I crabbed after him out the door, where he began to enjoy this little game. If I attempted to move, he'd get a two-step running start and tow me a few feet farther across the patio.

"Hurts, doesn't it?" he taunted. "That's what you get for breaking my arm, you sonuvabitch." *WHACK!* He swung at my head again. "Goddamn it, lay still. Let me put you out of your misery."

He was out of breath.

I was going into shock, which I realized in some faraway place in my head. This couldn't be happening—me, killed by an inept freak like this? I threw up both hands as if surrendering. "Okay," I said. "Let me sit up."

It surprised him. He stepped closer. The nylon line went slack just long enough for me to grab it, wrap it around my left hand, and give it a tremendous yank. The speargun rocketed free and damn near hit me in the face. Jayden started to charge, then reconsidered when he saw me reach and pull the small black 9mm pistol. One-handed, I took aim.

Instantly, his child persona returned.

"I didn't do anything wrong," he yelled, a pouting voice. "You can't prove it. Besides"—he spun around—"it's murder to shoot a man in the back. Everyone knows that. You'll go to jail. Are you insane?"

No, but I am methodical. "I won't be arrested if they don't find your body," I said. And I meant it.

The truth was in my voice and it scared him. To me, the next step—if required—was a question of methodology, not a moral dilemma. And I was very good at this unusual protocol.

Jayden, with a bawling cry of terror, ran for his life. I let him go. This was Florida, my home, not some foreign jungle three passports away. Pull the trigger, my life and the lives of everyone I knew might be forever changed.

So the situation became a training exercise. I'd had the Sig pistol refitted with Truglo tritium sights. From a sitting position, three green beads tracked the naked man to the stairs that led downhill to the dock. My mind squeezed off an imaginary crippling shot to the spine. I added a kill shot beneath the left shoulder blade before he was gone.

The speargun became a cane that helped me to my feet. My shirt showed only a splotch of blood. This was good. It suggested that the shaft had missed the brachial artery. The numbness in my left hand, however, signaled damage to a bundled nerve center located nearby.

Shoulder wounds are serious, the complications many.

I needed a knife to cut myself free of the nylon line. I needed access to my VHF radio and a QuikClot combat gauze to stem the bleeding. All three were aboard my boat.

Halfway down the steps, I paused for a cognitive update. I was dizzy. I feared I might pass out and bleed to death if I didn't get help. I fumbled for my phone and dropped it. It came to rest several steps below. On my butt, I scooted in pursuit while a more troubling scenario urged me onward. What if Jayden came back and found me unconscious?

Me, killed by a blathering adolescent?

My ego found the prospect insulting. Intellectually, though, I knew the truth. *It could happen*. This realization was more shocking than the reality of a stainless steel spear dangling from my shoulder. It was an awkward, nagging weight that, if the nylon line snagged, caused a whistling pain.

I regrouped. From where I sat, lights of the village where Hannah lived formed a halo above the mangroves.

Irony fueled a sudden sadness in me. We are all infinitely expendable. The world would not pause no matter the circumstances of my death, but, damn it, I cared. So why concede by giving in?

On my iPhone, I redialed Chris Bannister and got voicemail again. A list of previous calls offered options that might be speedier than a 911 request to scramble a medevac.

———

Hannah and her boat were only a few miles away, but I couldn't call her. The temptation reeked of emotional sabotage. Much closer were the flashing blue police lights.

I managed to get to my feet, hit REDIAL. It surprised the hell out of me when Tomlinson picked up. "Hey, amigo, we've been trying to raise you on the radio," he said. Then stopped. "Doc, you don't sound good. What's wrong?"

I didn't answer immediately. Jayden had reappeared. He was in water up to his knees, next to the dinghy. I watched him give the little boat a push, then climb in. Dumbass. Never cast off before starting the motor. In this case, the motor cranked on the first pull. But it wouldn't run for long—unless he figured out how to reattach the fuel hose.

To Tomlinson, I said, "I could probably use a doctor. Is Chris or one of the other cops handy?"

"How? What happened?"

I said, "Just put on one of the cops."

He did.

After we signed off, I sat and waited. I butt-scooted down a few steps and waited some more. I was aboard my boat when Deputy Bannister arrived. With him were Tomlinson and Delia. Had I known, I might not have followed first-aid procedure and spared them the shock of seeing me. No longer was I tethered to the speargun, but I hadn't pulled out the shaft.

Overhead, the police chopper prepped the area with a dazzling ray of light. They had already spotted Jayden and the dinghy adrift, not far from shore. Perhaps he thought it was an alien starship. He had waved with his one good arm and blown welcoming kisses.

More likely, it was an act.

"He's a con man and he's dangerous," I told Chris and another deputy, then referenced the fertility clinic attacks. "Find his car. He claimed to have a couple of pipe bombs in the trunk."

To Delia, who held my hand when they strapped me onto a gurney, I asked, "Why are you crying?" I'd just given her good news. In my opinion, Jayden, the lunatic, wasn't Tomlinson's biological son, nor her half brother.

"It's not obvious?" she sniffed. "I feel like an idiot because I was so wrong about you."

This made no sense. But it gave me something to ponder while I was prepped for surgery.

Then the lights went out.

TEN

In late July, Jayden F. Griffin and two unnamed accomplices were indicted by a federal grand jury. The U.S. Department of Justice formally charged Jayden, and the others in absentia, with terrorism under the Homeland Security Act of 2004, and added five counts of first-degree murder.

Lesser charges of assault and grand theft became trifles. Tomlinson considered this a reprieve of sorts.

"I won't have to testify," he said. "But you might."

No, I would not. The last thing my contacts at a certain federal agency wanted was to see my name and photo plastered across the international news.

"Could be," I replied. "But if they're going to serve

papers, they'd better hurry up. I'm taking off in a day or two for a conference thing. I'm giving a talk."

My friend's expression read *Bullshit*. "Where? The Bahamas, I suppose."

He knew someone had been trying to leverage information from me about Jimmy Jones's missing gold. I hadn't provided specifics, just enough to put him and Mack and a few others on the alert for nosy strangers.

"Cuba is nice this time of year," I countered.

It was a Friday afternoon, the second day of August—three weeks since I'd been choppered to a hospital. We were near the boat ramp. Figgy, shirtless and proud of his muscles, was eyeballing Delia, who sat in the shade, leafing through my folder on red tide. Her linen straw-colored blouse was loose-fitting in the breeze. It was a promising drama that I had taken pains to ignore. The girl had visited the marina a couple of times, yet we'd spoken only once since my shoulder surgery. She'd driven down from St. Pete, and was overnighting at one of Mack's cottages now that he was open for business.

Tomlinson glared at Figgy. "Don't you have better things to do?" he demanded in Spanish. "And put a damn shirt on. This is a family marina."

The little Cuban wasn't bright, but he recognized hypocrisy when he heard it. "Man, you ain't wearing no shirt and your *pinga* hangin' out 'bout half the time. When you ever get a chance to look at nice *chichis*, you didn't sit back and say, *'Gracias, Dios mio'*?"

They squabbled for a while before Tomlinson got back to me. "If the feds want you on the witness stand, they'll find you. Hell, amigo, let's be honest . . ." He lowered his voice. "We both know you've got some kind of CIA spook gig with those power-drunk devils. If they need the extra juice, though, they'll haul your ass in in a heartbeat."

"No doubt about that," I said. Which was true for most—but not in my case.

The Clandestine Services is a global consortium with power beyond my need to know. It was a subject I could not discuss. Nor could I explain that if the State of Florida had indicted Jayden, it might have been a different story. But the feds were in charge. So I was free—free within the constraints of a recent deal my contacts had offered. They wanted me out of the country—or at least out of contact—for a couple of weeks.

I didn't ask why. Never, ever ask why.

The timing was not good. Hannah didn't need another reason to dump me in favor of her new churchgoing friend. A more bankable excuse might have been my bum shoulder. Damage to a delicate nerve center—the brachial plexus—had caused my left arm to go dead for a while. Surgery had relieved a serious hematoma, yet recovery had been slow. I'd been out of the sling for a week. The feeling in my fingers was starting to return. But in the Clandestine Services an excuse is as untenable as asking why. So I had agreed to leave Florida in exchange for information on the extortionist, who, during his visit back in July, had claimed to work for the IRS.

Leo Alomar wasn't bright either. The guy had used his real name. That detail along with other information had been provided me in the form of a dossier.

Out of respect for Tomlinson, I confided, "By the way, you might be right about the Bahamas. Hurricane season's nice down there. You want to come along?"

Delia got up and walked toward us. "What about the Bahamas?" she asked.

"She reads lips," Tomlinson said, beaming. "Tell Doc about high school, the work you did with special needs kids. She's also an expert on hand signing."

The girl remained intent on me. She inquired about my arm. She made small niceties before asking, "Any chance I can borrow you for a few minutes? I think I mentioned those internships I applied for, and one of the interviews is tomorrow. Belle Glade, the Sugar Cane Growers Cooperative. Their aquatic biologist needs an assistant. Know anything about the organization?"

Delia had been reading my folder on red tide. She knew damn well I was familiar with the oldest collective of small farmers in the state. I consulted Tomlinson with a look. "Want me to come along?" he said—a suggestion, not a question.

"No thanks, Tomlinson," she replied. That was the end of it.

_____

The craft of reading lips is so notoriously inaccurate—in the real world anyway—that law enforcement views it as a tool best kept on the shelf with psychics. Baseball players and other pro jocks might believe that people can read lips, but I didn't—until Delia waited until we were alone to say, "What did Tomlinson mean about you being a spook? Something to do with the CIA. I didn't catch it all, but the _C-I-A_ part—individual letters, they're easiest—so I'm fairly sure. That would be so weird, but kinda cool, too. It might explain why I was so wrong about you."

We were in my galley, across from the lab. I waved the question away as if absurd. "I thought you wanted to talk about your interview tomorrow."

She was disappointed. "I do. But I was hoping . . . And it kinda fit, the way you handled that . . . the situation. You know what I'm talking about. You don't seem like the violent type."

"I'm not," I said. "It just sort of happened."

"Really? I don't know, Doc. Most people, me included, no way I could've done what you did. We still haven't talked about it, and I think we should. You mind?"

"I don't see the point, but . . . yeah, if you want."

Delia slipped into the chair next to my telescope. "I

get queasy when I think about what could've happened. That—whatever he is—that man would've killed us. Set us on fire. I mean, I'm sure you read about him in the news."

I had. There are a growing number of Jayden Griffins in this country. They are addicted to opioids, video blood sport, and immune to human carnage. Griffin had been violent enough to be expelled from middle school and remanded to a psychiatric facility in Pennsylvania. Twice he escaped. So he'd been moved to Shuman Juvenile Detention Center, a maximum security facility, and had stayed out of trouble until the recent bombings.

The feds had linked Jayden to a group of gamers he'd met on the internet. A couple of them discovered they'd been sired with the help of Mensal Cryonics, and the rage they shared had forged a violent obsession. After hacking the facility's data, they had created a hit list of the most prolific donors. The clinics they'd targeted were the same facilities where members of the group had been conceived.

Jayden, according to news reports, had been one of the ringleaders. The feds—or so the stories speculated— hoped his accomplices would testify against him. If not, the reports reasoned, they were fugitives and their names would have been made public.

I wasn't as certain. Another name the feds hadn't released was Tomlinson's. It was more than a lucky break. One of my sources had confided that Mensal Cryonics credited one of their donors with one hundred and seven successful inseminations. Maybe my pal, but my source wasn't certain.

I had not shared the information with Tomlinson or Delia.

There was something else on Delia's mind. First, though, she felt the need to rehash what had happened the night she'd been kidnapped. Trauma creates an intimacy, members only. We had yet to share the experience.

Mostly, I listened.

Tomlinson had told me the truth. They had been topside, under sail since sunset, when Delia had smelled smoke. "Weed," she said. "I smoke occasionally. Vape, usually. It's more private, but who doesn't know the smell?" She'd gone below to investigate, and there was Jayden in the forward berth, using a bong. He also had a hammer.

"We would've never picked him up," she said when I mentioned the abandoned kayak. "He'd been aboard the boat the whole time. When I first saw him, I froze for a moment, in total shock. And I said something stupid like 'May I help you?' It was dark, he had that hoodie thing on. I couldn't make out his face, but his voice, when I heard it, I knew we were in trouble. Deep, sharp, him totally out of his damn mind. And seriously pissed off in a cool, *I'm in control* sort of way. 'Wanna toke?' he said— like, laughing at me because I was so freakin' scared. Then said he was gonna rape me after he killed Tomlinson. Only that's not the word he used, *rape*. What he said was so disgusting, I'm not going to repeat it."

Other details were easier for the girl to share. Jayden, when he'd spotted the empty fish houses, had used the hammer to force them both into the dinghy. He'd claimed the sound of water slapping the hull were voices and the voices were ordering him to kill. He'd claimed he needed a wooden floor under his feet, not fiberglass. It was the only thing that could save them.

"From the moment he saw those old houses," she said, "I think he intended to burn us alive. Every night since it happened, I lie in bed and pretend I would've fought the son of a bitch. All the details, the smells, come back, and it's, like, he's trying to grab me again. And I know . . . I know the truth." The girl looked at me, then turned away. "That if you hadn't shown up, Marion, he . . . he would've—" Her voice broke.

I went to the fridge and got two bottles of water. "You can relax, it's over," I said. "The feds are going to send that guy away for a long, long time. And you don't have to worry anymore about the DNA. He's not your half brother and you know it."

Mensal Cryonics had confirmed this via their attorneys with a document provided to the police.

But the girl was still worried. "What about the guy who called himself Deville? He's still out there."

It was a possibility best not confirmed, so I kept quiet.

She continued, "Mack and everyone at the marina has

been so nice to me, that's what I really wanted to talk about. They expect us to hold the reunion at the cottages. Probably around Labor Day weekend and that's less than a month away. Doc?" She sat forward. "I want you to help me talk them out of it. Deville—the guy in the robe—he's already been there once. What if he shows up again and has a gun or something?"

I said, "The police have probably already found him by now. If they haven't, I doubt he's dumb enough to make an appearance. What about that DNA chat page you and your DNA siblings subscribed to? Any more crazy posts?"

No. And there had been nothing more about a class action lawsuit.

"Good," I said. "It's not proof that Jayden was behind it all, but it certainly suggests he was. And the reunion— is it really that important? Why not postpone it or just call it off? You and your biological siblings are adults now. And what's it really matter who—"

"Half sibs," Delia corrected. "And it matters more than you or anyone else could ever understand. That man out there"—Tomlinson, she meant—"he's part of who I am. My parents—my real parents—do you have any idea what it's like to find out the truth? My god, they paid top dollar. A stud fee. Like from a catalog. And you know what I got out of it?"

The girl didn't sound angry, just sad and a little bitter.

"A good home?" I suggested.

She managed a smile. "Christ . . . you're right. I shouldn't complain. But my whole life, I've felt like, I don't know, an orphan in my own home. I really can't describe the sense of emptiness? No, of missing something . . . an important piece of who I am . . . like twins separated at birth. And way before I did the DNA thing. Imogen—my half sister? She says she felt the same growing up. You don't know what it's like to live a lie."

I almost smiled when she said that. "Maybe everyone feels that way."

"It's not the same at all. Face it, Tomlinson's sweet and funny, but he is not, you know, my idea of the perfect father."

"Who is?" I replied.

"I'm not criticizing. It's the little things I see in myself that keep me coming back to see him. The way he pulls his hair when he's nervous. Our handwriting, the shape of our ears. And that goofy laugh of his. Our bio-squad— my bio sibs—they deserve an opportunity to . . . to . . ."

She began to get emotional again. There was a pause while she sniffed and took a drink of water. "What it comes down to is, we—the sibs—wouldn't be on this Earth if it wasn't for him. But Doc?" Her gray-blue eyes caught the light from the window. "I wouldn't be alive if it wasn't for you. I don't know why, but I feel closer to you than just about anyone I've met recently. The reunion, wherever we hold it, I'd like you to be there. Please?"

I got to my feet. "You're a tough one, Delia. That night in the fish house, you would've found a way out."

"Liar. I'm a coward," she said. "So's he, but in a way that puts other people first." Tomlinson, again. "I still haven't gotten up the nerve to tell my parents that we've met because . . . Well, that's obvious. Dad's sick and he's not getting any better."

I asked about her father's health—another tough subject.

She got up to leave. "Will you think about the reunion thing? And my interview tomorrow with the Growers Cooperative—Belle Glade is a two-hour drive. We could talk some more, and I'll buy lunch on the way."

Friday is the traditional party night at the marina. I said, "You're not sticking around for the cookout? We can talk later."

"I'd rather be alone, just the two of us," she countered, then realized how that might be taken. "What I mean is, tomorrow, in my car, it would be quieter. That's all. My boyfriend—my ex-boyfriend, really—doesn't want me to do the interview."

"Why?"

"'Cause he's a dick. He says legitimate biologists will blackball me if I go to work for the enemy. What do you think?"

She meant the Growers Co-op and the sugar cane industry. I said, "It's complicated, all the politics involved. What's he do?"

"Phil? Dr. Phil, as he likes to be called, Phil Knox—he's a philosophy prof at Windward College in Redington Beach. Big into ecology. We both are, that's how we met. He's twenty years older but acts like he's ten sometimes. Going to work for Big Sugar could ruin me, he thinks."

I said, "Why not do the interview and make up your own mind?"

"You'll go with?"

It was tempting. The girl was an interesting mix of certainty and sensitivity. I liked her. Rational people are always at war with their instincts. The most compelling link was Tomlinson. Children born to our friends—whatever the circumstances—become a shared responsibility.

My little seaplane was back from the shop. Its blue-on-white fuselage floated on pontoons outside, tethered to the mangroves. I said, "How about this? It'll be faster if we fly."

You don't know what it's like to live a lie.

Delia had no idea of the irony when she'd said this. I was going over Leo Alomar's dossier folder while I gave the subject some thought. It was late afternoon. Guys at the marina were amping up for music, beer, and food. A drum rimshot pinged through the mangroves. My block-headed retriever had been returned by Hannah's nephew, Luke O. Jones. A nice kid. The dog sprawled belly-up on the cool pine floor near my feet.

My whole life, I've felt like an orphan in my own home, Delia had also said. She could never know, but we had more in common than she realized.

At age nineteen, a clandestine agency—not the CIA—had plucked me out of basic training as a "candidate of special interest." Good-bye, Navy. Hello a lifetime of obligation and privilege that included college, postgrad, and any specialized school, worldwide, I chose to attend.

For a kid that age, it was a heady experience. Jungle Operations Training Center in Panama. Combat driving skills—escape and evasion. High-speed pursuit at BSR in West Virginia. Tactical weapons at Glynco. Close quarters combat at Moyock. There was a long list compiled over the years that included esoteric skills beyond my interests, my abilities, and sometimes my intellectual depth.

I'm not a genius or a gifted athlete. As I discovered later, "candidates of special interest" shared one key asset—our parents were either dead or estranged and we had no close family ties. My parents had died in a boat explosion when I was sixteen—murdered by a man my mother was having an affair with. So I'd lived with a crazed cowboy uncle until graduation, not that he was around much.

Highly trained and expendable. That was us. And if

the worst happened, there were no adoring folks back home to raise a stink or go running to their congressman.

"We have a franchise in every country," a friend of mine once said. "And to hell with politicians, they come and go. They have nothing to do with what *we* do."

My centrist view of politics borders on indifference. It dates back to those years. That has not changed nor have the rules of my employment. On those rare occasions when my expertise is needed, I do the job, come home, and live quietly under the radar. The role of an affable, slightly nerdy marine biologist has served me well. I have often wondered, however, if my clandestine life would end if Hannah, or any woman, said yes to marriage and became the family I'd never had.

The phone rang. Not the wall phone, the encrypted satellite phone in my bedroom. Pete the dog scrambled to alert and followed. It was Hal Harrington, my agency handler.

"You got a pencil and paper?" he asked. "I have that information. Not all, but it'll do for starters."

We don't use pens or personal computers. As he spoke, I wrote Leo Alomar's current home address on his dossier folder. "How far can I go to solve this problem?" I asked.

Harrington understood the insinuation. "Don't even think about. Be clever—I know that's a lot to ask from someone like you—but set him up, maybe, scare the hell out of the guy. Make him go away. He doesn't know who he's dealing with, that's obvious."

"They never do," I said. "Can you provide support?"

"We don't care about your personal problems," Harrington replied, "and we don't want to know. Understand?"

That was a provisional yes.

"I'll keep you out of it," I said, and hung up.

Leo's folder went into the floor safe. Pete pestered me while I showered and shaved, then bolted out the door as eager as me to have some fun.

Marina parties at Dinkin's Bay are interesting. The communal debauchery is spiced by locals who are quirky enough to live side by side on boats yet are convinced they've eluded the rat race in favor of seclusion.

Maybe they have. Water access only, along with a gate, make Dinkin's a private little enclave in a big, loud, busy world.

Fishing guides had trucked in a keg of beer. A bushel of oysters roasted over a bed of coals. There was smoked mullet, brats from Minnesota, mangoes from Pine Island, and a steaming cauldron of black beans. They had been made by the Esteban sisters and their mother, immigrants from Cuba whom I'd helped across the Florida Straits.

When I arrived at the party, a dozen or so liveaboards were on the docks beneath holiday lights, drinks in hand. Around the bonfire, a gaggle of others had cornered Delia. They were unaware of Jayden's assault, but they knew her connection with Tomlinson. Coupled with the marina's recent *Spit in a test tube* craze, I suspected that DNA would be the hot topic.

I got a beer and eavesdropped. Conversation ebbed and flowed with every few steps. Near the bait tanks, Mack was demonstrating a Māori war dance for Rhonda Lister and JoAnn Smallwood. The two women, over the years, had been business partners, lovers, sworn enemies, scorned wives, mistresses, and lovers again. They lived aboard an old Chris-Craft cruiser, *Tiger Lilly.* The vessel was one of the marina's gaudier floating homes.

Rhonda grimaced at Mack's antics. "For god sakes, Mack, shut your mouth before you bite off your tongue. That dance is idiotic. You want to hear something *really* interesting? JoAnn grew up thinking she was half Cherokee. With her big boobs and as short as she is, I believed her until—"

"Quarter Cherokee on my mamma's side," JoAnn interrupted. "I still don't think that damn test was accurate."

"Whatever," Rhonda said. "Let me get to the interesting part. Turns out that we're cousins. See, both our grandfathers netted mullet back in the day. Hers fished out of Chokoloskee, mine lived north on Estero—"

"Third cousins," JoAnn corrected. "And it's not like we're talking incest or . . ." She paused. "What about my boobs? Plenty of Indian women have—"

Mack hadn't finished his Māori dance. The wooden totem in his hand suggested he'd been practicing. "Jesus bloody hell," he cut in, "show a little respect for the Kiwi Nation or—"

Rhonda hooted, "No incest, my ass," and stepped toward JoAnn. "Your grandfather screwed his way up and down this coast—same as you'd do, given the chance. That itch between your legs didn't come in a bottle, sweetie, and you know damn well—"

JoAnn turned to me with a hurt expression. "Doc, you think my boobs are too big?"

"Last time I saw them, they were perfect," I responded. "I'm willing to take a closer look, if it'll help."

Rhonda chastened me with a laughing profanity.

I moved on to a group of fishing guides. Jeth, Big Alex, and Neville had gathered near the fuel pump. Guides are like ballplayers—they prefer to cloister themselves in privacy, apart from those who don't know a damn thing about what they do.

Jeth was talking about Bavaria. For a man who stuttered, *Bavaria* was a challenging word to pronounce, but not impossible because he was with friends. "Never heard of that country, so I looked it up. No ocean, just mountains. That's probably why my people left. A real fisherman's not gonna waste his time hiking uphill for some piddly little trout in a stream." Then, aloud, he wondered what Bavarian women looked like compared to, say, women in Europe.

Neville spoke up on behalf of the U.K. with an enthusiasm that Alex did not share.

"You every eat kippers? That's what they consider fish over there," the big man said. "Ireland is where I'd put my money. Redheads and smoked salmon, gentlemen. Without them, why go to war?"

From group to group I roamed, and it was the same. People talked with pleasant intensity, their faces glazed by firelight. They would consult the stars and visualize the forebearers who had guarded them through a risky millennium that lesser souls had not survived.

DNA, on this evening, became a communal lifeboat. Against all odds, it had delivered each and every person to this small bay, on this small island, at an intersection of space and time, so precisely that there was no way in hell it could have been an accident—or so everyone wanted to believe.

By then, the keg was nearly empty. Alcohol added a glow of divine certainty. People began to dance. Not as couples, as a group, bonded by Coors Light and destiny.

Fun? Yes it was. It had been a tough summer because of the red tide. For months, locals had suffered economic loss. The stench of fish and bad PR had lingered beyond reality or reason, and this seemed the first break in a long streak of bad luck. The Cuban kids, Maribel and Sabina, shamed me into a clumsy salsa. When Figgy swept a smiling Delia into the mix, I knew that the limbo stick would soon come out. It was time to leave.

Tomlinson, who had yet to make an appearance, was in the parking lot dismounting his bike. Pete charged the man, sniffed the bag in his hands, then trotted away.

"That's the rudest, most antisocial dog I've ever met," my pal said. "A perfect match, you two."

"Or a good judge of character," I responded. "You're going to limbo dressed like that?" Instead of a sarong and a tank top, his normal party attire, he wore linen slacks and a yellow surfer's shirt.

"No way, man. I'm done with limbo. Delia thinks I'm batshit crazy as is. No more womanizing either. I've got to set a good example for that girl." He stood taller, his head gesticulating like a turkey. "Hey . . . is that Capt. Neville she's dancing with? Why, that sneaky Buckeye scum . . ."

"She's dancing with Figgy," I said. "What's in the bag?"

Tomlinson unveiled a rare bottle of twenty-one-year-old El Dorado Rum. I looked at the bottle while he remained intent on the bonfire where silhouettes danced. "Dear Jesus, Mary," he muttered. "That Cuban Casanova has the morals of a wild dog. Hey, you're flying Delia to Belle Glade tomorrow? Explain the facts of life to her, would you? All men are swine."

"It would be more convincing coming from you," I

replied. "Besides, there's been a change of plans. I'm just dropping her off in Belle Glade. Something about her ex-boyfriend being pissed off. He's going to meet her there."

"Boyfriend?" My pal's expression communicated a fatherly contempt that I've yet to experience. "That's a disgusting misnomer," he muttered, "for yet another rutting boar. While you're at it, would you mind scaring the bejesus out of the pushy asshole adolescent who's been pestering her?"

"According to her, the guy's in his mid-forties," I said. "He teaches at a small college near St. Pete."

"That's even more disgusting. No violence, just a mild threat or three, and give him that look of yours. Like you'd bite off his nose and stick it under a microscope, given the chance. You know the one . . ." He paused. "Hey, how's your arm doing? You sure you're fit to fly?"

I opened and closed my left fist. "Stop worrying, Daddy-O," I said. "Delia's a big girl now."

ELEVEN

Leo Alomar's home was in a cookie-cutter suburb of Palm Beach County on the Atlantic Coast, thirty miles east of Belle Glade Municipal, where I had dropped Delia.

I did a slow drive-by. Alomar's house was a clone of tens of thousands of orange-roofed stuccos I'd viewed from altitude on the flight in. His property, though, showed signs of neglect usually not tolerated by gated communities. The yard was a mess. Out back, weeds had taken over a children's playhouse and swing set. Among a triad of garbage bins, a pink bicycle was missing a tire.

That hit me for some reason. I knew the guy had children, but until then they'd been just data specs in a dossier.

As I passed, the garage door opened. There he was,

dressed for a day on the links. I got a glimpse of a golf cart and a motorcycle among stacks of boxes, the big kind people use when moving out.

The Alomar family had lived at this address for a decade, according to the dossier—more evidence that Leo's life was unraveling.

I continued on. At Palm Beach's Jet Aviation Executive Terminal, I'd gotten a courtesy car with nav. It had guided me three miles west on Okeechobee Boulevard past Plantation Mobile Home Park, then right, across from a La Quinta Inn, if I needed to overnight.

It was possible. I'd had no guarantee that Leo hadn't fled after being charged with two counts of tax fraud. This was a recent revelation that, timing-wise, meshed with his visit to my lab. The charges had ended his career as an IRS agent at the Federal Building in West Palm.

All the more reason to risk a recon. The treasure savant, Jimmy Jones, had operated his salvage vessel out of nearby Palm Beach Shores.

I wanted to watch Leo's face when I asked about Jimmy. What was the connection? In the mind of a desperate man, brokering a deal with me might be his last financial hope.

The street curved along a fairway, houses separated by the minimum setback. Emerald lawns with sprinklers formed a fertilized blanket from driveway to drive, mile after mile. On each patch were the requisite ornamentals—

palms, hibiscus—shallow-rooted to a limestone base where, twenty years ago, palmettos had grown.

History and biology often intertwine. Flash back a hundred years, before the Corps of Engineers went to work draining the Florida peninsula. This had been sawgrass, a flooded prairie that flowed southeast down the Anastasia shelf toward the Gulf Stream. Eighty miles west across the Everglades were carbon copy communities. They would also be underwater if not for the Army Corps of Engineers, but water would have flowed south into Florida Bay.

I crept along at idle speed as if shopping for property. Around a bend, a sign welcomed residents to the *Polynesian Isles Country Club*. It was a white oversized building with pillars. Rocking chairs on a porch were empty on this hot Saturday morning. When my mirror showed Leo behind me, alone in a golf cart, I parked, went inside, and told the clerk, "Just visiting. Can I buy a day pass?"

The woman was perky and professional. "Sorry, not unless you're the guest of a member," she said, then noted my creased khakis, my gray Egyptian cotton shirt, my aviator sunglasses—it was the casual uniform of anonymous success. She reconsidered. "You know . . . between us, we do have a special get-acquainted provision if you're here looking at real estate. A flat fee, you get eighteen holes of golf, use of the spa, the pool, whatever you want. How does that sound?"

"Didn't bring my clubs," I said, which was misleading. I've never owned a golf club.

"No problem," she said. "Our pro will set you up. That's part of the deal for special drop-ins. Would you like to use a credit card? I'll need some ID, Mr. uhh . . ."

I removed my sunglasses and produced a money clip. "I'm Morris Berg," I said. "Is cash okay?"

"Sure, but we'll still need a driver's license, because you'll be taking a cart."

I handed her the same fake license I'd used in Guyana. "Capt. Berg," she said, impressed.

"No need for that," I smiled. "I'm trying to keep a low profile. My plane's at the Executive Terminal and I don't want my staff to know I'm playing hooky. But, so far, I like what I've seen . . . Isabelle?" Reading her name tag, I realized, had required a long, studious look at the woman's breasts. "Sorry . . . Uhh, I didn't mean to suggest . . ."

Isabelle stood a little straighter and laughed. "I'm sorry you didn't."

Behind me, double doors whooshed open. Leo entered, carrying a Callaway bag. He glanced at me with zero recognition and clinked his way toward the dressing room. The man's green suede loafers, with their cleats, were distinctive.

Isabelle called after him, "Mr. Alomar? The office manager would like to speak with you regarding your—" Discretion stopped her in midsentence. It suggested that

the problem was financial, an overdue bill or member-
ship fee.

"Why don't you stick to handing out score cards,"
Leo snapped without looking back.

The woman bit her lip and didn't respond. I waited
until he was gone to say, "You handled that very well.
Unhappy people are always looking for a fight."

"Takes all kinds, Capt. Berg."

"I'm Morris. Or Moe, if you want."

We shook hands to confirm our bond of informality.

I asked, "How's the club doing? I mean, is there a
vetting process for new residents?"

"Him?" The door had just closed behind Leo. "Oh,
he's not typical, and I don't think he'll be here much . . .
Well, I can't say any more." There was a clipboard on the
counter where I'd placed a pair of folded hundred-dollar
bills. "Would you mind filling this out while I get your
change?" She started toward the office, then stopped.
"This is way too much."

"I'm paying for guidance, not just golf," I said.

The woman responded with a smile. Not too much,
confident, still professional, but she was open to the possibility of a drink when I suggested that we meet later to
discuss local real estate. "Glenn—he's our pro—he'll get
you all set up."

"Do you have left-handed clubs?" I asked.

"Of course, whatever you need. I can give you a map
or walk you to the pro shop. It's slow this time of year.

Most members are up north or they're out at sunrise because of the heat."

"No need," I said. "If I get lost, I'll ask Mr. Alomar."

Isabelle thought that was funny.

The locker room was empty, stalls next to the urinals. Green suede shoes told me the former IRS agent was seated inside on the corner toilet. His pants were around his ankles.

I tapped on the door. "Leo? I told the nice lady out front that we'd partner up. It'll be easier to talk."

The man made a barking noise of surprise. "What the . . . Who are you? . . . Look, pal, I'm trying to take a dump in here."

I said, "A few weeks ago, you paid me a visit on Sanibel Island, remember? You planted a GPS on my truck."

There was long silence. Then: *"You."*

"That's right."

"Get the hell away from me. I didn't plant anything on your truck, you idiot. I'm surprised you have the balls to show up here."

I leaned against the door. "For starters, Leo, you have no idea who I am. Not really."

He laughed at that.

I said, "Know what I did once? This was in Cuba, the baseball stadium in Havana. I can't go into detail, but this guy—he was a real badass—same thing, in the locker room, on the crapper, when I walked in, so I grabbed him by the ankles and dragged him under the door. Leo, it's not the sort of thing I want to do twice."

I heard a hasty scramble for toilet paper. "Try it, you pompous prick."

I did. Dropped to one knee, grabbed his belt with my good arm, and pulled him halfway out. "I'm surprised you're still alive," I said when the door was finally open. "If you didn't plant that GPS, we really need to talk."

We were on the third tee before Leo got his color back. His attitude and a mild barrio accent returned with it. "You're the worst excuse for a golfer I've ever seen. Jesus Christ, almost nailed a house back there, fuckin' birds flying. Why do people like you even bother?"

I said, "No kidding. Last time I played, I hit I don't know how many cars. Really. I sliced a shot across six lanes of traffic. After that, I told myself never again. But I do enjoy hunting golf balls—which makes you the perfect partner."

The man had triple-bogeyed the first hole and was already 8 over par.

"Go to hell," Leo replied. "Like you've got a broken arm, with that swing of yours. An old lady with a stick up her butt. I shoulda kicked your ass in the clubhouse." He was teeing up.

"Yeah, I'm a little stiff. A couple days after I met you, a guy shot me in the shoulder with a speargun. They did an outpatient procedure, then I had to go back because of complications."

"A speargun? Sure . . ." The man chuckled.

"Yep, but maybe some good will come of it," I said. "Turns out, I golf a little better left-handed than right-. Baseball, I used to switch-hit. So it's the same except the ball's not coming in at eighty miles an hour."

"You are so totally full of shit, man." He took a practice swing. "You couldn't be any worse if you used a croquet mallet, hit the damn thing 'tween your legs. You know what they say about excuses and assholes."

I said, "It wasn't in the papers, but maybe you read about the guy who shot me. The same one the feds arrested for those clinic bombings? Five counts of murder. Another badass, but crazier than the guy I took down in Cuba."

That got Leo's attention. He looked at me, "Ford—that's your name, right?—are you trying to tell me . . . Hold on a sec." He paused and gave it some thought. "I did read about some freak who heard voices. Some test tube kid who grew up and . . . Yeah, but guess what? Your name wasn't mentioned, I would've noticed. Who names a boy Marion? So enough with the—"

"The feds kept my name out of it," I interrupted. "You were with the Treasury Department. You know how some of those agencies work."

He gave it some more thought, and it wasn't long before he chuckled again. "Sure. A small-time biologist who got lucky in the Bahamas. You want to talk, that's what we talk about. Do you mind?" He gestured to the white Titleist at his feet.

I surveyed the fairway. "Stay to the right. To me, that pond looks like gator country."

Leo squared, squinted, and hit his tee shot. The ball hooked left and bounced into a marshy area a hundred yards short of the green.

"Sonuvabitch." He pantomimed throwing the club, a 3 wood. "You did that on purpose. I can't concentrate with someone dogging my ass. Every Saturday, the one peaceful day I have to look forward to. A little fun—I'm a scratch golfer—then you show up."

"Every week the same time?" I asked.

"That's a mulligan on you. Doesn't count." He fished another tee out of his lime green slacks.

"Sure, do-overs, like on the playground," I said. "Every Saturday for how many weeks in a row?"

"Shut up, *Marion*. Don't talk, goddamn it, when a man's trying to drive."

I said, "You're missing the point. Put the ball in your pocket and walk it to the green, for all I care. Tell me who gave you those security cam shots of me and Jimmy's girlfriend. Maybe I can help you out."

It wasn't the first time I'd asked about the video during this golf outing. Nor was it the first time I had warned him that whoever it was might consider him a liability now that he'd been charged with tax fraud.

Leo went through his practice swing ceremony. I ignored the phone buzzing in my pocket while he shanked another drive. It was a mole killer. The ball sizzled across thirty yards of rough, then vaulted into a clump of trees. This time, he did it—he threw the 3 wood. "I am sick of this shit. The whole goddamn month has been a nightmare, you have no idea. So get your ass outta here unless you want to talk money."

I looked beyond him where his ball had disappeared. The club had sailed into the same clump of trees.

"Who's he?" I asked.

"Who?"

I used a driver to point.

A man had been flushed out of the foliage. He was striding across the fairway toward stucco houses on the other side. Over his shoulder was a golf bag, no clubs visible. He wore his hat in a way that hid his face, until he stopped abruptly, turned, gave us the finger, then kept going.

Leo stared, following the man until he had vanished among the houses. "Oh . . . Christ . . ." he muttered. "Why would he . . . You can't walk this course, you have to use a cart."

"You recognize the guy?" I asked. "He's not Treasury Department and he's not golfing. He's got something else in that bag."

The disgraced IRS agent appeared to be nervous. "A

fishing rod, maybe. I hear they catch a lot of fish in these lakes." The man wanted to believe it.

"Or a camera," I said. "Or a rifle with a scope . . . You come here at the same time every Saturday. Leo, for a man in your position, that's not smart . . . Are you still under investigation?"

The anger had gone out of him. Suddenly, he looked tired. "Ford . . . Okay, we'll talk. But first, I need a favor. You mind riding with me back to my house? It'll just be us. My wife took the kids when she walked out three weeks ago."

"You're afraid. Who is he?"

"I don't know. Could be . . . But why the hell would they . . . Unless it's my wife's . . ." He mulled it over in his head. "She's been screwing around on me for at least a year and she knows I can prove it."

Again, my phone buzzed. It was Delia calling for the second time. To Leo, I said, "Sometimes things have to bottom out before they get better. I'll follow you in my car."

On the phone, Delia said, "This is embarrassing. I'd get a rental car but the closest one available is twenty miles east. Loxahatchee, I think they said."

She had called on the chance I hadn't returned to Sanibel yet and could give her a ride in the plane.

I said, "Your interview's already over? What happened to . . ." I had seen her boyfriend from the tarmac—a fortyish shaggy man with an attitude—but now blanked on his name.

"Phil? At the Growers Co-op, he got pissed off in the waiting room and made a big scene even before they called me in. That son of a . . . He did it intentionally, I know he did. The HR woman—he got in her face, too. But she's cool. Impressive, actually. She understands. So she postponed my interview until after lunch."

"He went off and left you?"

"Supposedly. But I know Phil. He'll drive to the nearest Starbucks, have a latte, read the paper, and chat up the girls at the counter. Then try to time it right and call like he's ready to forgive me—if I'm done being emotional. You know, all calm and reasonable." She literally growled in frustration. "I can't tell you how sick I am of his Dr. Phil act. But I don't want to be stuck here either."

I said, "I don't know if he'll find a Starbucks in Belle Glade. Some good barbecue, maybe. Any idea when you'll be done?" I was in my courtesy car almost to Leo's house, where the garage door was open, the golf cart parked inside.

"This so totally sucks," she said. "I don't want you to change your plans on account of me."

I explained that I had no plans and it was only a ten-minute flight from West Palm. "Relax, take your time. They might want you to tour the operation. As long as we take off before five or so, no problem. This time a year, you know how squalls build over the mainland."

Delia said she would text as soon as she knew more, then added, "Marion, I'm sorry for being such a pain in the butt. We both know I—"

The front door of the house flew open. Leo stepped out, summoned me with a wild wave, and rushed back in.

"Call me," I said, and muffled her words, which might have been *I owe you.*

S omeone had broken into Leo's house via the patio, where more boxes were stacked, and the water in the swimming pool was a stagnant green. A pry bar had been used to breach the sliding door. Leo's office had been rifled. His laptop was missing, along with other stuff, maybe, he wasn't sure.

"That bitch," he said. The man had been rushing from one room to another. "I bet it was her. I don't have any money, who else would bother?"

"Your wife? Doesn't she have a key?"

The question stumped him, until he decided, "Wanted to make it look like a robbery. Her boyfriend, that's probably who did it. He's a cop . . . well, a customs agent. He knows how to do this crap and make it look real."

"This *is* real," I said. "Is that who gave us the finger?"

The man smiled for some reason, a bitter smile. "Definitely not him. A mile away, I know what that sonuvabitch looks like."

"Then who?"

Leo said he didn't know. A birdwatcher—could be— or a guy whacking off in the trees, he suggested, until a golf ball had almost knocked him senseless.

I told him, "Call the police and don't touch anything else."

That made him madder. "What? Now you're a crime scene expert, too? This is personal, goddamn it. My computer—I think what they were after is video of them in the bedroom."

"Your wife and—"

Red-faced, Leo yelled, "Who do you think we're talking about? I planted another camera in the garage. Her going down on the guy, him humping her all over this house—one time when my daughters were asleep in the next room. Now do you get the picture?"

"Do you know where he lives?" I asked. The flat inflection startled him.

"Lives . . . Uhh, yeah, not far from here. Temporarily anyway. But we can't . . . What are you getting at?"

"Yes we can, Leo."

"Go after him, you mean?"

I said, "Why not? Any chance your wife and kids are with the guy? If not, he hasn't gotten much of a head start."

"Jesus Christ, Ford!" The idea terrified him, but he

wanted to do it, I could tell. Leo said, "Are you . . . No, Nanette and the girls, they're staying with her parents in Jacksonville. But I can't get involved in . . . Aren't you paying attention? I've been charged with a felony, we're in the middle of a divorce, I can't just walk up and . . . Oh, this so sucks."

We were in his office. The place was a mess. He squatted and retrieved a photograph that had been knocked from a shelf. Two cute little kids—sisters—grinned out through the pane of broken glass. The man's face contorted. "Oh . . . that sick S-O-B has ruined . . . my poor little girls . . ."

"Leo, maybe you can't go after him, but I can," I said. He gave me a strange look when I suggested, "Come on, we'll take my car."

With the back of his hand, the man wiped his face. "You already know, don't you? That's why you're pretending to help me." In reply to my blank stare, he explained. "The guy's a Nassau customs agent, a lieutenant, and he's got very heavy connections. He's the one screwing my wife. You really didn't know?"

I said, "Now I get it. A Bahamian official. The guy has access to security footage of someone who looks a little like me. Tell the truth, Leo, how clear is the video? The freeze-frame shots, I assume they were blown up."

"Not that clear," the man admitted. "There's a resemblance—a big guy with glasses. Probably you, but the face is blocked. The way we made the connection is, you left a note at the mailboat office for a friend or some-one. Marion Ford, don't tell me it *wasn't* you."

I said, "The customs agent made the connection and he came to you and offered to cut you in."

Leo nodded.

"Did the customs agent seduce your wife before or after you two cut a deal? What's his name?"

"Ray . . . Rayvon Darwin . . . He's a mobster in a uni-form. You don't want to mess with him. I mean, a serious headbanger. Ray . . . One time I saw the guy . . ." Leo's eyes widened. "Hold on, I've gotta check on something." He hurried down the hall. A bathroom medicine cabinet banged open. "Oh Christ . . . he stole them, too."

Prescription drugs, I guessed, but said, "Tell me about it on the way."

TWELVE

We took Okeechobee to North Dixie Boulevard, turned left toward Rivera Beach. It was five miles of fast food, corporate start-ups, and failed sixties surf shops. Next we drove through residential housing, mid-income, on a gray three-lane that, in the heat, sparkled with flecks of melting tar.

Leo was jittery and argumentative—signs of withdrawal. He demanded to inspect my phone to make sure I wasn't recording our conversation. My questions about his wife and Rayvon—Did they sometimes ride a Harley? etc.—were evaded. I got the impression he was scared of the customs agent, dreaded an encounter that might soon happen. And Leo refused to acknowledge details about himself until he saw the three-page dossier I'd been provided.

He leafed through the pages in a rage. "This is confidential information, man. I ought to tear it up and throw it out the window. Where'd you get this?"

I countered by referencing the medicine cabinet. "I don't know what you're on," I said, "but would a beer help?"

"Just drive," he snapped. "I'm not a goddamn junkie." But changed his mind, so we pulled into a CVS. Leo came out, not with a six-pack but an over-the-counter med for menstrual cramps. "I haven't had a drink in two weeks and I'm not falling off now," he said, opening the packet. "But getting off the pills, man, that shit's harder. But I've got to if I want my kids back."

He washed down two Midol with a Pepsi. A few stoplights later, he sighed, and said, "Oxycodone—yeah, I was hooked, off and on, but I'm done with that crap, too . . . It's that obvious?"

"The way you snapped at Isabelle," I lied. "That was my first clue."

"Who?"

"The woman at the pro shop."

"Oh, her, the attractive . . . Yeah . . . Anyway, my doctor gave me a script to help with the symptoms—naproxen. My wife knows, and she wouldn't have had Ray steal my last bottle. I wasn't a perfect husband, but I'm a helluva good father, so it had to be his idea. The asshole wants me to crash and burn. That ain't gonna happen either, pal."

I was starting to like Leo a little bit.

I said, "Some of the best ones fall into that trap. Friends of mine. More and more, it seems. They start taking painkillers because of an injury, then find out they can't stop."

"Four years ago," Leo said, "same with me. Ready for this?" He looked over while he popped another tab from the blister pack. "Jimmy Jones—that's when my life started to go to hell. Jimmy was a curse to anyone dumb enough to trust him. Including me."

The Midol was doing its magic. Leo sat back and explained.

When word got out that Jones had found one of the richest treasure ships ever, the SS *Panama*, all sorts of governing agencies had gotten involved. Archaeologists and state accountants were mandated to record every artifact recovered. Customs agents from the U.S. and Nassau also monitored the project. The Palm Beach office of the IRS had sent Leo and a pair of other agents.

"We split shifts," he explained. "Three days on Jimmy's salvage boat, three days off. He was a likable guy—until you got to know him. The year before, I'd had rotator cuff surgery and was already hooked on oxy. Jimmy said he'd been through the same thing and offered to help out."

"He gave you pills?"

"Jimmy didn't give anyone anything. Ray was our connection. You name it, Ray could get it. Pills, coke, women—especially women—all you wanted when we docked in the Bahamas. Ford, you ever get tied up in something that makes you feel dirty? In your head, you know you're wrecking your life but you can't stop?"

I didn't respond. I made a right onto Flagler. A forest of boats, oceangoing yachts, and commercial cranes came into view. He kept talking. "What was that story about the badass in Cuba? If it's true, you've been through some crap. I doubt if you're still married."

I said, "Never been. What did Rayvon do, blackmail you?" I was thinking of surreptitious videos of Leo and a string of hookers. Threaten to send them to Leo's wife if he didn't pry information about the gold out of me.

"Not married, even once, a guy your age?" Leo asked. "Are you gay?" He didn't sound opposed to the idea, just curious.

"No, I'm selfish. I have three children, all by different women. The two oldest, one won't even talk to me. The mother's convinced the girl that I work for the CIA. For some people, depending on their politics, that's like working for the Devil. The other, a son, he's almost twenty, lives in South America, and we don't talk much. It sucks. The older I get, the more I think that family is all that—"

Leo interrupted. Told me to slow down, look for the Rybovich complex and go another few blocks. Then couldn't wait to ask, "No offense, but why would the CIA hire someone like you?"

"They didn't," I replied. "Now I've got a little boy, not even walking yet. From here on, what's best for him comes first."

"Two girls"—Leo smiled—"daughters eight and ten. Why don't you marry the kids' mother?"

We were having a conversation, I realized. Two strangers, safe to say any damn thing we pleased, because we knew we'd never be friends. Probably never see each other again.

I said, "She's a great lady, but she's very religious. A devout Christian. A person who doesn't just talk it, she lives the life. I've tried, gone to church a few times, but it's just not—"

"The born-again types," Leo said, "that's lame. They drive me nuts."

"She's a lot saner than you or me, Leo," I said, giving him a look. "Hey, where's this guy live?"

The street had narrowed. Palms, hedges of purple bougainvillea, and bus stops with green awnings and freshly painted benches—this was money, not a place where a Nassau customs agent would buy or rent an apartment.

"A couple more blocks on the right," Leo said. He popped another Midol, nervous again. "How are you gonna play it? Wait for him if Ray's not here? I already said I can't risk getting involved."

After a stoplight, a high chain-link fence separated us

from the bay and a maritime compound. Yachts towered above the quay, floating high-rises in billion-dollar rows.

"He lives on one of those?" I asked. "Where's he get his money, selling drugs?"

Leo explained no, three years ago the U.S. and Bahamian governments had both issued seizure papers on Jimmy's salvage vessel, *Diamond Cutter*, a hundred-ton trawler. While the courts wrangled for control, Ray lived aboard as security, but had to switch off every few weeks with another customs guy from Nassau.

I stopped short of the compound entrance, where there was an electronic gate—aluminum, not government-grade—and a sign that read *Owners and Crew Only*. I didn't have to ask which boat Rayvon lived aboard. The *Diamond Cutter*, with its towering wheelhouse, a massive crane and blow boxes aft, was distinctively utilitarian. She was set apart from the other vessels, moored alone in a landward slip. Egress was barred by a galvanized chain across the bow. Seizure notices in bright yellow had been posted, compliments of the U.S. Marshals Service.

"You know the gate code?" As I asked, I consulted the GPS. It showed the street address of our location. The first four digits were of interest.

Leo had slumped down in his seat. "Four-zero-something-something, unless they changed it. Man, why we doing this? What you gonna do, ask Ray nice and polite to give me my shit back?" He stared out the window. "I don't see anyone around."

"Could the code be four-zero-nine-eight?"

"The code? No . . . Well, hey." Leo sat up a little. "How'd you know?"

The gate's installer had reversed the street address. A common ploy that to me signaled lax security. There was no car near *Diamond Cutter*'s gangway, which was also chained and flagged by the Marshals Service. "What's he drive?"

"Ray? A Corvette, usually, but a rental. It varied. He likes shiny shit. But it's not like we saw much of each other once I found out he was banging Nanette. Dude, come on, he's not here."

I replied, "If Rayvon's the one who robbed you, a Corvette's too flashy. What about a motorcycle? You didn't answer when I asked about him and your wife going for rides on a—"

"Because it gives me ulcers to even think about. Yeah, sometimes he did that, too, rented a bike. Not always a Harley, but that's what Nanette liked—Harleys."

"That was her bike I saw in your garage?"

"Uh-uh. Mine, an old Triumph. I bought her a Super III, entry-level. We'd cruise around the neighborhood. You know, slow and safe because of the girls. When we split, she had her bike put in storage along with about everything else we own."

Across the street, half a block down, was a bus stop bench that was shielded from view by acacia trees. I pulled ahead, did a U-turn, and stopped in front of the bench. "Get out," I told him. "Sit here and just watch. We'll give it twenty minutes."

"To do what?"

"Probably nothing if Rayvon's in a car," I said. "But if he's on a motorcycle, I want you to steal it if you get a chance."

Leo's expression: *Are you nuts?*

"Steal the dude's fuckin' bike?"

"You heard me. I'll say something to make sure he leaves the engine running."

"Jesus Christ, you're out of your damn mind."

"Leo, you're starting to irritate me. Do you want your shit back or not?"

The man nodded dumbly.

My Maxpedition tactical bag was on the floor in the backseat. I reached for it. "Okay, then do exactly what I tell you. When the timing seems right, I'll give you a sign. Or use your own judgment. Get on the damn thing and drive, but not too far, just a few blocks. If we can pull this off, what we're doing is a type of street con." I went into more detail, before adding, "Leo, if you start to lose your nerve, think of that broken picture on the floor."

His daughters, I was referring to.

Rayvon Darwin lived up to his billing. He was six-three and change, two hundred pounds, a block of muscle with a head to match when he removed his helmet—a checkered racing model, silver on black, that I recognized.

He didn't recognize me from the Bahamian security video. Probably wouldn't have even if we'd stood face-to-face the day he'd come looking for me on Sanibel. I was inside the fence when he pulled up on a Harley and saw that my car blocked the entrance. The gate was open just wide enough for me to squeeze because I'd shorted out the wires to freeze the mechanism.

"You work here?" I asked, half yelling over the rumble of his motorcycle. "I think I messed up the code or something. I was just about to go hunt for someone in Maintenance."

The look on Rayvon's face, like I was a bumbling doofus. He glared at my car. He dismounted, then strode to the gate and punched in numbers. Punched in numbers a couple more times before finally addressing me. "My friend, what the hell you do? I never seen you here before. How'd you break the damn gate?" Bahamian accent, suspicious, but cheery like a cop ready to spring a trap.

I tapped my ears, and said, "You mind turning that off?"

"What?"

"Your motorcycle. Turn the damn thing off. I can't hear a goddamn thing you're saying."

"*What?*" Ray's smile was the equivalent of the middle finger. "Man, don't tell me what to do. This here's my home. What's the problem?" He tried the key code again, then banged it with his fist. "A year I been here, and you're the first one to— Shit! How'd you manage to screw this up?"

By then, I'd joined him at the gate. He was on one side of the narrow opening, me on the other.

I said, "Don't know. I punched in the right code. It started to open, then I must've hit something else."

"Huh?"

I said it again, louder.

"Why you mess with the damn gate when it's opening? You do dumb stuff like this all the time?" He hammered the electronic box with his fist. "Man, your car's blocking the damn entrance. What I think is, I'm gonna have you towed for my trouble."

A pair of computer bags were looped over the Harley's backrest. One of them was stuffed full. It was similar to the Maxpedition bag I'd left on the ground nearby. Leo was across the street, slump-shouldered in the shade, as if waiting for a bus.

"I'll pay for it, don't worry," I said. "I'll call someone. Triple A—you think they might help? Unless— Hey, you live here. Let's go find someone in Maintenance."

I reached for my bag. Intentionally, I grabbed it by the bottom, not the strap on top, then backed away to give Rayvon room enough to squeeze through. "Come on. They know you."

No way. The customs agent wasn't going to join me inside the compound—until the flap of my bag came open. My wallet, my phone, and a roll of money spilled out onto the ground.

There was a light breeze. Loose bills—mostly ones, fives, and a few twenties—went kiting across the cement toward the water. I grabbed my wallet and my phone, then charged after the bills, hollering, "That's close to five grand . . . Damn it, I could use some help here."

Rayvon, grunting from the effort, was soon beside me. Hunched over like kids at an Easter egg hunt, we lunged at and stomped the bills into submission. Most, though, sailed off the wharf and into the bay.

Behind us, the Harley revved. There was a clank of a kickstand. We both turned. The motorcycle was already moving, Leo's back visible for an instant as he roared off.

The customs agent screamed, "Dude just stole my bike." He lumbered in pursuit after it.

I got to the gate first and slid through. "Call the police," I yelled over my shoulder. "I'll follow him."

From the courtesy car, I got a snapshot look at Rayvon before I drove away—a big man in a tank top, a fistful of bills in one hand. His other hand slapped at his jeans as if he couldn't find his phone.

Leo said through the open window of the rental car, "I'm not leaving the bike here. Hell no, it's my wife's Harley, and the son of a bitch stole my computer, too. I didn't know when I agreed to . . . But, goddamn"—he sounded giddy, was laughing—"that was the most fun I've had since, hell, I don't know when. Wish I could've seen the look on the asshole's face."

"That's not the way it works," I said. "Get in the car. The police will be here soon. If you take the bike, they'll find you before you get home."

"But I own the goddamn thing."

"Yep, then Ray will know it was you. How do you think that'll go?"

Leo decided to focus on the positive. "When I took off, what did he say? Geezus, I wish I could've heard him. Bet he screamed like the bitch he is. That big bag of . . ." His giddy grin faded. "What the hell does Nanette see in that guy? Giving away the Harley I bought for her? A birthday present, you believe that? Until then, she didn't want to have kids."

"Get in. You can sit in the front for now," I said.

"For now, right," he said like I was joking. "Why're you wearing gloves?"

"If you enjoy this sort of thing," I replied, "you should buy some."

The motorcycle was parked on a quiet side street a block away. The computer bags still hung from the backrest. Before getting out, I asked, "Did you take anything? Don't lie to me."

Reluctantly, the former IRS agent produced Rayvon's alligator-hide wallet. I opened it. "Where's the cash?"

"You kidding? After what he did to me and my family? I've gotta get something out of this." He thought for a moment. "Hey, just exactly what are *you* getting out of this?"

"You get what Ray stole from you and you're done threatening me with that whistleblower crap," I replied. "And if you hear any more about this, you give me a call. We stay in touch. Understood? Now give me the money."

I held out my hand, palm up. Leo dug into his pocket and handed over a sizable wad of bills. I counted it— close to a thousand dollars—fifties and hundreds, not new.

I returned the money to the billfold. "Wait here," I said, and got out. I removed both computer bags from the backrest, then gently laid the motorcycle on its side. "Which bag's yours?" I asked when I was back in the car. "Open it, take a look. Make sure everything's there."

He did while I rifled through Rayvon's bag. Inside was the man's passport, an iPhone, his Nassau customs ID and shield. There were also condoms and some other stuff that made me glad I wore gloves. I made a mess of the contents and left the main zipper open.

"From here, you've got to ride in the trunk," I told Leo. "Fifteen, twenty minutes tops."

"No way."

"I mean it, Leo."

"Screw you. Why? It's gonna be a hundred degrees in the trunk. Let's get the hell out of here." In his bag, he had found the bottle of naproxen. His hands shook when he opened it.

"Take a bus," I suggested. "Or you can introduce me to Rayvon. How's that sound?"

Leo's eyes widened. "Whoa! Don't tell me you're going back there. What, for that roll of bills you dropped? You told me it was less than a hundred bucks."

"A little over," I said. "Mostly ones and fives."

"So what! Hell, I'll split Ray's wallet with you—five hundred each. Cash and credit cards, we'll both make out."

Leo still didn't understand.

R ayvon was pacing the parking lot and charged the gate as I got out of the car. "You see where that asshole went?" he demanded. "What the hell took you so long, man? I thought you'd run off. We gotta call the police."

I said, "You were supposed to call. Where are they?" I looked around as if unnerved by what had just happened.

"Damn phone's on my bike, dumbass, with everything else. Shit! You get a look at him?"

"Close. Must've just missed him," I replied. "About five blocks from here, he dumped your bike and took off. Probably had a car waiting. An accomplice—I don't know—but he was in a hurry. I found this in the middle of the street." I reached into the car and carried the second computer bag to the gate, where the big man had just wiggled through.

"Hey, that's mine." Rayvon yanked the bag from my hands and started pawing through it. "My bike still there? Did he wreck it?" He paused. "Shit . . . someone's gone through all the pockets."

"I did," I said. The man looked up and glared. "It was already a mess when I found it. Your bike's on its side, but it looked okay."

The customs agent puffed up, his manner threatening. "You went through my personal shit? Man, that's not cool."

I replied, "You could've had a kilo of coke in there, then the police show up? I'm not stupid. I found this, too." I reached into my pocket for the alligator-hide wallet. "It was under one of the wheels, probably fell out when the thief dumped your Harley."

Rayvon stared, snatched the wallet away, then turned his back while he counted the bills. "Goddamn it, there'd better be . . . Hey, yeah, looks like . . . Hmm, I'll be damned, it's all here." He pivoted, his manner not friendly, but less hard-assed. "You go through my wallet, too?"

"I had to make sure it was yours. Look, let's make this quick. I don't want to be here when the cops show up."

"Police?" He pronounced it po-LEESE, Nassau-style. "You got a problem with them?"

He was thinking about the wad of cash I had dropped.

"I've got a problem wasting my time if I get subpoenaed as a witness because of a stolen motorcycle," I said.

"That right?" The customs agent stuffed the wallet into his pocket. "Then don't expect no reward from me."

"It's not that," I said. "I live on the other side of the state. My plane's at the Executive Terminal, but it would still be a pain in the butt if I was subpoenaed." I motioned to the courtesy car. "Come on, I'll drive you to the bike, if you want, and wait until you get it started. Then I'm out of here."

Rayvon didn't know what to think of me. "You just an all-around nice guy, huh? Got your own plane, just doin' what's right. That's cool." His smile was pure cop. Still putting out snares, not convinced yet, but getting there.

"Nice has nothing to do with it. I'm a businessman, not a thief."

He laughed. "I didn't know there was difference."

"You got a point," I conceded. "For anything less than a quarter million, being straight with people is the cheapest investment I know."

"You read that somewhere? Man, that's pretty good— a reason to be straight." The big man was grinning. "But see what you just did? A quarter mil. Dude, you just named your own price. Must be rich to live on the west coast. Some big money over there, Naples. I played golf there once."

"Sanibel Island, part-time," I said, which got Rayvon's attention. "Agent Darwin, is it? I saw your badge and ID in the bag. I wouldn't have stolen your stuff anyway, but I like the Bahamas. It's not often I get a chance to help out a Nassau customs agent. Give me the bills you picked up, we'll call it even."

"Don't even want a reward, huh?" He was still testing me.

"Wouldn't accept it if you offered." I consulted my watch—a little after 3. "Come on, I'll run you back to your bike. We can take a look around, maybe the thief dropped something else, but then I have to go. There's a woman, a friend of mine. I've got to land in Belle Glade first and pick her up on the way home."

"Your own private plane, taking your lady for a ride." Rayvon liked that. Decided it was okay to get in the car, where he did what I hoped he would do. Opened the glove box and read the paperwork. He looked from the rental agreement to me. "Capt. Morris Berg, that you? Executive Terminal—yeah, says right here. What kind of captain are you?"

"Not the real kind. I've got a salvage business, but it's more of a hobby."

"Salvage, huh?" The man was impressed. "I know what that means. No wonder you carry around a ball of cash."

"We've all got to make a living," I agreed.

He took another look at the paperwork. "Berg, huh? That means you're one of the tribe?"

"Depends on which one," I said.

His smile broadened. "Sure it does. Me, I been thinking about having that DNA test thing done. Ya see, my people date back to the Lost Tribes of Israel. Direct descendants of Emperor Haile Selassie. Know of him? The Conquering Lion of Ethiopia? My gran'mama told me all about my family roots."

"Interesting," I said. "Personally, I don't want my DNA on some company's computer."

Rayvon got the message. Covert enterprises of all types communicate by subtext. Suddenly, we had a connection.

"Sanibel Island, huh? Know many people there?"

"A few. I try to avoid people. They can be a lot of work."

"For true, man. Always want something. But there's a gentleman lives on that island who—" He paused, looked over. "Hey, you saw my badge. I'm a sworn officer of the Great Commonwealth of the Bahamas. You need to understand the importance of my position."

"Of course. A lot of responsibility."

"Okay, then. This gentleman we're discussing—I never met him—won't share his name yet, but he lives there. He's a marine biologist, supposedly. Guy stole a bunch of shit from our national waters. Just ain't right, you know?"

"What's his name?"

Rayvon said, "That's what we're talking about now. A

foreigner steals valuable archaeological treasures, could be worth your while to help my government out with a certain matter."

I shook my head. "Something else I try to do is mind my own business."

"Business, yeah. Big business, if you'll listen. My friend, come on, you proved to me you're an honest man, can be trusted as long as your personal interests are taken care of. Am I right?"

"Maybe," I said. "How much are we talking?"

"Oh, buddy"—he grinned—"way, way more than your named price of a quarter mil. You cool with this so far, Morris?"

I let him watch me mull it over before replying, "Doubt it, but maybe. This biologist—I'd need to know his name."

"Dude named Ford. Dr. Ford. Sells fish and shit."

That required more time for thought. "Never heard the name, I'm fairly new on Sanibel. But fish? There's no money in selling fish."

"Could be why the dude went stole some of our treasures," Rayvon reasoned. "Morris, there might be half a mil in it, you find the information I need. What with your salvage connections and all."

I smiled a flat, tough businessman's smile, and said, "Call me Moe."

Ahead, on the side street, was the motorcycle just as I'd left it. The asphalt shimmered with heat. I parked in the only strip of shade available and listened to what the customs agent had to offer. Finally, he got out of the car, stood over a Harley that wasn't his to begin with, and inspected it before righting the machine.

"Bastard took another bag I was carrying," he said, meaning Leo's bag. "Probably not all he took. And screwed up the saddlebags when he dumped it. Gonna have to take them in the car."

The saddlebags looked fine to me. "Sure," I said.

Rayvon knelt over the straps, then gave a hard stare. "Moe, you one very helpful dude. Mind if I put these in the trunk?"

A final test. The bags weren't that big. "They'll fit in the backseat . . . Come on, I've got to go."

The cop smile again. "Paid five hundred for this set. Finest leather, man, they need to be laid out flat. What's the problem?" His eyes moved to the key fob in my hand. I got the impression that he would grab it if I didn't do something quick.

I did. Stepping aside, I pressed a button and the trunk sprang open. "Help yourself," I said.

On my way back to Palm Beach Executive, I phoned Leo. "We need to stay in touch," I reminded him. A little later, I admitted, "You were smart to take the bus."

THIRTEEN

From the air, I texted Delia. I had already received clearance to land at Belle Glade Municipal.

She responded, *ok, phils here, dont come inside.*

There was no need to come in. Glade Municipal serviced a fleet of yellow low-winged crop dusters parked in the heat 300 feet below my amphib. There was a small office, professionally kept, with AC and a Coke machine. That's all.

To the east of the runway was a massive complex, the sugar refinery and co-op. Six boiler towers spewed white plumes into the air. It was steam, not smoke, yet it resembled Pittsburgh during its industrial peak. Sugarcane is a tropical grass, mostly water, first brought to Florida in the 1700s. It was Prohibition and moonshiners, though, that caused it to spread across the Everglades. But it was the Cuban embargo of the 1960s that brought what is now known as Big Sugar to Florida.

"A noxious exotic," some claim. "A valuable food source," say others. Both arguments are espoused with a certainty more suited to theology than science.

I landed, pivoted my little amphib, tail to the office, and got the doors open before shutting down. Temperature on the tarmac had to be a hundred degrees.

Delia came out, a bag over her shoulder, taking long strides. She didn't glance back when Phil exited in a hurry to catch up. I had no intention of getting involved—until the guy grabbed the girl by the arm and spun her around.

Well, hell . . . I hopped out onto the portside pontoon and dropped to the tarmac.

A mechanic in overalls watched the scene from a busy open hangar. Delia pulled away. The shaggy-haired college professor towered over her and yelled something. Delia responded. Inside the hangar, a power ratchet suddenly went silent. The former lovers didn't notice. It magnified the volume of the exchanged that followed.

"That's exactly why I don't want to see you again, Phil. For god sakes, just leave me—"

"I'm not letting you get into a damn plane with a man you barely know, Delia. We'll talk in the car. Stop acting like a—" Again, he caught her from behind. The mechanic, whom I'd seen a few times but never met, started toward them, wiping his hands on a towel.

———

Delia noticed me. Red-faced, she yanked her arm free. Her computer bag slipped and fell hard on the pavement. Phil knelt to retrieve it. When he looked up, I was there.

"This is between us," he said. "Delia, tell this . . . whatever he is . . . to give us some privacy."

Delia said, "You know damn well who Dr. Ford is," then addressed me. "Sorry you had to see this, Marion. I'm ready to go if you are."

The mechanic kept coming. He might have been a boxer, one of those lethal little flyweights out of Tampico. I said to him, *"Tranquilo, mi amigo,"* then continued, also in Spanish, "I'm glad to know a good man works here and is willing to help a lady if she needs it. But she's okay now."

He stopped and gave Phil a burning look until the computer bag was returned to Delia. When he spoke, it was to me, also in Spanish. "That *culo*'s been back and forth, bothering our town all day. Some of the *mierda* he says . . . Brother, he thinks we're too dumb to know English."

The professor, in his Birkenstocks and white cotton Gillian hat, would have stood out on the streets of Belle Glade. It's an old cow town that still values cowboy ways.

Phil demanded, "What's he saying?"

The mechanic ignored that and spoke to me. "He flying with you?"

"Never met him," I said. "As soon as West Palm gives me clearance, the lady and I are taking off."

"Good, leave his ass. At the Prado Cubano—you know the lunch counter there? He told some tourists that we, people in this town, we're no better than slaves for the company. Ignorant, like mules."

"Said it in front of you?"

"Didn't need to, the Prado's so busy. Shows how ignorant *he* is. Man, I'm a citizen, twenty years now. Three of those Piper Pawnees out there, me and my brothers own. Had them built custom in Vero. But we still hear this sorta *mierda* from outsiders. You know, about how dumb we are."

Yellow crop dusters, he was referring to, half a million dollars' worth of aircraft moored in a row at the edge of the runway.

The professor had gone to work on Delia, trying to shepherd her away, until I wagged my finger at him— *Follow me.* This allowed us a private moment. "Phil, knock it off before my friend here has you arrested."

The mechanic was standing by.

"Has me . . . It's *Dr.* Knox to you . . . And don't think I didn't do some research. You're not a biologist, you're a pay-to-play hack . . . That's right, on the make for another naïve grad student. How much does Big Sugar pay for scalps these days?"

This was so outrageous, I laughed. Delia drifted toward us as I replied, "Think of me as a concerned uncle, okay? It's getting late, so why don't you—"

"Her uncle? That's a lie. She would've told me."

Interesting. Dr. Phil had not been entrusted with Delia's DNA revelation.

I looked at the girl. She shrugged and rolled her eyes in a confidential way, then continued across the tarmac. It only made Phil madder.

Behind us, he yelled, "I tried, I warned you. Delia, listen—in academics, sleeping with the enemy is a death sentence. Don't expect me to cover for you."

Had he really said that?

I motioned the girl further toward the plane. Had to motion again to keep her moving, then turned and didn't stop until I had stepped on the bare toes of Dr. Phil's left sandal.

He was outraged. "You did that intentionally."

Voice low, my manner friendly, I said, "That's right, Phil." Then issued a warning of my own.

T he enemy," I said. "He actually believes that?"

A small seaplane is loud. Headphones with filament mics allow for an exchange of short comments. But the noise makes thoughtful conversation impossible.

Delia, on my right, nodded. "Big Sugar and phosphate mining, you know what I mean. But Phil, he has to take everything too far. What did you say to him back there?"

"Enemies because of pollution?"

"Yeah, of course. Lake Okeechobee's become a sewer.

At my interview, I asked about . . . And what they said was . . . But I don't know whether to . . ." The end of every sentence was garbled until she gazed downward through the Plexiglas door. "How high are we?"

We were at 1,100 feet, ascending. Lake Okeechobee, to port, was ocean-sized at forty miles wide.

"This peninsula has a list of enemies so long, they're hard to rank," I said. "We've got time, weather looks good. Would you like to scout around a little?"

Tomlinson's daughter had recovered. In profile at the starboard controls, she emanated an Amelia Earhartish poise. Not as masculine, due to her build and cherry-black hair, but starched, attentive, and eager. She liked flying, I could tell, but didn't agree right away to a recon.

I took a guess. She hadn't had time to use the restroom because of Phil. "We'll be on Sanibel in less than an hour," I said. "Or I can find a private place down there, if you don't mind hanging off a pontoon."

"On the lake? Sure. I'm not the shy type. And I'd like a closer look."

The Maule's communication is closed-circuit unless I press a transponder button, which I did before advising traffic control there'd been a change of plan. Off Boomers Island, along the lake's western shore, I babied the flaps and set down. A water landing is a wild, rocking horse sleigh ride that kicks spray. It is also a demarcation of legalities. My plane was now a boat bound by nautical rules of the road just like any other power vessel.

"Beautiful," Delia said. We were motoring along a prairie of wire grass, as gold as Kansas wheat. Cabbage palms bloomed in the distance. There were shady hillocks that hinted of orchids and Spanish moss. No other boats around, just us in this secluded space where water hyacinth, pink blossoms, and white lilies bobbed in our wake.

I opened my door for air and signaled for her to do the same.

"Fisherman call areas like these the hayfields. They catch bass—huge ones. Shad, pickerel, bluegills. I've seen gar and bowfins the size of alligators. The whole basin's a spawning ground. And lots of gators, too, so be careful when you hang off the side. Wait until I give you the word."

When the engine was off, she scrambled out, did her business, and climbed back in. "Can we cruise along the shore for a while? This isn't what I expected. I've only seen the lake from the road—all those dikes and pumps, mile after mile. More like it's a giant holding tank for factories, it always seemed to me."

I said it was the same for most people. Even boaters who transited "the ditch" via the Intracoastal saw only the worst parts of Lake O.

"Let's get into the backcountry," I suggested.

We spent an hour hopscotching around what was once a lobe of inland sea. Harney Pond, the Monkey Box— remote areas known only to locals. Next was Buckhead Ridge, where remnants of the Kissimmee River—another engineered ditch—funneled the collective outfall from dozens of cities to the north. It was a massive area that included Orlando, ninety miles away. With it flowed water, treated and untreated, from septic tanks, citrus, horse and cattle farms, and an explosion of suburbs. These were gated communities and golf courses, mostly. Along the line was also a smattering of trailer parks, where toilets flushed directly into the nearest creek.

"I guess the lake really is a sort of sewer," Delia decided. "Parts of it are incredibly pretty, so I don't know what to . . ." She reconsidered. "Wait, Belle Glade and the cane fields are on the other side. South of us, right?"

I misunderstood this as a reference to the old maxim that water doesn't flow uphill. "The sugar companies do some backflushing. How much varies with the source. Some people—a few biologists included—don't trust the management district's data, but you're right. About ninety percent of all water that flows into the lake comes from the Kissimmee Basin north, not the cane fields. Personally, I think Florida would be better off without sugarcane, but, like I told you, it's complicated."

"No, south," she said. "I mean, that's where the Army Corps should send the water. South, the way it was before they screwed up the whole damn Everglades. Everyone I know, not just Phil, agrees."

"It's a respiratory process, not a sewer," I replied. "Like a filtering species. Yeah, the lake's struggling to keep up, but it's anything but dead. Polluted? There's no doubt. And the Army Corps flushes that crap to both coasts, but there're no easy answers . . . How about we fly south, then you tell me?"

"Tell you what?"

"You'll see."

Below were cane fields, a thousand square miles. The land was set aside in the 1940s as an "environmental district" that forbade development but allowed farming. Development is still forbidden in what is now called the Everglades Agricultural Area. I climbed to 2,100 feet, safe from the tallest radio towers, and followed Route 27 southeast. It is a rural highway that links Miccosukee and Seminole villages with the urban sprawl of Lauderdale.

Cane fields—industrial tiles of green—transitioned into sawgrass. The ancient flow of water had carved islands of cypress into amoebic shapes, a cellular progression that ended abruptly where Interstate 595 cleaved into concrete. Designer communities appeared, repetitious spiral enclaves. They linked and joined in genomic patterns that formed an airless crust without horizon.

Delia repeated the question she had asked twenty miles earlier: *Why not send the water south?*

I replied, "Okay. If you're the Army Corps of Engineers, tell me where you're going to get a half billion dollars to turn the east–west roads into bridges."

Through the Plexiglas door, she could see Alligator Alley beelining westward through sawgrass. It was ninety miles of asphalt, among the world's longest man-made dikes.

I said, "If you can't do that, tell me which communities you're going to flood. Those Indian villages back there? Or the people below us? Don't forget that the Tamiami Trail—headquarters of the Miccosukee Nation—is directly south. Before you flood anything, I suggest you talk to Billy Cypress. He's tribal chairman."

I began a slow bank, adding, "One more thing. The ecosystem here has had a hundred years to adapt to our screwups. And the land has adapted. Animal life, too. Sending freshwater south isn't a new idea. In the nineteen fifties there was an environmental push, so they dug what's called the Buttonwood Canal. A four-mile ditch that opened the flow of freshwater directly into Florida Bay. The shock to the ecosystem was an environmental disaster. It took people in charge seventeen years to admit they'd screwed up again and they finally plugged the damn thing. No one seems to remember."

The girl was taken aback. Then beguiled. She looked over. "Why, Dr. Ford, are you lecturing me? Or taking a shot at Phil?"

I smiled. "I try to stay neutral. But, yeah, your boyfriend really pissed me off."

Tomlinson opened the screen door without knocking and came into the lab. "Where's Delia?"

It was Sunday afternoon. I wanted to leave Sanibel in

a day or two but had some last-minute contract work to finish. "How would I know? Probably at one of Mack's cottages. Or did she stay at the West Wind last night?"

"You weren't with her? I happen to know you spent all day yesterday together flying around Florida, doing god knows what. From my boat, I saw you land, then you both disappeared. Not so much as a wave or stopping by for a beer." He pulled out a chair and straddled it. "Doc, I think we need to have a serious talk."

"Don't start with me . . ." I said.

"A perfectly innocent question. What about you landing somewhere in the boonies so Delia could take a whiz? Lake Okeechobee, I heard. Some private, shady spot, no doubt, just the two of you. *Mi amigo*, that is totally inappropriate."

This from a man who in Key West had taken a piss off the bow of *No Más* in full view of the sunset crowd at Mallory Square. In the past, he had also seduced at least two women I'd been dating and had failed with several more.

He ogled me for a moment, noting my slacks, collared shirt, and polished shoes. "Whoa, dude! . . . What are you all dressed up for? Taking her for a champagne brunch, I suppose."

In a Styrofoam cooler, I'd assembled jars and Ziplocs to take samples from what I'd been told was a suspicious algae bloom bayside on Captiva. I closed the lid, saying, "Just got back from church."

My pal chuckled, then sobered. "No, really. Dude, come on, you're wearing *socks*."

"It's what people wear to church. You ought to try it sometime . . . I've got work to do, okay? Help yourself to a beer—if there're any left."

To emphasize patience, Tomlinson transferred his ponytail from the left shoulder to the right. "I don't want to get heavy, but you ever think you'd see the day that we, the two of us, couldn't be honest and—" He leaned in as if in ambush. "Which church? Come on, that's a simple question straight from the shoulder."

"You've got a screw loose, you know that?"

"Doc, a father has an obligation to protect his—"

"Yeah, a father, parents, have obligations, not a seed vendor."

"Oh . . . that's just gross. You know damn well Delia has a thing for you. Man, I've been onto your act for years. Play hard to get, aloof, with all the emotional warmth of a brick. Then lay down the trump card, dress like some MIT nerd, and girls like Delia come running."

I'd had enough. Rather than laugh it off, I did my best to lapse into a moment of serious contemplation. "Okay. You asked for it."

"Damn right, I did. Uhh . . . asked for what?"

"Look, ol' buddy, this isn't easy. Delia wanted to be the one to tell you but—" I stopped as if reconsidering. "She should be here. Let's wait until—"

The chair toppled over when Tomlinson got to his

feet. "You swine, I knew it. You got into her knickers yesterday, didn't you? Pulled the *Let's land on the lake and go skinny-dipping* gambit—"

"No," I said, "but we will."

"You'll *what*?"

"Have sex—tonight, hopefully."

For a second, I thought he was going to punch me.

"Whoa! Take it easy," I said. "It's not what you think. All perfectly respectable."

"Bull hockey!"

"Would you just listen? Well . . . here it is. This morning at church, Delia and I got married." I held out a warning hand. "Don't overreact, look on the bright side. Depending on how the women in her family age, you could end up being my grandfather."

For a long, smoky moment, he believed me. Part of it anyway. Then his face reddened and he exhaled. "You *asshole*. Just when I think you're human, you prove I'm an optimist."

I began a laughing jag. It went on for a while.

"Church," he grumbled. "Should have known right then you were lying."

But it was true. I had boated to Gumbo Limbo and attended Pine Island Episcopal with Hannah and Izaak. It had gone fairly well—until I told her that I had to leave Florida again.

But this time, I'd suggested, *Why don't you come with me to the Bahamas?*

Hannah's response: *You're the second person this week to invite me to the islands. Marion, have you been spying on me?*

Sanibel and Captiva islands are separated by Roosevelt Channel. It is a tidal swale where the famous Rough Rider had lived on a houseboat while harpooning giant manta rays—the largest sixteen feet wide wing to wing.

Giant mantas, common on the coast not so long ago, are now rarities. In my mind, as I idled along the bayside shore of Captiva, I assembled a list of local animals based on how often I saw them now compared to two decades ago.

A game.

Bobwhite quail—gone. Bard owls, barn owls, and great horned owls—seldom heard. Small-toothed sawfish—uncommon. King snakes—rare. Florida panther—never had I seen one in the wild, let alone on the islands, although I've met many who make that claim. Mollusca—angel wings, junonias, whelks, horse conchs, alphabet cones—unchanged. Scallops—fewer. Bobcats, bald eagles, coyotes, swallow-tailed kites—often, depending on the time of year. Bottle-nosed dolphins, manatees, ospreys—daily, unless I was housebound.

It was a balancing act that provided reassurance until I began to include noxious invasive species. Pythons, noxious toads, and fire ants—probably the most destructive invaders since the arrival of Juan Ponce de León.

This took the fun out of the game and ended the list.

Complaints of a new algae bloom kept my eye on the surface. Water clarity in Blind Pass wasn't bad. It got worse as I motored along Buck Key. A humic turbidity shifted from rust to marl. Then, ahead, I saw why Harbor Branch Oceanographic had hired me to collect last-minute samples. Piled along the shore was an undulating mat of gunk. The stink of decomposition told me what it was even before I killed the engine and got out the sample bags.

I used a net and gloves. Dipped samples of festering green from the surface. Reached deeper and dredged slime that was anchored to a mucilaginous sheath below.

A friend of mine, Jeff Bromfield, appeared on a nearby dock. "It's the same crap all over again," he said. "Showed up about a week ago. It's not as bad as it was, but, my gosh, the smell. I thought the red tide was gone."

"It's never gone completely," I said. "This is something different."

"Some kind of algae," he said. "Think it's going to get worse?"

"Some call it that," I said. "Common usage—blue-green algae—but it's really a bacteria. Cyanobacteria. *Cyan*, you know, because of the yellowish green color. The genus is *Lyngbya*."

"*Ling* as in the fish?"

"Spelled with a *y*. No, nothing to do with fish. Well"—I sealed another bag, recorded time, date, and location with a Sharpie—"it can have something to do with fish. *Lyngbya* produces toxins that are thought to cause a type of tumor in sea turtles. It's nasty stuff, but the fish here will be fine once this crap blows out."

Jeff wanted to discuss what had returned this mess to his door. We talked until my satellite phone buzzed—Leo Alomar, the troubled ex-IRS agent, calling.

I welcomed this interruption of an unpleasant topic. Along with the recent red tide, Captiva and nearby Cape Coral had also endured a disgusting month dealing with this blue-green algae. It was a separate phenomenon, although easily confused.

Jeff was well informed. Most residents were unaware of studies that linked the blame directly to their own septic tanks. Their collective rage was reserved for agriculture and Lake Okeechobee.

FOURTEEN

On the phone, Leo said, "Ray has a new contact. A rich dude, sort of shady, lives on Sanibel. He's worked out a deal to have the guy spy on you. You said you wanted a heads-up if I heard something."

I had backed my boat away from the Captiva shoreline and anchored. Samples of *Lyngbya* were in the cooler, but I still needed photos and video. That meant getting in the water.

I tried to sound concerned. "You have a name? Hold on, who told you this? Don't tell me you contacted Rayvon, because that would just be—"

"Got the name written down here someplace," Leo said. "No, the man we saw yesterday. The one with no golf clubs, gave us the finger? He's the one told me about the guy Ray wants spied on."

"Gave *you* the finger," I corrected. "You're the one who almost beaned him."

"Whatever . . . He came to the damn house, just now left. I was in the garage, packing. He figured I recognized him yesterday, might as well clear the air. That part I believe. Sort of. Because I did recognize him once I saw his face."

The man, Leo explained, had worked aboard the *Diamond Cutter* as a representative for one of Jimmy Jones's major investors. An Iraqi via Saudi Arabia. Huge money, international connections.

"The guy we saw yesterday is rich?"

"No, works for one of the millionaire investors. I'm trying to give you some background, help you understand who we're dealing with. These people are dangerous. The Saudi team, is what we called them back in the day. They've spent the last two years tracking down every possible lead—hell, torturing people, for all I know. They're gonna find Jimmy's stash soon if we don't move fast."

"*We?*" I said. "I have no idea what you're talking about. Is this the same person Rayvon sent to Sanibel to plant the GPS on my truck? Or is this guy someone new?"

I expected to hear the alias I'd used, Morris Berg. Instead, Leo explained. No, the guy who flipped us the bird was Ellis Redstreet. He was Australian, an attorney, who had worked for the military overseas. That's how Ellis had met the Iraqi millionaire.

"I think him showing up today," Leo continued, "had more to do with the break-in here and them stealing my shit. He didn't mention me being robbed. The way he asked about Ray, though, I know damn well they were both involved. Ellis and Ray are the ones who had me check your financials. That was about a month ago. Now, since I lost my job, Ellis is pretending I'm still in on the deal, but that's bullshit."

"Back up," I said. "He's an Australian attorney? Which branch of the military was he with overseas?" I was thinking about Hannah and her new friend—a man who might be a vacationing Brit.

"What's it matter?" A refrigerator opened, ice clinked into a glass. "You and me need to discuss a deal of our own. I say we meet in the Bahamas, split all the coins, bars, whatever you can carry in your plane, before they beat us to it. And they will. Ellis says they have a new lead on Jimmy's ex-girlfriend. She's still alive, they think. Ford, come on, stop pretending. At least agree to talk. Maybe I can help you for a change."

I didn't like the sound of that for a couple of reasons. Jimmy's former girlfriend, Lydia Johnson, was a good person. More than a year ago, I'd helped her and the man she would eventually marry disappear into what they hoped would be happy, anonymous lives. They had adopted a local child. The last I'd heard, they were pregnant with a child of their own.

Another concern was Hannah. She was still considering my invitation to the Bahamas, but the name of the person who'd already invited her to the islands remained an unknown. I couldn't put her and the baby in harm's way if there was trouble.

I cleared my throat. "You didn't tell the Australian about what we did to Rayvon yesterday?"

"Ellis? Of course not. This is all about what I found out. Ellis said there's a guy who lives on Sanibel—I figured he was talking about you. But no, it's a new source Ray found to keep an eye on—are you ready for this?— the marine biologist they think knows where Jimmy's stash is hidden."

"But I don't," I said.

"Whatever . . ." Leo replied. "Now that Ellis has a solid lead on Jimmy's ex, maybe they'll lose interest. That's what I'm hoping anyway. Clear the way for us."

"Leo," I said, "there is no 'us.' But I do appreciate the heads-up."

"Look, Ford"—his breezy manner took on a hint of desperation—"I need to make this work. I'm off the booze, off the oxy, but I'm dead flat broke. For me to have any chance of sharing custody of my girls, I need money for an attorney. You know how it is."

I wanted to ask about Lydia, Jimmy's ex. Why did Ellis, the Australian, believe she was still alive? Were he and his associates closing in? But could only say, "Yeah, it's the way the world works."

Leo tried again. "How about a thirty–seventy split? Hell, twenty–eighty, and expenses come off my end? That IRS whistleblower thing is already off the table. I'm not going to screw you after what you did yesterday. My last three hundred bucks, plus my computer, was in that bag."

In my experience, it is sometimes easier to help a stranger. To convey debt to a friend, even as a gift, is to risk the friendship. I was trying to think of a way when Leo muttered, "Shit, okay. If we can't work a deal, how about helping me keep the deal I had with Ray and Ellis?"

"If I can," I said.

It had to do with the Sanibel resident, Leo explained, who had agreed to spy on me. "His name is"—I heard papers rustling—"Capt. Moses Berg. Sounds Jewish. You know him?"

Morris Berg was the alias I'd used, not Moses. Rayvon or Ellis had gotten it wrong, but that was okay.

"There was an old-time baseball player, Moe Berg," I said. "A catcher. But this guy, no. Is he new on the island?"

"All I know is, Ray trusts him for some reason. The idiot's got this racial thing about being from the Lost Tribes of Israel or some such crap. That could be part of it. Anyway, so far they haven't been able to find out a damn thing about any Capt. Moses Berg on Sanibel. With all my contacts, that's what I'm good at, so Ellis asked me to dig up everything I could. He has no idea I've been talking to you."

"Rayvon trusts a man he knows nothing about?" I asked.

"Ray's a degenerate crook. Crooks are used to working with scum they don't know anything about. This guy, Berg, supposedly is a multimillionaire. Flies a Learjet, Ray claims, and does salvage on an international scale, but always behind the scenes. No photographs of Berg either." Leo paused, perhaps linking this oddity to me, suspicious that Berg and I were the same person. But he was not. "Anyway, Ford, that's how you can help me out. Sanibel's a small island, right?"

"A Learjet," I said, half smiling. "Sure, Leo. I'll find out what I can about this Moses Berg and get back to you."

I arrived at Hannah's dock for the second time that day. The path led me up the shell mound to a house of old yellow pine, tin-roofed, where she had lived as a child, and had just put Izaak down for a nap.

Or so I was told from a distance. "Go away," an acidic voice called. "Baby's sleeping."

I replied, "Afternoon, Miz Smith," and kept walking.

"You deaf, mister? If you're after a poke, my daughter's a prude. And me? I'm spoken for by the king who rules these parts. Better men than you," she warned, "have died trying."

Something I hadn't considered before proposing to Hannah was that the woman who eyed me from the porch, Loretta Smith, might one day become my mother-in-law. The two refusals had given me time to reflect. Loretta had also been a single mother. With her oversized and active daughter, Hannah, who'd swum varsity and played the clarinet, the woman had spent a lifetime scraping by.

"Get the hell away from here," Loretta instructed with a flourish.

"Yes, ma'am," I responded, but didn't slow.

An aneurysm and two brain surgeries had clouded the woman's mind, not her spirit. She was also shrewd enough to know the surgeries were a handy excuse for all sorts of outrageous behavior. This included smoking weed whenever Tomlinson visited, cheating at bingo, fantasies about a pre-Columbian Indian king, and an artillery of profanities always kept at the ready.

I opened the door and stepped onto a screened porch that encircled the little box that was the house. There were ceiling fans, a hammock. Loretta, in a housecoat and fluffy pink slippers, sat watching a television so old, it had rabbit ears for an antenna.

"Oh," she said, looking up, "it's you again, the fish

doctor who can't take no for an answer. Since you're here, might as help me try and fix this goddamn TV. *Jeopardy!*'s due on after bowling."

Protocol permitted me to lean and kiss the forehead of my fiancée-to-be's mother, but I didn't. No way would I ever try embracing the woman again.

"Mama, please watch your language," Hannah's voice called softly from inside.

Loretta glared through dazzling rheumy blue eyes. "Shoulda had that girl's knees sewn shut and made her wear a raincoat—not that it woulda helped on a cold day, the way she's built. What'd you do, hypnotize her or get her drunk? Sure ain't your good looks. Hey"—she perked up—"where's Tommyson? That man's worthy of a good tumble and heartache. Did he send me a little something—you know, a present, maybe, to help me sleep?"

Something else I would never do again is deliver one of my pal's homegrown joints. Once was enough. Instead of sleeping, we'd tracked Loretta by flashlight to an archaeological site behind the house—a burial mound. She had been in a state of undress and was pleading for King Carlos to fly down from the moon and reclaim his vanished Indian nation.

"Darn, must've forgot," I said, kneeling in front of the TV. The screen was all snow and static.

"The hell you did," she growled. Then squinched her

face up and sniffed. "Damn, boy, you stink. You been rolling in something? Or fishing mullet?"

No, I'd been in the water, photographing *Lyngbya* bacteria. A dumb oversight on my part.

"Be right back," I said. "I left something on the boat."

At the rear of the house was an outdoor shower. Spare clothes were in the forward hold of the Pathfinder. When I returned, Loretta sniffed, then sniffed again. Cloudy eyes cleared. They speared me with a searing lucidity. "Hannah ain't never gonna marry you, Mr. Fish Doctor." She was keeping the subject just between us. "Know why? You're a heathen. A despoiler of the Lord's Word. And . . . you're a cold-blooded killer."

This was a charge never voiced before.

"Killer? That's a new one." I hoped she would notice my smile. "Why not let me bring you some sweet tea, Miz Smith?"

The woman shook her head. "Lie to me, but you can't lie to the Lord. You're a godless assassin. Yep, all the details came to me in a dream last week. There's blood on your hands—not that murder makes you a bad person."

"Oh?"

"Yep. I've kilt at least three myself."

Rumor was, this was true—more or less. When younger, Loretta had helped dispatch the abusive husband of her best friend. In the 1980s, after a net fishing ban, she had also joined her pinochle pals in smuggling "square grouper"—marijuana. It was a dangerous trade. At least one other pushy male had been added to the hit list of Loretta's female covenant.

"Hid their bodies, too," the old woman bragged.

"That right?" I said. This claim had more to do with a brain aneurysm than reality, I suspected.

"You didn't hear it from me," she whispered. "Hannah doesn't know, but don't let me catch you digging out back by the citrus grove. As a godless assassin, you'll understand my meaning."

I replied, "Miz Smith, most folks think I'm a nice guy. Certainly not a killer. Are you sure you don't want that tea?"

"Stop brownnosing," she sputtered. "Who hasn't lost his temper a time or two? Fact is, I sorta like knowing my only grandson might inherit fire in his veins."

"Then what's the problem?" I asked.

"You're not rich, dumbass," she snapped. "And selling fish ain't no way to make a living. Hannah's got another suitor, you know. What he knows about fish you could put in a thimble, but the man drives a nice car and carries Christ in his heart."

I lowered my voice. "Is he Australian?"

"Is he . . . No, he's a damn foreigner. Got a castle somewhere, I think. Flies all over the world when he's not worshipping the Lord."

"From Great Britain?" I pressed.

"All I know is, he don't sell mullet. Love might get a woman through the night, but it's money that gets her through the days. Propose all you want, Mr. Fish Doctor, Hannah won't say yes. Why? Because whatever I tell that bullheaded girl to do, she does just the opposite. And I ain't watching my grandbaby grow up poor."

After a final lucid glare, Loretta cackled and retreated into her handy camouflage. "Now, damn you, fix my TV. And where's that glass of sweet tea you promised?"

Hannah lowered her iPhone, and said, "What do you have against me taking pictures? Doc, I sometimes wonder if you're a wanted man." There it was again, her suspicions about my mysterious trips.

We were in the house. Loretta was still on the porch where I'd plugged in a VCR that was as old as the rabbit ears TV. Our son was a peaceful warmth in the baby carrier strapped to my chest. It was new, made by Mission Critical. Sort of resembled a bulletproof vest. I'd picked it out myself.

"Come on, just a couple of snapshots," she said. "A picture of Izaak and his daddy for the mantel." Hannah, barefoot, wore jeans and a loose blue blouse with a wet spot on the left breast. She had just finished nursing.

I looked toward the fireplace, once the only source of

heat in a house that had just recently gotten AC. The mantel was all too public, if my own suspicions about her new friend were correct.

"For his scrapbook, I guess that would be okay," I said to show my reluctance.

Again, she raised the phone—"Say *keys*"—then lowered it again. "Marion, what is your problem?"

I employed an excuse formulated months ago. Explained it dated back to high school, when I was living with my crazy uncle, Tucker Gatrell. "His partner, Joseph Egret—Joe, we called him—claimed a camera robbed a piece of your spirit every time the shutter clicked. For some reason, it stuck with me."

"Superstitious? You?" She wanted to respect the spiritual inference, but it didn't jibe. "He was Seminole? I've read that—that Native Americans don't—"

"Joe claimed he was the last of the Calusa," I said. "A huge man." The Calusa was a pre-Columbian tribe, as Hannah was well aware. They had built the mound on which the house sat, and other shell mounds on the back ten acres, where there was an archaic citrus grove—and possibly three bodies.

This connection to a Calusa king allowed me to seek help by calling through the wall, "Loretta, would King Carlos allow his picture to be taken?"

The woman couldn't hear me over organ music and a rerun of *Days of Our Lives*.

Hannah found my adolescent ploy irksome. Also sort

of funny. She laughed, touched the phone screen, and said, "Then how about video?" She started shooting.

An awkwardness between us varied in degrees but was always present. The temperature spiked when I tried to get personal. "Loretta mentioned the man you've been seeing—an Australian or from the U.K., I think she said, a foreigner."

"We agreed not to discuss our private lives" was Hannah's prim reply. "A *foreigner*? Why, that's just . . . And I don't appreciate you pumping Loretta for information. You know she's not right in the head."

"Your mother's just fine when she wants to be," I countered. "Is that who asked you to go to the Bahamas? I think it's fair to ask who our child is traveling with. Better yet, go with me. But let's go somewhere else, not there. Just the three of us."

Hannah's nephew, Luke, a nice kid newly arrived from the Midwest, was in the house, entertaining the baby. She had walked me to my boat after an otherwise pleasant afternoon. We'd talked and laughed and spent an hour on the porch listening to Loretta's mad ramblings about her "pot-hauling days" as the mistress of a rich man.

Details about her pinochle club and murder were omitted.

It was hard not to like Loretta. Her stories about smuggling were stitched with the woes of those who fished or clammed commercially. They had transitioned naturally into tales of past disasters. The worst, according to the old woman, was the lethal red tide of 1947, which had sent locals scurrying to church, convinced the End Times had arrived.

Now, though, on this late-August afternoon, a heavy chill was evident in Hannah's response to my prying. "Is that what you think of me, Doc? I'm so loose in my behavior, I'd accept an invitation from . . . That I'd fly off and sleep with a man while my baby's in the same room? *Oooh!*"

She made a sputtering sound and faced me. "Just because I gave in to you at a time of weakness doesn't mean I would ever . . . Not again anyway . . . Not as a single woman . . . Besides, he—my friend—he feels as strongly about such things as I do."

In light of modern standards, it was hard to believe we were having this conversation. "The sanctity of marriage?" I asked. "What's this paragon's name?"

"A very nice gentleman. And that's all I'm going to say. This morning at church, didn't you hear a word the minister said?"

She had me there. The sermon had had something to do with morality—governing one's passions, perhaps—but a buzzing fly, and the woman snoring in the pew behind us, had caused me to drift off.

"I'm not suggesting you'll hop into bed with the guy," I said, although that's precisely what I believed would happen. "Just tell me a little about him. If not his name, at least where he's from."

"Birdy Tupplemeyer's going with us," she fired back.

That threw me. Birdy was Hannah's best friend. She was a decorated sheriff's deputy and a SWAT team sergeant. Birdy had a very un-church-like wild side when it came to men—and just about anything else that wasn't illegal.

I said, "The guy invited her, too? Honey, ask around. To me, it sounds like a setup. Borderline kinky."

Fists clenched, Hannah looked skyward, then at my boat. "You got a bottle of water in there? I need to cool down before I lose my temper."

"Step aboard," I said. I had something I wanted to give her anyway.

She sat in one of the plush captain's chairs. It was shady under the boat's T-top. Over the mainland, towering thermals vacuumed a breeze off the Gulf. Useppa, Cayo Costa, and, to the north, Boca Grande were stolid outposts in the heat, all visible from the dock.

"Sorry, that was unfair," I said. "Birdy, sure, I can see her signing on for a trip like that. But not you. It's not that you're naïve, Hannah, just a little too trusting when it comes to—"

"Would you just park yourself and listen?" she interrupted. I returned from the forward hatch with my tactical bag, got a beer and a bottle of water from the cooler, and took a seat. She gave me a long, sad look of concern. "If you don't respect who I am by now, how can we—" She switched threads. "Okay, Birdy won some kind of contest. Six nights, all expenses paid, for her and a guest at a resort down there—Stanley Key, I think. She's the one who invited me and Izaak."

"Staniel Cay?" I suggested. The island was midway down the Bahamian chain. Forty miles, at least, from the remote spot where I'd found Jimmy Jones's stash. "What kind of contest?"

"That's the island's name," she said. "Very fancy. We'd have our own little beach cottage, room service. And there's a spa for pedicures and things—girl fun, you know? Birdy doesn't make much money. She could never afford a trip like this. And, Lord knows, I can't. Not after that awful red tide. And, for a fishing guide, this is the slowest time of year."

She talked wistfully about this opportunity to stay at an exclusive resort where the restaurant served high tea and people dressed for dinner. "Marion," she added with an innocence that squeezed my heart, "I've only been out of Florida once in my life—Atlanta, for a swim meet, back in high school. I'd planned to say yes to Birdy until you surprised me by asking if we—"

The woman stopped and regrouped, suddenly emotional. "You've been all over the world. A piddly little trip to the Bahamas might not seem like much to you, but"—she looked toward the house where, when she was growing up, her mother had barely managed—"it's the sort of thing I used to daydream about as a girl. I so wish you had asked me before."

My god, she was right. I had never invited her on a trip, even a weekend getaway. To me, *travel* was a euphemism for personal, unsavory business. Geezus, what a revelation. On the other hand, Hannah's own blue-collar sensibilities had negated any thought of destinations with elegant, expensive resorts. She was a jeans-and-boots girl who carried a toolbox in her SUV. And sometimes a gun. Why bother with exotic travel when we could stay right here and eat or fish whenever we wanted?

"I'm an idiot," I said. "Name it. Anyplace in the world."

"It's my fault for not mentioning it," she replied. "I don't need such things. But it is nice to be with . . . To be understood, you know? Accepted for the person I am. I'm done being ashamed for what I believe."

A meaningless apology, words of comfort came out of my mouth. I put my arm around her in the hopes she would lean against me. Instead, her muscles tensed. Then slowly, out of politeness, Hannah pulled away. We had been through our ups and downs, but this time I had a panicky sense that I had to make things right or I would never get another chance.

I said, "This is totally unrelated, but I brought you something. Take a look."

From my bag I removed a folder containing paperwork I'd planned to give her anyway. Next, I handed her a second gift. It was a leather bank portfolio embossed with *CFS*—Cayman Financial Services. I got up and pretended to be busy so she'd have time to go through it all.

The folder contained a Florida Prepaid College Plan for our son—four years' tuition, paid in advance. I'd also opened a modest 529 college fund account. "In case he wants to go out of state," I said in response to her stunned expression. "West Point or the Naval Academy, it would cover those, too. That's up to Izaak, of course."

The leather bank portfolio wasn't so easily explained.

"Doc"—Hannah stared at the amount—"this can't be right. Where in the world did you get so much money?"

For a woman who'd grown up on Gumbo Limbo and fished for a living, a dollar sign followed by six figures was an astronomical sum.

There's a lot more where that came from is what I wanted to say. Instead, I told her, "I set it up as an LLC and created a trust fund in Izaak's name. You're the signatory officer, though. What that means is, the money is yours to use whenever needed. Not just for him, for yourself." I made a show of cleaning my glasses. "I want you and Birdy to enjoy yourselves in the Bahamas. When do you leave?"

Thursday, she said, two days from now, because it would give Birdy a couple of extra days off.

"Buy yourself something nice," I suggested, "a dress,

whatever. You can wear it to dinner when you get back. Hannah, I want you to use this account."

I'm not sure what I expected. In this new century, there are very few Hannah Smiths left in the world. Tears and a kiss would have been nice. Another long, sad look of concern, though, is what I received. Her expression communicated affection, gratitude. Better yet, respect, when she said, "You're a good man, Marion Ford, and you're a great daddy. We'll always love you for that."

We hugged. Again, Hannah's sudden tenseness sent a message. On the boat trip back to Dinkin's Bay, I weighed, argued and reargued the subtleties, but could not dent the truth.

The woman I had asked to be my wife was already gone.

FIFTEEN

The next night, when the marina was asleep, I waded out to the end of my dock. A buoy there marked a chunk of submerged mooring anchor that had been cast from Dutch and Spanish artifacts. Maybe because of a big, bright full moon, my dog confused the mission with playtime. He galloped along the shore, barking. Roosting birds—herons, cormorants—bawled and hammered the water with wings and excrement.

I whistled. Sound carries over water. On Tomlinson's boat, a light came on. Somewhere at the marina, a door opened, then closed.

The dog kept going. It was a quarter to midnight on a Monday. If fun was to be found, I reasoned, Pete would have to track it down on his own.

I returned to the lab with a wedge of gold. On the scale, it weighed slightly more than two pounds—thirty troy ounces. Using a surgical saw with a jeweler's blade attached, I portioned the wedge into thirds. Next, I unveiled a desktop smelting furnace. I dialed it to fifteen hundred degrees centigrade and put on leather gloves. When the furnace was ready, welder's goggles were needed. Gold filaments, one by one, went into a carbon crucible, which was lined with a thin coat of borax. The crucible went into the little furnace.

It didn't take long. When the contents resembled a molten egg yolk, I poured the liquid into a grid of shallow carbon molds. Each mold was about two inches in length and an inch wide. After a few minutes for the rack to cool, I dumped it onto a black cloth.

Dazzling, the color. More lustrous than the copper moon floating outside the laboratory windows. Before me lay a dozen untraceable gold ingots. At two troy ounces each, they were more easily converted into cash than the four- and eight-ounce bars I poured next.

The precision demands of the work took my mind off Hannah. The moon and a cold beer helped. On such a night, a fanciful linkage was forged with alchemists. In medieval times, alchemists had attempted to meld science with religion in the hope of creating gold, as well as antidotes for imperfections of the human soul.

An argument could be made, I decided, that neither science nor religion had advanced a hell of a lot since then.

This, and a third beer, dulled my awareness of what was going on outside. A sudden, polite knock at the screen door—*tap-tap-tap*—caused me to spin around like a thief who'd been caught in the act.

Delia peeked in grinning, perhaps a little drunk. "Isn't the moon crazy tonight?" she said. "I'm glad I'm not the only one who can't—" She noticed my guilty reaction. "Hey . . . what's wrong?" Her eyes moved to the counter and the neat stack of bars. "Oh my god, are those real? No . . . can't be. What are you doing, making costume jewelry? Let me see."

I stood there like a dope. I, a man trusted by some as a security pro, had been caught in a situation that, by rights, should have gotten my butt kicked just for being so dumb. She came toward me, onyx hair agleam. She wore shorts over black yoga leggings and a white hoodie shawled across the shoulders. Her balance seemed wobbly. It was too late to throw a towel over sixty grand in gold bullion. And I was fresh out of lies.

Fortunately, three empty beer bottles in the sink snagged the girl's attention. She stopped and leaned against the counter. "Have you been drinking? I didn't even know you drank."

"One beer more than usual," I admitted. "Want one? Come on." It was an attempt to lead her next door to my cabin.

"Good," she replied, "I'm stoned."

"You're . . ."

"Earlier, yeah, but I'm okay now. I got high with Capt. Bio Daddy." She motioned outside to where *No Más* was anchored. "I asked if I could vape on his boat. We'd made lasagna for dinner—vegetarian, of course. He went into this whole routine, old-school stuff about reverence for the sacred herb, not my propaned artificial crap. Later—I was in the forward berth—he snored like a grizzly, so I thought, *Screw it.* I left a note, told him I was going back to my cottage at Mack's place." She talked a little more about Tomlinson, his eccentricities, then asked, "Got anything to eat?"

I sensed a reprieve. But no, she gave my arm a friendly pat and went straight to the gold ingots. "Damn, I was hoping these were Nestlé's Crunch bars. The ones wrapped in foil? They were my favorites at Halloween."

The little smelting furnace still radiated heat. The weight of a single ingot surprised her. She dropped another two-ounce bar into the palm of her hand and the leaden clink convinced her.

"Holy shitsky, these *are* real. Where did you . . . Or maybe I shouldn't ask . . . What do you do, collect old jewelry or something? I've read about people, they go to yard sales and stuff. Like, a hobby."

Delia had kindly provided me an out. After dealing with Hannah, however, more hypocrisy was distasteful. "Nope. What you see there, it was all stolen."

She smiled. "Sure it was. I mean, really? Do you buy stuff on eBay?"

"It's the truth," I said. "A few years back, there was a treasure hunter who was also a thief. He salvaged a wreck—I'm not going into the details or the amount. Now part of what he took is mine. Can we leave it at that?"

The girl sobered, her attention on the ingots. "Oh my god. Well, sure. Wait—you stole these from a thief?"

"Indirectly. He dumped what he'd taken and I found part of it."

"Like, Spanish doubloons and stuff?"

"Nothing that romantic. Tomlinson knows, but I'd prefer no one else does. I'm not a thief, it just fell into my lap."

"Of course not," she said. "Really, I'm not judging. In fact, it's sort of exciting. My god, what's an ounce of gold worth now, a couple thousand dollars?" She raised a single ingot to the light. "The only reason I know is, a few months ago Phil proposed and complained about the price of a ring compared to the price of gold. I totally turned him down. He really is a pompous jerk. Oh . . . he hates you, by the way."

"The people the gold belonged to," I replied, "died in a shipwreck more than a hundred years ago. The legalities are sort of foggy." With a towel, I moved to cover the ingots. "I'm done working for now. Need a ride to— where are you staying tonight?"

"A *shipwreck*." Delia was savoring the word. "Wow! That *is* exciting. In the Bahamas? It just makes sense, since you're going there. Seriously, I'm certified for nitrox, and I've always want to do that. Dive a wreck."

I replied, "I can make you a sandwich, then we'll take my truck," meaning *End of discussion*.

I finished putting things away and we went out the door.

"The world's most interesting man," the girl murmured, speaking to herself. Not flirting or convinced. Just surprised.

All I had at home to eat was dried beef and MREs, so we drove to the all-night 7-Eleven on Periwinkle. Delia was chatty because of the weed. Tomlinson had shared the story about how I'd reeled him in with the fiction about our church wedding. She thought that was hilarious, wanted each nuance of every detail. "He actually believed you?"

We were both laughing. "Just long enough. Where I screwed up was mentioning the women in your family— the big age gap. Told him if he play his cards right, he could end up being my grandfather."

A Styrofoam cup was to her lips. She coughed rather than spray iced tea through her nose. This added to the hilarity.

"He claimed . . . He claims . . ." The girl waited until she was under control. "He says you have no sense of humor. But he's the one with a stick up his butt. I pictured—because of his book?—what I imagined was this brilliant Zen Buddhist saint. You know, a halo almost, a man who's at perfect peace with the world. Can you believe how jealous he is? Totally a dweeb, sometimes—especially when it comes to you and Figgy."

"Figueroa?" I asked.

"Figgy Casanova, yeah—isn't that a cool name? The good-looking little Cuban guy. He's *fun*."

I let that go. "Tomlinson's protective, that's all," I said. She had bought a basket of nachos loaded with cheese and salsa. I reached, dipped, and crunched, before I hit the blinker, then turned left on West Gulf.

Delia, enjoying herself, argued, "As if Tomlinson doesn't have a whole string of women in that bed of his. But he plays it, like, *Hey, sex is a very serious decision*. Not these days, it isn't, and sure as hell not for him."

I countered, "The man's been around long enough to be selective. Plus, he's single and lives alone. A 'whole string' is taking it a little too far, I think."

"Now who's being protective?" she laughed. "On his boat, I was looking for a towel and found a drawer full of swimsuits, bras, underwear—you name it. Every size, from mini string bikinis to double X-L. Huge, you know? Almost bloomer styles that a woman in her sixties might wear. I'm not criticizing, understand. Phil's seventeen years older than me. Who cares about age?"

I caught a glimpse of myself in the rearview mirror.

My frozen smile was a reminder not to do anything stupider than I already had in the last twenty-four hours.

So I asked the girl about her parents. There was an immediate mood shift. Her father was enjoying what might be his last few weeks of remission. It was a bittersweet time. Delia's mother had booked a cabin near Asheville where they'd honeymooned almost thirty years earlier.

"He can't stand the heat this time of year," she explained. "It's terrible to say, Doc—I love them both, I truly do—but I needed a break. That's why I'm spending a few days here. For the last six months, since Dad started going downhill, Mom and I took turns looking after him. Us and a nurse. We all know what happens next—home hospice." Her voice caught. "Life can be so damn unfair, you know?"

I switched to a lighter topic. "How're plans for the reunion going?"

Delia told me that four of her seven bio sibs had already committed to a gathering the week before Labor Day. Mack had offered a special rate for the cottages. Tomlinson was all for it, but she was still concerned about their kidnapper, Jayden Griffin. If he and Deville were not the same person, the guy was still out there.

"What I suggested," Delia continued, "is that we rent a trawler or a big houseboat. There's a marina in St. Pete that rents both. I'd prefer a sailboat, of course. But something that size would require a crew, and my bio sibs aren't sailors."

She mentioned two names that were becoming familiar. There was Imogen, from Arizona, and the minister from North Carolina, Chester. The three of them had become the planning committee.

"An overnight for eight people, max, should do it. Inshore, never far from land," she said. "If the chemistry's not right, we'll cut it short and say *At least we tried*. Imogen's the wild one, she's fully stoked and all in. Chester, he's a lot more conservative. Know what's been fun? Finding out how much we have in common. Totally a genetic link. The whole nurture-versus-nature deal. Seriously, it's not what our prof preached in psych class."

A mile down the road, the *Grin-N-Bare-It* signage at Mack's cottages had been changed to

Playa del Temptation
An Internet-Free Refugee

Syntax and spelling suggested that Figgy had lent a paintbrush and his creative hand. My headlights swept across several cars with out-of-state plates, each cabin with its own sandy parking space. Not bad, for this time of year. Apparently, the no-internet angle had produced results.

"Which cottage?"

Delia pointed to the last one on the left, set off by itself among mango trees. No lights. I parked but left the truck running. "Where's your car?"

Back at the marina, she explained. "I can get it in the morning. The idea of coming here alone was sort of spooky, this time of night . . . Another nacho?"

I declined. She munched, in no hurry to get out, and returned to the subject of the Bahamas. When was I going? Where? For how long? She was a lip-reader, I had to remind myself. Then asked again, "Is that where you found the gold? What I don't understand is, why do you have to melt it down? Or maybe I shouldn't ask about that either."

My responses were as polite as they were vague.

I noted a girlish awkwardness when she continued, "Thing is, my parents will be in Asheville for another eight days. I'm . . . Well . . ." Her face, in half-light, turned toward me. "I'd like to go . . . as a diver . . . your assistant . . . whatever . . . There's not a boat I can't learn to handle, and I can take care of myself. With that bad arm of yours, you'll need an assistant." Her tone switched to caregiver mode. "No strings. And there's no shame in needing help."

No strings? No idea what she meant, so I asked her to explain. As she tried, I looked for cars with out-of-state plates. A few gooseneck lamps, old-style, were a new addition to the walkway that wound across the grounds. Those, with the help of a high white moon, helped identify an SUV from the Tar Heel State and one car, possibly two, from Georgia. For a clearer look, I cranked down my window.

"Did you hear what I said?" Delia asked after a long silence.

"Uhh . . . sure. About the Bahamas, yeah," I responded.

"Fine," she said, miffed.

Clearly, I had not been listening.

I took a last look at the vehicles, then consulted my watch. "It's late," I said. "Mind if I come in for a minute?"

The question startled the girl. What did not compute was her eager nod. We got out. I asked for the key. She followed me into the cabin through a creaky door. A wall switch illuminated gaudy rattan furniture. I went to the tiny kitchen and searched. A folding door revealed a food larder. The next closet contained a washer-dryer combo and spare sheets.

"If you're looking for beer, it's in the fridge," she said. "Or how about a glass of wine? But first . . ." She switched off the kitchen's bright neon in favor of a soft coffee table lamp. "There, that's better. Do you prefer red or white?"

I nodded toward an open door down the hall. "Is that the bedroom?"

Again, she was startled. "Uhh . . . Or we could split a bottle of water, if you're in a rush."

"Mind if I take a look?"

"Fine . . . Wait. Hold on, I don't think I made the bed." The girl hurried ahead of me. When I came in, she was holding balled-up towels and the top of a swimsuit—or a bra, possibly. I pretend not to notice. She watched me go into the bathroom and throw the shower curtain back, then open the closet. Next, I searched under the bed.

"All clear," I said, out of habit.

"What's clear?" she demanded. "It might be clear to you, but it's not to me. How many beers did you say you had?"

"Three," I said, "but I'll take one for the road. It's been kind of a tough day."

"The road? What do you mean? You're not leaving."

"I won't get any work done in the morning if I don't," I said. "Bolt the door and use the chain. You'll be fine."

Delia dropped the ball of laundry on the floor. She did a slow side step to block my passage. "Marion, you're still not paying attention. I *want* you to stay."

There were a couple of ways to interpret this, but I chose to respond, "Oh, that's too bad, but I understand."

"My god, I would hope so. Wait—what do you mean *too bad*?"

I said, "That you don't feel safe here. The only reason you'd want me to stay is because of Deville."

"No . . . I mean, yes." Now the girl was embarrassed. "Why else would I . . ."

"How about we sit down and talk for a while?" I suggested.

"Sure, why not?" she answered. Her attitude had changed, as in, *To hell with it, I don't care one way or the other.* Next came sarcasm. "We can talk about your kid, or the fishing guide you're apparently in love with, and I can bitch about Phil. We'll be drunk buddies, right?"

Delia's icy manner warmed halfway through a glass of wine. And that's the way it turned out. We became friendly confidants after a quiet hour, voices low, and some nice moments of laughter.

Rayvon called twice the next morning, a Tuesday, hoping to speak with his new and trusted friend, Morris Berg. Voicemail is not among my satellite phone's options. I didn't want Berg, my alias, to appear anxious, so I let it ring. Finally, in the afternoon, I answered, saying, "I don't have anything solid on the biologist yet. I'll call when I do."

"Cap'n Berg, it's me, Ray—Agent Darwin from Nassau," he insisted.

"I know," I replied, and hung up.

I wasn't as abrupt when Leo Alomar, formerly with the IRS, called. "Ray's hounding me for information on the rich guy, the dude with the Learjet he told to spy on you. I've got to tell him something about the man. You both live on the same little island, how hard can it be?"

"Not just hard," I said, "dangerous."

"You're saying you didn't find out a damn thing?"

"I'm saying I found out enough. Look, Leo, I'm sorry about your situation, but I had no idea what I was getting into until I started asking around about . . . I'm not going to say the man's name. I want nothing to do with him or—"

"Who, Moses Berg?"

I cupped my hand around the phone's mouthpiece. "It's Morris, not Moses, and do not mention that name again—understood? I'll hang up right now."

"Whoa! . . . Wait, Ford, you at least owe me for the heads-up about, you know, *him*. This dude, Berg, he's really that bad? Come on, Ray will cut me out of the deal if I don't—"

"He'll cut you out anyway," I said.

"Not if I come through. Listen, Ray's including me again—told me what they got going on in the Bahamas, him and Ellis. Would he bother if he didn't think I could help?"

I replied, "That's where you can help me. You don't happen to have a picture of Ellis? Or at least what Ellis looks like? His size, his age—that sort of thing."

Leo's reaction: *What's it matter?* "Let's stick with Berg for now. Moe . . . Morris . . . whatever his name is . . . Berg is the guy who's gonna get cut out once he forks over the money to fund Ray's project."

"Rayvon said that?"

"No, but that's the way that asshole operates," Leo

said. "I happen to know he's getting very close to finding Jimmy's ex-girlfriend. Find her, he'll find Jimmy's stash. But Ray's not a money guy. Before he can screw Ellis and the Saudis, he needs a financial backer. A partner with a Learjet—that's what I'm thinking."

I was in the lab, making notes on a legal pad. "Jimmy's ex . . . Are you talking about the girl that you accused me of murdering? Lydia—"

"Johnson," Leo said, getting impatient. "A while back, before the really bad shit went down, I gave Ray a list of people Lydia had been seen with before she disappeared. Ford, you were at the top of the list. Then he found the security cam video of you and Lydia together."

"But you're not sure it was me," I said. "You told me that yourself."

"Which might save your ass," Leo replied. "There are other names that Ray and his people are checking on. One is this old guy, a Bahamian preacher. He hangs out at the same mailboat dock where the security cam caught you and Lydia."

"It wasn't me," I insisted.

"You keep saying that . . . Anyway, Ray finally got off his dead ass and had his people find the old preacher. *Bingo! I gave him a winner,* Ray thinks. But the old man won't talk, so Ray flew to Nassau today to question the guy personally. Now do you understand why I need that information on the money guy and need it in a hurry?"

I was starting to. The preacher's name was Rev. Josiah

Bodden. Tomlinson and I had met him in the Bahamas. Bodden was a good man, respected on the outback islands. Without him, Lydia Johnson and her nerdy husband to-be—and their children—would all be dead.

I said, "What's Rayvon going to do, beat the information out of the preacher? That's just nuts."

"There you go," Leo said, "so's Ray. I'm not asking you to get involved with the rest of it. Just tell me what you found out about Capt. Learjet and I'll make Ray cut me in for a flat fee."

I put the pencil down. "Capt. Learjet—I guess that works, the guy we're talking about . . . Well, here's one way to explain it. Tell me what you know about Sanibel Island."

"Uhh . . . money, lots of birds and stuff," Leo said. "Come on, man, stop with the guessing games."

"I'm trying to educate you about the sort of people who live here. The Learjet types have been coming down since the fifties. Look up *Bay of Pigs invasion and the CIA*, then type in *Sanibel*."

"Huh?"

"Pay attention," I told him. "Search the internet. Type in *assassination attempts on Fidel Castro*. Add *waterboarding* and *the hunt for Osama bin Laden*. A couple of U.S. presidents and I don't know how many directors of major intelligence agencies live or vacation here. There's a saying on this island: *You can't tell a spook by his cover, but you can by his tan.*"

"Spook, sure." Leo thought that was funny until he realized I wasn't kidding. "Whoa! You're saying Ray's new buddy, Capt. Learjet, is—"

"I'm not done," I interrupted. "Harder to find, but the information's out there if you dig deep enough. It has to do with an organization called the Mossad."

There was a silence. Leo was putting it together. "You're screwing with me."

"Nope."

"The *Mossad*? Geezus. Okay, yeah, I've heard of it. Jewish . . . like, a spy agency. Wait . . . An Israeli spy lives on . . . Oh, this is bullshit."

"Morris Berg is an international investor," I replied. "He has connections I want no part of. Why do you think nothing comes up on the guy on the internet?"

That's all that Leo or Ray, the Nassau customs agent, needed to know about Ray's new and trusted friend.

"I'll be damned," Leo said in a musing way, but he was impressed. "My god, Ellis and the Saudis on one side and that dumbass Ray has gone and gotten himself hooked up with a captain in the goddamn Israeli Mossad! Damn, Ford, those are the dudes that assassinate people, right?"

"Pass it along," I said, and hung up.

Immediately, I called Tomlinson and told him about my concerns regarding Rev. Josiah Bodden of Cat Island, Bahamas. My pal knew the old man a lot better than I.

They were both Freemasons, a secret fraternity that, supposedly, had deep roots in the islands.

"Brother Josiah," Tomlinson groaned. "I've got to warn him. Damn, you know how tough it is to get a local on a landline down there in the islands. And Josiah doesn't own a cell."

"You've got to do something," I told him.

"For sure, man. So . . . what I'll do is start with the Masonic Lodge in Nassau. Get the word out. Yeah, that's my next play! Let the brothers know the Right Reverend Bodden needs looking after."

I switched off the ringer and finished what I was doing, which was getting the lab in order for an extended absence.

An hour later, Tomlinson came flip-flopping up the steps in sync with the first distant boom of afternoon thunder. From his body language, I knew something was wrong.

"Josiah's missing," he said. "I got someone on the pay phone at New Bight—you know, where the mailboat lands? Last night, the old man went out hunting land crabs and didn't come back. People all over the island are looking for the poor guy. Doc, what do you think we should do?"

"Pack a bag," I told him.

My pal grinned in agreement. "Yeah, right, man. We gotta move fast on this one." He began to pace, then muttered, "Crapola. I can't leave today. Delia and I are supposed to go sailing tomorrow. Her dad's in a bad way, and I don't want to go off and leave the poor kid. Unless—" He snapped his fingers. "Can she go with us?"

Bad idea, I told him. It took a while to explain the situation. "Two separate factions are figuring out where Jimmy dumped that gold. They're both dangerous. With that much money at stake, I don't think Lydia or the preacher will be safe until someone derails both factions."

"Derails?" Tomlinson didn't like the word. "Amigo, you're not going over there, you know, to snuff someone?"

He had to repeat the question. *"Snuff?"* I chuckled. "Don't be so dramatic. There's a better way, yeah . . . In fact, I'm surprised I didn't think of it before." A possible solution had just come to me. "You're the philosopher, you tell me—how much money is enough money?"

"Huh? I don't see where this is headed. For one person, you mean? Amigo, with my inheritance, I've got more than I can ever use."

"For a normal person, I mean."

Tomlinson found some humor in that. "Well, the rule of thumb is, when people start buying cocaine, they have way too much money. If you need me, I could fly over commercial on Thursday, maybe Friday."

The next morning, at sunrise, I turned my little Maule

amphib east. By noon I was across the Gulf Stream, thirty miles out from Cat Island. Somewhere down there among the blue lagoons and strands of beaches was Staniel Cay. Hannah, our son, and her friend Birdy would arrive there the next day.

SIXTEEN

On Cat Island, I cleared customs as Marion D. Ford. That afternoon, I caught a commercial hop to Nassau, where I used a different ID to register at the Grand Hyatt on West Bay.

"Welcome to the Bahamas, Capt. Berg," the clerk said with a smile right out of the brochures.

In the lobby I bought a cheap BTC mobile phone and a prepaid card. Used it to text Rayvon with the name of the hotel and told him to meet me at the Jazz Bar. The message was signed with the initials *M.B.* The customs agent called when I was in the shower. I let it ring. Three attempts later, I answered, saying, "What didn't you understand about meet me at seven? Not cool, Ray."

I sat with the phone to my ear at a quiet patio table.

Within view was an acreage of swimming pool that, in color, could not compete with the tumescent blues of Nassau Bay. A fleet of cruise ships, framed by palms, spilled out a nonstop flow of tourists, ant-sized, given the distance.

"This better be important," I added. "I'm in a meeting."

Flustered, Rayvon replied, "But, man, Capt. Berg . . . I mean, why didn't you tell me you were coming to Nassau? Coulda waited and flown over together in your plane . . . And, hey, I'd've had something special waiting for the two of us, know what I'm saying?"

His deference was striking. Leo, obviously, had passed along what I'd inferred about the Mossad agent, Morris Berg.

"That's another thing," I said. "I never mentioned my Learjet. Who've you been talking to?"

"I've got my sources, sir," the customs agent said. Proud of himself for what, in his mind, had been a lucky guess. Did I need anything? he wanted to know. The inflection hinted at women, drugs—anything at all. Just name it.

"A couple of things," I replied. "A boat. Can you requisition a vessel from Bahamian customs? Doesn't have to be big. In the thirty-foot range, with a derrick. Oh—I need a picture of Ellis Redstreet. Text whatever you have as soon as we hang up."

That threw him. "Ellis . . . Yeah, I think I might know who you mean."

"Don't lie to me, Rayvon. I'm not going to warn you again."

"Okay, okay, brother. But one of our government vessels, that's not . . . Well, of course I could, an officer of my rank . . . But there'd be a lot of paperwork. And"—he gave it a beat for emphasis—"certain people in my government would have to, you know, be *compensated*."

"I'm aware of that. The seed money will be provided."

"Yeah? Okay, then. What, exactly, we gonna do with this boat?"

I said, "My associates have confirmed that you're onto something good. If we're going to do business, you have to trust me. See you at seven."

"Whoa! Don't hang up, Moe . . . Can I call you Moe? . . . What I'm wondering is, that salvage project we discussed? It might be a few days or so before we know the exact location. Not a problem, understand. There's an old gentleman who . . . Well, none of your concern . . . But I don't see the rush for me requisitioning a government vessel—"

"Josiah Bodden?" I interrupted.

The customs agent didn't know what to say. I let it sink in. "I've got my sources, too. In the last twenty-four hours we've learned a lot more than you realize, Rayvon. And the deal is, no one gets hurt unless I say so. Where is he?"

"Who?"

"Not cool, Ray," I said, and hung up.

When he called back, I answered by saying, "Lie to me again, we're done. Rev. Josiah Bodden—where is he?"

"Moe, my friend, I don't know who you . . ." The customs agent lost his nerve. "Okay, yeah, the old man. I learned he has important knowledge regarding our project. So I instructed certain associates in my government to detain the man for—"

"You detained Josiah Bodden?" This was said softly but as a warning.

"Yes, Capt. Berg. For questioning."

"You idiot. He's not just some old man. Are you out of your . . ." I exhaled a long breath. "You, of all people, the Lost Tribes of Israel? You have no idea who you're screwing with. So what you're going to do is, let the Rev. Bodden go. Make the calls, whatever it takes. *Now!* And he'd better not be hurt."

Rayvon was getting panicky. "You mean, he's one of . . . Capt. Berg, I swear, I had no idea. The old gentleman, I was told, fishes for a living and used to preach at some no-account church. That he's nobody with no money or—"

"You heard wrong," I said. "We don't need him anymore. Same with Jimmy Jones's ex-girlfriend. She's dead—as of this morning."

A long silence was followed by, "Oh. Then you must know where Jimmy—"

"We do," I said. "Tonight, bring a briefcase. Something you can lock to your wrist."

"To the bar? For . . . What are you talking about?"

"Compensation," I replied. "Start-up money. I'm trusting you with a retainer. And your pal Ellis and the Saudis are no longer involved, is that understood?"

"Uhh . . . yes, sir," Rayvon responded.

"Especially Ellis Redstreet," I said. "He's out. Permanently. I need whatever you can tell me about his personal habits. His daily routine—that's important. Think you can manage that?"

"His *daily* routine," the customs agent repeated, aware of what that might mean. "Capt. Berg . . . Moe . . . all you got to do is say the word and I can take care of that matter personally."

After we hung up, my cheap little BTC mobile pinged with Rayvon's number. Two photos—one was a group shot from the Jimmy Jones salvage days, the other had been cropped to isolate the Australian.

Ellis was not Hannah's type—long blond hair, tats on his neck, a thin cigar dangling from his lips. This was reassuring. Even so, I forwarded the photo to Tomlinson. My pal's special relationship with Hannah's mother might confirm that Ellis was not the man who Hannah had been dating.

Next, via encrypted satellite phone, I messaged my State Department contact, Hal Harrington. In part, the message asked if we had a trusted asset embedded with the U.S. Department of the Treasury.

If we did, great. If not, that was okay, too. I was improvising, manipulating key players. I wanted Rayvon and the others to give in to greed and hang themselves. For me, this was a moonlighting project. It was backyard chemistry, not a precisely planned assignment. If people like Rayvon and Ellis fell for the ruse, all the better. If not, busting bad guys in the Bahamas was not my job.

At the hotel watering hole—the Jazz Bar, it was called—the music was too loud. Gaudy Miami architecture struggled but failed to re-create the boom town intimacy between the Bahamas and Florida during Prohibition.

Hotels, like everything else in the hospitality biz, are desperate for an identity. It's getting tougher and tougher for mega companies to convince clients that their travel experience is real, not a Disney PR contrivance.

The only reality I was aware of was moonlight, a half-filled room, and the redhead eyeing me from the bar. The bartender noticed. He crossed the room, leaned in, and spoke confidentially. "Sir, I believe the lady is alone this evening if you'd like to sit next to her. She's, uhh, a guest of the hotel, of course, not what you might be thinking." The man's voice was deep, melodic, formal, from the days of the Brits.

I reached into my pocket. "Looking after your customers. Very thoughtful."

"My job, sir. In Nassau, a night so beautiful, no one should be alone. And I couldn't help notice that she seems interested in . . ." He smiled. "Well, what's the harm in helping nice folks meet for the evening?"

The twenty in my hand disappeared into the bartender's with the deftness of a magician. I said, "I'm expecting someone. Works for Bahamian customs, but I doubt he'll be in uniform." After describing Rayvon, I added, "I'm going to move to the balcony. Would you show him out and see that we're not disturbed?"

"My pleasure. May I ask the gentleman's name?"

When I told him, the bartender's congenial manner vanished. With it, I suspected, went his invitation to meet the vacationing redhead. "As you say, sir."

He sniffed, pivoted, and was gone.

Interesting. The staff here knew the corrupt customs agent. They did not approve.

No wonder. Rayvon's swagger when he finally appeared, a thirtyish blonde on his arm, would set anybody off. And I'd been wrong about the uniform. He was in full dress, with gold epaulettes and trousers bloused. The woman struck me as a tourist from Minnesota rather than a pro, despite her low-cut, bouncy red cocktail dress and glossy heels. They both carried drinks in plastic cups. Dark liquor, whiskey or rum.

"Capt. Bcrg, may I present my friend Nanette . . ." Rayvon stumbled on the last name, which he finally said was Davis—an alias, I suspected—and nothing more until the conversation moved along. The woman was an investment wizard, Rayvon claimed. When he explained that she was the sister of a former business partner— strictly friends, of course—the name Nanette came back to me. The woman was Nanette Alomar, Leo's wife.

I suppressed a gag reflex when I stood to shake hands. "Nice to meet you," I said as if it were true.

It was quieter out here on the balcony. A salted Gulf Stream breeze spiraled up with the scent of frangipani and a hint of exhaust. Nanette took a chair across the table. To feel fortunate that she was sitting downwind from me was cruel, but I did. Way too much perfume.

"I know I'm intruding and it's all my fault," Nanette said a little too gaily. "I ran into Ray in the lobby, and when he told me he was meeting with a . . ." She glanced to her left. "How did you put it, an *international businessman*? Well, I decided to be bold and ask for an introduction."

Over the candle separating us, Leo's wife had an attractive face with smoker's lines that suggested more than one addiction. Nervous, too. Too much busty posturing. Too much laughter from a suburban mother, whom, I hoped, had not been forced into an all-too-obvious role.

Forced or not, that was the role she played when Rayvon left the table, saying, "Service always sucks here. I'll get us a couple more drinks."

"So, Capt. Berg, where are you from?" she asked. We made small talk. It went on too long. Rayvon had struck up a conversation with the redhead at the bar. This gave Nanette time to say, "Such a coincidence, both of us staying at the same hotel. I've been here nearly a week."

"Oh?"

"Looking for the right location. See, I'm opening an office in Nassau—as a consultant. Overseas capital flow. Bank contacts, mostly in the Caymans, which is the very best place in the Caribbean for . . . Well, why am I telling you?"

She laughed. Adjusted her skirt. Beneath the table, her foot found mine. Lingered just long enough that it might be accidental, then she pulled her foot away. "I'm looking for clients, but only the right sort. Discretion is what I specialize in. I don't suppose"—she was fumbling with her purse—"we could get together later for dinner? Or a nightcap? After your meeting with Ray, of course." She had found a pen and started writing something on a card.

"I fly out early," I replied.

Her pen paused at this possible slight. "Well, next time then. I'm a night owl, if you change your mind. Entirely up to you." She folded the card twice and slid it across the table. "This is just between us, do you mind? I barely know Ray. Wouldn't want him to get the wrong idea, now would we?"

For the first time, I allowed extended eye contact. "Is a customs agent worth worrying about?"

"In Nassau," the woman replied, solemn, not flirtatious, "it can be very dangerous not to take them seriously." Then she started to ask, "How much time have you spent—" when she noticed Rayvon returning from the bar. "Ray," she called cheerfully. "I was just explaining to Capt. Berg that I can't stay."

Nanette sipped her drink. More small talk, before she made her excuses and swayed away. Watching her, Rayvon confided, "My friend, I think she's jiggy jiggy for you. And that pretty redhead over there? I know a place we could all go and have some real fun. You want me to call Nanette back? All you got to do is say the word."

The customs agent was a fixer man, proud of his contacts and power.

I let him read my disdain. "Stick to business. What's the update on Rev. Bodden?"

The old preacher, Rayvon claimed, was just fine, back in his own home as of an hour ago. "He's a stubborn ol' gentleman, and I figured out your concern. Yes, I did, which I shared with the fellas sent to ask a few questions. Explained to them that Rev. Bodden preached the gospel of our Lost Tribe, Emperor Selassie, the Conquering Lion. Am I right or am I right?"

"You're a smart guy," I replied.

The customs agent took that as approval from me, a supposed Mossad agent. He lowered his voice. "Moe, you need something done, just tell me, understand?"

I retrieved a small black satin sack from my pocket. It made an alluring clank when I put it on the table. "I've had these tested," I said. "Test them again, if you want. Start-up money. Open it up. It's yours."

Six freshly minted ingots, two troy ounces each, glittered in the big man's hand. His eyes widened. "Oh, my, my—these here be the brightest of lights, brother. For true? Where'd you—"

"Street value," I said, "the legitimate way with fees, you're looking at sixteen to eighteen K. With the right connections, more like twenty. Or would you prefer the low end in cash? I can do euros or dollars."

The man's big hand squeezed shut. "You say they good, my brother, they good. Trust is what we already proved, ain't that right?" He had an equally big white smile. "You got more of these? Reason I ask is, I can get us the best price anywhere, including New York. That's something we can discuss in the future, huh?" The hand opened again for closer inspection. "No mint marks." Rayvon thought for a moment. "Could cause a problem, Moe—what with there being no provenance. Where'd you say you had these tested?"

"We found Jimmy's gold," I replied. I watched those

words register, before adding, "My associates took just enough for a sample and expense money."

"Whoa! Hang on. You only had, what, a week to—" He was suddenly irritated. "Moe, without telling me? Man, what'd you do, melt down some coins? Ain't right, dude. Tell your friends that's just stupid, in my opinion. Coins from Spanish times, they in good shape, they worth twice the weight of these if you know where—"

"What you're holding is untraceable," I interrupted. "What's smarter, you think? Risking arrest or a nice, clean profit margin? My associates found most—maybe all—of what Jimmy stole. Three or four tons is the figure most often quoted. We don't give a damn about coins. The melt-down price is close to two hundred mil. Now the challenge is how to salvage it all and stay under the radar."

Rayvon sensed his control slipping. "See, that's where you're wrong. With me in charge—a man in my position?—that problem goes away. For an outsider such as yourself, though, Moe . . ." He gulped half of his drink and squared himself to face me. "Yeah, my government would be all over you and your people. What I'm suggesting is, we sell the coins. Buyers come through here all the time, no fees, no taxes. We split four hundred mil instead of—"

He stopped midsentence when he noticed me shaking my head. "Think about it," I said. "What I'm trying to explain is—no, you tell me—how much profit is enough profit?"

He sat back, looked at me like I'd gone soft. "You kiddin'? Man, there's no such thing as too much. I thought we was on the same wavelength regarding that matter."

"Apparently not. The difference between a business-man and a thief is, people like me choose the safest ap-proach. You need to change the way you think, Ray, because, fact is, we don't really need you anymore."

I watched the custom agent's face change. He started to get to his feet. I waved him down, saying, "Relax. You're in for the whole ride. A deal's a deal."

He was furious, but played along. "But see, where you wrong is, you do need me. Bahamian customs agency, man, we do shit to folks stealing our national treasures that newspapers never find out. I mean *nasty* shit." Star-ing, he added, "Anyone else but you, my brother—'cause of what you just said—I'd be worried about some kind of con job."

I nodded at the little black satin bag. "I just gave you twenty thousand in gold. That strikes you as a con?"

The man seemed to have forgotten the ingots in his hand. "Well . . . no, as long as they're—"

"Have them tested," I said again. "Deal is, you get thirty percent, same as me. Expenses come out of my associates' end and they keep the rest. Sound fair?"

Rayvon did some quick math and was stunned. After

what I just told him, he didn't expect anything close to a profit share of sixty million plus. But still he had to say, "I thought fifty percent is what we discussed, but, yeah, that'll work, thirty off the top. You sure your people are cool with this?"

"Doesn't matter what they think," I replied, "because it's fair. You forget what I told you the day your Harley was stolen? Being straight with the people I do business with is the cheapest investment I know." I placed a twenty on the table and signaled the bartender. As I did, Nanette's folded card went into my pocket.

"Whoa, brother! You leaving? Come on, lighten up. We got us cause to celebrate."

I was on my feet. "Only when we're done. Get us a boat. Make sure it has a derrick rated for at least a thousand pounds. Just you and maybe one other crew. Today's Wednesday, so let's say by Sunday latest. A boat with government markings—that's important. Can you do that?"

In Rayvon's head, it was party time, his attention back on the redhead at the bar. "Hell yes, bro, whatever you say." He pantomimed putting a phone to his hear. "Hit me up, man, anything you might need."

I waited until I was in the elevator to unfold the card. Nanette had written her cell *and* room number. The only surprise was that Rayvon carried a lot of last-minute weight with hotel management.

The woman's room was next to mine.

T here are a lot of little tricks regarding personal security in a hotel. Techniques that employ *discreet alignment* or *cardinal bearings* are as low-tech as they come. Because they're old-school, they've become simple, unexpected tools in an age of electronics-savvy bad guys.

One look at my door, I knew someone had been inside. The corner of the *Do Not Disturb* sign was no longer discreetly caught in the doorjamb.

Okay . . . the maid had come in to turn down my bed. A caution flag, nothing more.

I entered and did a quick walk-around as I unbuttoned my shirt. One by one, I clicked off small inconsistencies. It was possible the maid had moved the water bottle I'd left a thumb's width away from my computer's USB port. Same with the drawer I'd left open a quarter inch. But why was the pen atop my carry-on bag no longer pointing precisely north–south?

Someone had searched the room. And they'd had some training.

In my head, the caution flag signaled full alert. It caused me to test my damaged left arm, as I already did a dozen times a day. With some effort, I could touch the back of my head, but movement was slow, fingers numb.

Not good.

Hidden aboard my plane on Cat Island was a 9mm pistol, but I'd flown commercial to Nassau. A gun was too obvious anyway if my visitor had planted a camera. So, carrying an innocuous little Benchmade pocketknife, I checked the bathroom before brushing my teeth. Next, the bedroom of my spacious sixth-floor suite.

My visitor had done a thorough job. Left everything as neatly as I'd left it. Almost.

A final concern was a spy camera. In my bag was a DefCon Hunter Sweeper, palm-sized. I switched off the lights and activated the unit. Tiny red LEDs pulsed as it scanned for transmitters and wireless cameras. The micro-pointer singled out a USB charging plug with a full view of the room.

Okay. I hefted my bag, carried it into the bedroom, and showered. Returned and placed the bag squarely in front of the USB mini lens.

It was now safe to inspect my laptop. In *Systems Library*, I opened *Console*, then *User Diagnostics*. At 16:23 hours, someone had awakened the screen by opening it. Twice they had attempted to hack my entry password, but wisely chose not to risk a third attempt.

An hour before this failed breach—around 15:00 hours—I'd been at the pool on the phone with Rayvon. The man worked fast. And the power he wielded, even here at a five-star hotel, was disconcerting.

Finally, I deployed my *Iron Key* firewall data. Someone had attempted a systems dump via USB, which had temporarily put my computer on lockdown.

I was not dealing with clandestine pros, but they certainly were not amateurs. These were dangerous people, Leo, the disgraced IRS agent, had warned. Sleazy, too, as I soon found out.

Nanette tapped on my door at a little after 9. I had just changed for dinner. Through the peephole, she appeared to be wearing only a towel. No, it was a swimsuit, a gauzy black one-piece. She feigned surprise when I opened the door. "Oh my god, *Capt. Berg.* I had no idea. This is so embarrassing."

She claimed that she had stepped out for a late swim and the door had closed before she realized she'd gone off without her key or phone. "I can't go to the lobby like this," she said, "and I, well, I panicked. Would you mind calling the desk?" I didn't respond immediately, so she added, "Or I guess I could wait out here, if you have company. But I've got to get into my room."

"Come in," I replied. When she ducked under my arm, I got a whiff of vanilla perfume and alcohol.

How far was Leo's wife willing to take this?

She didn't appear to know where the camera had been concealed, but was, perhaps, looking for one as she entered. Her eyes moved from wall to wall as she said, "I had no idea your room was next to mine. God, *so* embarrassing. But better, I guess, to look up and see you than some stranger, huh?"

"A dangerous world," I agreed. "Want me to call the desk?"

"I can do it. You're probably on your way out." Her

eyes settled on the mini bar. She looked up, already a little drunk, and gave me a bold, smoky look. "Or we could have that nightcap, Capt. Berg. Probably not a good idea to swim at night anyway. You know . . . because of sharks . . ."

I thought, *How damn sad*, but said, "Sure. We can talk."

SEVENTEEN

Tomlinson arrived at the sun-bleached airstrip at New Bight, Cat Island, before noon two days later—a Saturday.

"I'm stoked about seeing Josiah," he said, shouldering a red, yellow, and green Rasta bag. "Does he know you're the one who got him sprung? I'm still not clear about the details."

He had asked the same thing last night on the phone. During the last two days, we had kept each other updated. I'd shared info about the local players and just enough about our objective to prepare my pal for his role when he arrived. In the same conversation, he had provided welcome news: Hannah's mother had confirmed that her daughter's new friend was not Ellis Redstreet.

What Tomlinson might know—if his biological daughter had bothered to tell him—was that Delia had called me several times. Usually late, the only time reception was passable here, midway down the Bahamian chain. Cat Island is fifty miles long, rarely more than two miles wide, sparsely populated and far off the tourist trail.

"I haven't spoken to Josiah," I said, "and keep my name out of it when you do. The less he knows about my deal with Rayvon, the better . . . Is that all your luggage?"

He replied, "Dude, I can't lie to a Masonic brother, you know that. Hey"—we were walking toward the parking lot—"you got anything to drink? I could go for a couple of Kaliks about now. What's the beach like? A swim would be nice, too." Tomlinson was in tropic travel mode. Eyes a tad brighter, a bounce to his step.

"Shallow up," I told him. "The car's over here."

It was a breezy trade winds morning. Temp, low eighties, a wisp of lingering noctilucent clouds adrift in the jet stream. There were more stray chickens than cars in the gravel lot outside the airport terminal, which was one room with a window AC, seating for eight.

"Put your stuff in the trunk," I said. "We'll stop at the store on the way."

Our Toyota was a patched-up rental with a nav system that insisted we were somewhere in midtown Tokyo. A clone of most vehicles on the island—and there weren't many. I waited until the engine was started to talk. "I left a message for Josiah at the mailboat office. Hopefully, he'll meet us at the wharf this afternoon. I said around two. If not, we'll have to track him down because we need—"

"I know, I know, his boat," Tomlinson said. "I still don't know if Rayvon's people beat the crap out of the old guy when they questioned him. Geezus, the least you could've done is brought me a roadie."

"We need his local knowledge, too," I said. "Most of all, his church congregation's approval. We're screwed if he says no. Or we'll have to do the salvage work at night."

"Marion, chill. This idea of yours about how to end the battle over that missing gold, it's so simple, no wonder I didn't come up with it. No one gets hurt or killed, and Lydia will be left alone." He looked over and grinned. "*How much money is enough money?*—dude, that is a very heavy abstraction. Clean, like a razor exposing the soul. You have actually evolved beyond greed."

"Don't be so sure," I said, and meant it.

The only store for miles was Cindy Moss's grocery, north on a narrow road that ran the length of Cat Island. I'd already bought supplies for the beach house I'd rented. Tomlinson needed a cooler, ice, and a twelve-pack, so I waited outside.

My BTC cell phone rang. When I answered, Rayvon said, "It's about time," meaning it was his third attempt this morning. "Got the report back. Twenty-two-karat, bro. The shit's real." He was referring to the gold ingots. Seldom have I heard a grown man giggle, but he did.

"What about requisitioning a government boat?" I asked.

That was a problem. I could tell by his airy optimism. "Oh, I'm all over that. I've got a line on a forty-one trawler, commercial, out of Hawksbill. It's only a thousand bucks a day. There's no crane, but it's got outriggers—you know, those booms that netters use. We can rig something. It's a short run to Cat, so how about we meet tomorrow afternoon?"

I was too pissed to respond. After a long silence, he asked, "Moe? You still there?"

"A Bahamian customs boat," I said, "that's what we agreed on. I couldn't have been clearer about that. Don't put me in a position where I've got to change our deal at the last minute."

"Whoa, brother! No need for talk like that. I didn't know it was such a—"

"It is," I said. "A *big* problem. I'm not doing a salvage project like this without a government boat on the job. One of your planes flies over, or the local cops show up, then what? What do we tell them?"

"Oh," he said, "an *official* vessel with the markings and shit. My bad. I was thinking one of our undercover boats so we wouldn't draw any—"

"We don't want any attention," I said. "That's the point. Someone sees a customs boat anchored, they're not going to ask questions. Ray, can you handle this or not?"

"Now that I finally know what you need, hell yes," he said, flustered but already working on it in his head. "Yeah . . . Yeah, I know just the one. It's been out of service for . . . Never mind, leave it to me."

"Out of service where? I need specifics or I'll put my associates on it, and we'll find our own damn boat."

"Hold on, Moe. When I say I got this covered, I . . . Damn, man, okay. North of George Town in the Exumas—the port at Moss Town. We got a cutter there, forty-some feet. It's an older vessel, been up on the ways for about a year, but she's ready now. Fresh paint, all the markings and lights." Rayvon sounded more confident. "It'll take a day for me to work my magic, so not tomorrow, but Monday, Tuesday latest. How's that sound? Now all I need is the GPS numbers where Jimmy hid the stuff. You know, approximately—so we can meet up. I got a pen handy when you're ready."

No way. I wasn't going to reveal the gold's location until the last minute.

Tomlinson exited the store. He'd bought so much beer and ice that Cindy's husband, Alfred, was lugging one of the boxes. Through the open window, I signaled for him give me a second. To Rayvon, I said, "Not so fast. The boat at George Town, does it have a derrick?"

"A crane to lift shit? Oh hell yes."

"And it runs? Don't screw this up, Ray."

"Dude, the vessel's got twin inboards, runs like a scalded cat. All kinds of electronics and—hey, you ready for this?—a fifty-cal machine gun mounted on the bow. The boat was a present from your DEA."

"That ought to do it," I said. I was mildly amused—a DEA assault cruiser. "What about scuba gear and the guy you're bringing as crew?"

Rayvon's ego was tired of being on the defensive. "Whoa! Come on, man. You do your job, I'll do mine. Where Jimmy hid the stuff—how far we talking from George Town?"

"About fifty miles from where you'll pick me up," I guessed, "then another twelve to the spot."

"To the north of Cat Island?" he asked.

"Northwest," I said, which was true.

I could picture the man narrowing it down in his head. "From George Town, that's right on my way," he said. "See? It's all gonna work out. I'll hit you up in the afternoon—but, damn it, answer your phone for a change."

Tomlinson got in the car, popped a Kalik, in its clear bottle, and waited until we were driving to ask, "Suppose you were talking to Delia, huh?"

"Nope."

"Oh." He drank in silence for a while. "Seemed sorta secretive, that's all. She got mad because she wanted to come along. Don't worry, I took the heat. Figured she might have called you. Man, I was tempted to say yes. Know who's still hitting on her? That damn *bomba* hound, Figgy. That Cuban's got the morals of a Republican love bug."

"No need to take the blame," I said. "I already told Delia coming here was a bad idea. You want to stow your gear at the house and go for a swim? Or try the wharf first? Josiah might show up early."

"Told Delia when?"

"Yesterday, maybe. No, late Wednesday night, when I was still in Nassau."

"You called her?" He tilted the Kalik bottle. "Kinda weird, ol' buddy, you ask me, calling my daughter all hours of the night from a town where most normal people are paired up and drunk by sunset."

I turned onto a rutted limestone lane toward Fernandez Bay. "Don't start with that nonsense again. Delia has called me, I've called her, we're friends, so what?"

"Just catchin' up on the local gossip, I suppose, you and her?"

"Some. She and a few of your other biological kids did a FaceTime session. Fun, she said, but a couple of them still won't share their real names. I find that a little disturbing, don't you? I didn't say anything. Didn't want to worry her."

"Sounds like you two talk almost every day. What's up with that?"

"She needs advice," I replied. "The sugar co-op in Belle Glade invited her back for a second interview. She's worried it could damage her reputation—political internet stuff. And her ex-boyfriend has been hounding her to the point of stalking. Delia's smart, very rational, objective way beyond her age. But we all need an outsider's view sometimes."

"Phil's *stalking* her? That pompous academic quack. You were supposed to scare the hell out of the prick. Now you've suddenly lost your badass skills, too? She didn't say a word about it to me."

I was pulling up to our rental house—one story, two wings of native limestone with a commons. It was an isolated property built on a lagoon of electric indigo, miles of distant mangroves, wind-sheared.

"Why would she bother?" I countered. "So you can debate Phil into submission?" I jammed the car into park, done with the man's insinuations. "Let's clear the air here. Her dad has rallied, so her mom booked another week in Asheville. That's why she pressed the issue about coming here. Oh, you're gonna love this." I reached over and got a beer for myself. "Promise you won't get pissed off?"

"Oh, *please*. Long ago, I mastered my anger by embracing—" He stopped. "Hold on, poncho. What kind of ugly kimchi are you gonna lay on me now?"

"Not ugly, just the opposite. Before I left, Delia and I spent part of the night together at one of Mack's cottages. We talked, had a nice time. Just thought you ought to know."

Tomlinson stared. His Adam's apple bounced as if in eloquent speech, but all he got out was "Wha—"

"Yep, just the two of us."

"You . . . her . . . *alone*."

I said, "Unless you count the two bottles of wine. We started in the bedroom. I told her I needed to search the cottage—which was true. She's still worried about Deville. Then we ended up on the couch and almost finished the second bottle."

"Of wine, two bottles . . . What kind of wine?"

"Red, I'm pretty sure. Hey, pay attention. When you two talk, don't let on you know unless we're all together. No more secrets between us. I think that's a good rule from now on."

Tomlinson continued to stare while his mind dissected all this. "You and Delia . . . all night drinking wine." He attempted to finish a beer that was already empty. With the back of his hand, he wiped his mouth, then his face rebooted with a slow grin. "You *asshole*. Doc, you don't drink wine, you hate wine. And a couch? Oh, come on. With a perfectly good bed available?"

"It was more comfortable," I said. "She had one of those little electronic smoke things—a vape stick. We passed it back and forth a couple of—"

Tomlinson started to laugh before I could finish. "Oh, right . . . Doc Ford, smoking a bone, drinking some red. Grooving on some Grateful Dead, were we?"

"No, a vapor pipe, maybe it's called," I said. "Marijuana. It was in kind of a tube. Had a little button."

"A little button! Hilarious." My pal threw his head back and roared. "Geezus frogs, Doc, think I'm gonna fall for this bull—" He had to get himself under control before continuing, "I know, don't tell me—then you got married again. What, you fly to Vegas and rent the Elvis Chapel? Had to be hell landing your seaplane in the freakin' desert." He opened the door, his chest heaving. "Okay, okay, I've learned my lesson. Just one question: When's my grandkid due? By the time we get back, I hope."

More laughter.

I switched off the engine and sat for a second. "Well, at least you know the truth," I said, which I doubt my friend heard.

Josiah wasn't at the wharf when we arrived that afternoon. We waited on the quay. Tomlinson had another beer while I paced the water's edge, tallying life-forms along the seawall. From a cluster of food shanties, a woman called out. She offered us a map, drawn with a shaky hand, saying, "Ol' Rev. Bodden, he ain't doing so good after what that Nassau trash done to him. You tell him Miss Mary said 'Hey,' you hear? I'll carry him some fish stew tonight. Tell him that, too."

In the car, Tomlinson fumed as we drove north. "Wonder how bad they hurt the old guy. Geezus, the man's in his nineties. Who are these assholes you're dealing with, Doc?"

"People who don't know who *they're* dealing with," I

replied. "Saddest part is, Josiah doesn't even know where Jimmy dumped the stuff."

"Yeah, but he knows where Lydia is," Tomlinson reasoned. "I wonder if she's had her baby yet? Josiah wouldn't let anything happen to a mother and her kid."

A short distance north, I turned inland onto a single rock lane hacked through an impossible thicket of vines and dwarf trees that clawed at the car. A twisting half mile led to a clearing that invited sunlight. Goats, a pig or three, wild chickens, scratched in the shadows of a crooked block home probably built in the 1800s. Walls of stick and wattle, freshly whitewashed, a roof of tin.

"You think Josiah has family here or is he hiding out?" I asked. I knew that he and his congregation lived on a remote private island an hour's boat ride away. The island was off-limits to the public, including me. But he and Tomlinson were tight. There was the Masonic connection. And they both had a fondness for quoting the Bible.

My pal replied, "I'll go first and wave if he's willing to see you."

No need. The Rev. Bodden appeared in the doorway of the cabin. He was a leathery beanpole of a man, bent over a cane that he used as he shuffled toward us. Baggy, torn overalls, no shoes, a massive straw hat. He also wore a black frock coat as if dressed for Sunday service.

The old gentleman waved, grinned, but appeared weak. Tomlinson met him halfway. They exchanged a secretive handshake. They embraced, and Tomlinson whispered something, mouth to ear. A mitten of medical gauze, I noticed, covered the old man's left hand.

Josiah was a talker. He was an animated antique from the days when islanders built their own sharpies and fished under sail. Tomlinson installed the old man in the passenger seat. My pal curled himself into the back. I listened to a nonstop, singsong exchange of topics, but Josiah often had to stop and take a few breaths before rejoining the conversation. They discussed the weather, apocalyptic clues from Revelations, and the price of snapper. Tomlinson asked about the Masonic Lodge, which had fallen into disrepair, then made a vague reference to a married woman who Bodden had been seeing on the sly off and on for forty years.

Finally, I interrupted to ask how Rayvon's people had handled the interrogation. The old preacher pretended it was no big deal. Tomlinson disagreed. "Tell him what they did to you." Then told me himself, saying, "Bastards cut off two of his fingertips, for Christ sakes!"

Josiah seemed okay with that, too. "Still got eight left. That ain't bad," he said. "Lost only two in the last ninety years. What's that come to? My math ain't good—one finger every forty-some years? Never told them boys a damn thing either." The man thought about it, then reconsidered. "Now, if they'd applied those odds to my pecker . . ." He allowed the sentence to fade into contemplative silence.

"Can you describe the men?" I asked.

Josiah banged the tip of his cane on the floor. "Oh yes, one of them was Nassau trash. The other, a foreigner of some kind. His name was . . . Ellis . . . I believe."

"Ellis," I repeated.

"Yep. Don't you worry about those two. As the Book says, 'Blessed be the Lord who trains my hands for war, my fingers for battle.' If those boys woulda known their Scripture, they woulda kept cuttin'."

"Book of Isaiah?" Tomlinson suggested. He wasn't sure.

"Psalm 144," the old man replied. "The Good Lord's gonna jumby-fuck them fellas, yes siree bob. And I'm gonna be there when it happens." He inhaled a heavy breath as if he was about to pass out.

"You want to stop and rest for a while, Reverend?" I asked.

In reply, he whapped me on the shoulder. "Damn it, boy, pay attention. Slow down, take the next left. My boat's down yonder, all fueled and ready to go. I want to hear about this plan of yours that's gonna rid us of the burden my people bear."

There was no need to explain the backstory. Josiah had played a key role in helping Jimmy's ex-girlfriend, Lydia, and her husband disappear into their new lives. I said, "How often do treasure hunters come poking around, looking to get rich?"

The old man addressed Tomlinson. "Ain't no way to stop that, the greed of the modern world. Poor girl still lives in fear, especially now they got the baby. What's your friend getting at?"

I said, "About a year ago, I found it—Jimmy's gold. I probably should've told you, but I didn't. It's just off-shore on the east side of your island. Marl Landing. That's why I'm here. To show you."

Marl Landing is how locals refer to an island that, on charts, is unnamed. Josiah, his congregation, and their forebears had inhabited the place since a shipwreck in the 1700s. Generation after generation, their families had lived there in isolation—by choice.

"You knowed about this all along?" he asked Tomlin-son.

"About the gold. Yes, brother. It was Doc's secret to share, not mine. But if your people had been in need—"

"Guarding your friend's secret," the old man inter-rupted. "That there's very righteous. As it was said, 'No man shall question the faith of others, for no human being can judge the intentions of God.'"

My pal guessed. "Book of Matthew, verse 51?"

"You thinking of 'Judge not, least ye be judged,' verse 7," Josiah replied. His voice had deepened as a melodic sermon. "No, the wisdom I just shared was spoke by Brother Haile Selassie. Worshipful Master of Ethiopia's Ancient Masonic Lodge, by the grace of Prince Hall and JAH Almighty. Treat thy friends as brothers in the hope one day they seek the light. Good for you, Brother Tom-linson."

Tomlinson nudged me from the backseat. "Isn't that cool? Wish I could explain, but it's, like, totally cryptic shit."

The road had widened, potholes unavoidable. Ahead, a giant land crab scampered sideways but was in no rush. I said, "Jimmy melted down the treasure he found and made mooring anchors, about a hundred pounds each. They're spread out over about half an acre of bottom in the shallows off your island's main dock. He probably worked at night."

"You joshing me?" Josiah asked. "Water's so clear at the Landing, surprised my people didn't notice 'em."

"The anchors? I'm sure they did. Probably still do. But they're flat, spoon-shaped, with a kind of gray coating. Last time I was there, most were buried under a couple of feet of sand. You probably see them every day, just don't know what they are."

"Oh yeah, Mr. Ford, I remember our time together here." Josiah twisted around to address Tomlinson. "Right off, I read your friend as a sinner, but a good heart when it come to that poor lost girl and her idiot husband. You still vouch for this man?"

"Doc? Yeah, I do . . . Well, as long as we're not talking about some of the truly nasty kimchi I'd rather not get into."

The Rev. Bodden smiled his approval.

I said, "I'm not sure how the law works in the Bahamas, but in most countries property rights end at the mean low-tide mark. The Bahamian government owns everything on the bottom. That seemed like a problem, until I really thought it through."

"Marl Landing," the old preacher replied. "We our own government. All that gold out there waitin' to be took . . . Well, I'll be dog-blessed . . . Maybe we'll salvage it for ourselves . . . Hmm . . . Tell me what you got in mind."

I did. It took a while. I parked in the shade of casuarina trees on an inlet with a view of old docks. The docks were built with planks and raw poles. Getting out, the Rev. Bodden asked over the roof of the car, "You bring that gizmo that scares the deacons away?"

"Repels sharks," Tomlinson translated. "At the landing they're, you know, considered spiritual visitors, deacons who come to collect tithes."

The preacher was referring to an ankle strap with co-axial cable I'd been experimenting with—a "shark zapper"—that emitted a continuous low-voltage electrical field. Fish were not fazed, but sharks, if they came too close, received a shock because their noses are dotted with supersensitive pores. I'd used the device on my last visit.

"Yes, sir," I replied. "Not with me. But tomorrow, if you're willing to help on our first dive."

"You gonna need it," the old man cackled. "The deacons don't like outsiders no better than we do."

EIGHTEEN

We were at the Starlite Restaurant—an eloquent name for a place on an empty stretch of road that needed no sign because the food was that good. It was a single room with a bar, doors open to the trill of frogs outside. On the porch, Tomlinson slapped dominoes with a gathering of his Masonic buddies—strangers until tonight, yet that didn't seem to matter.

Josiah, after a long afternoon on the water, was too weak to join the group. He had instructed us to meet him at sunrise, but had yet to agree to my proposal.

My phone buzzed. Surprise, surprise—Hannah was finally returning my call. "How are things on Staniel Cay?" I answered cheerfully. I was inside the restaurant, where there were ceiling fans and a menu that varied with the luck of local fishermen.

Static—*buzz-buzz*—then a sentence fragment that sounded like "Izaak's having a fun . . ."

Back and forth we went, a failed conversation that consisted mostly of "Can you hear me now?"

Three dropped calls later, I switched tactics.

A boom box filled the restaurant with the music of choice, which was country-western or gospel, not reggae, on this agrarian island where everyone it seemed attended church and went to bed early. I signaled for Rusty, the bartender, to lower the volume, then went outside and I tried my local BTC mobile phone.

"Who's calling, please?" Hannah answered. She was wary of the unfamiliar number.

"Finally," I said. "I've missed seeing you and Izaak. Got a minute?"

"I called you, remember?" There was a warmth in her voice. In the background were steel drums and occasional hoots of laughter.

"Is there a party going on?"

"Always, with Birdy around," Hannah said. "Doc, guess what? Izaak and I caught our first bonefish this morning."

"You brought a fly rod?"

"A little pack rod, an eight-weight. I put him in the tummy sack, waded out right in front of our cottage.

Had to be a hundred fish in that school of bones. You ought to see this place."

"Where are you sitting?" I asked.

"I'm not, I'm standing. Are you asking if I'm with someone?"

"No, look to the east. I doubt you can see the lights, but I'm on Cat Island about forty miles away. If you and Birdy want to go for a plane ride, I can pick you up . . ." I had to think. Tomorrow, Monday—maybe Tuesday, too—was booked. So I finished lamely, "Why don't you stay until Wednesday? You can all fly home with me."

That created an awkwardness until the conversation swung back to fishing.

"The first bonefish, I'd guess four pounds," Hannah said. "And that first run . . . My Lord, not even snook compare. A man here—one of the managers, I guess, nice man, British—he watched me catch a couple more and asked if I'd be interested in working here as a guide. Isn't that funny? You know, because he saw me cast. I'm a licensed instructor, and they get a lot of tourist ladies who want to learn—"

"The man, is he British or *Australian*?" I asked a little too sharply.

"What's it matter? From London, I think. For heaven sakes, he was paying me a compliment."

"Plus, you're beautiful," I said, hoping to gloss things over. "Is his name Ellis? I used to know a guy who—"

"Good Lord, Doc, don't tell me you're jealous of him, too. I swear."

"Then his name *is* Ellis?"

"No!"

"Too bad," I lied. "The guy I'm thinking of—he's probably mid-eighties by now—knows more about bone-fishing than anyone around. I was hoping you two had run into each other."

Some warmth returned to the woman's voice. We talked for several minutes. When Delia's ID flashed on my personal phone, I hit DECLINE. Hannah and I talked for another ten. I told her that Tomlinson and I were treasure hunting because no one takes such a subject seriously.

"What about your shoulder?" she wanted to know. "Is it healed up enough? You can't go in the water with an open wound."

I dodged that.

She asked, "What sort of treasure?" not really interested until I described Marl Landing as a place that was forbidden to outsiders. "How's that possible?"

I sensed a chance to lure her over on this trip. Or the next. "By international agreement," I said. "Thirty years ago, the island was designated as something called an Indigenous Protected Area, an IPA, and now it's under government jurisdiction. The program's based on the Australian model created in the nineties to protect Aboriginal culture. There now are IPA preserves in South America, Polynesia—"

"Indians live there?" she asked. "How'd you and Tomlinson manage to—"

"They're mixed race. Unusual people, very striking," I said, then explained. In the 1700s, a Scottish ship had foundered on an uncharted shoal in a thousand fathoms of water. Survivors included men and women. The island was far off the known shipping routes. They were marooned. The survivors intermarried with the last remnants of the indigenous people, then with slave castaways from later shipwrecks.

A century and a half passed before inhabitants saw the first airplane pass overhead. By then, after generations of isolation, farming the land and living off the sea, the islanders had morphed into a unique subculture. They no longer cared about outside contact. In fact, they discouraged it. The Maroons of Jamaica were an example. The blue-eyed, copper-haired progeny of the Pinder family on nearby Eleuthera were another.

"The captain of the Scottish ship," I continued, "was a man named Marl Bodden. The Marl People—that's what they're called locally. He and most of his crew were members of the same fraternity. This is where it gets strange."

"Already sounds strange enough," Hannah replied. "Doc, have you been drinking?"

"I'm on my second beer," I said. "The fraternity is

very old—nothing to do with colleges. Ready for this? Tomlinson belongs to the same fraternity. Masonic, the Freemasons. On Marl Landing, it's evolved into a kind of a weird Euro–Afro–Knights Templar sort of religion."

Hannah found this interesting. "Just on that island or everywhere? Reason I ask is, some churches—the one Loretta and I used to attend—claim the Masons worship the Devil."

"Witchcraft, more likely," I said, "knowing Tomlinson."

"You're not serious?"

I chuckled the question away. "He's friends with one of the direct descendants—an old guy, a preacher. You'd like him. If you'd like to visit the place, I might be able to get permission."

"A preacher?" Hannah asked. She wanted to talk about that, so we did. The topic had shifted to her friend Birdy when she suddenly was interrupted by a whooping noise, and said, "Guess who just woke up? That boy sleeps less than you do."

"Call me back," I said.

"Tomorrow maybe," she replied, and hung up.

I returned to the bar, where Rusty had just delivered a basket of fried conch and potato salad. After I ate, I wandered out to watch Tomlinson and his friends bang domino tiles.

Delia phoned me a second time. If her bio dad had not been present, I might have answered. No, I was in a jaded mood, nothing to do with Hannah, just people in general of late. Rayvon had thought nothing of having an old man tortured. Nanette, an estranged wife and mother, had disgusted me with her willingness—no, eagerness—to trade sex for profitable information. In Nassau, I'd gotten a perverse satisfaction out of sending her away. It had more to do with two daughters I'd never met and her husband, the poor fool, who inexplicably was still in love with the woman.

Ironic—I felt pity for the IRS agent who had threatened me with extortion. Leo, at least, was trying to kick the pills and booze and salvage what was left of what he perceived to be good in his life.

As a species we are, at once, complex and idiotically myopic. To judge is to risk an inspection of one's own skeletons. I'm a hypocrite and know it. This might have been worth discussing with Hannah despite her tough personal code of morality. Delia, on the other hand, was more open-minded. She would've been a better choice had I needed someone to talk to.

But I didn't. Not the ever-self-sufficient Marion Ford.

I declined the girl's call again and ordered another beer. But she was persistent. A text arrived. It contained several images. I carried the phone to the end of the porch and swiped through them. Tomlinson was still playing dominoes with a cluster of locals. Their table was illuminated by a single bulb where moths the size of bats collided blindly. I noticed him checking his phone.

Good. Delia has sent him the same text.

In the rental car, my pal delighted in sharing what she'd sent. Photos of a 60-foot two-story houseboat. Twin outboards, a galley, plus four tiny staterooms, with bunk beds, and a screened party area topside. Perfect for the bio sib reunion they were planning.

"Plenty of space. Couches up there fold out into beds," he explained, delighted that Delia had contacted him. "She wants to rent the thing for an overnight, all of us together. The Bio Launch, they're calling it now. Get it?"

Launch, as in *boat.* "Clever," I said.

"The marina's out of St. Pete Beach," he continued, "but I'll rent Mack's cottages anyway. You know, September is slow season. Don't want to piss him off. And some of the kids might want to hang out, spend a few extra days." He pushed the phone toward me. "Read it yourself. I'm getting sort of excited about this."

I already had. Or so I thought. But, in Tomlinson's version, Delia had not included what she had confided to me: *I'm still worried about you-know-who. Please be there.*

Josiah's 28-foot tri-hull was a bad risk, if Rayvon didn't provide a government vessel. I decided this the next morning after a rough twelve-mile crossing. It was our second attempt to get to Marl Landing.

Yesterday, we had turned around because of the seas and the old man's health. Today, the weather wasn't much better. The deck of the preacher's boat felt as soggy as a trampoline when whitecaps met us outside Cat Island's lee. Its twin Chryslers predated four-stroke dependability and its CB radio was no match for an area so isolated.

Finally, we raised Little San Salvador, a misty knoll on the horizon. Closer, to the west, Marl Landing revealed itself as a low bank of clouds girded to a single limestone peak. The island was a seamount that pierced the surface from 4,000 feet below, the water velvet black where it plummeted into an abyss only a hundred yards from shore.

"How're you holding up?" I asked Rev. Bodden. Last night, someone had changed the dressing on his hand. It was already leaking blood.

"Fine, fine," the preacher replied. "Sit your ass down."

Wind was a steady fifteen out of the northeast. Frigate birds, black on a high sapphire horizon, shadowed flying fish that skimmed ahead us.

As we drew nearer, the island took form. There were ridges grazed green by goats, a low tangled forest. A limestone bluff was capped by a seemingly miniature church. At the base of a hill, hidden by palms, was the largest of three villages. Even from a distance, I could see people. Some were working on their haunches in fields among papaya and corn. Woodsmoke, cooking fires—it was the scent of life, of contentment, that I associated with rain forest cultures in Brazil, Micronesia, Vietnam.

We didn't tie up, just idled around the island's main dock, where a sign warned

Federal Indigenous Preserve
No Visitors, No Cameras, No Trespassing

"Shut the engine off and let's drift," I suggested. It took a while for Tomlinson and the old man to train their eyes to see what I could see. Here, on the windward side, water was a hazy green lens but clear enough to see the bottom 20 feet below.

"All those little splotches?" I said. "Some with pieces of rope still tied. See, the rope sort of looks like ribbons of seagrass. The buoy markers are long gone—if there ever were any."

This is where Jimmy had dumped his homemade anchors, I explained. "He probably chose this spot because he knew Marl Landing is off-limits to the public."

"He had to have had some help," Tomlinson pointed out.

I had researched this oddity as well. "Two of his employees died in a dive accident, just before he was arrested," I replied. "It didn't make big news in the U.S."

Josiah displayed a stubborn reluctance to admit that a thief could've done such a thing so close to where he, like the Boddens before him, reigned as captain.

"Seems my people woulda noticed," he said, not for the first time. "Must be a hundred of them things down there. They all pure gold?"

I replied, "That's my guess. I only took one. It assayed out as twenty-two-karat. Like I said, the anchors weigh just over a hundred pounds apiece."

"Only *stole* one," the old preacher corrected with a stern look. He pulled out a red neckerchief, removed his hat, and wiped his face. The man wasn't doing well. "How many more you plan to steal?"

"At least two," I said. "What happens to the rest? That's your call."

Tomlinson was surprised, but the old man seemed to appreciate my honesty. "Twenty-two-karat, huh? Same as Spanish coins. Over the years, we found thousands of those on the north shoal." He wasn't exaggerating. As an aside, he glanced at my pal and said something indecipherable over the noise of the engines.

"The shoals here are the Marl People's private bank," Tomlinson explained. "Question is, preacher, how much is enough? The two dudes who tortured you—and who knows how many of those vultures are still looking for Lydia—it'll never end until word gets out that Jimmy's stash has been found. Doc's plan is brilliant, I think. It's the only way."

I hadn't said my plan was the only way, but it was workable. Better yet, it was simple. When a cache of gold is measured by the ton, the news media would not quibble over an exact amount. Nor would the ruthless factions racing to find it.

"Yeah, but found by who?" Josiah muttered to Tomlinson. "I've got my people to think of. You got no idea the bribes we have to pay to cowans of all types to keep this island private. Government thieves, they the worst. Always snooping with their hands out."

I opened my phone to a photo of Rayvon. I had found the image on the internet. "Recognize this man?" I asked.

Josiah had cataracts, a translucent gray. I had to shade the screen from the sun. "Oh yeah. Wears a uniform. The man's been here a few times askin' about Ciboney."

"Who?" I was lost.

"That's the girl—Lydia Johnson. Ciboney is what was given as her Marl name. Last couple months, had to run that gentleman off several times. She still scared to death of being found."

"Did he see her?"

"Wouldn't've mattered, the way Ciboney looks now," Josiah said. "You wouldn't recognize her either."

Actually, I probably would. The last time I'd seen Lydia was from the shadows, her unaware of my presence. She'd had wild spiked hair, her face, in the sunlight, soot-covered. In white rubber boots and a baggy sarong, she might have been born on the island.

"He's Rayvon Darwin," I said, "a Nassau customs agent. He's the one who had you tortured."

"For true?" Josiah was unconvinced. "He weren't the one who done it. When the time comes, I'll recognize those two. Ellis—did I mention that bastard's name?"

"Doc knows the dude," Tomlinson put in. "He's setting Rayvon and Ellis up for a big fall."

"Maybe. Don't count on it," I said. "I'm not sure how this is going to work out. Rayvon's greedy, and he can't be trusted, that's all I know." I scrolled through my phone and found the photo of Ellis Redstreet. "Is this him? He and Ray were partners for a while. Now they're supposedly on the outs."

Josiah looked from the screen to the bloody gauze on his hand. He flexed what was left of his fingers. His voice dropped a spooky half octave. "The foreigner. Man with the snippers. Oh yes, sir, I recognize that Ellis. You wanna make me a deal?"

"That's what we're talking about now," I said.

"A different sort of deal," Josiah responded. "Deliver that gentleman here, my people will never speak a word of your help. Or what we do with him." He nodded to a huge commercial reel bolted to the gunnel. It was loaded with braided cable, not monofilament, for deep drop fishing. "Take four of them gold anchors as a reward, we'll haul 'em up right now."

I said, "I can't promise that either. What I hope is, Rayvon shows up here tomorrow night, early Tuesday maybe, in a government boat and tries to steal it all for himself. I have no idea who will be with him. That'll give your people all day tomorrow to take, let's say, half of what's down there?"

"Ain't gonna let that happen," the preacher said. "Not some damn government boat. Rayvon's his name? A man you say had my ass kidnapped, me out hunting crabs, not botherin' nobody?" He glared up from his injured hand. "As the Book says, 'To me belongeth vengeance and recompense.' That's from Deuteronomy, I forget the verse. Those two Babylon filth will be jumby-fucked. My people will take every damn ounce what's there before giving it to that spawn with the snippers."

The preacher had a temper.

I looked at Tomlinson for assistance. "Brother Bodden," he said, "you have to let it happen. Listen to Doc. He'll explain how things will go if we pull this off."

I corrected, "*Might* go," then turned away to allow the men privacy as they talked back and forth, mouth to ear.

Finally, Josiah put the boat in gear. "I'll listen," he said to Tomlinson. "Owe you two that much, I guess."

We idled a crisscross pattern and scanned the bottom while I laid out what I had in mind. Bodden dressed like a peasant but had an elite IQ. The old man listened, he asked the right questions, including a few that stumped me. Finally, when we were closer to the island, he told Tomlinson to get the anchor ready.

I helped. When the anchor line was taut, Josiah killed the engines. Onshore, a hundred yards away, a cluster of men had gathered on the pier. Beyond was a warehouse and a large fish-cleaning table. One man signaled with his arms—a right angle, then a slow flap. Josiah's response was lengthier—a series of precise movements with his arms.

Semaphore—it was an old nautical form of communication but without flags.

"You got a mask and fins?" the old man asked me.

I said, "It's sort of deep. There's a bunch of those anchors in the shallows. Last time, I waded out from shore. A hundred pounds doesn't sound like much, but it would be a lot easier."

Josiah stared at me until I grabbed my dive bag, sat, and began taking off my shoes. "If you can't bring me the foreigner with snippers," he said, "you're back to two anchors, not four."

The man was already stripping off cable from the big commercial fishing reel. Tomlinson held the cable's working end, where there was a huge snag hook, all of it attached to a metal batten that served as a fishing rod. They swung the rod outboard, the old man saying, "I ain't convinced about your plan yet, Mr. Ford, but I'm getting there . . . Give this a couple of tugs when you're ready."

I had uncoiled the electronic shark zapper, ready to strap it to my ankle. "You ain't gonna need that," Josiah added.

My last visit, I had done several dives here. Never had

I seen so many oceanic whitetip and tiger sharks. Was this a test?

Yes. It was in the old man's hard stare. If I didn't trust him, he couldn't trust me.

"I'll get my gear on," Tomlinson offered. "Doc's got a bad shoulder."

"No need," I said, and went over the side.

Water clarity improved as I neared the bottom. A thatch of mooring anchors resembled stingrays hidden beneath the sand. I fanned one clear. The limited mobility of my left arm made it difficult to secure the hook to the mooring fluke's shackle. Twice I had to surface for air.

"Haul her up," I said when it was ready.

The electric reel was geared to land fish five times the weight of the anchor. Tomlinson wrestled the thing into the boat. The old man helped. When a second anchor was aboard, I made another dive and shot some video, then climbed over the transom and took off my fins.

"Any visitors?" my pal asked. He meant sharks.

"Nope, but the deacons will appear," Josiah responded. "Hand me that there knife."

The anchors were furred with benthic growth, anemones, a few barnacles. He knelt and peeled away a strip of rubberized coating. The metal beneath the coating resembled liquid sunlight.

"Looka there," the preacher mused. He swiped at the second anchor until he saw gold, then took a seat. "A damn fortune lying there right off our dock." He took a moment to wipe his face and think. "But with Ciboney in a family way again, I guess it's a curse, too. On the other hand, money is money."

Josiah nodded as if he'd made a decision, then addressed Tomlinson. "I don't want to hear no nonsense about camels climbing through needles neither. My people have been poor and my people have had money. Only a fool would choose to be poor. There's a passage from Ezekiel I'm trying to recollect. . . ."

"Ezekiel's pretty heavy going, man," Tomlinson said.

The old man searched his memory, then gave up. Next, he wanted to discuss logistics.

I told him, "Rayvon can't do anything until I give him the GPS numbers for this spot. The timetable is up to us."

Josiah said, "Okay, then. We're gonna take about half of what's down there and leave the rest." He looked to see my reaction. "Most of what we leave will be out here in deeper water. You ain't gonna be aboard when that Babylon filth shows up, are you?"

I shook my head. "If you leave half, that's more than enough to make headlines if they get arrested."

Arrested. That was the part Josiah still didn't understand. Who would challenge a Nassau customs agent salvaging gold from a government boat?

"I've got some contacts" is all that I could tell the man. I was thinking about the U.S. Treasury Department and Leo, who was trying to get back in the good graces of the IRS.

Josiah replied, "Mr. Ford, you just make sure you're not on the boat with them bastards. Here . . . Watch . . ." He stood and signaled the men on the pier. It was built of heavy timber, planked with boards. One man, then several of the men, began stomping their feet.

Tomlinson perked up and threw his hair back. "I love this part." He smiled. "Let the dance begin."

We had both witnessed this phenomenon before. Build a fish-cleaning table over an abyss 4,000 feet deep, oceanic predators will develop a Pavlovian response. Wood conducts sound in low-frequency ranges that few animals other than sharks can hear. To the south of where we were anchored, a lemon cusp of sand plummeted into indigo shafts of light.

On that lemon cusp, a shadow appeared. Then a slow flight of shadows topped the shoals and cruised shoreward. Oceanic whitetip sharks, massive, their pectoral fins maneuvering as wings, their bodies languid missiles. Each shark was accompanied by a squadron of remoras.

Rev. Bodden was still trying to remember the Bible passage. "Something about 'Their gold shall be removed and they will not be spared the wrath of the Lord,'" he said. "Only the passage was longer, filled with God's pissed-off wisdom from the Old Testament."

He turned to me. "You gentlemen are welcome to spend a few nights on my island, you want. Rules are simple. Maybe even lend a hand—we got a helluva lot of work to do."

Tomlinson and I already knew the rules. There were areas on the island we were allowed to go and a few that were forbidden.

"Mind if I land my plane in the lagoon?" I asked.

Josiah was contemplating the sharks. "I'm gonna have to look that passage up. Well, tomorrow night—or whenever that filth gets here—we'll watch for their boat and let the deacons decide."

NINETEEN

On the phone, Leo said he was worried about his wife. His daughters spoke to the woman daily, but they hadn't seen her in more than a week. "That's not like Nanette," he said. "She's got her faults, but she's a damn good mother. Ray says he hasn't seen her either."

"You're still talking to Rayvon?" I asked. It was Monday morning. Tomlinson and I had just made the fifty-mile flight from Fernandez Bay to George Town in the Exumas. I had moored my plane at a resort in the lee of February Point, a busy tourist area compared to Cat Island.

"Ray calls, I answer," Leo explained. "So what? He's trying to cut a deal with that salvage honcho, Moses Berg. You really think the guy works for the Mossad?"

"Morris Berg," I said again. "And I told you not to mention his name on the phone."

"Then it must be true," Leo reasoned. "Ray, he's upped my percentage to ten, if they find what they're looking for. I think Ray's a little afraid of Berg. Suspicious, you know? Oh, here's something else—it's all over between him and Nanette. Ray actually apologized, said it only happened a couple of times and they'd both been drinking—not that I trust that asshole. Guess she finally came to her senses, huh?"

"I wouldn't believe anything Rayvon tells you," I replied.

"I don't. I just said that. Thing is, Ford, when I really think about it? I've slept with three different women—not counting massages and blow jobs—since we got married, but somehow that's okay? Double standard, man. We talked about that at the last AA meeting. Every human being is entitled to a few mistakes, don't you think?"

It was weird how easy it was for Leo to confide in me, a stranger. Honesty came easily because strangers have nothing to gain by lying. I said, "I'm going to tell you something and you're not going to like it."

"Let me guess," Leo said. "Ray's planning on screwing me over. Like that's a surprise. Hey, man, I'm not stupid. Every conversation we've had, I've got him on tape—well, on my phone—bragging about a cocaine deal he just did. And his plans for Jimmy's gold, if he finds it. Black market, and pays zero taxes. He pulls that crap, I go straight to the feds if he doesn't cut me in."

This was surprising news. "Good for you. That could be useful."

"What do you mean?"

I took no pleasure in sharing what Leo deserved to know. I told him that I'd seen Rayvon with Morris Berg at the Grand Hyatt in Nassau. "It was in the bar a couple nights ago. This is the tough part, Leo. Your wife was there. First with Ray, but she ended up in Berg's room."

"What? *Bullshit*."

"A pretty blonde, early thirties?" I said. "She smokes Marlboros, I think."

"Nanette, she . . . What the hell are you . . ." The man couldn't get his brain around it. "Hold on. What do you mean she ended up in the Mossad agent's room? Like a goddamn hooker?"

I started to say, "As far as I know, nothing happened. I think Rayvon forced her into—"

"You're a fucking liar!" Leo yelled, and hung up.

Tomlinson had found a shady spot beneath a poinciana tree that had rained a few scarlet petals onto his hair. We were waiting for a cab. Before taking off from Cat Island, I had exchanged several texts with Rayvon. I'd included underwater video I shot of the mooring anchors, two dozen in a line—more than a ton. I'd also included photos of an anchor I'd salvaged with the coating stripped off.

The photos had done the job. Rayvon was gut-hooked. Now—if he wasn't lying—he was a few miles north, near Moss Town, doing the final prep on the government boat he claimed to have requisitioned.

I hadn't told him I was coming to George Town. I wanted to eyeball the situation first. After that, I would play it by ear.

"Sounded like you were in a yelling match," Tomlinson said, referring to my conversation with Leo.

I took a seat next to him. "I think love is the biggest time waster in the world. If it's not kicking your ass, it's humiliating somebody you know."

"Well, I suppose stalking is more efficient," Tomlinson reasoned. "But I'd miss the cuddling." He gave me a sideways glance. "More Hannah problems? You know, it wouldn't kill you to at least pretend you believe in God. What's the worst that could happen? You're struck dead, wake up, and have to beg God for forgiveness? Hell, I do that most mornings anyway."

I said, "I was talking to the IRS agent who tried to extort me. If the dumbass would cooperate, I wouldn't have to bother a friend at another agency."

"Who?" When I didn't answer, he said, "Oh, racking up more debt to Spook City, huh? That should add to your frequent-flyer miles."

"I'm trying to help the IRS guy," I said. "It would cost me a hell of a lot less down the road. And might even solve some of his family problems."

Tomlinson found this amusing. "Marion Ford, look at you—founder of the He-Man Womanizer's Broken Hearts Club."

I flipped him the bird. My phone buzzed. I answered and walked away, saying, "Leo, take a deep breath and let me explain. You could come out the winner in this. *Really.*"

North of Grand Isle Resort was an undeveloped area. After another mile was a complex of cement piers, where there was a fuel depot. An oceangoing tug was moored there, and a dilapidated tri-hull next to a row of garbage bins.

Signage read *Government Use Only.*

I got my first look at Rayvon's boat from a distance. The garbage bins provided cover. His DEA "cutter" turned out to be an outdated police patrol boat. I recognized the design. It was a 31-foot Interceptor from the early years of Pablo Escobar. The paint and official markings were fresh.

No sign of life aboard, but there was a car. A Toyota, blue on white, the door stenciled *Bahamian Customs Service.* There was also an oversized cargo van, the sliding rear door open. The bed was empty except for a stack of blankets. They were the type people use when moving furniture—or, in this case, two dozen or more mooring anchors that Ray planned to steal from me, his trusted associate, Morris Berg.

Tomlinson was in the resort parking lot, waiting in the cab. I glanced back, before moving closer to the boat. A couple of rusty air conditioners were mounted on the boat's roof next to the radar tower. The AC compressors rattled against the heat on this hot August morning. Forward, covered by a blue tarp, was the .50 caliber machine gun, as mentioned. Aft was a derrick, and a dozen scuba tanks secured near the transom.

Ray was way ahead of schedule, almost set to leave. No surprise there. But who had he brought along as crew? That's what I needed to know before deciding my next move.

I waited, I watched. Still no movement aboard the boat, so I sent Rayvon another text. It read *just landed george town, be there in 10, driver knows location.*

That got some action. The cabin door opened. First came Nanette. She was wearing shorts, a big floppy hat, sunscreen goo on her arms. Standard dress for a two-day cruise. Next came a boney-looking man, blond hair to the small of his back, and tattoos.

It was Ellis Redstreet, the Australian attorney. This was unexpected. I couldn't see Rayvon sharing his windfall. My guess was, he would use the Australian's diving expertise, then kill him.

I snapped photos, then switched to video. Rayvon stepped out on the deck. He looked like an ad for steroids, in his white bikini underwear. Redstreet slammed the cargo van's rear door closed. He and Nanette got in, and the van bounced away. Rayvon did not respond when the woman looked back and waved.

Uh-oh, I realized. *He's going to kill her, too.*

Could I let that happen? No . . . But to warn Nanette was to warn Rayvon. I argued the options back and forth in my head. There was no good option. I returned to the parking lot and told Tomlinson I needed the cab and to wait in the resort's bar.

"You got a very heavy vibe about you, man," he replied. "Black karma going down . . . What's the problem?"

I couldn't talk in front of the driver. "Not now," I said. "Call me in thirty minutes. Speak loud, I want you to be heard by the person I'm with. Tell me my plane's cleared for takeoff. Got it?"

Tomlinson gave me his Zendo clairvoyant look. "Whoa, dude! Whatever it is, you can't let it happen," he said. "No violence. You promised."

This made no sense until I had returned, solo, to the dock and was getting out of the cab. Then I remembered that three days ago, at the airport, I had told him that no one would be hurt or killed.

Not a promise, exactly, yet those were my words.

Rayvon had changed into official attire. He wore blue BDU pants and a white shirt with epaulettes, lieutenant bars pinned to the collar.

"Ready for inspection," he said with a grin and a mock salute when he saw me. "Come on, come on," he said, waving me aboard. "Moe? That video you sent? We gonna have us a party, my friend, when we done with this. How much gold you think's down there? I mean, *really*?"

He was buzzed on something—cocaine, I guessed. It brought out the showman in him. He wanted to tour me around, but first apologized for repairs just done to the deck. It was an excuse for all the clutter—tools, cans of paint, a roll of fiberglass, open tubes of epoxy.

I said, "I'm in kind of a hurry. We need to coordinate our timing. You got a GPS chartplotter aboard?"

Rayvon loved that. He couldn't wait to get me seated in the wheelhouse, where there was a midsized Garmin. On the screen, a lucent nautical chart showed our location. "Glad we're doing this, yeah," he said. "Business first. You want to give me the numbers or punch them in yourself?"

I ignored that and instructed him to zoom out. He did until the chart included Cat Island to the east. I said, "I want you to pick me up around sunset—here." I touched the screen. "It's about fifty miles to Fernandez Bay—a two-and-a-half-hour run, tops. How soon can you be there?"

It threw him, which I expected. "*Today*? Man, you told me be ready by tomorrow or Wednesday. I still gotta take on fuel and shit."

"You'll have time," I said. "What about crew? Who's coming with you? My people want to run a background check."

"Background check? Oh man"—he made a theatrical gesture—"it's just some local kid. A good diver, that's all we need. Pay him a couple hundred bucks and say good-bye. Moe, lighten up, man." He got up from the captain's chair. "You want a beer? How about a beer?"

As he went to the ship's fridge, he explained how he expected it to go. We'd meet tomorrow around noon, take our time, he said. He had plenty of air aboard, but other gear was needed. A slow, fun day that would make us very rich.

Still talking, he returned with a couple of Red Stripes. "No one's gonna bother us out there. Man, you were right all along about using an official boat. But see"—he handed me a beer and took a seat—"this vessel is now my personal responsibility. The Bahamian government, we got strict rules and such. You know, got to file a float plan, all that crap."

He swiveled around to face the chartplotter. "That's why the *first* thing we do is enter all the waypoints. The course we gonna take tomorrow—our destinations, in other words. Okay"—he hunched forward—"where, exactly, you want to meet me at Fernandez Bay?"

I knew what he wanted, but I couldn't give in too quickly. "Your float plan has to be approved before you leave the dock?"

"Moe, my brother, you a pilot. Same as your Learjet, man. When you ever take off without permission? This ain't some damn little pleasure boat we're on."

"How about just write in the Fernandez Bay waypoint for now?"

Rayvon effected the patience of an adult dealing with a child. He produced a clipboard of protocols required before leaving port. Nothing on there about a float plan, but I finally conceded, "Rules are rules, I guess. I've got the GPS numbers on my phone." I swiped it open. "You ready?"

Oh yes, he was ready. The man's right hand had a slight tremor as he waited. I gave him coordinates for the mailboat dock, even though I knew he wouldn't show up tomorrow. Then I read off a series of numbers that began "North latitude two-four-four-zero-zero-four . . ."

The Garmin zoomed in like a missile. A flashing red waypoint anchored itself amid the pile of gold that was waiting a quarter mile off Marl Landing.

"Goddamn, man," he muttered. "Always suspected that's where Jimmy's ex-girlfriend escaped to. But no idea the sneaky fool—"

"She's dead," I reminded him. "We had her journal stolen and got the numbers from there. Problem is, people on that island don't know about the gold. Not yet, they don't. But when they see us out there, salvaging something, they're going to be damn suspicious."

"The shit wouldn't still be there if those people

knew," Rayvon reasoned. "But, hey, what they gonna do, call the po-leese? Not on a Bahamian customs vessel, they won't. You one very smart gentleman, my friend."

He sobered. "I don't know, though, man. The Marl People—they bad news. People say they still cannibals, like in back times. Dude, when I used to patrol? We avoided the damn island. Cruise past at night, they'd be up there, dancing around fires, all savage-like.

"That can't happen," I said. "We can't afford a confrontation of any type. No violence—understand?—or the deal's off."

Rayvon was ready for another beer. He got up. "That's what you say now, but this here vessel is government property. They pull some kinda aggression . . ." He glanced forward, where the machine gun was draped in a blue canvas duffel, then decided he'd best change the subject. "Know how that island got started? A ship come over from England carrying witches—for true, man, it's in the history books. Laws had changed over there, said they couldn't burn witches no more, so the Brits was gonna dump them but ended up shipwrecked."

He sat down heavily, something else on his mind. In texts, he had glossed over what had happened to Josiah, unaware that I knew already. So I took a chance. "How's that old preacher doing? I was hoping to run into him."

Rayvon was relieved that I had not. But the problem was something else. He finally got to it, asking, "On Marl Island, anybody see you—what was it, yesterday—

when you shot that there video?" His focus did a slow shift from the GPS to me. He had small, limpid eyes that were flecked with green. "What I'm wondering is, why you only took two of them anchors, Moe?"

"Because I'm not stupid enough to go after something I wasn't sure was there," I said. "It was a quick recon. I rented a seaplane. We were in and out." I waited for the man to blink. "You don't trust me?"

His wide grin returned. "My brother, trust is what we got going for us. First day we met, we both prove that."

The mood lightened. The man couldn't wait to get me off the boat yet still played the role of host. He made a ceremony of assigning me a locker in forward berth, saying, "Stow your gear here, brother. Consider this your home."

My phone buzzed—Tomlinson calling. I declined the call, but said, "I've got to take this," meaning I needed privacy.

Rayvon claimed he had to use the head anyway.

I hurried up the companionway. Outside, I paused, knelt, and snatched two tubes of epoxy from the clutter. Then, with the phone to my ear, strolled forward as if interested in the machine gun.

The gun's cover was loose. It was an M2 .50 caliber Browning. The boat's forward windshield gave me a clear view inside the cabin. Rayvon was still using the toilet. I'm not a firearms expert, but I've been through close quarters combat schools and I have shot a variety of full autos. The basics couldn't be much different. I hoped . . .

Phone to my ear, I carried on a merry conversation with myself while I moved fast. The gun's retracting slide handle slammed back. I flipped the cover assembly clear. The chamber was empty. I squirted one tube of epoxy into the chamber, eyeballed the empty cabin, then added the second tube—a chemical hardener.

Quietly, I allowed the weapon's bolt to slide back into place.

Tomlinson called again. I was so startled, I damn near dropped the phone because the thing was still against my ear.

"Plane's cleared for takeoff, boss!" he yelled.

From the main cabin, Rayvon made his way aft and walked me to the gangway. "Brother, we gonna be rich. See you around noon tomorrow."

In my head, I was thinking, *More likely, in about four hours.*

M y guess was way off. That evening on Josiah's island, a little after sunset, I confessed to Tomlinson, "I think I might have seriously screwed up. They should have been here by now—in the water and almost done."

Rayvon and his crew of one—not two, hopefully— had yet to appear.

"She had to be warned," my friend said, referring to Leo's wife. "Want me to send another text? Like from a normal person's phone. There's no guarantee she got the first one."

I still had Nanette's card, her cell and room number written on the back. My conscience had battled my good judgment into submission. Yes, I had warned Leo's wife. The message she'd received from my satellite phone was succinct—*go home, your daughters need you.*

There had been no reply.

"It was too damn obvious," I said. "She probably showed it to Rayvon and he spooked."

Until now, all the little pieces seemed to be falling into place. This afternoon, Leo's contacts at the IRS had alerted the FBI attaché's office at the U.S. Embassy in Nassau. Two days ago, as backup, through my connections, the clandestine branch of the Bahamian National Intelligence Agency had also been notified. They had been warned that a government employee, in a government vessel, planned to heist a fortune in gold.

Tomlinson was smoking a joint—perfectly acceptable here on Marl Landing where village law ruled. "Shallow up," he said. "Marion, dude, you really need to relax. Besides, we can't see diddly-squat from here. Come on. Let's find Josiah."

The old man had left us alone on a footbridge with an east-facing view of the pier and fish-cleaning table. The last silver thread of daylight was being pushed westward by a purple veil of stars. Locals had avoided us. They remained shadow people, fleeting images, backdropped by huts, tethered goats, cooking fires. I trailed Tomlinson up a path into the gloom of coconut palms where there was no light. Halfway up the hill, a charcoal figure emerged.

It was Josiah. "Government boat's coming, gentlemen," he called. "That Babylon filth is finally here. Follow me."

It *happened*. From a limestone crest, we watched the refurbished DEA Interceptor round the point, lights out. It slowed and began a robotic search under GPS control. When the vessel was a quarter mile offshore, a figure appeared on the stern. A marker buoy was dropped. Underwater lights flared, yet the boat continued a slow search grid. Back and forth . . . back and forth . . .

After ten minutes, Josiah muttered, "Idiots. They either blind or too drunk to see what's down there on the bottom."

"Or scared," I said. "I sent the customs guy a video. Told him that from up on the surface the anchors looked a little like stingrays covered with sand. Geezus—maybe he's afraid of getting stung." I was getting frustrated.

After another pass, the 31 Interceptor circled back to the marker buoy. There was a reverse thrust of engines. A chain rattled, the anchor splashed. Engines idled for a time, then went off.

In the abrupt silence, the vessel's black hull floated on

a mushroom of LED submersible light. The foliage around us roared with trilling frogs.

A second figure exited the cabin. The clank of air tanks, the rubberized thud of scuba gear being readied, reached us across the water.

"Can you make out who's aboard? I only see two people." Tomlinson had binoculars to his eyes.

Josiah had never tried night vision technology before. "Take a look," I said to him, and offered him the little monocular I'd been using.

The old preacher marveled at the increased number of stars. Their infinite galactic swirl seemed to take the breath right out of him. Then he focused on the cabin. "Two men . . . Yeah, just two of 'em so far. But we're too damn far away for me to make out . . ." He paused. "Wait . . . One of 'em is lighting a cigarette now." He lowered the lens. "Could be him? The foreigner with the snippers?"

I knew what he was thinking. So did Tomlinson. "Brother Bodden, if you start stomping around on that pier, you might be trading one problem for another."

By calling the sharks, he meant.

Josiah wanted to get closer. I remained alone on the crest with the NV lens. When I was convinced that Leo's wife wasn't aboard the Interceptor, I joined my friends on the footbridge. For the next hour, we took turns using binoculars and night vision. Rayvon and his helper had hoisted twenty-one golden anchors aboard—more than a ton—when the old man wandered off and returned with a brass ship's spyglass.

"Shoulda used this from the start," he said. "It was my great-granddaddy's." The bridge's handrail served as a brace. He extended the tube, focused, then began to pace and fume. Tomlinson took a look, then handed the telescope to me.

Rayvon's partner, as I'd anticipated, was Ellis Redstreet. I confirmed it just before the Australian somersaulted backward into the water.

"The man with the snippers," Josiah said again. His bitter monotone raised the hair on the back of my neck. "I've showed the Lord my patience long enough." He started toward the pier.

Tomlinson whispered to me, "Can't blame him."

By some unseen signal, a group of villagers joined the old man at the fish-cleaning table. What I at first perceived as drumming was not. It was a dozen bare feet stomping in perfect, rhythmic unison.

Maybe Rayvon heard it in time. More likely, he had decided there was no more gold to salvage. He was mounting the boarding ladder when, suddenly, a flood of underwater shadows ascended.

I moved closer and watched. They were oceanic whitetips. Unlike tiger sharks, whitetips sometimes hunt in packs. The speed, their bulk, was sufficient to cause the 31-foot boat to rock in their wake of displaced water. Behind Rayvon, the surface exploded. There was a second explosion off to port, where Redstreet had just entered the water.

In a panic, the customs agent scrambled aboard. The man tripped and fell . . . wrestled his fins off. He took a quick look over the side, where a dark froth had clouded the glare of LED submersibles.

Rayvon didn't bother hauling up the anchor, breaking the chain free with a pry bar. Alone in the cabin, he buried the throttles. The vessel reared, fishtailed, nearly out of control. The hull's chines gradually found purchase, and he turned southwest toward the Exumas, where his cargo van awaited.

That was okay—or so I believed at the time.

The night vision lens revealed something the customs agent would see soon enough. From the direction of George Town, a helicopter had levitated itself over a fast, distant boat, blue lights flashing.

TWENTY

Two weeks later, Tomlinson said something that stuck with me. It was the same day I found out that Lt. Rayvon Darwin had been promoted to captain, not jailed, for "heroic action while intercepting contraband." It was cop-speak for the gold stolen by the con man Jimmy Jones.

The *Miami Herald* had picked up the item from the *Nassau Guardian*, the largest newspaper in the Bahamas. Internationally, the recovery of the missing fortune had already made headlines. Most stories focused on Jones and the fascinating backstory. A *Mystery Finally Solved* video on the internet had gone viral, even though it misrepresented old underwater footage of the treasure as being recently shot.

RANDY WAYNE WHITE

From story to story, details had been provided by a spokesperson from the island government. Credit for the discovery was given to the Royal Bahamas Police Force, which "for many years" had been working in concert with the Ministry of National Security to unravel the case.

So far, there had not been one written word that mentioned Rayvon. Or had hinted at the truth.

I'm not a newspaper reader. Lately, it's tough to even find a paper, so many have gone out of business. But I'd grabbed the last *Herald* at Bailey's General Store, more interested in a headline about human trafficking in South America. I had finished with the paper, I thought, and was busy with a siphon hose, cleaning fish tanks, when Tomlinson flip-flopped into the lab. He took a seat, then folded the *Herald* to a section that was headed "Caribbean News Briefs."

We talked about things friends talk about. Delia's father had moved on to home hospice, which I already knew. Figgy had lied about his age—again—and had been booted out of a Red Sox tryout hosted exclusively for high school prospects. Rhonda and JoAnn, aboard *Tiger Lilly*, had had another raucous lovers' spat. The rumor was, they were putting their soggy floating home up for sale—for the third time in five years.

"It'll never happen," I said.

Tomlinson chuckled and folded the paper into quarter sections. "If those two don't get married, they'll end up

320

adopting a bunch of damn cats and making everyone miserable. The relentless flow of life," he said. "Everyone's afraid of getting stuck in a rut."

Somehow, the subject of marriage—or being stuck in a rut—swung back to me in the devious form of a question. "How are you holding up? I know Hannah's been chartering almost every day."

It was true. All the guides were busy because fishing had never been better. Tarpon, cobia, snook, redfish had returned, and more tripletail than most locals had ever seen. A freak summer, some were calling it. But there was nothing freakish about it. I motioned to the desk and the folder I was still assembling on historic references to red tide.

"I'm fine, fishing's great, and it's no mystery—take a look for yourself," I suggested a little too sharply. "After the worst lethal blooms ever recorded, fish have always rebounded in a big way despite all our human screw-ups and pollution."

"Geezus, you don't have to bite my head off," my pal replied. "Stop being so sensitive. And stop avoiding the subject."

He was right. "Okay, I'm in a rut. And it sucks." I wrung out a towel, dumped a bucket of turbid water over the railing, then returned and took a seat. "Every day, I'm up before sunrise. If Hannah needs bait for a charter, I put a cast net in the boat and meet her halfway. Then I look after Izaak. Feed him, change him, take him for a boat ride if he really gets pissed off at nap time. That part's fun. I love it, really. But dealing with Hannah's crazy mother . . . Those goddamn soap operas of hers . . . Do you know she claims to have killed three men—helped kill them anyway—and buried them out back?"

"I like her stories about the King of the Calusa better," Tomlinson chuckled. "That woman truly is a pisser."

I took a breath, miffed at myself for allowing Loretta's tactics to rattle me. "That's putting it kindly. Fact is, she doesn't want me around, so we're interviewing nannies. Well, *she's* interviewing nannies. Loretta's going to win. I know it and she knows it. And I think Hannah is falling in love with the guy she's dating . . . There, end of rant, end of confession . . . On the bright side, Hannah's taking the next few days off—maybe a whole week—so I'm free. For a while."

Tomlinson had drifted off, his attention suddenly on the *Herald*, but recovered enough to make the remark that would stick with me. "Beautiful," he said. "It's the days that pass by unnoticed that are probably the best days of our lives."

More Zendo nonsense, I thought.

He focused on the paper and sat straighter in his chair. "You believe this shit? When's the last time you talked to Rayvon? Or that IRS dude, Leo what's-his-name?"

I hadn't. Protocol after a con job is the same as concealing a covert act. With rare exception, all contact had to be suspended. I'd trashed my BTC cell phone and had refused Leo's many calls, nor had I spoken with Hal Harrington, my agency handler. "What's up?"

"You really want to think karma sucks? Read this."

He handed me the newspaper, and there it was:

NASSAU CUSTOMS AGENT HONORED

Rayvon Darwin, a fourteen-year veteran of the constabulary, was promoted to captain Tuesday in a ceremony held at Government House, New Providence . . .

I looked up from the paper. "You've got to be kidding me."

"Keep reading," Tomlinson said. "That Babylon spawn is being treated like a hero."

The story was only two paragraphs. Rayvon had been awarded a citation for taking part in a classified operation. He'd played a key role in the recovery of a "substantial portion" of contraband that was of "inestimable" value to the Bahamian government.

No shit.

"What they awarded Ray was a bounty. Or he bribed someone," I said. "Had to be more than one person. I doubt if he's got much, if anything, left. How the hell did he weasel out of that jam?"

"Go big or go to jail," my pal reasoned. He gave the story another look, then tossed it aside. "Josiah's happy.

No more treasure hunters snooping around—not after the first couple of days anyway. And no more reason for bad guys to search for the girl. That's all we care about, right?"

Lydia Johnson, her husband, and two children were doing just fine, as we both knew.

I couldn't help being curious about Leo. Presumably, his wife, Nanette, was still alive. One way or another, they would make their own way. All people do. I said, "As far as I'm concerned, it never happened. Well"—I made vague gesture toward the dock—"except for . . . you know . . ."

Beneath us, in chest-deep water, lay a pair of befouled mooring anchors worth, give or take, four million dollars.

"I'm trying to picture what kind of truck you'll buy Izaak for his sixteenth birthday," Tomlinson remarked later. It was dark by then, a few days shy of the new moon. He had made a round of the bars. There was rum and weed on his breath.

I had just gotten into my own truck—the same old blue GMC. I said, "Have you checked your messages lately?"

He wrestled with his phone and took a look. "Oh crapola. Delia's dad died. But she didn't say . . . I don't know, Doc. Think she wants me to—"

"Don't offer. It's not appropriate," I said. "We'll send flowers and a note from the marina. Anything else?" He looked at me blankly. "In her text, did Delia say anything else?"

I waited for him to read it again. "Uh-uh. Just that he died peacefully . . . You know, probably copied and pasted to a bunch of friends and family."

In her text to me, the girl had added *could use my guardian angel, Phil scares the hell out of me, really think I'm losing my mind.*

To Tomlinson, I said, "Take a look at what she wrote to me," and handed him my phone.

"That swine," my friend sputtered when he finished reading. He flopped his arms and tugged his hair. "Delia never heard of something called a restraining order? Hell, husbands have filed them against me for less cause. In a way, a relief, you know? God's way of saying, 'Time to move along, dummy.'" He rambled on about Phil, a man he'd never met but accused of being a fraud, who used Rasputin wiles to seduce his students.

I thought, *And you haven't?*

I said, "I'll call her, then I'm staying out of it."

"Right," Tomlinson shot back.

No, I meant it.

The days that passed by unnoticed flowed into late August. Hannah and I fell into a routine that was too pleasant, too friendly, and sometimes even sweet, to feel like a rut. I had learned not to pry about the man she was dating. But me being me, I made backdoor inquiries and found out that he was a widower, a respected orthodontist, with a medical ministry that provided free care to poor kids in Central America.

Well, *damn*. How do you compete with a saint who drives a Jag and likes to fish? For a week, I was in a foul mood.

Florida Trend magazine ran a feature on Mack's quirky little internet-free cottages. As a result, Playa del Temptation was booked almost solid through the holidays. The island got a nice business pop—badly needed. The ladies aboard *Tiger Lilly* reconciled and made up. The *For Sale* was taken down. Figgy somehow wangled a tryout with what turned out to be a women's professional softball team. Results were predictable, but rejection resulted in new friendships. The marina had been populated with lithe female athletes at recent Friday-night parties.

A Thursday that month was memorable for a different reason. Delia called. We were in the habit of talking about once a week, but I'd never heard her so excited. "They caught him," she said. "Did Tomlinson tell you? We just hung up. He's probably on his way to your place now."

"Caught who?" I asked. From the window I could see my pal's little yellow dinghy puttering toward the lab.

"Deville," she said. "It's on the internet, his picture.

His real name is . . . Hang on . . ." She had to check. "His name's Alonso Arkham. Christ, he looks like a Viking methhead. Best part is, I don't think—well, there's no proof anyway—that Tomlinson is his biological father. Just that his parents probably used the same fertility lab as mine and that other freak, Jayden. Isn't that great news?"

I'd been in the middle of trying to wrestle a dead mullet away from my dog. It took a second for my mind to reboot. A month ago, the guy who'd shot me with a speargun, Jayden F. Griffin, and two unnamed accomplices, had been indicted on five counts of murder. Terrorist bombings.

"He's in jail?"

Delia said, "Deville—the one *we* call Deville—yes. Well, in the picture, he's wearing handcuffs. The FBI caught him. Guess where? Bradenton, just across the bay from my apartment in St. Pete. Jesus Christ . . ." Her voice began shaking. "I just realized, that's only about fifteen minutes from the marina where we're renting the houseboat for the reunion. Doc, you don't think . . ."

Again, I had to put it together. She and her half siblings were only a week away from a party they'd been planning for a month. Rent a luxury houseboat out of the Skyway Boat Basin and overnight off some deserted island.

I said, "The FBI would've contacted you," which I believed, but was guessing, when I tried to reassure her.

Told the girl she had no reason to worry, the man was in jail, relax.

It didn't seem to help. "You're coming, aren't you?" she asked. This wasn't the first time she'd mentioned the reunion, which, in the written invitation, was now being called the Family Bio Launch Mixer.

I have a horror of social gatherings where I'm trapped in a confined space. In this case, a beating was preferable to a night on a houseboat loaded with my pal's genetic offspring. But I said, "Of course. I'll stay as long as I can."

"What's that mean?"

I said, "It's a safety issue. Tomlinson thinks—and I agree—it would be smart if I trailered my boat up there. Or rented one. A faster boat, in case someone needs to get back to shore in a hurry. I mean"—I tried to make a joke out of it—"what if you run out of beer?"

Delia didn't laugh. "Guess I can't argue, since he's paying for everything. Just as long as you're there . . . Doc?"—I felt the rubbery thud of a dinghy bang outside as she continued—"I'm starting to think you really are some kind of security ninja. I haven't heard a peep out of Phil since you did whatever you did. Are you sure you didn't threaten him?"

"Don't be silly," I said. "Hey, Tomlinson's here, gotta go."

"Hang on! The week before Labor Day, think you could come up to St. Pete a day early? There'll be eleven bio sibs. We're meeting at the Vinoy Thursday night, and I'm—"

"Eleven?" I was startled by the number.

"I know, the emails keep coming in, but only four of us are doing the Friday overnight. I'm so damn nervous, I could use someone to talk to before they start showing up. Meet at the hotel on Thursday before seven?"

It seemed a minor concession. "I'll try," I said. "Unless something comes up."

My dog, with the mullet still in his mouth, greeted my pal at the door by jamming the fish into his crotch. Tomlinson winced. "You damn brute . . . Geezus, it smells like a Liverpool whorehouse in here."

"You would know," I said. "Come on." My pal followed me across the breezeway into the lab. "That was Delia on the phone. No way in hell I'm spending a night on that houseboat, so I told her you wanted me to trailer my boat up there. Like a crash boat, for safety reasons. When she asks, you've got to back me."

"Coward," he said. "She told you about Deville?"

The dog plopped down at my feet as I opened my laptop. "And that she's somehow sure you and the guy aren't related. I don't understand how she arrived at that. How do you spell his name?"

"The most detailed story so far," Tomlinson replied, "was in this morning's *Washington Post*. An FBI sting got him and two other guys. Terrorists, anti-fertility-clinic nutjobs."

"I don't want to read about him, I want to see him," I said. "How do you spell his damn name?"

We could find only three photos of Alonso Arkham, all mug shots. He was as Delia had described: blond hair, matted Rasta-style, his neck a scarf of tattoos. The man had dull, dead eyes, black slits, as if something alive was in there waiting to crawl out. The jail wall had his height at six-foot-six.

"You sure it's the guy who jumped you at the cottages?" I asked.

Tomlinson was sure. The deflated look of pain on his face told me what I already knew. "He's your son, isn't he?"

"God help me . . . afraid so," he said. "But I didn't lie to Delia, exactly. There's no proof. See, the way it works is, the children of donors have a legal right to the records. Sperm donors don't have diddly-squat. I tried to confirm it, man. I really did. Even hired an attorney, but we got nowhere. That was back when I first found out I had a bunch of test tube kids out there."

My friend had not shared any of this with me.

I skimmed the *Washington Post* story. "Good. He's in on five counts, first degree. No bond. At best, federal prison for the rest of his life. And I agree. Why upset Delia by confirming what she's already scared shitless of?"

"Insanity," my pal said. The words came out as a whisper. "It's true, Doc. Insanity runs in families."

"So does genius," I countered, and closed the laptop. "As far as I'm concerned, this never happened. Just let it go."

"You keep saying that."

"It's a way of life," I responded.

Perhaps he thought I was referring to the mooring anchors hidden beneath the dock.

I wasn't. And I couldn't let it go. After an afternoon jog and rehab drills for my arm, I reviewed my research on Mensal Cryonics. This led to searches on other clinics. The practice of "confused insemination" was still being used to give fallow couples hope that both were the biological parents. Once a woman was pregnant, a more deceptive technique was to advise the woman that her blood levels showed she was probably pregnant before the procedure.

Well . . . who wouldn't want to believe?

A kindness, it seemed, until I typed in *lawsuits* and found out otherwise—all thanks to the popularity of DNA testing. Children conceived through artificial or in vitro fertilization who were now adults were suing the clinics. They were also suing the donors who had fathered them and, in some cases, the parents who had raised them.

Not all who had gotten pregnant with the help of the clinics were happy about the results either. Some claimed that embryos had been switched or the sperm donor had been misrepresented. It was a *No way can this child be ours* reaction that had resulted in an abnormally high percentage of kids put up for adoption.

There were a lot of pissed-off people out there still numbed by the results of their DNA tests and the shock of learning the truth. The numbers were unexpected. Since the early 1980s, about sixty thousand donor-conceived children a year were born in the U.S. alone. Multiply by five decades—three million test tube babies.

Wow. The mathematical probabilities weren't troubling, but the possibilities were.

I went back to Mensal Cryonics. I searched deeper. It was an international, multimillion-dollar company with a stable of attorneys, presumably, to block prying eyes. I wondered if they were aware that at least one of their "Ivy League matches" had produced a terrorist accused of multiple homicides?

I phoned an old and trusted source, Donald Piao Cheng. He's a computer wizard and sometimes analyst for various intelligence agencies. He owed me a favor, which the man acknowledged when he called me back.

"How are things in D.C.?" I asked.

He wasn't in D.C., he was in Maryland.

"Shitty," he replied. "That's why we're all moving to Florida. What do you have for me?"

Donald was not a man for niceties. I referenced today's story in the *Washington Post*, then Mensal Cryonics.

"I don't think they'd want the story to go public," I said. "Tell me what you can find out about the perp."

Donald replied, "Front door access is asking for trouble. I'll have to set up a gray hat conduit. When do you need it?"

I had no idea what a "gray hat conduit" was.

The sooner the better, I told him, but definitely before Labor Day weekend.

Donald asked, "How do you spell Alonso Arkham?"

TWENTY-ONE

On the first day of September, a Thursday, I dropped my boat at O'Neill's Marina on the St. Pete side of the Skyway Basin. Two hours later, I was waiting for Delia in the lobby bar of the Vinoy Hotel. The Vinoy is a city landmark, a classic old matron, ornate with marbled history. The structure resembles an eight-story wedding cake that's been frosted Easter egg pink. The veranda overlooks the waterfront of one of the most beautiful and vibrant cities in Florida.

I wore khaki shorts and a clean polo beneath a baggy, unbuttoned fishing shirt. When Delia entered, it took me a moment to recognize the aspiring ecologist and sailor. She was elegant in a black cocktail dress, heels, and pearls. Her cherry-black hair was layered up, a waterfall of curls that spilled onto spaghetti straps and bare shoulders.

An image flashed to mind—an oil painting again. She was one of those timeless, haunted beauties from the Renaissance. It was the fragility of her eyes more than anything.

"I'll go change," I said. Already I was thinking, *Change into what? Slacks and a different polo?*

She gave me a hug, a kiss on the cheek. "Don't bother. I just want to sit here and drink until the party starts. Have you seen Tomlinson yet?"

Their group had reserved one of the smaller ballrooms for this first meeting of the bio siblings. A buffet and an open bar. Doors opened at 8. It was now ten till 7.

I said, "He's holed up in the Presidential Suite on the top floor."

"Presidential? You're kidding. That sounds extravagant for a . . . It's hard to believe he really is a Buddhist monk."

"The mad monk, he calls himself," I replied. "Ordained. He really is. But the vows of poverty, chastity, and obedience—I think he sees them more as loose guidelines. The suite's got a balcony, and two bedrooms in case the party goes late. Now the dope's worried about how to dress . . . Risk being too splashy in a tux? Or come like the boat bum he is? I told him it doesn't matter, just not one of those damn sarongs."

Laughing, the girl swiveled to face me. She seemed

nervous, emotionally on edge and delicate. "Thanks. Thanks for being here. I feel better already." She placed a tentative hand on my knee, then used it to inspect the bottle the bartender had just delivered. "What are you drinking?"

I had a Beck's NA beer.

"Must be a sign," Delia said. "Yesterday, my shrink told me to avoid alcohol. Among other things. It was a tough session. You ever do therapy?" She got a tissue from her purse and dabbed at her eyes.

I asked, "Are you okay?"

"I will be. Oh hell, no. I've been a mess lately, Doc. Dad's funeral, and all the nitpicky details for this party. And that goddamn bully Phil, he's always a worry. I don't think the guy's right in the head."

"Bully? He's still calling you?" This was unexpected. Weeks ago, in a pointed yet polite phone conversation with the man, I had referenced Tomlinson's idea about a restraining order. After some blustering, Phil had been contrite, damn near on the verge of tears.

"That's the weird thing," Delia said. "Not a peep out of him, but, you know, it sorta hangs over me, the idea he could show up and make another big scene. It just adds to this thing that's been happening to me lately. The counselor, she says they're panic attacks. Tells me they're harmless. But that's impossible . . . She doesn't understand . . . There's no way to describe how it feels when . . . when all of a sudden, for no damn reason—"

The girl's voice broke. Tears welled. I watched her face go pale, and she began to hyperventilate. "Is it happening now?" I asked.

She nodded rapidly. "I've got to get out of here."

"Come on," I said. I signed for the beer. I also asked the bartender if I could take the pen and a blank order pad. On the way out, I put my arm around her waist. "I want you to try something for me."

"Can't," she said. "Have to walk. When it happens, it's like a chemical . . . this feeling, my head. I can't breathe. Like I'm dying."

We walked Bay Shore Drive past a flotilla of yachts. The streets were alive with sunset joggers, people with pets who smiled and actually said "Hello" or "Nice day." Could be their friendliness helped the girl. Or maybe it was what I suggested when we found a shady bench in the park across the street. I gave her the pad and pen and told her to write down a couple of math problems, then solve them.

She looked at me like I was nuts. "Can't hurt," I said. "Here, try this one." I scribbled a multiplication problem that contained decimals and equivalent fractions.

"This is stupid."

"We'll see," I replied.

Delia, when she concentrated, was a tongue biter. She solved the problem quickly, and I gave her another. Then a third problem, more complicated. Midway through, she paused, looked up at me. In a wedge of copper light, her eyes widened. "My god, it's gone. That chemical sensation. Like a wave—that's the way it feels—and I can't even . . ." She put her hand to her breast as if checking her heartbeat. "Doc, it *is* gone. How'd you know?"

"I didn't. Just that it works for me," I said. "Sometimes, for no good reason, our fight-or-flight response kicks in. It's a chemical thing."

"I don't know, man," she said. "No way, it can't be that simple."

"There's nothing simple about survival coding," I said, then tried to explain. "When it happens, our lizard brain takes charge and gathers data from the right brain, the creative side. Usually, the data is imaginary bullshit. But the lizard brain doesn't know the difference between fact and fiction, so we're flooded with adrenaline anyway. The reason this little trick works—when it works— is that math requires a shift to our left brain, the linear side. There's no emotion in the left brain, no fear. The lizard brain is immediately disengaged."

The girl sat back and gave me that look again: *Who are you?* "Will it come back?"

"If it does, try the math trick again. Your counselor was right—scary as hell, but it's a response to false data. Absolutely harmless."

She wanted to believe it. "Did you learn this in therapy?"

"It was more like a class," I said as an evasion. "Fear management, high-pressure situations, that sort of thing. A practical approach to dealing with panic."

"Why would a biologist take a class on fear management?"

That required a longer conversation. Terms such as *breath control* and *trigger press mode* could not be used. We talked on the way back to the hotel. Delia, as a precaution, also calmed herself with an occasional puff of cannabis oil from a vaporizer that she held like a cigarette.

The doors to the ballroom were open. Inside milled a dozen people, a few with familiar Tomlinson-esque features. "Go have fun," I said. "I'll stop back later."`

"You'd *better*," the woman said with emphasis. And a very different type of smile.

I made a slow lap around the hotel grounds. It was a security measure that also allowed me to skip the inevitable formalities. The group had had an hour to loosen up with a drink or three before I returned. In the corridor was a chair with a view through open double doors into the ballroom. It was an innocuous spot to sit with a Corona and observe before risking an entrance.

Inside, thirty people mingled, half brothers or sisters, some with their partners in tow. Genetic similarities were not obvious. The partners were easier to pick out. They stood apart, shielding themselves with fixed smiles. A few spun off into small groups of their own. They weren't part of "the test tube kindred."

Gradually, the siblings were separated, most near the bar, where Tomlinson held court. He wore baggy belted slacks and a sea-gray shirt, collar starched. His hair was tied back in a respectable ponytail. There was a lot of laughter, some raucous, most reserved. My pal appeared to be enjoying himself, but I could tell he was struggling emotionally. Around him were men and women, all in their mid- to late twenties, but with whom he had no real connection save for the salted flow of DNA.

A father orphaned by his past—that was the impression I got. He was the mystic cult hero who had written a book between visits to a sperm bank. Now here he was, live, a brilliant but haggard clown on exhibit.

The siblings knew the truth. Some resented it. They began to drift away to form their own group in this brightly lit space beneath crystal chandeliers. Among the disenchanted, there were no unifying flags. Expensive business suits mixed with blue-collar Levi's, sandals, and just-off-the-golf-course attire. A man with bushy blond hair wore a Red Sox cap. A woman with Asiatic features was dressed as if her next stop was the gym.

Delia sensed trouble. As hostess, she began to ping-pong between the various factions. A red-bearded man in a wheelchair also worked the room—the Baptist minister from North Carolina that I recognized from his church Facebook page. There was a brief, contentious exchange between him and a large woman with hibiscus blossoms woven into her hair—Imogen, I guessed, the holistic medicine practitioner from Arizona.

Tomlinson realized the vibe was turning sour. He panned the room in desperation, then made a decision.

He stood, grabbed two bottles of liquor, and turned them into bells by banging them together.

The place went silent.

"I've got an announcement to make," he said. "No . . . Actually, it's a confession. Let's get down to the ugly bones of the matter." Attendees cleared their throats while he struggled for words. "I'm . . . I'm not your father, not really. I never will be, and we all know it. So at least be kind to each other. You want to disagree with someone, choose me because I'm the most disagreeable goofball in this room."

Nervous laughter was the response.

"Look . . . think of me as the guy who happened to live upstream of the great futures I hope you all have. You want the truth? Okay, here it is—I'm a selfish, egocentric asshole. A boat bum who didn't realize how lucky I could have been all these years."

His audience began to warm.

"I wish I could go back in time and somehow change what I"—my pal began to choke up, so I started into the room while he kept talking—"I really want to somehow make amends. And I'm gonna try, that I promise, in a way your kids and grandkids might appreciate."

In the corner of the ballroom, an isolated trio suddenly paid attention.

"On the other hand," he continued, "I can't file this away as just another one of my major-league screwups. Not now. Not after having met you all. My god, I've never seen a more beautiful collection of people in my life. You could paint freakin' Disney World with the far-out auras in this room." He gazed and grinned.

Delia, the guy in the Red Sox hat, and a few others smiled back in response.

Tomlinson continued talking, shared some of the dumb mistakes he'd made in his life. A story about getting lost in a Key West cemetery with an escapee from a Cuban psych ward—Figgy—got a pretty good laugh. Then, tears streaming, he clanged the bottles together again. "No one gets to choose their genetics. But free will gives us other choices. Great choices, and tonight the choice is between rum and tequila. So let's drink up and have some fun."

The speech didn't win everyone over. Several couples left. But it did get the party started. I joined in for a while. Delia wanted to dance—no thank you. Imogen wanted to debate politics after a snide comment about my clothes and the length of my hair. Up close, she was an oversized woman in a gauzy, gothic gown bejeweled with stars. And she was wearing ruby red heels. Her offer was declined.

I gravitated to the minister and the guy in the Red Sox cap. I liked them. They were smart. They stood back and took it all in. Chester—"You can drop the 'Reverend' stuff," he instructed me—and Carlton, a financial adviser from Boston. Their questions about Tomlinson were general, at first, then more pointed. Mental health was a concern, since Chester already had a child and Carlton was engaged to be married.

I told the truth—a polished version—and they seemed to deal with it okay.

"Guess there's a bomb of some kind buried in most people's heads," the former Marine reasoned with a Carolina accent. "Or maybe some talent, a genius—could be—waiting to pop up like a flower. It's all about choices, like Daddy Tomlinson just said. That's the way I see it."

The mention of a bomb caught my ear. I also suspected that beneath the minister's baggy, unbuttoned shirt there might be a gun. A decorated combat vet with a prosthetic arm and a wheelchair had every right to take precautions. Even so, I stuck around until the room was cleared so the bio siblings could meet privately. By then, I was convinced that Chester knew a lot more about his internet kindred than he was willing to share with me, a stranger—a reticence that was protective, not threatening. He'd even come to Imogen's defense when I had asked about their confrontation.

"Don't blame her," he replied. "That girl's had a harder time than most of us. She's got a good heart, I'm hoping, and that's about all I can say for now."

His abruptness did not invite questions.

At 11, I did another security lap, then jogged up the stairs to my room.

———

A lively tapping on my door got me out of bed around 1 a.m.—Tomlinson stood there, grinning. "Hermano, did I wake you up?"

I replied, "Don't be silly. I had to get up and answer the door anyway." The irony went right over his head.

"Staying busy, that's my ol' pard. Got anything to drink in here?" He shuffled past me and began rummaging around in the honor bar. "What about ice? You mind calling room service?"

"How drunk are you?" I was pulling on my shorts in case there were stragglers.

"You kidding? I was on my best behavior tonight. Rationed myself to two beers and four tequila shooters. Dude, that Imogen can drink. Challenged me to a chugging contest. No way—not dignified, you know? She's still down there in the bar with a couple of the staff she took a shine to. What I'm afraid of is, that girl inherited one of my other weaknesses, too."

"It's a long, dangerous list," I agreed.

He stood, holding a handful of mini bottles. "Hey, tell room service to bring some kosher salt and a couple of limes, while you're at it . . . No, have them send it to my suite." Then fixed me with a pointed look. "She's in love with you, you know."

"Imogen?" The thought made me grimace. "She accused me of being a war criminal. Well, implied it any-

———

way. Those tequila shooters—were you drinking them out of a beer mug?"

"Not her, numbnuts. Delia. She's head over heels." Mini bottles clattered as he placed them on the desk where I'd been studying a chart of Tampa Bay. "I know sensitivity isn't your strong suit, but have you gone batshit blind, too? The poor kid gets all moony-eyed. I saw the way she pressed up against your arm—you *know* what I'm talking about. Want me to spell it out? *Elbow tit.* There, I said it. And it's damn disgusting, you ask me."

"Don't be crude," I warned.

"See?" he said. "There you go again. Doc, you've got to stop acting so noble around that girl. A few examples of what a tight-sphinctered dweeb you can be ought to set her straight. Is that too much to ask?" My pal sat on the bed I hadn't used, slapped at the desk, and caught the phone in midair.

"She has a crush," I said. "Nothing has happened. Nothing will."

Tomlinson had already moved on. He ordered a bunch of stuff from room service, instructing with a flourish, "That's right . . . Presidential Suite. Don't bother knocking, someone might be on the throne. No, using the head, amigo. The *toilet*." He hung up and his attention shifted to the chart of Tampa Bay. "What do we have here?"

"The houseboat party tomorrow night," I said. The chart had been folded to show a collage of islands off the southern tip of St. Pete. The Skyway Bridge separated the islands from the shipping channel and the bay, with the mouth of the Manatee River to the southeast.

"I know this area pretty well," Tomlinson said.

"Then tell me what you think. Delia wants to run the houseboat—just her and a couple of others aboard—from the Skyway Basin and meet you and the rest of the group here a couple of hours before sunset." I touched my finger to Madeline Key. "It's only about four miles. What bothers me is, why leave the dock so late?"

"You kidding? Hangovers," Tomlinson replied. "Besides, they don't want me along. Not really. And I don't blame them. You and me, we'll make an appearance, then split."

He hunkered closer to the chart. "It's a great area. Fort De Soto Park—yeah, man. Madeline Key is the entrance. It's a gunkholing paradise. A thousand acres of some of the most beautiful beaches in the . . . And I don't know how many islands . . . The kids will really get off on all the places to—"

I interrupted, "Yeah, but there's car access from the mainland. A road and a boat ferry. There'll be RV campers and tents. Not many people this time of year, but still . . ."

"So?"

To explain, I opened my laptop to a new chat page that Delia hadn't mentioned until tonight. Already, the page was loaded with party photos taken earlier in the ballroom. I ignored them and went straight to something else she or Imogen had recently posted.

"A calendar of events," I said. "Anyone can go to this page and find out when and where your group is meeting tomorrow afternoon. I didn't even realize until I got back here."

Tomlinson gave it some serious thought. "Deville—yeah, I get it. The worst of my bad seeds—Alonso Arkham. But he's still in a federal pen somewhere, isn't he? Unless you know something I don't."

I had yet to hear from my intel pal, Donald Piao Cheng, but I'd kept tabs on Arkham. "They had him at Wildwood Federal—that's up by Ocala. Yesterday, they shipped him to maximum security in Atlanta. He's gone for good. You would've been notified if there was a problem."

Tomlinson relaxed visibly, but agreed, "Still, yeah, potentially bad juju. The calendar of events—it needs to be deep-sixed. Too many prying eyes in this crazy ol' world." He glanced up. "Did you try calling Delia?"

"At this hour?"

"Why not?" The Zen guru bio dad fumbled around for his phone. He dialed and gave me an adolescent grin as he said to Delia, "Hello, beautiful lady. Are you awake and sober? Well, that's to be expected. Here—Mr. Excitement wants to speak to you. Say hi to Doc."

He pushed the phone into my hands, Delia, already midsentence, saying, ". . . so funny, isn't it? I was hoping you would call."

I replied, "It's me, Marion, not your . . . Not Tomlinson."

"I know. Where'd you disappear to, you strange man? Get your butt up to the Presidential Suite. Really nice marble floors, where, you know, a person can just stretch out and stay nice and cool."

Her speech was slurred.

"It has to do with your new chat page," I said. "Something needs to be removed, but it can wait until morning, I guess. What time are you leaving for the houseboat?"

The woman made an unpleasant mewing sound. Then she burped. "Ooooh, yuck. When I get up off the bathroom floor, I guess. Where are you?"

"In my room," I said. "You're not really laying on the floor, are you?"

"What room number?" she replied.

"Me? I'm on the second floor. Don't worry, Tomlinson is on his way." I pointed my friend toward the door.

Delia groaned a sleepy groan, asking, "But Doc, how are you going to hold my head out of the toilet from way down there?"

TWENTY-TWO

Spend the early-morning hours with a mop, a bucket, and a beautiful female drunk, any diversion at 5 a.m. was a welcome relief after standing guard over a woman who was finally sober enough to no longer be defenseless.

So I went for a lonely walk—or intended to. But across from the hotel entrance, in the shadows of the park, sat the Baptist minister and former Marine in his wheelchair, unattended.

It was two hours before sunrise. I would've kept going had he not spotted me first.

"Morning, Chester," I called out as I approached. "Are you up late or out early?"

The man waited until I was closer to speak. In the silence of a distant street sweeper, this struck me as odd.

He didn't want to be heard for some reason. Even odder was his response after a quick glance my way. "Morning, Doc," he said softly in his Carolina drawl. "How's Sister Delia doing?"

I was surprised he knew where I'd spent most of the night. "She'll have a headache," I said. "I ordered coffee and some tomato juice for her."

"V8 and Advil." He nodded. "Lord, I don't miss those days—'shrooms and beer used to be my weakness." I stopped to Chester's left as he noted my baggy, unbuttoned shirt. "Ask you something?"

"Sure."

"At the party, I wanted to, but we both know it's breaking the rules. What are you carrying? Glock woulda been my first guess—until I had a sit-down with Tomlinson last night. Now I'm thinking Sig."

His attention returned to a dark stretch of sidewalk that separated the park from Van Gogh swirls along the waterfront. Boats were moored there in a grid beneath a gaseous halo cast by the city across the bay, Tampa.

I answered, "And I'm supposed to say, 'What makes you think I'm carrying a gun?' Chester, what are you doing out here at this hour?"

He had inherited Tomlinson's gauntness, but his nose was more Lincoln-esque. Up close, facial scarring beneath the beard was more obvious. I wondered if the man had stepped on an IED.

"Watching her," Chester said. Someone had just appeared from the shadows and was walking away. "Come on. Pretend like you're pushing me."

"Well . . . okay."

"No, dummy, just pretend. Get your hands off my damn chair."

The man pivoted the wheels around and took off in pursuit. I had to trot to keep up. Only two possibilities came to mind—"Is it Imogen? Or did you have a fight with your wife?" I'd gotten only a quick look at his spouse in the ballroom. She was a thin woman with a good smile, but whose outdated clothing had added to her discomfort in an already awkward situation.

"Mama and me don't fight," he hooted. "We're too busy makin' love." Laughter, his voice low. The minister was enjoying himself. Gloves on both hands, he had found a rhythm on the chair's racing wheels—*slap-slap*—glide—*slap-slap*—glide. "Hurry up, Ford." This went on for a while. Then he hissed, "Okay . . . Stop, stop, stop!"

The man braked so abruptly, I nearly stumbled into the back of him. We had traveled the length of the park by then.

It *was* Imogen. For an instant, a streetlight colored her gown and ruby slippers. She crossed into the shadows, backdropped by the glass wall of a museum. Within a lighted room, an antique biplane was frozen in midair, suspended from the museum's ceiling. Imogen took a seat on a bench beneath a massive banyan tree as if waiting for the next flight out.

"Why are you following her?" I whispered.

"'Cause that girl's in trouble and my wife's plane doesn't leave until seven" was the reply. "Good—see there? She snuck out for a smoke. That's all." He made a clucking sound as Imogen lit a cigarette. "Crazy girl, she was all over my butt last night for dipping snuff, yet there she is. Gave me a lecture on vitamins, herbal cures, too—she really is a doctor, you know."

Chester sounded genuinely proud. He added, "From what I heard, she took a dislike to you, too, the moment you met, God bless her little heart."

Imogen flicked something off her tongue. She crossed her legs and blew smoke toward the stars.

"What kind of trouble?" I asked. "As in drugs? Or—I hope not—suicide?"

The minister made a *Hush!* gesture with his prosthetic hand. "Just watch for a second. That girl's been depressed—didn't come right out and admit it, but I can tell. Highs and lows. A lot of my new sisters and brothers got the same problem, turns out. Not so strange when you think it through."

He produced a can of Skoal and thumped it with his thumb. "We never saw each other until yesterday. Now I feel like I've been worried about them kids since the day we were born, just didn't know it." He offered me the can. "Care for a dip? I use pouches. Don't have to spit with pouches."

Since the day we were born—the remark stuck with me

as we observed the woman in silence. When Imogen lit a second cigarette and angled through the park toward the hotel, Chester decided it was okay to return via the sidewalk. Loose cover, he termed it, as if I would understand. Which I did.

"What, exactly, did Tomlinson say about me?" I asked. There was enough room on the sidewalk for us to travel hip to shoulder.

"You'd have to ask Tomlinson" was the reply.

Hannah had often used this same stubborn, Southern device to warn me about prying. But he loosened up when I responded, "Imogen's got a point. We're both judgmental jerks."

"Lord knows, ain't it the truth?" He laughed.

Suddenly, we had things in common. We talked about the military and guns for a while—he preferred Berettas but Glocks were cheaper. I mentioned Alonso Arkham and got the reaction I'd hoped for. Arkham was a disturbing subject that he and the others had discussed last night—a private conversation. That was made clear to me. He asked about Delia in a leading way. Then, without any prodding, told me more about Imogen. Not only had her DNA test revealed the truth about her biological father, the girl had received another shock—after being born to one set of parents, Imogen had been put up for adoption.

"Happens to a lot of us test tube kids," Chester said. "Folks don't get the sporty model they think they ordered, so they send the kid back. Son, you'd be amazed at some of the stuff I've learned since I found out. Me, it didn't matter so much. I was never close with my folks. Enlisted when I was seventeen, been on my own ever since. Why would I care who my real daddy is?"

This was something else we had in common. To encourage him to keep talking, I shared a blurred account of my own past.

"Yeah"—the man smiled—"Tomlinson hinted around, but, buddy ruff, you've got the eyes. Adapt, overcome, and improvise, huh? Three years after I said good-bye to the Rock Pile"—he was talking about Afghanistan—"I emptied my last bottle. Fish House Punch . . . Thunderbird. Got up, looked in the mirror, and told the worthless S-O-B staring back at me there's only one honorable way for a gimp to cure a headache." He tapped his hip. It had nothing to do with the catheter bag strapped there.

We were at the corner of Bay Shore and Fifth, waiting for the light to change at an hour when there was no traffic. Chester gave me a frank, searching look to confirm that I understood.

I said, "You made the right decision, Rev. Pickett. I'd like to meet your wife and son one day."

He appreciated that. "Oh, brother, I am blessed more than you could possibly know—unless you'd *like* to know. I'm not the sort to push—same, I've heard, with that fine woman you're trying to court. A fishing guide, is she? Now, that there would be quite a catch." He had a bubbly kind of laugh.

We crossed the street. It was nearly 6 a.m. Valet parking had come to life. A uniformed doorman waved from the distance. I feared the topic would switch to religion thanks to Tomlinson's big mouth. He had obviously shared my problems regarding Hannah, another born-again Christian.

Instead, the minister offered me his hand, and said, "Give Sister Delia a kiss for me, you hear?" Then gripped my hand harder so I couldn't pull away. "Doc . . . About her, you know, loose cover?"

I said, "Uhh . . . I don't how that applies."

"Think about it, buddy ruff. None of us are children—no matter what our Zen Buddhist daddy says." Chester's familiar gray eyes tightened a millimeter when he added, "I'm not a gimp and they're not cripples—we can take care of ourselves."

This was said so genially that only later did I wonder, *Was that a threat?*

I waited until a respectable 9 a.m. to place another call to my intel pal, Donald Piao Cheng.

Still waiting to hear something about the Alonso Arkham matter, I reminded him via voicemail. *Even if you don't have anything, give me a call.*

That afternoon, a Friday, I played the role of maritime tender for Delia and Imogen. They were aboard the

60-foot houseboat they'd rented, and I followed them to the gathering of hungover millennials awaiting us at Fort De Soto Park.

I was alone in my Pathfinder. Delia steered from a nifty little console atop the houseboat's upper deck. She was wearing shorts and a white tank top over a crimson two-piece swimsuit.

By then, the group of bio siblings had rallied. As we approached, there was a lot of waving, even a few shouts. Tomlinson, who had convoyed over by rental van, had staked out an isolated stretch of beach at the north point of Mullet Key. He motioned us toward a fishhook-shaped basin of sand. I scouted ahead to confirm the water was deep enough for a floating house that drew only three feet.

On the four-mile passage from the marina, Delia and I had stayed in touch by VHF. Our vessels were close enough now, I could look over and see sweat glistening on her long tanned legs. I pressed the squawk key and used the radio anyway. "Looks good—six feet plus in the middle," I informed her, "and the tide's still coming in."

"The chart's a little off," she replied into her handheld radio. "But, water's so clear . . . Yeah, I can see we've got good bottom. What an incredibly cool spot. I'm gonna swing around bow to the beach." She spun the wheel. Aft, twin Evinrudes clunked into reverse.

"Want me to set the anchor for you?"

Without looking over, the girl replied into the transceiver, "No, we've got it, Doc. Really. You've been such a help. Hey—if you stick around, maybe talk later?"

Delia was embarrassed, I decided, not dismissive. After the clumsy silence we had shared over lunch, our communication by radio almost resembled sparkling repartee.

"You bet," I replied, and signed off.

Gulfside, spaced along the beach, were picnic shelters with white-domed roofs that resembled Frisbees. The only shelter in use had been claimed by the bio siblings and their partners. A few hours ago, they'd fired up the grills. Coolers waited in the shade near a volleyball net. Missing was the boom box music I associate with such events. But then realized many attendees wore earbuds—reclusive, even here, among brothers and sisters they were just getting to know.

One by one, as I idled away, I matched their faces with the memory of people I'd seen last night. Not a stranger among them. Rev. Chester Pickett, in his wheelchair, had become their rallying point. He waved to me from the group clustered around him. I replied with a thumbs-up and kept going.

Tomlinson was waiting bayside where I tied up. "These kids today, huh?" he chuckled. "They're grilling tofu and bean sprouts instead of hot dogs. About half of them are into the health deal—holistic, none of that GMO crap. That's one of the interesting things I've noticed. We're a polar species in a polar universe, and genetics be damned. See where this is going?"

I was tired and preoccupied with what had happened last night, in no mood for a tutorial on human behavior. "I'm going to hang around and check the houseboat one more time before they head out," I replied. "Then I'm starting back to Sanibel. I don't see any threat here."

Fort De Soto Park is comprised of five islands linked by narrow asphalt roads. There'd been very little traffic on this Friday before Labor Day weekend. Only a handful of tents and RVs at the campground.

Tomlinson hesitated as if struck by something I'd said, then continued with his insights on polarity. Imogen and Chester became examples. They were siblings coded as spiritual and linear opposites, yet good people both. He mentioned three or four more of his DNA offspring by name and said they, too, were a study in contrasts.

I said, "I don't have your mystical gifts. What's your read on Chester? He carries a gun, did you know that? I like him and all, but he's wound pretty tight."

"So are you. What's the problem?"

"Uhh, I'm not sure. He'll be on the houseboat tonight. It's got wheelchair access to the lower deck." That didn't explain my concerns, so I tried to re-create the conversation we'd had that morning. Even as I went through it, the things Chester had said didn't sound the least bit sinister.

"In other words, you're worried about Delia," Tomlinson summarized. He stared at me, did a thing with his eyes, allowed them to glaze. His voice softened. "I appreciate the way you took care of her last night. Even when I'm drunk, I recognize patience when I see it. The respect you showed, too. There aren't many guys who would've tucked a woman that pretty into bed, then slept on the couch after mopping up the bathroom. Don't think I didn't notice."

I replied, "And don't think I didn't hear you snoring when you fell asleep." He knew what I was implying—I could've climbed into bed with her unseen. Delia had invited me to do exactly that, but only the lowest of the lowlife types would've accepted.

"That's cool," he said, and seemed to mean it. "As of now, it's officially none of my business."

I almost started to say *It never was* but held back. "Look, Delia's an unusual person, and I like her. She's had some problems, but we have a few things in common. That's all. End of story."

My pal has an irritating way of effecting an air of deep understanding. "If you say so. There are no rules when it comes to love."

I said, "Actually, there are, you've just never followed them. Okay, she's got a crush on me, I agree. If I let myself, maybe I could fall into that trap, too—rationalize all kinds of excuses that we'd both regret later. But she's your daughter, for god sakes. That means something to me. Besides, it's not worth screwing up my chances with Hannah."

"DNA," he replied, "doesn't constitute parenthood. That much I've learned. What I think is, you should stay on the houseboat tonight. I'm not going. Those kids like me in small doses, and who can blame them? But Delia wants you there." The smile on his face was irritating. "Come on, poncho. Why don't you just admit you're halfway in love with the girl already?"

I said, "Because I'm not, which is why I'm heading back to Sanibel. Do you really think I'd go off and leave her if I was?"

I could feel my friend's shrewd old eyes on my back as I walked away. What he might have said, but had the kindness not to, was *Don't you always?*

Imogen was in the galley, with a phone to her ear, when I stepped aboard the houseboat. Her voice contained a gaiety that cut through fiberglass walls. "Of course I'll meet you at the gate," I heard her say. "Oh hell, don't worry about the money. The old dude . . . Yeah, he's paying for everything."

I didn't like the woman to begin with, and that really pissed me off. I stood there, hoping to hear more of this one-sided conversation. Unfortunately, she turned and caught a glimpse of me through the bulkhead window.

"Gotta run," she said, aware that I could hear every word. "Tommy's buddy, Capt. America, just showed up. Yeah, probably wants to play cop again. No . . . it's a mystery to me . . . I'll tell you about it when we have more time."

The woman hung up as I did the polite thing, which was to knock before entering. She had changed into modish black harem pants, tied at the ankles, and a black T-shirt that read *Heavily Meditated.* "Delia's taking a nap," she informed me. "I made her some valerian tea from Starbucks, so don't wake her up. We have a long night ahead of us."

I said, "Mind if I ask who you were talking to?"

Of course Imogen minded, which I was prepared for. "See, the thing is, the way the houseboat contract reads, we need to turn in a list of names of people who will be aboard tonight. If someone plans on showing up late, might as well tell me now, huh?"

"That's idiotic," she replied.

Cheerful concession can be the best way to deal with contentious people. "Oh, I agree," I said. "But if it wasn't for stupid rules, there'd be no need for attorneys or insurance forms, and all that crap. I feel like a dope for even asking."

That got the pretense of an understanding nod, at least. "It'll just be four or five of us," she said, "no one you haven't met."

I couldn't tell if she was lying. "Very helpful," I said.

"Now all I have to do is write down the names. Or . . . I don't suppose you could make a list? Just names and phone numbers. I need to take one more quick look around, then I'll be out of your hair."

Up close, Imogen had a wide, handsome face, a hint of Tomlinson's jawline. She also had his theatrical gift for employing paranormal bullshit when needed. She took a moment to inspect my aura. "Who are you? I mean, who are you really in the deepest seed that people like you always try so hard to hide? Not that it matters. Last night, the moment I saw you, I knew you were a narc, a cop—one of those—the same thing. You've already snooped through every part of this boat. What are you really after—bust us for so-called drugs? Or is this about getting into Delia's pants?" She watched the insult hit home, before adding, "If it makes you feel better, that asshole minister of a half brother will be around to make sure we don't have too much fun."

What Tomlinson doesn't have is a mean streak.

An angry, troubled young woman—Chester had been right about her. I remained unruffled. Explained that the beach area closed at sunset. Outside, the group was packing up. Some would move to the camping area that had all-night access. Those who didn't leave would have to come aboard the houseboat soon. I smiled and extended my hand. "Why don't we start over? I'm just trying to make sure you have a safe trip."

I might as well have been offering her a snake. Fortunately, Delia came down the spiral staircase that led top-side. She had just showered. Wet hair stained the gray beach wrap tied at her neck, and she was barefoot.

"Hey—what's the matter with you two?" The girl eyed us both, then came toward Imogen with her arms outstretched. "Come on, sis, he's not the enemy. Doc's like a big old harmless dog, just trying to help. Don't be cross with him."

They embraced. Imogen held on tight with real affection before pulling away. "They're all dogs," she muttered, teary-eyed, for some reason, but then laughing. "Okay, if you say so. Apparently, it's time to pack up."

Delia waited until the woman had stepped off the gangway to say, "Don't be hard on her. Imo has some issues she's trying to work through. We all do."

I said, "She's meeting someone at the gate later—the campground, I assume. Any idea who it is?"

This question was mildly irritating, I sensed. "Carlton, probably. The Red Sox fan? He didn't get up until four this afternoon . . . Doc"—she gave me a friendly hug—"could you just lighten up a bit? I was hoping we could talk in private, just the two of us, for a while."

"No problem," I said. "In fact, why don't you anchor the houseboat here for the night? You're not actually on the beach, so they can't kick you out of the park."

"Mind your own business," she seemed to joke, but she wasn't joking. "I've got the trip all charted. In a way, I'm glad you and Tomlinson aren't going. The sibs and I have some serious stuff to hash out. I'm afraid there's going to be a lot of tears, all sorts of dramatic crap I normally hate, but we've got to get through it."

"If you're worried," I said, "I can follow you in my boat, curl up on the deck for the night. Really, I wouldn't mind. I always carry mosquito netting, all the emergency gear, in case I get stranded."

Delia found that humorous. Her eyes sparkled in a coquettish way. "Of course you do, dear. Give me your hand. And no more questions. I want to show you something."

"What?"

"You'll see."

She led me up the stairs, topside, on a boat I'd already gone through, every nook and cranny, at the boat basin three hours earlier. Forward was the tiny captain's suite. She opened the door and didn't close it until we were inside. The settee table had been collapsed to form a queen bed. The bed was recently made, the cabin still steamy with the scent of shampoo from the closet-sized shower.

I did a slow one-eighty. "Show me what?"

Even before Delia did what she did, I knew what would happen. "I was going to pretend not to remember details about last night," she started softly, "but I do. If you hadn't gotten all noble and cold, what I wanted to show you is this—"

I caught her wrists just as her fingers found the bow

that held the beach wrap taut on her shoulders. "Delia, let's not—" I started to say.

Too late. She pulled the string. Sheer gray cotton snagged momentarily on her breasts, then dropped to her ankles.

The woman maintained eye contact as a challenge to me. "I felt like an adolescent fool last night when you walked away. Treated me like a helpless little I-don't-know-what. Then you promised me something, remember?"

"You were drunk," I said.

"I asked you to kiss me good night. You wouldn't do it. Said, 'In the morning, if you don't change your mind.'" She stepped back, wanting me to see her body, the swollen secrecy of tan lines, the salted contours. "I haven't changed my mind," she said. "And I'm sober now."

I stood there dumbly for several uncomfortable beats—far too many. The woman's expression slowly changed. Then her face contorted, mortified by her behavior or yet another rejection. "Oh my god, how stupid can I get? I'm acting like a crazy woman again."

As she lunged for her dress, I took her in my arms and stood her up so we were face-to-face. "Good morning, Delia," I said. Then I kissed her.

TWENTY-THREE

The boat ramp at O'Neill's Marina on the St. Pete side of the Skyway Bridge closes at 8, so I couldn't linger until sunset with Delia and her siblings while they decided who was going to overnight on the houseboat and who wasn't.

"What are you so damn antsy about?" Tomlinson asked me. "If I didn't know better, I'd guess you've been snorting Adderall. Don't have any, do you? I could use a pick-me-up."

We were alone aboard my Pathfinder. The deck was piled with bags of post-party trash to be dumped before I started back to Sanibel. He staggered forward toward the cooler. "Geezus, remind me to never whack off in a test tube again . . . Got any beer left?"

I said, "It's right next to the cocaine and illegal weapons. I'll take a Diet Coke, while you're there."

He returned to the swivel seat to my right, his Corona already half empty. "I told you they don't want us around," he confided. "Like kids waiting for the adults to leave so they can tell secrets. Nothing weird about that." When I took yet another look over my shoulder, he chided, "Hey—what is it with you? They'll be fine. Cripes, it's not like you'll never see her again."

Delia, he meant. He sensed that our relationship was different now. And it was. Instead of the looks and nudges we had shared for weeks as secret confidants, there was a new and palpable coolness between us. To me, it signaled that I'd done something really stupid and she resented the embarrassment I had caused us both.

Was I reading too much into the sudden change? The woman had been eager to say good-bye and be off with the family she was just getting to know—it wasn't my imagination.

"I guess that might be possible," Tomlinson said agreeably, "if you *had* an imagination, which you don't. Stop worrying. Life flows on, man. That's about all I can tell you."

By then, we had cleared the no-wake zone off Indian Key. I was turning toward the boat basin inside Maximo Point. To the west, the sun cast a molten funnel that darkened the first shadows of dusk. To our right, the lights of the Sunshine Skyway streamed on. The bridge was a circus tapestry of color that resembled a galactic trapeze act. The shipping channel provided an animated gray net below.

"Something's not right," I said. "I like Chester, I really do"—I had to organize my thoughts—"but this morning we were talking about Imogen, and he said he'd been worried about her since the day she was born. No . . . said he'd been worried about 'those kids' since the day *we* were born."

"That's pretty darn articulate for a Southern Baptist," Tomlinson joked. "Hey—we've already been through this." He was getting impatient. "Man, you don't think my sensory receptors would be on fire if my own flesh and blood were in danger? Give me some credit. My powers aren't what they used to be, but I haven't lost all my Indian skills."

"And how often are you wrong?"

My pal has a gift for articulate observation, it's true, that sometimes appears to border on mysticism, but he is occasionally far off the mark—as we both knew.

"Well . . . shit the bed," he conceded. "If you want, call the guy. Tell Chester what you're worried about. Talk to him, lay it all out. There's still time."

"What do you mean?"

Tomlinson said, "On the phone, coconut head."

"I know, but there's some kind of time limit?"

"They're doing the kumbaya thing," he explained. "All phones off, once the houseboat leaves, but they might still be waiting on the pizza delivery guy. The campground doesn't close at eight."

I was idling into the boat basin. Immediately, I shifted into neutral. "Delia didn't mention anything about pizza. And I asked her—made of point of asking—if anything had been delivered to the boat. She said absolutely not. In fact, I warned her not to accept any deliveries."

"It's just pizza," he replied. "That was my going-away surprise. Five big pies, all vegetarian. Imogen knew. I told her to make excuses until the delivery guy shows."

"Imogen? Are you out of your mind?"

Tomlinson was getting flustered. "One of us sure as hell is. Geezus frogs, shallow up, dude. There's nothing dangerous about pizza—" He hesitated, suddenly uncertain. "Well . . . depending on the mushrooms, I guess. Yeah, you're right. Go ahead, call. Call Delia, see if they've already left."

I reached for my phone. It was in my tactical bag, not my pocket. I ripped it out of its waterproof case. Notification alerts vibrated in my hand.

I swiped the screen open. There were several voice messages. One was from Hannah, the second from Delia, and another from an unknown area code—910. Only one message demanded immediate attention. It was from Donald Piao Cheng.

I hit play and pressed the phone to my ear.

"Damn . . . this is not good," I said softly. Cheng had just provided me with some shocking information.

Now my pal was worried. "What's wrong, Doc?"

I spun the boat around, then throttled onto plane. "Take my *phone*," I said over the noise of the engine. "Hit Delia's number on REDIAL. Tell them to get the hell off that houseboat."

"Why?"

"Just do it, damn it."

Tomlinson redialed. The blank look on his face told me the call went immediately to voicemail.

"That guy—Alonso Arkham?—when he was born, it was a multiple delivery," I said, which might have been heard as an accusation. "Arkham has a twin. They were separated at birth. That's all I know for now."

My pal either didn't want to believe it or couldn't pull the threads together. I took the VHF mic from the console and pressed it into his hands. "Sorry, buddy. Try to raise someone on the houseboat."

We crossed Boca Ciega Bay doing fifty-plus, the lighted Skyway to our left. High above, miniature cars traveled at Interstate speed, which gave the illusion that we were being held back by a dark, unnatural tidal anomaly.

Tomlinson tried over and over on the radio, calling, "Break, break, channel 16. I'm trying make contact with a houseboat in the Fort De Soto Park area. A double-decker with twin Evinrudes. Does anyone have a visual?"

He tried other descriptions. He tried channel 21 alpha, his ponytail flagging in a wind that swept his words away.

"Crapola," he muttered, and gave up. "Doc, maybe we're worried for no reason."

"Use your cell and call Delia again. Anyone who might be aboard," I said. Our next move—although I didn't say it—was an emergency call to St. Pete Coast Guard.

My friend ducked behind the console and started dialing.

The sun was gone. The entrance into Tampa Bay is a major shipping channel. Night markers blinked on, a horizon of robotic, pulsing colors—red, white, green. Confusing colors, unless you have spent a lot of time at night at sea. A cruise ship was being piloted outward bound. It was a towering neon skyscraper that could crush a houseboat if the skipper had lost an engine or made the mistake of allowing a novice to take the helm.

Someone suicidal, perhaps.

I found the cut into Bunces Pass. Roared beneath the bridge to Madeline Key, indifferent to the bobbing *No Wake* buoys. From a quarter mile away, I confirmed that the houseboat was no longer anchored where we'd left it. I slowed and made a hard turn toward the Fort De Soto

Park camping area, then buried the throttle because of what I saw.

"What the hell are the cops doing there?" Tomlinson wondered.

Blue police strobes echoed off trees midway down the shoreline. The shore was dotted with RV campers, and flickering Colemans marked a row of tents. An EMT vehicle was there, too. But not the houseboat.

"Is that where your group is camped?" I asked.

I knew it was. Tomlinson tugged at his hair. "Drop me off, I'll run up and see what's wrong."

We were in a narrow bay, no docks, just shells and mangroves. A good place for kayaks, not powerboats. I trimmed the bow and tilted the engine high. Doing thirty, we skated around a spoil bank on a skittish starboard chine in a foot of water.

The hull of my boat banged hard on the bottom. Tomlinson didn't wait for me to shut down before going over the side. He put a fist to his ear to mimic a phone and hollered, "I'll call you. Don't go off and leave me, man." He slogged toward shore.

"Find out where Delia is," I hollered back.

It was so shallow, I had to get out and push my boat into deeper water. From shore, a Q-beam flared. The beam searched and damn near blinded me. "Sir . . . Hey, you! This is a no-wake zone. I need to see your registration."

In the glare was the silhouette of a policewoman.

I shielded my eyes, and called, "Sorry—talk to my friend, Officer. He'll explain what's going on."

The spotlight tracked me until the woman had intercepted Tomlinson. The light went off. When I was in muck up to my knees, the Pathfinder's hull shifted with buoyancy. I climbed aboard and fired the engine. Wooden stakes marked the channel out of what my chartplotter identified as Mullet Bayou. At the mouth of the bay was a view of the Gulf of Mexico, an inky rim attached to a high, fading strand of orange.

It was an hour after sunset.

With the engine running, I waited. An outgoing tide tried to carry me westward, so I anchored with the power pole. Finally, Tomlinson phoned.

"Everyone's going to be okay," he said. "I know where the houseboat is. Pick me up, we'll go together."

"What the hell happened? I can't get in that bay again, the tide's falling."

"Food poisoning," he replied. "At least, the cops are willing to buy it for now, depending on what the EMTs say."

Geezus, the pizza! I thought. "You're covering for someone. Tell the truth."

"I am, so stop being such a hardass. It's nothing serious. Two of our people are going to the ER just in case. The rest are sort of, you know, strung out."

"You mean strung out or hallucinating?" I demanded. "You wouldn't have mentioned mushrooms if you hadn't suspected. Damn it, Tomlinson, someone's trying to kill your whole family . . . Is Imogen there?"

"We don't know it was her," he argued. "Doc, we're not squealing to the cops about this. The 'shrooms could have been a sort of bonding experiment. Or an accident. I'm eating a piece right now and it's actually pretty good."

"I didn't accuse Imogen," I responded, "I said 'someone.' And you're a fool if you don't spit that crap out right now. Where's the houseboat?"

Tomlinson refused to answer. "How about I catch a ride to the bridge? There's plenty of water at the parking lot. Pick me up there."

He meant the ferry landing. It was only a few hundred yards up tide. I was tied there when the headlights of a Pinellas County Sheriff's cruiser panned the area, then accelerated toward me.

Oh damn . . .

But it was okay. Tomlinson hopped out of the cruiser, waved his thanks, then waved again after he had stepped aboard.

"The houseboat's supposed to be anchored off Egmont Key," he said. "Know where it is?"

I did. The illuminated screen of my GPS confirmed the island's location. It was Gulf side, a few miles southwest.

"Hold on," I said.

Tomlinson grabbed a windshield bar. "And, for god sakes," he said, "pay attention to the no-wake buoys. That cop's got the hots for me and I don't want to have to lie to her again."

TWENTY-FOUR

Egmont Key sits offshore, alone at the mouth of Tampa Bay. It is an uninhabited barrier island, amoebic in shape, narrow, two miles long, with an abandoned lighthouse station at the northernmost point.

"See it?" Tomlinson stood on bare tiptoes and pointed.

"What?"

"The lighthouse, man. It's right there."

Ahead was a confusing array of night markers—red, white, and green beacons.

"Are you hallucinating?"

"No . . . Yeah, a little. Very mild, but I'm cool. The tallest light, man. It blends in with the stars."

I said, "You shouldn't have eaten that stupid pizza," but then had to agree. Visible from two miles away was the old Egmont light tower, 80 feet high. Every fifteen seconds, a fixed white flasher strobed.

"We'll have to get closer to find the houseboat," I said. "I hope to hell you're right."

My friend was. The houseboat was there, anchored to the south of what the GPS showed as Quarantine Pier. But first we raised the tower itself and the remnants of the keeper's quarters.

That building, too, had been abandoned after twenty decades of hurricanes, wars, and tropical hardships that included a bout of yellow fever in 1878. As I knew from my files, the fever had started concurrently with one of the worst red tides in history. Lethal algae had plagued the peninsula for more than a decade.

I increased speed to 4,500 RPM. The island shrunk the horizon into charcoal strokes of casuarinas and palms. Stars formed a canopy. Jupiter was bright on the elliptic, Saturn a thumb's width behind. I nudged the throttle back when I saw double-decker lights anchored close to a beach half a mile away.

"That has to be them," I said. "Take the wheel." We switched places. I opened a locker on the console and found the night vision headgear. A 9mm Sig Sauer went into a holster belted to the small of my back.

"Oh . . . shit-oh-dear," Tomlinson said several seconds later. He was looking to starboard. "I hope to hell that's the mushroom fairy playing tricks and not that lady deputy sniffing around."

In the distance, flashing blue lights hobbyhorsed toward us. I didn't need night vision to confirm it was law enforcement of some type.

"Darn it, Doc! Please tell me you didn't call the cops. Delia—all of them—are going to be seriously pissed off."

I had tried to summon help. From the bridge, I'd radioed St. Pete Coast Guard, but had been unable to provide the houseboat's location or details of an actual emergency. The watch officer had told me to check back. "It wasn't me," I said. "Maybe there's something else going on out here." I gave him a nudge. "Move—I'll take the wheel."

Blue lights continued to close as I dropped the Pathfinder off plane and plowed toward the houseboat. It became a tactical race. I wanted to get Delia and the others ashore in case something—an explosive, perhaps—had been planted to supplement the poison mushrooms.

A bomb . . . ?

I backed the throttle to idle. "We can't just go charging up there," I said. "We'll use the trolling motor."

"Why?"

"What if the wrong person sees us? They might spook and do something really stupid."

Tomlinson didn't get it. A bomb could be detonated manually. A cabin doused with gasoline could be torched. I killed the engine—but too late. On the upper deck, houseboat windows flickered with what I hoped was an array of candles. A door on the boat's lower level swung open. A hunched figure exited outside onto the aft patio deck. The figure seemed to pivot toward us and waved with both arms.

"Who's that?" Tomlinson cupped his hands to his eyes. A moment later, he hollered, "Hello, boat! It's us, me and—"

I threw the throttle ahead before he could finish.

"Jesus Christ!" my pal yelped.

"Get ready to fend off," I told him.

Pulling abeam another vessel at speed is tricky. I powered forward as if my intention was to ram. Just before impact, I spun the wheel in full reverse. My boat skated sideways, came to a stop until our wake caught us, then we banged together, hull to hull. When Tomlinson grabbed the houseboat's safety railing, I used the gunnel as a step and vaulted aboard.

"Hey—whoa, stop right there, mister! Who the hell are you crazy people?" a man's voice demanded.

The galley lights were on, not bright. I was looking down at Chester Pickett in his wheelchair. The pistol aimed at my chest was a Glock, him having admitted as much that morning.

"Ford . . . That you, buddy ruff? My Lord . . ." Uneasy laughter allowed him to take a deep breath. "I thought you were drug pirates, the way you charged up here." He lowered the weapon, adding, "You can show me your other hand now. You ain't gonna need that Sig."

I made a show of straightening my shirt until the Glock vanished somewhere beneath the man's catheter bag.

I said, "Where're Delia and the others?" The boat's lower cabin area appeared to be empty. No music—an odd silence on a vessel that smelled faintly of weed and vomit.

Tomlinson was cleating off, starboard to portside.

Chester replied, "You sure enough don't check your phone messages, Ford. You're the first one I called." He peered beyond me, where blue strobes showed a boat dropping off plane. "Thank the Lord," he said. "I been on the phone with the Coast Guard for half an hour. Doc"—he spun his wheelchair around—"get up there and check on 'em. They're all either sick or freaking out because of some bad pizza, I'm pretty sure. And my gimpy ass can't make it up the winding staircase."

I had started inside when a chilling thought stopped me. "Why aren't you sick, Reverend?"

Chester didn't appreciate the insinuation. "'Cause I'm not a damn vegetarian. What the hell, man! Didn't I already tell you I'm wary of 'shrooms and that sort of crap? Now, get going. Imogen's in a bad, bad way."

Tomlinson came in, saying, "She'll only freak worse if she sees Doc. Trust me"—he gave Chester a pat on the shoulder—"I've dealt with this too many times to count. Talk the freaking souls down gently, that's the key."

"Hold on," I said. Next to the microwave was a fire extinguisher. I snapped it free. "Take this just in case," I told him, and he went clumping up the stairs.

The Coast Guard response vessel was still several hundred yards away, coming toward us. "The first thing they'll ask," I said to Chester, "is, do you have weapons aboard? That will take up a whole lot of time. But they've got no reason to check my boat. So what's our smartest move, you think?" I extended my hand, palm up.

To my relief, the former Marine agreed with a shrug. He cleared his pistol and handed it to me butt first. Next came the magazine. I locked both of our guns beneath the console of the Pathfinder, then returned to the houseboat and asked about Delia.

"She's the one who felt it first," he said. "They ate pizza on the way out—her, too, I guess, while she was topside driving. After we anchored, we met down here as a group." He indicated a sitting area inside. "I had something important to say. I was telling them the hardest part. And she . . . Well, I'd already told Imogen, which was a big mistake. Then Delia got this weird look on her face. She started to panic, then Carlton puked. It was like dominoes after that. That's when I knew what my sister had probably done."

"Your *sister*?" Until then, I thought I'd understood Donald's message about multiple births. "They're both your *half* sisters."

Chester shook his head no, and his attention shifted to what we would soon have to deal with.

On the Coast Guard vessel, a spotlight flared and began to search. The duty officer used the PA to identify herself and asked if there was a Rev. Pickett aboard. Together, Chester and I waved the Coasties in. We were very busy for the next hour. A medic with a red gear bag came aboard, demanding, "Where are they?"

I led him up the spiral staircase into a bizarre tableau of tiny staterooms, doors open, and a party deck. There, Carlton and two other men sat in their own upchuck. They had their arms around each other, giggling, as they stared at a bank of guttering candles.

Behind us, Tomlinson exited a room and summoned the medic. "In here. She's the worst, I think," he called. "She might need to be medevaced."

He sounded panicked. And I was starting to panic, too.

I got to the door first. Imogen lay on the bed, breathing, but deathly pale. My friend had turned the woman on her side to prevent aspiration. "Delia?" I asked, "Where is she?"

Now I was worried that Delia had possibly leaped from the top deck. But no, she was in the captain's suite, curled up in the closet-sized shower she had used that afternoon. There were more candles. I put them out and carried her to the bed. At first, she battled me. Then her eyes focused, but they were terror-crazed. "Oh, Marion, I tried and tried," she wept. "We're all crazy . . . I don't blame you for not wanting me."

I pulled the woman close and made comforting noises. There was a long wait for the ceiling fan roar of a helicopter. A pair of EMTs in jumpsuits arrived. While they worked on Delia, they reassured me. Before they made me leave, I noticed writing inside the shower stall done with a Sharpie—a whole wall of cryptic figures.

Math problems.

On the aft deck, Chester was thumping his can of Skoal. I told him what I'd been told—Delia and the others would be okay. Imogen, though, would have to be airlifted. Tomlinson had found an empty bottle of Ambien next to her bed.

"My sister couldn't handle what her conscience wouldn't let her do," the minister reasoned softly, then explained.

He, Imogen, and Alonso Arkham—a brother they had never met—were triplets. They'd been separated at birth by a disappointed couple who had demanded a refund from Mensal Cryonics. That was the tough news he'd had to share with Imogen. The psychedelic mushrooms, Pickett believed, was her misguided attempt to provide a bonding experience. When the night started to go terribly wrong, he told me, Imogen had freaked and overdosed on pills.

"I don't want Tomlinson to know," he added. "Not about what I think Imogen tried to do, but the other part. It's not his fault some rich people chose some guy named Deville from a catalog."

Touched by this good man's kindness, I replied, "As far as I'm concerned . . ." and let the sentence trail off.

He understood.

TWENTY-FIVE

That autumn, blocks of time passed by unnoticed—and they were good times indeed. I worked at being a responsible father. Days when Hannah chartered, I was there. Nights, too, when she would allow me to stay. This ended when we came close to reconsummating what had been a crazed chemical attraction.

Close. That's all.

The celebrated fishing guide had been plied with a glass of wine. I had sent her mother, Loretta, to the guest cottage with a smuggled freshly rolled joint. The village of Gumbo Limbo was decorated for Halloween. It was a black, windy night with a moon. Hannah, in my arms, had caught herself just before teetering over the physical brink.

"Marion . . . stop. I'm dating someone and you know it. I can't do something that I won't do with . . . *Please* . . ."

Do with him. This was implied—that damn respectable orthodontist again. The widower. The saint with the medical ministry.

While the woman gathered her blouse and bra, I had risked an ultimatum.

"Darling, I'm the father of our son. You've got to make up your mind."

Hannah is one of the independent ones.

She did—a third refusal to marry me.

That winter, the flow of day to day was interrupted by a few memorable parties, a booming holiday season, and a second reunion of the bio siblings in late December. The event was held in St. Pete at the Vinoy Hotel. I didn't attend. Five additional Tomlinson heirs did attend, along with the original seven, including Imogen.

Why are you avoiding me? Delia had demanded in a voicemail message from the bar. *Doc, you can't just go off and disappear.*

Actually, disappearing is part of my trade. On that night, I'd been packing to leave Nassau. As Morris Berg, I had spent several days brokering a deal with an all-too-eager Rayvon Darwin. Revenge is not part of my trade. Nor is exacting justice.

But Delia was right. I was avoiding her. The girl's persistent phone calls, her unexpected visits to the lab, had become too much to deal with. We had been confidants, not lovers—aside from one single and all-too-memorable kiss.

Even my tattered sense of morality knew that such a relationship was wrong. I feared that Delia's determined dependency on me, a much older man, was an unhealthy tangent that might stunt the future she deserved.

Or so I told myself. This rationalization became a handy excuse to escape to the Bahamas and tie up loose ends.

Five days after I left Nassau, Rayvon was intercepted at Palm Beach and charged with drug trafficking by U.S. customs. They'd found ten kilos of cocaine in a bogus diplomatic pouch. The drugs had been paid for in advance with untraceable gold ingots.

My conscience was clear. As Tomlinson had said, when big money is involved, even the best people can turn dangerous. This was a warning that I repeated to my pal on a cold, windy night in January, a few weeks after the party in St. Pete. We were alone in the parking lot and had just returned from the rum bar. Down the shoreline, the marina was buttoned up, the temperature a frigid fifty-some degrees.

"They know you plan to leave them a bundle in your will," I said. "And I still don't trust Imogen. What makes you think she's not lining up a bunch of deadbeats to take advantage of your millions?"

I blew into my hands for warmth. The marina's Christmas lights gave the illusion that it might snow. I was eager to get going. Via text, Hannah had requested that I deactivate the lab's alarm system so she could wait for me inside, but I wanted to impress upon my friend the danger he was inviting.

Unlike me, Tomlinson's idea of "personal protection" did not require a holster.

He replied, "I don't care if they take advantage. That's what I want to do—give every penny away. Doc, you don't appreciate the big picture. This all fits in with my ultimate goal—to one day disappear without a trace. Like, you know, man"—his fingers opened to illustrate a wisp of smoke—"just vanish without ties of any sort. You'd have to study Buddhism to understand."

I countered, "What did the Buddha have to say about getting robbed some dark night by a methhead who claims you're his biological father?"

"Oh, the big guy was all over that," Tomlinson assured me. "Uhh"—he turned inward for proof—"people can only lose what they cling to. How's that? Or, wait, this one's better. When you realize how perfect life really is, you will tilt your head back and laugh at the sky."

My pal did just that. Threw his head back and laughed.

"Give Capt. Hannah a big kiss from me," he added, walking away.

"Unlikely," I said, "but I'll try."

The path to my lab tunneled through mangroves to

the water. Dinkin's Bay was a windy mirror of stars. My stilthouse, a genial silhouette, cast a rickety reflection. Hannah's boat was moored there. Window lights showed dimly in the cabin, and I could smell woodsmoke.

She had lit a fire. I had insisted that she drive my brand-new pickup truck home because it was too damn cold, after her all-day charter, to return across the sound in a boat. Loretta and the new nanny were taking care of Izaak, so there was no reason for Hannah to rush home. *Perfect.*

Yes, I had ulterior motives. Yes, I had purchased a bottle of wine. And yes, I had loaned out my stinky, bullheaded dog for the night to her nephew, Luke.

The warning gong had been deactivated, so I called, "Hello, the house!" as I crossed the boardwalk.

There was no need for a response. And I didn't expect one.

I went merrily up the steps. The cabin door was shut tight against the cold. I straightened the collar of my jacket. With a cupped hand, I tested the minty scent of the gum I was chewing. The gum needed to go. And so did I.

Rather than waste this private moment, I unzipped my pants and walked to the railing. Nice stars to gaze upon on this winter night. The gum had been jettisoned, and I was in midstream, when the door behind me opened.

___

"I'm writing your initials," I joked over my shoulder. "Done in a minute."

"Marion!" Hannah's voice screamed from inside. "He's got a gun!" This blended with the bang of the screen door crashing open.

I spun. A huge silhouette was there, coming toward me, arms extended as if about to pull a trigger, the glint of a chrome gun barrel visible. My response required no thought. Muscle memory. It had been hardwired into my brain during close quarters combat drills, over many years and many tens of thousands of rounds fired under stress.

Holstered against the small of my back was the little 9mm Sig Sauer pistol. The pistol was up, level, and locked in my hands. Trigger pressed soundlessly. A double tap—*pop-pop*—two shots fired, yet I heard nothing, my attacker so close that a chunk of his skull stung my face.

Jesus Christ. "Hannah!" I yelled. "Are you hurt? Where are you?" Gun ready, I moved sideways, my eyes seeking threats to the right and left.

No one there. Just me and a grizzly-sized body at my feet. A man. Black boots. BDU military pants. A black leather motorcycle jacket. His left leg spasmed, contracted, then lay still. The back of the man's head was gone.

The porch lights came on, and there was Hannah, holding a kitchen knife, ready to come to my rescue. "My god," she whispered, staring. "Oh dear Jesus, is he . . . Do you know him?"

I rushed to her. "Are you okay? Did he hurt you?"

"No . . . Well, I don't think so. He came in just now, less than a minute ago. I thought it was you. I tried to make him . . . But he had a gun." She looked at me, then averted her eyes.

With a finger, I tilted the woman's face to get a better look. Her cheek was starting to swell, the skin already bruising. "What did he hit you with? Did he—"

Hannah pulled away. "Doc . . . we've got to do something. Is he . . . Do you think . . . Oh my god, he has to be dead. Who is he?"

It was Rayvon Darwin. A nickel-plated revolver, large-caliber with ivory grips, lay nearby. As Leo, the IRS agent, had said, Ray was dangerous. And he liked shiny objects. *Leo* . . . I wondered if the man was still alive after revealing my true identity?

I said to Hannah, "You can't be any part of this. Listen to me! Take my . . . No, take your boat and get out of here."

"Absolutely not!"

"You have to."

I had shifted into plausible deniability mode. If I called the police now, the mother of my son would have to give evidence. Later, Bahamian attorneys might be allowed to hammer at her testimony. And there was my own future to consider. Why had a decorated Nassau customs agent come gunning for a low-profile marine biologist?

I paused. I looked toward the mangroves. Beyond was parked the very expensive Ford Raptor truck that I had ordered in June on a lark. Submerged beneath the dock lay more than two hundred pounds of stolen gold.

"Turn out the porch lights," I decided. "Let's calm down first and get some ice for your face." I was thinking, *Maybe no one heard the shots.*

Inside, I put a kettle on for tea. Hannah couldn't sit still. She paced, she fretted—an unnerving sight—a frightened woman with an ice bag to her cheek. I said, "The smartest thing for you to do is to go home." We argued about it back and forth. "Forget everything," I insisted. "Pretend you weren't here and let me take care of it."

"You're going to lie to the police?"

My silenced caused her to stop pacing. "Doc . . . you *are* going to call the police?"

I nodded vaguely and shrugged. It had been twenty-five minutes since I'd fired two rounds. No sirens. No sudden flare of lights at the marina on this cold, cold windy night.

Now on my mind was the vehicle that had carried Rayvon to my doorstep. A motorcycle, I hoped.

I plopped down in the reading chair of my tiny library—the best place to think. Hannah came closer, knelt, and put her hands on my knees. "Marion, please!

Why did that man come here to kill you? My Lord, after all we've been through, you still don't trust me?"

Maybe it was time, I decided, to trust someone other than myself.

"If he came here on a motorcycle," I said, "I'm not going to call the police. To tell you anything else would be stupid. Hannah, darling"—I touched her face gently—"go home to our son. Please, pretend this never happened."

Why do most people find the concept so difficult to embrace?

But Hannah Smith was not most people. I watched her eyes widen, then narrow, cat-like, with understanding. "You're going to hide his body?" she whispered. "Marion, you'd better have a damn good reason."

"I do," I replied. "I've got four million dollars' worth of reasons hidden under this house. In gold. All stolen."

"Holy shitfire," Hannah murmured. Fear had vanished. She was a practical person who had not lived an easy life. It was time to get up and pace again. "Loretta got away with worse," she reasoned after a while. "I guess we can, too."

The decision was made. She took my hand and pulled me up. "Come on. *Hurry*. Check the parking lot for his motorcycle. I'll grab some bags and start cleaning."

It was 3 a.m. when we started across the bay in my heavily laden boat. We rode in a determined silence until the mounds of Gumbo Limbo came into view, the citrus grove with its buried secrets out back.

Hannah huddled close to my shoulder. She was wrapped in a blanket on this frigid night. Suddenly, as if startled, she pulled the blanket away and remarked, "Doc, know what I just realized? Oh my Lord, honey—now I guess I *have* to marry you."

The celebrated fishing guide didn't sound too thrilled with the idea.

RANDY WAYNE WHITE

"The master."
—*The Florida Times-Union*

For a complete list of titles and to sign up for our
newsletter, please visit prh.com/RandyWayneWhite